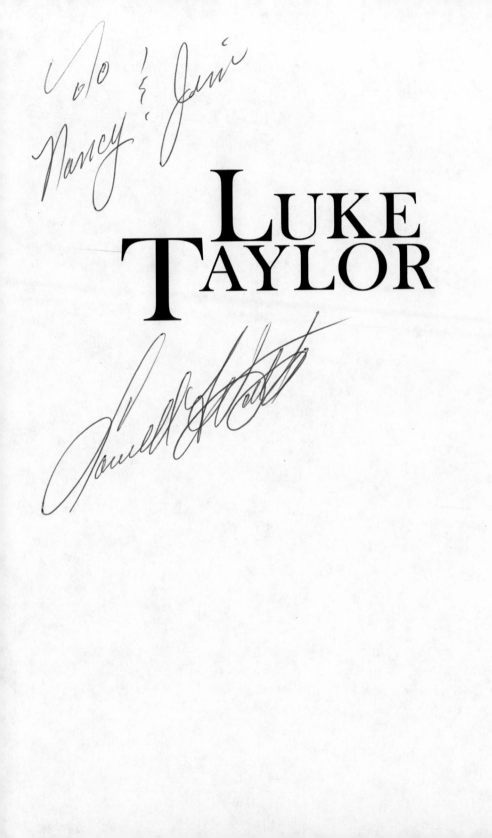

To
Nancy & Jim

LUKE
TAYLOR

LUKE TAYLOR
westward bound

Lowell F. Volk

TATE PUBLISHING & Enterprises

Published by Tate Publishing & Enterprises, LLC
127 E. Trade Center Terrace | Mustang, Oklahoma 73064 USA
1.888.361.9473 | www.tatepublishing.com

Tate Publishing is committed to excellence in the publishing industry. The company reflects the philosophy established by the founders, based on Psalm 68:11,
"The Lord gave the word and great was the company of those who published it."

Published in the United States of America

ISBN: 978-1-61777-314-3
1. Fiction / Westerns   2. Fiction / Historical
11.03.09

To those who have read *The Taylors' Civil War,* thank you.

introduction

The year was 1865. The war between the states had just ended. Now was a time for healing. Both the North and the South needed to recover from the heavy tolls put on them by the war. Southern plantations and farms had been totally destroyed during the war by northern troops. Fathers and sons had been killed, leaving widows to take care of themselves. Those who had slaves before the war to help with their land were now without help.

Most of the fighting had taken place in the South. Buildings, crops, and livestock had been destroyed. As the troops from the North marched through the South they burned fields and any crops that the plantations or farms had stored. Now a new type of man from the North was coming south to prey on those less fortunate. Because of the cases they carried, which looked like they were made out of carpet, they became known as carpetbaggers. These men came with the idea of getting rich off of the sufferings of others. Several of the farmers who had lost their crops and livestock during the war could not pay, so they lost their homes to these carpetbaggers. Taking what they could, farmers and their families started west, hoping for a new start.

The Taylor family was no different from many of the other Southern farmers. Jake, the father, had gone off to fight with General Jackson. He was one of the lucky ones. He did return, but a wound left his left arm almost useless.

While he was gone, Jake's family had been attacked by renegades dressed as Union soldiers and led by a man they called Captain Fry. During the attack, they beat Abigail, Jake's wife, and his oldest son, Luke. They killed Jake's middle son, Tyler. Jake's three remaining children, Milton, Sue Ann, and Mary, were not hurt. Luke went to find his father to tell him what had happened.

After Jake and Luke returned home, carpetbaggers came after the Taylor farm. When they arrived to try to take the farm, Luke killed one of the men escorting Mr. Jones, the carpetbagger's guard, and wounded a second guard. Mr. Jones reported to the army that Luke had killed his man in cold blood. The army swore out a warrant for Luke's arrest. Knowing that Luke would not have a chance to save himself from being hung by the army, Jake and Abigail talked Luke into leaving home and going west.

Because he left, they would never believe that he was innocent if he was caught. If Luke had stayed, he would have been hung. At least the family was safe and still had their farm.

Luke had heard stories about Oregon and rich farm land. There had been rumors about gold in California. There were several other stories that he had heard from the men who had returned from the West before the war. They also told stories about wagon trains leaving from Independence, Missouri, going west. Some other rumors were that wagon trains were started as far east as St. Louis. If he headed for one of these locations, he might be able to hire on as a scout.

Luke knew that if word got out that he was a murderer, he would be a target for anyone trying to get some quick money. He would be alone as he had never been before. Still, the only chance he had was to leave.

westward bound

Luke had wanted to go out west before the war had started, but his ma and pa had stopped him for being too young. Now nineteen, Luke had grown into a man. He had killed several men, making him cold and hard against death. Some of the men he killed while defending against raids, and others he killed face-to-face while searching for his father.

While searching for the men who had raided their farm, Luke practiced with his pistols and had surprised himself at how fast and accurate he had become. When he killed the man he was accused of murdering, it had been while defending his folks' farm and family. Carpetbaggers were trying to take the farm from his pa and were going to kill him by shooting him in the back without giving him a chance. When they drew their guns, Luke outdrew them, shooting both men, killing one and wounding the other.

Based on a report filed by Mr. Jones, the carpetbagger, the army came to their farm looking for Luke.

When the army rode into the farm, Jake went out to see what they wanted. "What can I do fer ya, Colonel?"

"Sir, I am Colonel Anderson with the Union Army here to oversee the area maintaining law and order. Are you Mr. Taylor?"

"Yes, I am, sir," said Jake.

"Well, sir, I'm looking for a man named Luke Taylor. Is that you or one of your sons?"

"He's mah son. What do ya want him fer?"

"Mr. Jones swore out a warrant for his arrest stating that when they came here to peacefully talk to you about your taxes, your son Luke murdered one of his men in cold blood and wounded another."

Jake looked at the colonel. "Luke didn't kill da man in cold blood. They done drawd on us, and Luke shot him in self-defense. If anyone was trying to kill another in cold blood, it was them trying to kill me."

"I need for your son to come in so we can let the courts decide what happened," said Colonel Anderson. "If he runs, there is no court in the country that won't call him guilty and hang him. Turning himself in, Mr. Taylor, is the only way. By law, I have to serve this warrant to him. Now is he here?"

"He done left a couple days ago fer da West. He figured that now that da war was over, it was time fer him ta go. I don't think he'll be com'n back soon. When he left, he weren't running from ya."

Colonel Anderson said, "If you don't mind, we'll take a look for ourselves. If he isn't here, we'll leave. If you see him, tell him I need to see him if we're going to get this cleared up."

The soldiers spread out and started searching the farm looking for Luke. Going through the barn, they counted the horses and asked Jake's son Milton if they had any others. Milton told them that the horses they saw were the only ones they owned, except the two horses Luke had taken with him. Some of the soldiers even checked the house. Not finding anything, they rejoined the colonel.

When all the troops had returned without finding Luke, they mounted, preparing to ride back to town. The colonel turned and looked at Jake. "If your boy comes back, he'll have to turn himself in. Tell him it's the only way." As they rode away Jake turned, wondering how much of a chance Luke would have with the colonel.

After they got out of sight, the colonel halted the troops. "Private Yantz, I want you and Private Miller to find a spot in those rocks back yonder and watch the farm. Make sure you stay out of sight. If you see anyone who looks like the son, I want one of you to stay here watching and the other to come back to camp to report to me."

Private Yantz said, "Yes, sir," and they headed back to the rocks.

Jake knew that Luke had not left but was out hunting and would be returning later that day. He told Milton to go find Luke and warn him. Jake didn't feel comfortable about the colonel leaving and suspected that he might have left someone behind to watch the farm. He thought that he had seen some movement up in the rocks. "We gotta be careful in your leaving ta find Luke. They got ta think that ya got some work ta do in da field. If they suspect that ya are go'n ta warn him, they're go'n ta follow ya. If ya take fencing tools, they may think yer go'n ta fix da fence."

Milton turned, going to the barn to get the wagon. Jake followed to help him. Before bringing the wagon out, Jake told Milton that they needed to load all of Luke's gear stored in the barn. After loading Luke's gear, they pulled the wagon out in the open where they loaded it with the fencing material. Milton put his rifle on the seat and climbed onto the wagon. Taking the reins in his hands, he turned the horses toward the field.

Milton knew that Luke would be going by the cave that he always used. Once out of sight of the house, he headed for the woods where the cave was located. Arriving at the cave, he unloaded Luke's gear, putting it into the cave, and sat down to wait. It was the middle of the afternoon before he heard Luke. Coming out of the cave, he saw Luke riding up.

Luke was surprised to see Milton waiting for him. "What's wrong? Did something happen ta da folks or da girls?"

"Na, da folks and da girls are fine," Milton said. "We done had a visit from da army taday.

Milton told Luke about the colonel showing up that morning and what he had said about the warrant that Mr. Jones had sworn out. He told Luke that Pa had said for him to stay at the cave until dark before making his way to the house. He told him that Pa had a feeling that there was someone watching the farm waiting for him.

Milton looked up at Luke's packhorse and said, "I see da war hasn't changed ya. Ya got a deer."

"Yap, and she should be nice and tender as young as she is."

"Let's load her in da wagon."

They lifted her off Luke's packhorse and put her in the wagon. Once the deer was loaded, Milton picked up his rifle and fired a shot in the air.

"What did ya do that fer?" asked Luke.

"Well, if someone is watching da farm, they might wonder how I got this deer without shooting her."

Milton waited for a while before heading back to the farm. When he arrived at the barn, Jake came out. He helped Milton with the deer before putting the wagon away. They hung the deer on the side of the barn where the men watching them could see, and they butchered the deer. Milton told him that he had talked to Luke and that he would be coming in after it got dark.

That night Luke returned to the farm after it had gotten dark and before the moon came out. The clouds made it darker than usual, making it easier for Luke to make his way to the house. Leaving his horse tied out of sight in the trees, Luke went to the house.

Entering the house, his ma gave him a hug and put some food on the table for him. Luke sat down and started to eat and asked, "What did da colonel say?"

"Da colonel said ya gotta turn yerself in ta him or ya gonna be hung if yer caught," said Jake. "From da way da Colonel was talk'n, dis Mr. Jones said ya were a cold-blooded killer."

Sitting down with Luke, Jake and Abigail talked about what they had discussed after the colonel left. They figured that if he turned himself in he wouldn't have a chance to prove his innocence and he would be hung. The best thing he could do would be leave and go west. Luke said, "If'n I run da Army will say I'm guilty without a trial. Maybe I should go in and talk ta da colonel. Maybe he will listen ta mah side of da story."

"From what da Colonel was saying, we don't think ya got a chance ta prove it was self-defense," said Jake. "They've been watch'n da place. Ya got ta leave tonight while it's dark."

"Luke, you know I don't want you to go," said Abigail. "But I gotta agree with your pa about this."

Luke finally agreed that it was the only way that he and the family would be safe.

Abigail gathered Luke's things along with some food and placed them by the door.

He said his good-byes. He told his ma that when he figured out where he was going he would write and let her know. He told his pa not to worry, that the last couple of years had taught him how to survive in a hostile world. Before his pa put the lamp out, Luke saw a tear in his ma's and sister's eyes. They knew that this would be the last time they would see Luke if he was to remain alive.

Jake blew out the lamp, making the house dark. The moon was behind a cloud as he opened the door, making it impossible for anyone watching the farm to see them. Picking up some of the supplies with Luke getting the rest, they left the house, going around back to where Luke had left his horse.

After Luke tied his supplies on his horse, he again said good-bye to his pa. Taking the reins in his hand, he turned and started leading his horse back to the cave. Jake stood in the dark looking in the direction that Luke had gone listening to him getting fainter as the horse walked away. Jake knew that it was the last time he would see his son. He turned and headed back into the house. He could hear Abigail crying when he entered the bedroom. Jake went to comfort her before they went to bed. Both Jake and Abigail were restless throughout the night. At one time, Jake heard the dog let out a low growl. He made his way to the window without lighting a lamp and looked out. The night was not as dark as it had been earlier, and he thought he saw someone going away from the farm. He stood there watching for a while and again saw someone just before they got to the rocks.

When he got back to bed, Abigail asked, "What's wrong?"

"The dog heard someone and let out a growl. I was right. They have someone watching the place. Now with Luke gone, they're going ta have some cold nights with no luck of finding Luke."

The colonel continued to have the farm watched for several days, during which time there wasn't any sign of Luke being there. Not finding Luke by watching the farm, he pulled his men. During the same time, he had sent out word to other units in the area and to the west describing Luke and what he was wanted for. Maybe someone would come across him if indeed he had headed west. Not hearing anything, he figured that Jake had been truthful when he said that Luke had gone west prior to their arrival at the farm.

After saying his last good-bye to his pa, Luke returned to the cave, leading his horse loaded with the supplies his mother had put together for him. It was good that he had taken his packhorse with him when he went hunting that morning. At least there would not be a change in the number of horses and the way they had gotten his supplies to him; anyone watching would never know that he had been there.

When Luke arrived at the cave, he unloaded his horse and moved him to where he had left his packhorse. Going back into the cave, he built a fire so he could check his gear and supplies.

He started going through the supplies his mother had put together. He stopped short when a picture fell out of some clothing his ma had packed. Picking up the picture, he turned it toward the fire. When the light of the fire lit up the picture, he almost dropped it. The picture was the one that they had taken of the complete family, including Tyler before he was killed.

When the war broke out, Luke's mother had insisted that they have the picture taken in case something happened so they would always be together. Luke knew that it had to be really hard for her to have given up the last picture with Tyler. Luke knew that he would keep it near him as long as he lived.

Luke finished checking his supplies, set out what he would eat in the morning, and packed everything else, making it ready to leave in the morning.

Sleep did not come easily. He kept thinking about his ma and pa as well as his brother and sisters. The war had been hard on Luke, and now that it had ended, it was taking the only home he had known from him as well.

Luke's need to get out of the area was more than just the army being after him. The chance of someone recognizing him and turning him into the army for the reward had become an even greater risk than the army finding him. If the army caught up with him, his life would be over. The supplies he had would last him for a month. If needed, he could avoid civilization until he was well into Kentucky. Once in Kentucky, his chances of being recognized would be far less. If he had to, he could change his name, but he was proud of the name Luke Taylor and had no desire to be called anything else.

Sleep finally came to him, but it was a restless sleep. Morning found him tired. It was not good for him to be tired because once he started making camp in the open, he would have to be alert. Falling into a sound sleep could cost him his life.

After making breakfast, Luke brought his horses nearer to the cave. Moving his gear to the mouth of the cave, he saddled Buck and loaded his packhorse.

Mounting his horse, Luke turned and rode away, heading west into the unknown. Looking back, he figured that this would be the last time he would be home or see his family. Thinking about the supplies he had, he felt that he was prepared for anything that he would come across. Besides clothes and food, he had an extra rifle and a couple of extra pistols. He also had one hundred Yankee dollars that he had collected from the men he had killed.

He was a wanted man, and he would have to be extra careful whenever he came across others, especially any Union soldiers.

When Luke had been talking to his pa, his pa had suggested that he follow the old Wilderness Trail from Virginia into Kentucky. He hadn't heard of many people using it, and with it being traveled by few, he might be safer. He would have to be extra careful between home and the Cumberland Gap, but once he reached the gap, his chances of being recognized were slim.

The first week of travel since Luke left home went without any problems. Luke knew he was getting close to the Cumberland Gap but didn't know much about it. When he entered Estillville, he figured that the blacksmith shop was the best place to get information on the gap. When he was looking for his pa during the war, it was at the blacksmith shops where he got his best information.

Not paying attention to his surroundings and thinking about what he needed to find out in town, Luke rounded a curve and came upon a troop of cavalry taking a noon break. Seeing them, Luke almost turned around to head back the way he had come, but his better sense took over, and he kept riding. He could see an officer talking to one of his men. Without looking directly at the men as he rode, he saw the officer look up at him and then turn back to the man he had been talking to. Luke felt that he was going to be all right when he heard the officer call out for him to stop. Stopping, Luke turned to see what he wanted.

The officer was walking toward him with his arm raised. As he got closer, Luke asked, "What can I do for ya?"

"My name is Lieutenant Jordon, and we got word to be on the lookout for a man traveling this way. Where did you come from?" asked Lieutenant Jordon.

"I come from Dublin way," answered Luke, thinking of his friend who was killed.

"What's your name?"

Quickly thinking again of his friend, "John Hicks," replied Luke.

"Have you come across anyone traveling alone heading this way during your travel?"

"Can't say that I have. Most of da people I come across were headed ta other way," said Luke. "Who you look'n fer?"

"We're looking for a fella going by the name of Luke Taylor. He killed a man near Greenville, and the army's looking to put him on trial and hang him," said the lieutenant. "If you come across him, you need to be careful. Chances are that he has already gone through these parts and you won't run into him. Good luck to you, Mr. Hicks."

"Thanks. I sure will. Hope ya find yer man," said Luke as he rode away.

Luke had been lucky. If the lieutenant had received a better description, Luke might have been caught.

Entering town, Luke looked for the blacksmith shop. Seeing it near the edge of town, he rode up and dismounted. As he was tying his horses, the smithy walked out.

"What can I do fer ya?" asked the smithy.

"I need ya ta look at mah horses. I think they got a couple of loose shoes," said Luke.

"It will be a bit fer I can get ta them," said the smithy. "I got a couple ahead of ya."

"That's all right," said Luke. He walked over to his horses and started to unload his packhorse. After setting the packs by the fence, he loosened the cinches on the horses before asking, "Where's there a place ta eat?"

"Just up da street, a place called Ma's Café," said the smithy.

Luke figured that with the smithy being busy he would get something to eat and talk to him later about the gap when he came back. He walked up the street, keeping an eye on who he met along the way. It didn't take him long before he saw the sign for Ma's Café.

Entering the café, he noticed that it was still half full of diners. Taking a seat off to the side and out of the way, he waited for the waitress.

When the kitchen door opened, Luke's heart skipped a beat. The girl coming through the door looked like Helen. Luke knew that it couldn't be her, as Helen had been killed when a bullet meant for him missed, hitting her. She had died during the night, leaving a deep sorrow in Luke's heart. Seeing the waitress brought back those deep feelings and memories.

Putting the thoughts of Helen out of his mind, he tried not to think of her while waiting for the waitress. When she arrived, Luke wasted no time ordering his meal, and he waited for his coffee to be served. After his meal was served, he ate thinking about all the things that had happened in his life bringing him to where he was today. By the time he had finished, the café was empty except for him.

Just as he was about to leave, the sheriff walked in. Spotting Luke, he walked over to his table and said, "I don't recall see'n ya in town befer."

Luke said, "Na, ain't been here befer. I am just pass'n through. As soon as yer smithy finishes mah horses, I'll be moving on."

"Mind if I set?" asked the sheriff.

"Help yerself," said Luke.

When the sheriff sat down, the waitress came over with a cup and the pot of coffee. Setting the cup in front of the sheriff, she looked at Luke and asked, "Do ya want some as well?'

With the sheriff just sitting down, Luke figured he just couldn't get up and walk out on the sheriff without raising suspicion, so he said, "Sure enough, ma'am. I'll have some more. Thanks."

After the waitress refilled Luke's cup and walked away, the sheriff asked, "Where ya from?"

Luke said, "I come from Dublin way."

"What brings ya our way?" asked the sheriff.

"Well," said Luke, "da war took all we had. Mah folks only had enough left ta support them, so I thought I would go out west."

"Seems like a lot of folks are do'n that since da war ended," said the sheriff. "What folks didn't lose during da war they lost ta them carpetbaggers who come through."

"Da war was hard on mah family. It killed mah brother and hurt mah folks," said Luke. "After I made sure that they would be okay, I packed up and started west. Can ya tell me anything about da trail through the Cumberland Gap? I figured that it would cut off some distance head'n west."

"Well," said the sheriff, "the trail ain't been used for travel much these past years. I heard during da war the North and South took turns controlling da gap, make'n sure that no one got through who they didn't want ta let through. Some say a fella named Boone blazed the trail. Others say that da Indians have stories about buffalo using da gap ta migrate befer white man was here. Ain't seen no buffalo here about, so couldn't say fer sure."

The sheriff went on. "At da end of da war, I heard tell of a large explosion come from da Gap. I couldn't say if they closed da Gap to stop anyone from come'n through. Do ya have a wagon with ya or just horses?"

"Na," said Luke. "Just mah horses."

"Well then, ya should be able to get through," said the sheriff. "By da way, what's your name?"

"John Hicks," said Luke.

They continued to sit, drinking coffee and talking about stories they had heard coming from the West. Some of the stories were about rich land that ran for as far as a man could see. Others were about men getting rich with gold or silver. Some said that there was so much gold that you could find it lying on top of the ground. You had to be careful drinking from streams so you didn't choke on the gold. Still there were other stories about the sun-bleached bones of livestock and graves of people that marked the trails heading west.

After sitting and talking to the sheriff for an hour, Luke told the sheriff that he needed to go check on his horses. Standing up and paying his bill, he said good-bye to the sheriff.

The sheriff got up and wished Luke good luck in his travels and walked out of the café with him.

Heading down the street, Luke decided to stop by the general store to get more salt and coffee. While he was there, he decided to pick up some more shells for his rifle. Picking up his purchases, Luke went to the blacksmith's shop.

The smithy was just finishing the bay packhorse as Luke arrived. Luke stood by waiting for the smithy to finish before asking, "How were da buckskin's shoes?"

The smithy said, "I had to replace his front shoes. Da backs just needed reset."

Luke paid and thanked the smithy. After tightening the cinches, he loaded his supplies on the packhorse. Mounting, he said good-bye to the smithy and rode through town.

Luke saw the sheriff walking down the street, and as he rode by, the sheriff waved and wished him luck again.

With his horses rested, Luke rode until it started to get dark. Finding a spot where there was feed and water, Luke stopped. After tending to the horses, Luke set up his camp and started a fire to cook his supper. After supper, Luke sat back thinking about what he had heard about the Cumberland Gap. Both the North and the

South had occupied the gap during the war, but he believed that they had both abandoned it since the war ended.

The explosion the sheriff had talked about had come from people who had heard about it but had not been able to explain what had caused it. Most people were too afraid to investigate the trail because of stories that they had heard about travelers who had tried to go through the gap and didn't make it. Others had no need to go down the trail. If the explosion had been to close to the trail, Luke would have to find a way around it. Being on horseback, he could ride around it if they had tried to block the trail.

Finally, Luke fell into a sound sleep.

cumberland gap

Luke woke with a start when the horses were snorting and stomping their hoofs. It was not quite daylight. Lying still listening for any sound in the dark that would tell him what was bothering the horses, he waited. It wasn't long before he could hear something moving around the edge of camp. With his rifle in hand, he sat up to see if he could get a look at what was out there. Luke finally realized that it had to be an animal. As soon as Luke got up, he could hear it moving away.

While he was cooking his breakfast, Luke saw something moving out of the corner of his eye. At first he thought it looked like a coyote lying off in the brush watching. Luke continued to cook his breakfast while watching what lay in the brush, hoping to get a better look at it. While eating, Luke saw the animal move closer to the camp. This time he could see that it wasn't a coyote. It was a dog, and one that looked like it had not eaten in some time. Taking a piece of meat, he tossed it where the dog could smell it but would have to come closer to get it. When he tossed it, the dog jumped back to the brush and waited.

Luke continued to sit and wait to see if the dog would come back and get it. He didn't have to wait long. Soon the dog started creeping closer toward the meat while keeping his eyes on Luke. When he got to the meat, he jumped up, grabbing it, and ran back into the brush. Luke saw that when the dog ran he was running on three legs. He didn't use his right front paw. Luke took another piece of meat bigger than the first one and tossed it where the dog would have to come even closer. Again the dog started toward the meat, keeping his eyes on Luke. When he got to the spot where the first piece had been, he jumped up, grabbed the meat, and ran out of sight. This time Luke saw that the dog had hurt the paw he was favoring. If he could get close to the dog, he might be able to help him.

Luke set a trap that would hold the dog so he could take a look at his foot. This time he put more meat where the dog would get caught if he took it. Again the dog came back and, seeing the meat, started creeping toward it. When he jumped up to grab the meat, he sprang the trap. Fighting to get free, Luke waited for him to tire before approaching.

Once the dog quit fighting the trap, Luke approached him. Growling at Luke, he tried to get free without success. When Luke got closer, he tried to bite Luke but missed. Luke, with the help of the trap, got the dog by the head and tied his mouth shut.

Once the dog had been rendered helpless, Luke held him down while he took a look at his foot. Luke could see that he had a twig that was stuck in between his toes. Taking out his knife, Luke was able to remove it and drain the puss. Going to his pack, he got some salve to put on it, something that would help to heal the wound.

When Luke returned to the dog, the dog again tried to get away, but the trap continued to hold him. Luke put the salve on the wound and wrapped the paw. By now the dog seemed to have calmed down some. Making sure that the wrap would stay in place, Luke freed the dog from the trap, still holding him so he couldn't run. Untying the dog's mouth, Luke made sure that he would not be bitten when turned loose.

Once the dog was loose, he ran for the brush. As he ran, Luke could see that he was putting weight on his right paw again. Once the dog realized that Luke was not chasing him, he stopped and looked back before going behind the brush. Luke watched him as he tried to remove the wrapping that was on his foot. Not being able to, he ran off.

Luke stood laughing at the dog. He could tell by how thin he was that he had not been eating properly, figuring that because his foot was sore he could not catch his food. Even so, he was a big dog. Luke figured that he had been raised by a family but had been abandoned for some reason. Maybe he had been abused by the family, making him afraid of humans and causing him to run off. Or it could be that the original family had to move, and the dog had been left behind. No matter what had happened to the dog, he didn't trust humans now.

Luke cleaned up his camp, saddled his horse, and loaded the packhorse. He looked around and did not see the dog. With the twig removed and the paw wrapped, the dog should be all right. The wrapping would come off after a while, but hopefully it would stay on until his paw was healed.

As Luke rode that morning, he noticed that the horses would keep looking back every once in awhile as if there was something on their back trail. Maybe someone was following them, but he had not seen anyone. One time when he looked back, he thought that he saw something running off the road.

Keeping a closer watch, he soon recognized that the dog was following them. Seeing that it was just the dog, he relaxed.

When Luke stopped at noon to rest the horses and eat, he moved off the road. He unloaded and unsaddled the horses, letting them roll before starting a fire and putting on coffee. While waiting for the coffee to finish, Luke noticed that the dog had come into view and lay down where he could watch Luke. Luke could see that the wrap he had put on was still there.

Luke started talking softly to the dog, and his ears came up as he listened. When the coffee was done, Luke took out some jerky and leftover biscuits from breakfast. Breaking off part of the biscuit, he tossed it to the dog. This time he threw it far enough that the dog did not have to move to get it. As the biscuit came toward him, he waited and caught it without moving. Luke figured that he would run off again, but he didn't. He stayed there and ate the biscuit. When he finished, he lay there waiting for more.

Luke tossed him a piece of jerky, but this time it was short of where he lay. The dog got up and moved to where the jerky fell. Picking it up, he went back to where he was lying and lay back down. Looking up at Luke, he started eating the jerky. When he finished, he again lay there looking at Luke, waiting for more.

While Luke ate, he continued to toss the dog food. Each time the dog would get the food and return to where he had been lying to eat it. It appeared that the dog was losing some of his fear of Luke but kept his distance.

When Luke felt that they had rested long enough, he started to clean up his camp. After putting the coffee pot back in the pack, he saddled the horse and loaded the packs. Meanwhile the dog continued to lie where he had been eating and watched. Luke mounted and rode away with the dog still lying and watching. Luke turned looking at the dog and said, "Well, are ya come'n with us or not?"

The dog got up and started to follow. Now instead of hiding, he stayed on the road with Luke. Whenever they would meet someone, the dog would go off into the brush. After they had passed, he would again follow behind the packhorse.

That evening Luke had not reached the gap as planned. Stopping to make camp, his new companion was still with him. After unloading the horses, Luke led them to water. While Luke was watering the horses, the dog came down to the stream as well and drank near the horses on the opposite side of Luke. When Luke took the horses and hobbled them, the dog followed.

Leaving the horses, he went to set up camp; again the dog followed Luke. Finding a spot, the dog lay down, watching Luke as he set up camp. After cooking his supper, Luke sat down to eat.

Luke had taken out some extra meat, and as he was eating, he again tossed some of the meat to the dog. Each time he tossed the meat, he would talk to the dog, throwing it a little closer. By the time he had finished eating, the dog had moved to within a few feet of Luke. But when Luke got up to clean up his camp, the dog moved out of the light of the fire.

Luke took out his bedroll and lay down. While lying there, he kept watching for the dog to see if he would return. It wasn't long before the dog worked his way back into camp. This time he came into the dimming light of the fire but on the opposite side away from Luke. There he lay down, facing Luke. Luke could see that even though the dog had laid his head down, he was continuing to watch him. The dog was still lying there when Luke fell asleep.

When Luke woke up in the morning, he noticed that the dog was not in camp. Looking around, he did not see the dog anywhere. Luke thought that maybe he didn't want to be a companion after all. While Luke was making breakfast, the dog returned, carrying a rabbit. Luke also noticed that the wrap was now missing and the dog was not favoring his paw.

While Luke ate breakfast, the dog lay nearby eating his rabbit. Now that his foot was not hurting as much, he may have a chance to survive on his own. When Luke had finished eating, so had the dog.

While Luke was breaking camp and loading the horses, the dog again lay there and watched. He did not run off like he had yesterday with Luke moving around camp. Leaving camp, the dog walked alongside the packhorse.

Watching the dog, Luke figured that he had picked up a new traveling friend. Besides the horses, a dog would be able to alert him if someone was approaching. Riding along, they met fewer and fewer people traveling, which was all right with Luke. They did meet one other traveler, and Luke noticed that the dog did not run off but stayed by the packhorse and watched the stranger until he was out of sight.

The sheriff was right; now that the war had ended, anyone traveling would take an easier route to travel. The army had been the only ones using the gap during the war.

As he approached the entrance to the gap, he could see several trees scattered about. At first, it looked like a storm had gone through the area, knocking down the trees. Thinking about what the sheriff had said, that there was an explosion reported coming from the gap, maybe the explosion had knocked down the trees. Riding closer, he could see that the trees had been cut and left lying in all directions. No one was going to travel through them in a hurry. Maybe they were placed that way on purpose.

Making his way was slow going. When he reached the far side of the downed trees, he could see an old army camp. Stopping, he gave the horses a rest.

After unsaddling the horses, he made a fire. Taking out some jerky, he sat down and ate. The dog came in close to Luke and sat down to watch him. Again Luke tossed the dog some jerky.

The dog was getting used to Luke, staying where he caught the meat and eating it. Luke talked to the dog while they ate. Finally Luke held a piece of jerky in his fingers for the dog while talking softly to him. The dog looked at Luke, not moving. Luke continued to talk to the dog until it stood up, taking a step toward him.

After a while, the dog took another step and stretched out his head trying to reach the food Luke was holding. Still not able to get it, he took a couple more steps. Grabbing the meat, he backed up and lay down to eat it.

After they had finished eating, Luke got up to look the area over. Walking around, he found evidence that the armies from both the North and South had been camped there. He found that what the sheriff had told him was true about the area.

Returning to the camp, he saddled his horses. Starting up the trail again, he was getting into a routine. The dog continued to walk with the packhorse. Luke would turn and talk to the dog as they rode. The more Luke talked to the dog, the closer he would move toward Luke's horse. The trail wound back and forth as it climbed. It was hard on the horses, tiring them quickly, so Luke decided to stop early.

Finding a campsite near the top of the gap, Luke stopped. He found a stream with fresh water and grass for the horses. Hobbling the horses, he went hunting for fresh meat.

Returning to camp, Luke saw the dog lying by his pack. Luke picked up his rifle and headed for the trees looking for game. While hobbling the horses, he saw a fresh deer track that he wanted to follow. As Luke followed the deer trail, the dog followed. Luke wasn't sure what the dog would do when they came across any game, but he would wait and see.

Picking up the trail near the horses, Luke followed it to a wooded area. Once in the woods, he stopped and listened closely for any sounds. He noticed that the dog would stop and lie down when he stopped. When Luke moved forward, the dog would follow again. Soon the dog jumped in front of Luke, stopping, his ears pointing forward. Luke stopped and looked where the dog was looking. At first he didn't see it, but then the deer moved, and Luke caught the movement. Taking aim, he dropped the deer.

Once Luke fired the shot, the dog dashed forward to where the deer lay, watching it until Luke got there. Luke saw that the deer was a young one that would make good eating. Luke cleaned and hauled the deer back to camp. Back at camp, Luke cut up the meat.

Some of the fresh meat Luke cooked for supper. While Luke's supper was cooking, he finished cutting up the rest of the deer. Luke cut it into strips that could be dried into jerky. As he cut it up, he tossed pieces to the dog, which was sitting nearby watching.

When the meat was finished, Luke ate. When he finished eating, he laid the strips on a rack he built, setting it over the fire to dry the meat overnight. Before retiring for the night, Luke brought the horses closer to camp. The dog had even moved closer to where Luke was sleeping.

During the night, the dog started to growl, waking Luke. When Luke looked at the dog, he saw him standing, looking toward the area where the deer had been, the hair on his back standing up. He kept growling and showing his teeth. Luke picked up his rifle, looking in the same direction. Luke heard the horses moving restlessly as well. Taking a log and putting it on the fire, Luke could see coyotes lurking around the deer remains. He fired just over their heads, and they scattered.

After a while, the dog lay back down, and Luke knew that the coyotes were gone. He checked the progress of the meat drying. He would rest easier knowing that the dog was now a friend. Taking a piece of meat, he held it out for the dog. The dog did not hesitate before coming to Luke and taking it. Standing next to Luke while he ate, Luke reached down, petting his head. The dog looked up at Luke and finished eating.

When Luke lay down, the dog lay even closer to where Luke was. In the morning, Luke finished drying his meat and packed. Luke had some of the fresh meat left that he cooked for dinner and breakfast so he could eat it on the trail.

Finishing breakfast, he watered the horses before loading them to travel. They had only gone a short distance when Luke saw a large hole off to the left of the trail. Taking a closer look at the hole, Luke could see that it was not a hole created by nature. Realizing that it must have been the explosion the sheriff had talked about, he stopped to take a closer look. There he found pieces of destroyed ammunitions and equipment. So it was the army destroying supplies that had caused the loud explosion.

Moving on, he reached the top of the gap and stopped to look at the view. This was the new world that he was heading into. It looked green and peaceful. It was hard to believe that the war had caused so much destruction to so many people. It almost made him forget that he was still a wanted man.

Starting down the trail and coming out of the woods, the trail made twists and turns. As he rode farther down the trail, he saw what looked like a chimney. Maybe there was a farm up ahead. Soon the building with the chimney came into view. It wasn't a house but looked like a large furnace. He decided to stop and check it out before going on and give the horses a chance to rest.

Tying the horses, he went back to the furnace to look it over. He could see that the furnace had not been used in some time. He wasn't sure what it had been used for, but there was what looked like some type of metal lying around. Making a dry camp, he ate while he continued to look around.

The dog followed along as Luke walked around. Luke tossed the dog some meat while looking the place over. Once he finished looking around, he sat down in the shade to rest. The dog sat next to him. Without thinking, Luke reached out and scratched the dog's head while it lay next to Luke and seemed to go to sleep.

After resting, Luke started down the trail again. It wasn't long before they came upon the town of Cumberland Gap.

Cumberland Gap was a small town, so Luke figured that he would not have to worry about anyone recognizing him as the man wanted in Greenville. As he entered town, he saw a cavalry outfit riding in from the other end of town. Not wanting to meet up with them, Luke stopped at the general store. Keeping an eye on the dog, he could see that he was not comfortable being in town as well. Calling the dog to his side, he entered the store, the dog tagging along.

"Can I help ya?" asked the clerk in the store.

"I need some supplies," said Luke. "Do ya have any salt pork, a slab of bacon, beans, flour, and salt? Do ya happen ta have a map of da trail go'n ta St. Louie?"

The clerk said, "Ya, I can get da food fer ya. We have a map that a fella drew up sometime back. Ya might be able ta copy if ya can write. Yer not from hereabouts 'cause I ain't seen ya in here befer."

"Na, just pass'n through. Head'n west. Do ya have many come'n through here? I seen da cavalry com'n inta town just now."

"Since da war, we haven't had many through here. During da war, them Northern troops would be here trying ta keep our boys out of da Gap. Then our boys would drive them out fer a while. Now da Northern boys keep hanging out here. I heard they're look'n fer a fella. One said that he had killed another fella there in cold blood. Where did ya come from?"

"I come from Dublin Way," said Luke. "Seems I talked ta a lieutenant near Estillville. Seem to recall they were look'n fer a fella named Luke Taylor. Is that da someone these are look'n fer?"

"I seem ta recall da name being mentioned," said the clerk. "Didn't pay much attention ta them. I couldn't turn in one of our boys fer killing a Northner."

The clerk went to the back room and returned with a piece of folded paper. Opening it on the counter, Luke could see it was a hand-drawn map of the trail he was following. Taking a pencil and piece of paper Luke copied the map and put it in his pocket.

Just as Luke finished putting the map away, the door to the store opened, and a Union captain walked in. He stood by the door looking the room over. Seeing Luke standing by the counter talking to the clerk, he walked over to them.

The clerk said, "I'll be with ya as soon as I finish with this customer."

The captain said, "Take your time." Turning to Luke, he asked, "Are you from around here?"

"Na, I am just pass'n through."

"What's your name, and where are you coming from?"

"My name's John Hicks from Dublin Way," answered Luke.

"Have you come across a fella by the name of Luke Taylor?"

"Can't say I have," said Luke. "I ran inta a lieutenant near Estillville look'n fer the same fella. I'd thought ya had caught him by now."

"Some are saying that because he is from the South that people are hiding and feeding him, so he cannot be found," said the captain.

"What did this fella do?"

"Word has it that he killed a man who was escorting a tax man when he went to their farm. When the army came back to talk to him, he had gone."

"Why did he kill da man?" asked Luke.

"No one knows for sure. Some said that the man he killed was trying to kill his father when he shot him. Mr. Jones said that the boy was a hot-headed kid. Said he didn't even give him a chance to explain why they were there before the kid opened fire, or so the report said."

"Wouldn't that be self-defense, not murder, if the fella was trying to kill his pa?"

"That's up to the court to decide. We just have orders to bring him in when we find him," answered the captain.

The clerk had gotten Luke's supplies together and wrapped them for him. Luke paid for his supplies and said to the captain, "Hope ya find yer man." Taking his supplies, he headed for the door, calling the dog.

As Luke reached the door, the captain called, "Luke. Luke Taylor."

Luke opened the door without turning around and walked out. Going to his packhorse, he loaded his supplies. Untying his horses, he mounted and rode out of town. The captain came to the door of the general store and watched Luke as he rode out. He still wasn't convinced that he was not watching the man they were looking for. Luke rode down the trail, keeping an eye on his back trail. He continued to ride until dusk when he stopped to make camp.

When Luke lay down that night, the dog came and lay next to him. Luke was thinking if he was going to have the dog with him, he at least needed to give him a name. Looking at the dog, he said, "What do ya think I should call ya?"

The dog looked up at Luke and tilted his head as if to say, "I don't know what you are saying." Luke laughed at the dog and said, "How about calling you Rex? I think that would be a good name for you, mah friend. I met ya like mah friend Hicks when he was wounded. Now yer stay'n by me like mah friend Hicks did before he was killed. From now on, I will call you Rex."

The dog looked at Luke and then put his head down on his paws, indicating to Luke that he approved of the name.

Luke remembered the map he had copied in the general store and took it out. He figured that if all went well tomorrow they could reach the cave marked on the map. There was no indication of how big the cave was, but it must have been used by whoever drew up the original map.

Putting the map away, Luke lay back and closed his eyes. Bringing up the idea of naming Rex brought him back to thinking about his lost friend and how they had become friends. They had met in a strange way, but Hicks had been a true friend to Luke. He was still thinking about him as he drifted off to sleep.

Rex stayed by Luke's bed all night. When Luke got up, Rex continued to lie where he was at until Luke untied the horses and headed for the stream. Rex then got up and followed. Leaving the horses on fresh grass, Luke went to make breakfast.

Rex was getting used to being fed by Luke and was putting on weight. With the renewed energy, he would go off and chase rabbits whenever he got a chance. After eating and cleaning up their camp, they were again on their way.

They were in Mipplesboro by early afternoon. Luke did not want to encounter the army again, so he rode straight through town. As he rode through, he noticed two men looking at him. One of the men pointed toward Luke, saying something to the other who shook his head. Luke didn't like what he had seen but didn't want them to think that he was watching them.

Riding out of town, he kept an eye on his back trail to see if those two were following him. Neither the horses nor Rex gave Luke any indication that they were being followed.

He rode on until he found the cave from the map. There he decided to stop for the night. There was grass and water for the horses, and he and Rex could sleep inside the cave.

After dismounting at the mouth of the cave, Luke and Rex entered the cave. Luke could see that the cave had been used by several people before him. There was even evidence that it could have been used for the wounded during the war. Unloading his horses, he placed his gear inside the cave before hobbling the horses on grass with water.

Returning to the cave, Luke built a fire. With the fire going, Luke could see that there was something carved on the wall of the cave. After eating supper, he wrapped an oil rag around a stick and lit it to explore the cave. Further in the cave he found names and dates carved into the wall. The dates indicated that they had been carved during the war. Maybe it was used for a hospital. Anyway, it looked like a warm place for the night.

That night before lying down to go to sleep, Luke and Rex took a walk, bringing the horses closer to the cave. Luke could tell that Rex liked being out of the cave where he could move around. Maybe his family had kept him locked up in a small room, causing him to not like being inside. As they headed back to the cave, Luke heard something out of the norm. Leaving the horses out of sight, Luke and Rex made their way to the cave.

Stopping, Luke heard two men talking from behind some rocks overlooking the front of the cave. Working his way around to where he could see them, he saw that it was the two men from town sitting on their horses.

"Leroy, I told ya he would stop at da cave fer da night. Ya can see there's a fire go'n in there."

"So what we gonna do, Jed?"

"We need ta set here and see if he's in da cave. If he be there, we get him when he comes out," said Jed. "Now go tie them horses outa sight."

Getting down from their horses, Leroy moved them behind some trees while Jed took his rifle, moving behind rocks where he could keep his rifle on the opening. Luke continued to watch until Leroy had returned.

Keeping Rex quiet, they made their way around the two men. Rex let out a growl, and the two men turned with their rifles pointing toward the sound behind them. Seeing the dog, Leroy raised his rifle to shoot just as Rex jumped, grabbing Jed by the arm.

Luke said, "Drop da rifle fer I shoot."

Leroy saw Luke and dropped his rifle, and Jed said, "Call yer dog off me."

Luke called Rex off, and Rex let Jed go and returned to Luke. Luke said, "Unbuckle yer gun belts, and let them drop."

Both of the men unbuckled their gun belts and let them drop. Stepping away from them, Luke went over and picked up their belts and rifles and motioned them toward the cave. Once inside the cave, Luke tied them while Rex watched. Luke left the cave as Jed called out, "Ya ain't gonna leave yer dog here with us, are ya?"

Luke continued to walk out of the cave, going to their horses. Bringing them as well as his horses back to the cave, he knew that he could not stay there now but would have to move on.

Luke unsaddled their horses, turning them loose. They did not want to leave till Luke fired a couple of shots and they took off toward town. Leaving the tack where he had dropped it, he went back into the cave.

When Luke entered the cave, Jed asked, "What were them shots fer? Did ya kill our horses?"

Picking up his gear, Luke loaded his horses to leave. Rex continued to keep an eye on the two men while Luke loaded the gear. If their horses went back to town and someone knew who they belonged to, there could be someone coming to look for them, if not tonight then in the morning.

After loading all his gear and tying their guns on the packhorse, he went back into the cave and called Rex. Jed asked, "What about mah arm? Yer dog done bit me, and it's bleeding. Ain't ya gonna wrap it fer me?"

"Y'all were gonna shoot us. You'll live if ya don't die of hunger first."

Luke did not like traveling during the night in new country. He figured that his best bet was to follow the road where he could make the best time. He wasn't sure how long it would take those two to get free. They might remain tied up all night, or they could be loose by now. Whichever, they would still have to find their horses, and with no saddles on them, they would be harder to catch. If the horses made it back to town, they would have a long walk.

After Luke had gone, Jed told Leroy, "Make yer way over here, and see if ya can untie me."

Leroy rolled over next to where Jed was tied, and moving to where Leroy could get his hands on the knot, he started working to untie Jed. Once Jed was untied, he untied Leroy. Stopping long enough by the fire to look at his wound, Jed wrapped his arm.

Leroy went outside to see if their horses had been shot and to look for their guns. Coming back into the cave just as Jed had finished wrapping his arm, Leroy said, "He done turned our horses loose and left our saddles here. I checked, and he done took our guns with him if'n he didn't throw them in da dark. What we gonna do, Jed?"

Jed looked at Leroy and said, "We gonna get that fella. First we gotta get them horses back and find our guns. When da moon comes out, we gonna see if'n we can track our horses. Move our gear inta da cave till we can come and get it."

Leroy went out, got their gear, and moved it into the cave. By the time he was done, the moon had started to come out. Finding some wood and cloth, he was able to make a torch where he might be able to see which way the horses had gone. They each took a rope. Lighting the torch, they walked out of the cave. Leroy showed Jed where Luke had saddled his horses and where he had unsaddled their horses. Following the tracks from their horses, they could see that the horses had headed toward town. The shots they had heard must have been to scare the horses off. If they followed the road, maybe the horses didn't go far. By now the moon was up high enough where they could see the tracks on the road.

Now that the moon had come up, Luke felt better, as he could see what was around him. Rex was still walking alongside Buck. He didn't seem to be nervous about anything, so Luke figured that they were alone. He wanted to get some distance between him and that cave in case they did get free and find their horses close by. He had checked their saddlebags for extra guns and didn't find any. The guns they had on them were now tied to his packhorse. If they were going to come after Luke, they would have to get new weapons.

Luke rode until midnight when he saw a place, leaving the road to camp. Making his way through a grove, he came to an open field. Working his way around the field so he didn't leave a trail crossing it, he found a spot where he could set up a cold camp and still watch for anyone approaching.

After unloading the packhorses, Luke tied them near camp. Rolling out his bedroll, he lay down. Rex came over and lay next to Luke. Luke looked at Rex and said, "We done had a nice warm cave befer them two showed up. Now look, we got ourself's a cold bed."

Luke went right to sleep.

Jed and Leroy kept walking toward town. They were in luck. About an hour after they started walking, they found their horses grazing alongside the road. Putting a rope on them, they started toward the cave and their saddles. It was after midnight before they reached the cave. Tying the horses, Jed decided that they should wait till morning and look for their guns before going after Luke.

Rolling out their bedrolls, Jed said, "I want that fella now more than ever. He done made a fool outta us, and he ain't gonna get away with it. If'n I gotta, I am gonna foller him ta hell."

Leroy said, "I heard in town that da army thinks he's headed west. How fer are ya will'n ta foller him?"

"He ain't gonna get away with this. He owes us now. If he got our guns, I aim ta get em back," said Jed. "We should be able ta pick up his trail in da morning."

They both rolled over and went to sleep.

kentucky

Luke woke with a start. He had been sound asleep when he was startled. Rex was lying next to him, looking toward the field. Looking there, Luke saw a deer grazing. Relaxing, Luke got up and made a fire for a hot breakfast. While eating, Luke took out the map. Luke tried to decide if he should change his route. He figured that the two would again try and catch up with him now that they knew who he was. Maybe the next time he would have to kill them.

He would head for London, avoiding any towns on the way. Putting the map away, Luke finished breakfast.

After breakfast, Luke cleaned up camp and started down the road. He had taken their guns. Maybe he could find a place in London where he could sell them or trade them. He didn't need any additional weapons as he already had spares.

Jed and Leroy were awake at first light. Building up the fire, Leroy started making breakfast while Jed went out to look for their weapons. When Jed returned, Leroy had finished breakfast. He asked, "Did ya find our guns?"

Jed said, "Na, he must have taken them with him. We're gonna have ta get some new ones. I did take a look at da road and saw he headed north. He won't be thinking that we will be follering him with no guns."

After finishing eating, they saddled their horses and started. Just before noon Jed saw a spot where two horses left the road. Following the trail, they found the place where Luke had spent the night. Looking around the campsite, they did not find anything that would help them.

Returning to the road after resting their horses, they headed north again. Jed kept watching the trail, tracking Luke's horses. Hurrying, they needed to make up time during the day when they could see his tracks. In late afternoon, they met a man riding south. Stopping him, Jed asked, "Have ya come across a fella traveling with a packhorse head'n north?"

The man said, "Na, ain't seen no one but you taday."

Leroy asked, "Might ya have a couple of spare guns ya could sell?"

The man said, "I might have one ta spare."

Jed said, "Let me see it."

The man got off his horse and took a pistol out of his saddlebags and handed it to Jed. Jed took a look at it.

"How much ya want fer it?" asked Jed.

"Ten dollars," said the man.

Reaching into his saddlebag, he took out the ten dollars and gave it to him. It turned out that it was the same caliber of his own gun, so he had ammunition for it. Thanking the man, they rode on.

Leroy said, "That done took all our money. How we gonna get another gun, Jed?"

Jed said, "Ya just leave that up ta me."

Jed and Leroy continued. They at least had one gun again, but they would need another weapon if they ran into Luke.

Luke was a lot more cautious riding the open road after the two from the night before had tried to capture or kill him. Keeping an eye on the trail ahead of him, he thought he saw dust rising.

Moving off the trail into some trees, he waited. It wasn't long until he saw a lone man riding south. He continued to watch until he had passed.

Returning to the road, Luke continued on toward London. By midafternoon, Luke could see Pineville. Not wanting to be seen in town, Luke skirted the town. He knew that by doing this it would take longer, and the two men, if they were following, would gain ground on him. His only hope was that he had enough of a lead that they would give up on him.

Reaching the north side of town, he returned to the road. Riding until it was close to dark, he stopped and set up a cold camp.

Making sure there wasn't anyone else in the area, he picketed his horses after seeing that they had water and feed. They needed to rest, as they did not get much the night before. He wanted them as fresh as they could be if they caught up to him.

Keeping an eye on Rex while he was setting up his camp, he was sure that they were alone. Rex lay down like he had every night since they had become friends. After eating, Luke laid down to get some sleep. Rex came over to Luke and lay down next to him.

Jed and Leroy rode into Pineville as evening was coming on. Seeing a few people still on the street, they stopped asking if anyone had seen a man heading north with a packhorse and dog. No one had seen Luke going through town. They rode on, making camp outside of town.

When Luke had turned their horses loose, at least the food they had was in their saddlebags, and now with a gun they might be able to get some fresh game. While Leroy set up camp, Jed went hunting. Not too far from where they had stopped, Jed found a farm that had chickens. Making his way closer, he didn't see anyone by the buildings.

Going behind the barn, he entered from the corral. Inside the barn, he saw some chickens walking around, pecking at grain on the floor. Keeping an eye on the doors, making sure that no one came in, his eyes spotted a rifle hanging on the wall. Taking the rifle, he saw that it was in good shape and loaded. The farmer must have left it where he could get at it in a hurry if something happened while working near the barn.

With the rifle in hand, he started to leave when he saw a pitchfork leaning against a stall. Taking the pitchfork in hand, he speared one of the chickens near an empty stall. He was able to spear the chicken without it making enough noise to raise an interest from the house.

They now had a second weapon and fresh meat for supper. He headed back to camp. At camp, Leroy had a fire going with coffee brewing. Looking up as Jed came into camp, he saw the chicken before he saw the rifle.

Reaching for the chicken, Leroy asked, "Where did ya find that rifle and hen?"

"Found them at da farmer's place just across da field."

"Didn't they object ta ya taking them?"

"Na," said Jed. "They ain't gonna miss them till morning. We need ta get go'n early fer they come'a look'n fer them.

Leroy cleaned the chicken and then put it on the fire to cook. While the hen was cooking, Jed went and moved the horses closer to camp. If the farmer came looking for them, he wanted to be able to leave in a hurry. They would have to sleep light this night.

Once the hen was done, Jed and Leroy ate. Glad for the fresh meat, they were quiet while they ate. Once they were done eating, Leroy said, "Where do ya think that fella is headed fer? Ya don't think that we rode past him and he might be come'n look'n fer us, do ya?"

Jed said, "Naw, I don't think he stopped ta wait ta see if we were follering him."

"Well, no one seen him go'n in town. Do ya think he went around?" asked Leroy.

"It makes sense ta me that he might not want ta take da chance of being recognized in town like we done. He might want ta stay where he ain't gonna be seen by anyone," answered Jed. "We'll go north in da morning and see if we can pick up his trail again. Ya know that da one horse had new shoes on his front, so we can look fer that. Put out da fire befer turning in. If that farmer come look'n, we don't want ta give him any help."

Leroy and Jed rolled out their bedrolls and lay down. Jed woke before the sun had started to come up. Waking Leroy, he said, "We need ta get go'n."

Leroy said, "We ain't et yet."

"We ain't gonna be here when that farmer comes look'n fer his rifle neither."

Breaking camp, they quickly saddled their horses. Jed gave Leroy the rifle. Leroy felt better that he again had a gun.

Riding for a couple of miles, they stopped to make coffee and eat the leftover chicken. By the time they were done, it had gotten light enough so that they would be able to see any tracks in the road. Walking back to the road, Jed took a close look for fresh tracks. Most of the tracks were heading toward Pinesville, but his eyes caught a set of tracks heading toward Barbourville that he recognized.

Turning to Leroy, he said, "I done told ya he was just avoiding town. Come look at these tracks. They belong ta them horses of his. I'd say they were made sometime yesterday evening. We gotta be close ta him. From da way he's traveling, he ain't in a hurry. I bet he don't think he is being follered."

"How far behind him do ya think we are?" asked Leroy.

"Maybe only a couple of hours," said Jed.

Mounting, they headed north, moving at a faster pace, trying to close the gap between themselves and Luke.

In the morning, Luke got up and checked on the horses. Seeing that they still had grass to eat, he left them and returned to camp. He decided he would make some coffee and biscuits. Luke and Rex sat down and ate. Luke was cleaning up his camp when he heard horses traveling on the road, heading north at a rapid pace. Leaving his horses, he made his way to where he could see the road and remain hidden. Rex came with him, staying by his side. Luke got in place just in time to see the two who he had left tied up at the cave. He also saw that they again had a couple of guns.

Rex also recognized them and let out a low growl. Luke put his hand on Rex's head to quiet him. After they had passed, Luke returned to camp to think on what he was going to do next. He had been lucky that they had missed where he left the road. He knew for sure now that he was being followed. Now he had to worry about an ambush if they realized that he was behind them.

Taking time to study the tracks that they had left, he saw that each horse had its shoes marked. One had a bar across the bottom of his left front shoe. The other had a defective hole in his right rear shoe. Luke would be able to spot them anywhere.

Leaving the road, Luke started to follow a path that was somewhat parallel to the trail that the men were following. As he rode, he looked for any tracks that crossed the path he was taking. With the path not as open as the road, travel was slower. That did not bother Luke, as he was not meeting up with anyone.

Every hour Luke would go back to the road to see if the two men were still in front of him. At noon, he checked the trail. Seeing they were still ahead of him, he stopped to rest and eat. Luke made a cold camp just in case they were close enough to smell smoke or coffee. According to the trail they were leaving, they were still in a hurry.

Luke began to think maybe they had gotten into trouble of their own and were not looking for him. No matter; he would have to be careful. Taking a longer break, it gave them time to get farther ahead.

It was midafternoon when Luke started traveling. He decided that he would stay on the road and follow their trail.

Jed and Leroy had kept moving at a fast pace trying to overtake Luke. At noon, they moved off the road to rest their horses and eat. Before leaving the trail, Jed searched the road for Luke's trail, not finding it. This began to worry on him as they built a fire.

Sitting down, Jed said, "I didn't see no sign of him befer we stopped. I wonder if he got behind us or left da road."

"What we gonna do now?" asked Leroy.

"We keep go'n north, only we gonna slow down. We need ta keep an eye on our back trail and see if he is follering us," said Jed.

They finished eating and resting their horses, all the while keeping an eye on their back trail. Not seeing anyone, they headed out with Jed keeping an eye on the road ahead, searching for any sign of Luke while Leroy kept watching behind them.

They rode all afternoon, entering Barbourville late in the day. Jed figured that if they stayed near town they wouldn't have to worry about Luke, as it looked like he was avoiding towns. In the morning, they would again head north, and if they did not see any sign of Luke, they would head for home.

Luke kept following their tracks for two miles until he saw where they left the road. Getting off his horse, he followed their tracks to where they had stopped. Back on the road, he saw that they had slowed their pace.

Stopping to study their tracks, he figured that they finally realized that they had passed him and were waiting for him to catch up to them. Luke would have to think about how he was going to proceed. Maybe he should change his route to avoid them completely.

Taking it easy, he continued following their trail, making sure they did not double back or leave the road. Luke also kept an eye out for a place where they could set up an ambush.

Riding all afternoon, he followed their trail. When evening came, he stopped before dark, making camp. Looking the area over, he found a farm. Going up to the house, the farmer came out carrying a rifle. Luke could see that the rifle that the farmer was carrying was old and not in good shape. As Luke rode in, he kept his hands out where the farmer could see them, showing that he meant no harm to them. Stopping short of the farmer, the farmer asked, "What can I do fer ya?"

Luke said, "I was wondering if ya might spare some feed fer mah horses and me? I'd be willing ta pay fer it."

"Who ya be?" asked the farmer.

"I am Luke Taylor," said Luke.

"I heard that name mentioned in town. I believe they done said something about a murder of some carpetbagger. Are ya da one who killed that carpetbagger fella?" asked the farmer.

"I am," said Luke, putting his hand on his pistol. "Is that gonna be a problem?"

The farmer lowered his rifle and walked up to Luke before saying, "Not with us. Yer welcome here, son. Step down. Ya can put yer horses in da barn. There is hay and grain in there. When ya are done, ya can wash up back of da house befer ya come in."

Luke thanked the farmer and stepped down before leading his horses to the barn with Rex following. He stopped and watered them before putting the horses in the barn. Before entering the house, Luke washed up in back of the house where the farmer showed him. While he was washing up, the farmer came out to wash up himself.

"By the way, mah name is Samual Perry. Ya can call me Sam." Looking down at Rex, he said, "That dog of yers don't let ya out of his sight, does he?"

Luke said, "We kind of grew on each other."

"Come on in. Mae Belle has some supper on. Ya can join us." Then looking at the dog, he added, "Ya can join us as well."

"Thanks," said Luke. "I sure think it mighty kindly of ya and yer wife."

Going into the house, Mae Belle was just putting a platter of meat on the table. Luke could see that there were only three places set at the table. From that, he figured that they did not have any children. Luke removed his hat, nodding toward Mae Belle.

Sam said, "Ma, this here is Luke Taylor, and that thar is Rex. Luke, this har is mah wife, Mae Belle."

"Good ta meet ya, ma'am."

Mae Belle said, "You can hang your hat on the peg by the door and take a seat at the table. Do you want some coffee?"

"Thank you," said Luke as he hung up his hat and told Rex to stay by the door before sitting down at the table. Sam took the seat at the end of the table while Mae Belle poured coffee before she sat down with them. Both Luke and Sam waited until Mae Belle had joined them before they started eating. While they were eating, they talked about what Sam had heard.

Luke asked, "What have they been saying about me?"

Sam said, "While I was in town about two weeks ago, I stopped in da saloon fer a beer. While I was there, this army officer came in and talked ta da barkeep ask'n if he had seen a man by da name Luke Taylor come inta the saloon or any strangers traveling alone during the past two months.

"The barkeep asked, 'What ya look'n fer him fer? We had several stranger pass'n through here since da war ended.'

"The army officer said, 'Received a dispatch on this fellow saying that he had killed a man. If you see him, send a telegram to the nearest army post. There is a reward for him.'

"The barkeep asked who he had killed.

"'They said it was a government man working with an agent collecting taxes on their farm,' said the officer. The dispatch said that when they rode up to the farm, you were hiding in the barn and started shooting before they could say who they were or why they were there."

Sam went on to say, "After da officer left, I talked ta da barkeep, and he agreed with me that if we come across ya, we wouldn't turn ya in. Them carpetbaggers done some mean, dirty things ta a lot of people, and if ya killed one, ya did good. Do ya mind telling what happened?"

Luke told Sam and Mae Belle what had happened, explaining that it was in defense of his family. Now he had people after him, so he had to be careful of who he talked to. He went on to tell them about the night in the cave and about the two men following him.

When they had finished supper, Mae Belle got a plate and put some meat in it and put it down in front of Rex. Rex looked at Luke, and when Luke nodded, he started eating.

Sam said, "We ain't got room fer ya in da house, but yer welcome ta sleep in da barn."

Luke said, "That would be nice. I ain't had a roof over mah head since I left home. That sure was a mighty fine meal, ma'am, and I thank ya kindly fer feeding mah dog as well."

Leaving the house, Luke and Rex went to the barn. Finding an empty stall, he put some fresh straw in it before laying his bedroll on top of the straw. When he lay down, he remembered how nice it was to lie in a soft bed at home and how hard the ground was. Some day he would be able to sleep in a soft bed every night again.

In the morning, Sam came into the barn just as Luke was waking up.

Sam asked, "How'd ya sleep?"

"That was the best night's sleep I have had in a long time," said Luke.

"Come on inta da house. Ma has breakfast on," said Sam

Stopping to wash up on the way, Luke felt refreshed and well rested. Rex had seemed more comfortable in the barn than he did when he was in the cave with Luke. Entering the house, the table again had been set; only this time before Mae Belle sat down, she took food over for Rex, placing it on the floor where he was lying. This time Rex started eating right away.

Luke said, "Ya gonna spoil that dog."

Mae Belle sat down, and when they started eating, she asked, "Have you had Rex long?"

Luke said, "Na, we met on da trail. One night he came inta mah camp with a sore paw. Since then he has been tagging along with me. We kind of keep each other company and look out fer each other."

After they finished eating, Luke again thanked Mae Belle for the good meal and for feeding Rex. Luke offered to pay for the meals, but Sam turned it down.

In the barn, Luke saddled his horses while Sam went and put some grain in a sack for Luke to take along. By the time Sam had the grain ready, Luke was loading the packhorse. Sam handed Luke the sack of grain.

Luke said, "Ya need ta let me pay ya fer the feed."

Sam said, "Na. Ya gonna need yer money where yer headed."

Luke picked up one of the rifles that he had taken off the two men at the cave and handed it to Sam, saying, "Here, take this extra rifle I have. I got it from those men who tried ta kill me. I seen yer rifle, and ya could us a new one. I don't know if I would shoot that one ya got in da house."

Sam said, "That is a mighty fine look'n rifle. I sure could use a new one. Thank ya."

As they came out of the barn, Mae Belle came from the house carrying a package. She walked up to Luke, handing the package to him, saying, "The way you were eating my bread, I figured that you could use some to take with you. There is a little something for Rex in there as well."

Luke took the package, thanking her and putting it on the packhorse with his other food. Mounting, he turned toward them and said, "I sure do want ta thank ya fer all yer kindness."

Sam said, "Best of luck ta ya. I hope ya don't run inta them fellas again."

Mae Belle said her good-byes before Luke turned and rode off.

Turning in the saddle, he waved one last time to them as he rode away. He knew he was getting close to Barbourville, so he again left the road to circle around town. When he reached the other side of town, he rode back to the road. Before entering the road, he looked for any sign of the two men. It didn't take him long to see what he was looking for. There, just as plain as day, was the shoe with the bar and the other one with the hole. They were still ahead of him.

Jed and Leroy started out of Barbourville in the morning. Jed remembered that they had gone a couple of miles out of Pinesville before he tried to pick up Luke's trail at the last town. After going a couple of miles, he stopped looking around and did not see any sign of Luke. After going five miles they still had not see any sign of Luke.

Jed turned to Leroy and said, "We done lost him, Leroy. I ain't see any sign of him since Pinesville. We need ta head back."

Leroy said, "I think yer right. We ain't got any money left and we're running outta food."

Turning around, they started back, disgusted that they had lost that easy money and their guns did not sit well with Jed. He kept grumbling under his breath while Leroy kept shaking his head as they rode. If they had been paying attention, they might have seen the dust rising on the road heading their way.

Luke had kept an eye on the road and saw the dust coming his way. Not knowing who it was, he cut off the road, getting out of sight. It wasn't long before the riders came into view. Luke was surprised to see that it was Jed and Leroy. Luke watched as they rode pass.

Jed was still mumbling to himself when he saw the track in the road that he had been looking for. Stopping, he turned to Leroy and said, "He's on da road. Keep riding, and we will circle back ta find him."

Continuing, they rode out of sight of Luke. Luke decided to wait to make sure that they did not return before going on. He waited to see if they saw his tracks.

After Jed and Leroy were out of sight, Jed said, "I seen his track go'n off da road back there. We need ta leave da horses here and go back on foot."

Taking their horses off the road and tying them, they made their way using the trees for cover. As they got close to where Jed had seen the tracks, he heard a horse snort. Stopping, he waited. It wasn't long before he heard a horse stomp. Now being even more cautious, they headed in the direction where they had heard the sound. It wasn't long before Jed spotted Luke's horses. Seeing his rifle still on the packhorse, he decided that he was going to get it.

Rex had been lying next to Luke when all of a sudden his head came up and his ears were pointed toward the south. Luke knew that Rex had heard something. They got up and moved to where he could keep an eye on the horses. He didn't have long to wait before he saw movement coming through the trees. Luke put his hand on Rex to keep him quiet.

Jed looked around, and not seeing Luke or the dog, he moved into the open. When he was headed for the packhorse to get his rifle he heard the growl from Rex and froze in his tracks. Leroy had been following Jed and was just coming into the opening when he saw Jed freeze before he heard the growl. Looking toward the sound, he saw Rex and raised his rifle, aiming it at Rex.

Luke saw Leroy raise his rifle. Luke fired, hitting Leroy in the chest and knocking him back and to the ground. Jed, hearing the shot, turned and, seeing Luke, raised his pistol. Luke, seeing Leroy was hit, turned and, seeing Jed had a pistol, fired at Jed. He saw Jed spin but remain standing. Jed again started to raise his pistol when Luke fired a third time, hitting Jed in the head, killing him instantly.

Luke walked over and checked Jed; seeing he was dead, he went to check Leroy. Leroy was also dead. Picking up the rifle Leroy had with him, he went over and picked up the pistol that Jed had. Checking their pockets for any money and finding none, he got his horses and went looking for their horses, leaving the two men lying where they fell. Following their tracks, he found where they had left the road. It was there that he found their horses. Leading them back to his horses, he took a rope off their saddles and tied them to each other before tying them to his packhorse.

Now he had another problem. He had killed two more men and had their horses. He would have to get rid of their horses the first chance he had before someone called him a horse thief as well as a murderer. With the two men dead, chances were no one would recognize the horses. They had come some ways from Mipplesboro where he first saw them. Chances were they were strangers here themselves.

Luke wanted to put some distance from those two bodies before anyone found them. He decided that he needed to stay off the main road until he had gotten the distance he wanted.

Late that afternoon, Luke found a campsite that was well hidden. Unloading his packhorse and unsaddling the other horses, he hobbled them in a field with fresh grass and water. Setting up his camp, he started a fire and made supper. Looking in the package that Mae Belle had given him, he found fresh bread and some leftover supper from last night for Rex. Putting the food down, it didn't take Rex long before he had consumed it.

Luke enjoyed some of the fresh bread with his supper. Finishing eating, he picked up the saddlebags from the extra horses and went through them. He found some extra ammunition, salt, and flour that he put with his supplies. Looking at the saddles, he took the scabbards to put on his packhorse. They could be used to hold the extra rifles. There was some extra clothing but not much more.

Maybe he should have taken the time to bury the bodies. Luke figured that the only reason they would have done anything with his body would have been for the reward. If he had waited around and buried them and if anyone had been in the area, they would have asked a lot of questions that Luke did not want to answer.

Putting the two men out of his mind, he put the saddlebags aside and lay back. Rex came over to Luke and put his head in Luke's lap. Luke reached down and started scratching Rex's head and began thinking about what the next day might bring. He was still two days from London where he figured he might be able to sell his extra guns. He might be able to sell the horses as well.

Luke lay back and went to sleep. During the night, Rex got up and walked out of camp, waking Luke when he got up. Seeing that Rex was not growling, Luke figured that nothing was wrong and continued to lie still. He did reach up and put his hand on one of his pistols just in case. It wasn't long before Rex returned and lay down again.

The next morning Luke got up and made breakfast. Early that morning he had gotten restless thinking about what to do with those extra horses. Maybe he should just turn them loose. Luke decided that he would split up his gear between the three horses, putting the pack saddle on one of the extra horses and his saddle on the other extra horse. Using one of the extra saddles, he would tie some of his gear on the bay, leaving the buckskin with just a saddle on him. That way if he ran into someone on the trail, they may not be as curious about his extra horses.

That afternoon Luke stopped early to hunt, as his meat supply was running low. Finding a wooded area, he tied the horses and unloaded them before hunting. Luck was with him. When he got to the edge of the trees, there was an open field with a nice doe grazing. He dropped her. Going out to where she lay, he started to dress her. Rex had followed and lay nearby watching Luke work. While he was working, Rex started to growl. Looking up, Luke saw someone coming from the other direction carrying a rifle. Luke kept working while the man approached and told Rex to be quiet. Rex settled back down, still keeping an eye on the man as he arrived.

"Nice doe," said the man. "I heard yer dog growling. Is he okay?"

"Thanks. He'll be all right. Don't take kindly ta strangers at first though."

The man asked, "It's good ta have a companion when yer out. Do ya need any help ta get her back ta yer camp?"

"Could use a hand if yer a mind ta. Ya live here abouts?"

The man put his gun down before saying, "Mah place is just on da other side of that grove over there. Heard yer shot and came ta see what was go'n on."

"Got a farm there?" asked Luke.

"Yup," said the man. "Mah wife and two kids live there with me."

"Could ya use some fresh meat? This here doe is bigger than I need," said Luke.

"Wouldn't mind some," said the man. "Here, let me give ya a hand."

They finished cleaning the deer, and the man asked Luke, "Why don't ya come up ta da place fer da night. I'll have da wife cook us up some of this fresh meat fer supper, and yer welcome ta spend da night in da barn."

Luke said, "Thanks. I sure would enjoy that. What's yer name? I'm Luke Taylor."

The famer said, "Mines Isaac Green."

Luke said, "Let me get mah horses, and we can load her on them ta take her ta your place."

Luke went back to camp, returning after loading his gear again. Isaac was surprised to see Luke coming with four horses but didn't say anything about it. After loading the deer on two of the horses, they started heading to Isaac's place.

As they came into the yard, a young boy came running out to meet them with a girl following. As they reached Isaac, he turned to Luke and said, "Meet mah children. This here is little Isaac and mah daughter, Dorothy."

Luke said, "Howdy, kids. Ya have some nice look'n children here, Isaac."

Little Isaac asked, "Can I pet yer dog, mister?"

Luke called Rex to him. Rex had been following behind the horses as they approached the farm and had moved off as the children came running out. Once Rex was by Luke's side, he said, "Son, ya want ta be careful with this here dog. He don't take ta strangers right off. He got ta get ta know ya first. If ya come here, ya might be able ta pet him."

Little Isaac walked over toward Luke, and Luke heard Rex give a low growl. Reaching down and petting his head, Rex quit growling and leaned against Luke. Little Isaac reached out to pet Rex while Luke told Rex it was okay. Once little Isaac started petting Rex, Rex started to relax and move closer to little Isaac. Dorothy, seeing little Isaac petting Rex, reached out as well and started petting him. While the kids and Rex were getting to know each other, Isaac's wife came out of the house.

Isaac said, "This here's mah wife, Anna. Anna, this here fella is Luke Taylor. I invited him ta supper, and he done brung us some fresh meat. As soon as we get her hung in da barn, we'll cut ya some ta cook fer supper."

Luke said, "Nice ta meet ya, ma'am. Hope I ain't gonna be any trouble fer ya."

Anna said, "Nice to meet you. You won't be any trouble at all. It's going to be nice to have some fresh meat. I was just telling Isaac this morning we could use some fresh meat. While you two are cutting up the deer, I'll go get supper started. Kids, you say out of your pa's and Mr. Taylor's way."

Anna turned around and headed back to the house while the kids ran off with Rex chasing after them. Isaac and Luke went to the barn where they hung the deer.

Isaac said, "Ya can turn yer horses loose in da corral. There is some hay in da loft ya can throw down fer them."

Luke thanked him and unsaddled them, putting the gear in the barn before turning them loose in the corral. By the time Luke had thrown down the hay and returned to the deer, Isaac had it skinned. Cutting out some of the back strap, he took it to Anna for supper. Returning, they continued to cut up the deer until Anna called that supper was ready. Stopping by the side of the house, they washed up before going in for supper. Luke looked around for Rex and didn't find him. Maybe he went with the children.

When Luke entered the house, he saw that Rex was already in the house with the kids, and they had made sure that he was fed. Seeing that Rex was busy eating, he smiled. Thinking to himself, he thought it sure would be nice to know what had happened to Rex before they met. Getting his attention, Anna pointed to a chair, indicating that Luke should sit there. Hanging his hat, he sat down.

During supper, Anna asked, "Where are you from?"

Luke said, "I'm from Greenville, Virginia."

"What brings you our way?" asked Isaac.

"Head'n west," said Luke.

"Seems like there's lots of folk's head'n west these days," said Isaac. "The war has hurt a lot of people. I talked ta a family a week or so back that was moving west. Said that they were gonna meet some of their relatives who had gone ahead of them near St. Louis or Independence, Missouri. Da fella said his name was Frank Daily, I believe. Said that what da war hadn't destroyed da carpetbaggers were taking. He packed what he could and left. Seemed like a right nice family too."

Luke said, "Mah folks were able ta save their farm from da carpetbaggers but only had enough ta take care of them. Lost a brother ta some outlaws during da war, and mah pa was wounded. They still got mah brother and two sister's help'n with da farm."

"Mind me ask'n why ya didn't stay and help yer folks if they still had their farm?" asked Isaac.

"I killed a man who was trying ta kill mah pa. They said it was murder. Knowing I didn't have a chance with them northern folks, I am heading west," said Luke.

After they had finished supper, Isaac and Luke excused themselves and went back to the barn to finish butchering the deer. Isaac salted the meat that they were going to keep to cook and wrapped it, putting it in the root cellar. While Isaac was putting their meat away, Luke continued to cut his meat into strips that he could jerk. When Isaac returned, he told Luke that he had a smoker out back where he could dry the meat he wanted.

Taking his meat, they headed for the smoker. While Luke was laying his meat on the racks, Isaac started a fire to dry the meat. When everything was completed, Isaac told Luke that he would have to add wood during the night. If he stoked the fire about midnight, it should continue to burn the rest of the night. Thanking Isaac, Luke headed for the barn while Isaac went to the house.

When Isaac opened the door, Rex came running out looking for Luke. Seeing Luke, he ran to him. Luke looked down at him and said, "I thought ya were gonna leave me fer them kids."

Rubbing Rex's head, they went into the barn and laid out Luke's bedroll. About midnight, Luke woke with a start. At first, he didn't know why, but then remembered that he needed to stoke the fire in the smoker. Getting up, Rex followed Luke out to the smoker. Putting more wood on the fire, Luke felt that it should be good until morning. Returning to the barn, they lay down and went back to sleep.

In the morning, Isaac came into the barn calling. When Luke sat up, Isaac said, "Ma's got breakfast on. Checked yer meat, and it should be ready by da time we eat. Get washed up, and come in da house."

Luke got up and rubbed the sleep from his eyes and headed for the wash stand. After washing up, Luke went to the house. Opening the door, he could smell the aroma of fresh bread baking. As Rex entered, the kids ran over and started petting him. He stood there waging his tail and started licking little Isaac's hand. Dorothy ran to her ma and got some food for Rex. Returning, she set it down and went to the table while Rex enjoyed his breakfast.

Anna had made some donuts that were sitting on the table. Luke had not seen them before and asked what they were. Anna laughed and said, "Try one."

Luke took one, and taking a bite out of it, he thought that it tasted very good. It almost tasted like a cake his ma use to make. By the time they had finished breakfast, he had eaten eight of the donuts along with three eggs and half a dozen slices of bacon.

Anna said, "I have not seen a man eat like that for some time. I would have to say you like the donuts as well."

Luke said, "Yup, ma'am. I can't say I ate anything like them befer. They sure are good. Mah ma use ta bake, but she never made donuts."

Getting up, Isaac went out with Luke to help him collect his meat. Wrapping it, they took it to the barn where he could put it with his gear. Luke had also salted some of the meat that he could cook for his meals the next few days.

While Luke was in the barn, he saw a packsaddle in the corner of the barn that looked like it had not been used for some time. Turning to Isaac, he asked, "Would ya like to make a trade fer that pack saddle?"

Isaac said, "Ain't used it in some time. I use a wagon ta do our hauling now. I could use a saddle fer da boy. He's get'n old enough ta ride. "

Luke said, "Take yer pick of these two, and ya got a trade."

Isaac picked the saddle that he felt little Isaac could use while Luke went over and picked up the pack saddle. That would look better when he rode into London.

Taking the horses out of the corral, Isaac helped Luke saddle them and put his gear on two of the horses. Luke again used one of the extra horses for a packhorse as well as the bay, putting saddles on the other horse and buckskin.

Isaac asked, "Don't mean ta be stickn mah nose in where it don't belong, but how come ya got three saddle horses anyhow?"

"Couple of days ago two men jumped me. When they tried ta shoot me, I had ta kill them. I couldn't just leave their horses there ta die, so I brung them along. Figured on selling them in London," said Luke.

"Ya might try da stable in London. I heard he does a lot of horse trading," said Isaac.

Luke asked, "How far ta London from here?"

Isaac said, "Ya could be there sometime tanight or midmorn tamorrow."

After finishing putting his gear on and tying it down, Anna came out carrying a package. She said, "Seeing how you like my donuts so much, I put enough to last you a couple of days if you don't try and eat them all at once."

Luke put them on the packhorse, thanking her. Mounting, he said good-bye to Anna and Isaac while the kids said good-bye to Rex. Riding out, he waved one last time before they turned to go about their work.

Luke rode most of the day, stopping early in the afternoon so he would not enter London until midday.

london, kentucky

In the morning, Luke saddled his buckskin and put packs on his bay and one of the sorrels and saddled the other. When he entered town, he would try and sell the one sorrel and keep the other one as an extra packhorse.

When Luke started breakfast, Rex went out hunting and caught a rabbit. Returning to camp with his catch, he lay by the fire to eat his breakfast while Luke ate his.

Putting out the fire, Luke headed for London. It was late morning when Luke reached the edge of town. Stopping before entering, he watched the main street. There seemed to be a lot of activity going on with a group of soldiers halfway down the street. Not wanting to draw attention to himself, he rode down the street looking for the stable. Seeing it just past the soldiers, he rode around them and up to the front of the stable.

Going by the soldiers, he saw they had three men tied up in the back of a buckboard. One of them looked to have been beaten quite badly, and another had been wounded. It didn't look like they had been treated, nor did it look like anyone was getting them help. Some of the soldiers watching the prisoners kept an eye on Luke as he rode by. He watched the sergeant, who was walking over to where the wagon sat. The sergeant turned to take a second look at Luke. He raised his hand to stop Luke and started to say something when one of the soldiers by the wagon called for the sergeant to come to the wagon. Luke felt relieved when he saw the sergeant turn towards the wagon without saying anything to him. He wondered if the the sergeant had recognized him. While he was in town he would have to be careful.

Stopping at the stable, Luke asked the man, "What's gon'n on with them fellas?"

The man said, "Them soldier boys brought them three in this morning. I heard one say something about these three being part of a raiding party they caught."

"Where are they take'n them ta?" asked Luke.

"They ain't going anywhere. If it's like the last fellas they brought in, they'll be hung come morning," said the man.

Luke asked, "Are ya da fella who owns this stable, or do ya know where I might find him?"

The man answered, "I own it. What can I do for you?"

Luke said, "I got me a horse I'd like ta sell."

"How did you come about to have the extra horse?" the man asked, suspiciously looking at Luke.

Luke didn't want to tell the man how he really got the horse, so he said, "Me and mah friend were riding up from da Gap a few days back and got ambushed by a couple of men. They wounded mah friend. We were able ta run them off, but mah friend was bleeding real badly, and I couldn't stop it befer he died. If I can sell his horse, I'll send da money ta his folks."

"Let's take a look at him," said the man.

Luke dismounted and tied his horse to the hitching post before bringing up the sorrel. The man looked him over and saw that he was a sound horse. He did some figuring and said, "I'll give you twenty dollars for him."

Luke said, "Make it thirty, and I'll throw in da saddle."

The man said, "Twenty-five with the saddle, and you can leave your other horses here till you leave."

"Throw in some gain fer mah other horses, and we got a deal," said Luke.

They shook hands on it, and the man drew up a bill of sale for the horse.

"What name do I put on the bill of sale?" asked the man.

"John Hicks," replied Luke.

The man handed Luke the money, and Luke signed the bill of sale. Putting the money in his pocket, the man took the sorrel and entered the stable.

Turning to Luke, he said, "Get your horses and follow me."

Luke untied his horses and led them into the stable.

The man pointed to three stalls near the back of the stable and said, "You can put them there."

Luke unloaded his horses, putting his gear on the ground. Unsaddling the horses, he put them in a stall. Turning to the man, he asked, "Can I leave mah gear here till morning?"

The man said, "Ya, you can put it in the corner next to the box there with the grain in it, and it will be all right."

Luke thanked the man and put his gear next to the grain box. Taking some grain in a scoop, he gave some to each of the horses before picking up his bedroll and saddlebags. Walking out of the stable, Luke saw a hotel up the street in the direction he had come from. Again walking around the soldiers, avoiding the sergeant, Luke and Rex headed for the hotel.

Luke stopped at the entrance to the hotel, wondering what he would do with Rex. He decided that Rex would stay in the room with him. Entering the hotel, he went straight to the desk where the clerk was sitting. As he walked up to the clerk, Luke could see the clerk eyeing his dog. Reaching the desk, he said, "Do ya got a room?"

The clerk said, "If he stays, ya gotta pay fer him too."

Luke paid the clerk and signed the register as John Hicks. The clerk gave Luke a key, indicating that they had to go up the stairs. Luke and Rex went to their room.

His room was at the end of the hall with a window overlooking the main street. Looking down the street, Luke could see that several people were gathering around the soldiers. A man was talking to one of the soldiers, pointing at one of the men in the buckboard. Luke figured that he might know that one. The soldier kept shaking his head at whatever the man was saying. Finally the man angrily walked away, shaking his head and not looking back.

Looking beyond the stable, Luke saw a sign that said General Store and below in smaller letters it said Gunsmith. Luke decided that he would see if he could sell some of his extra guns. Leaving the hotel, he stopped at the café to get something to eat.

Entering the café, Luke took a seat in the corner where Rex would be out of the way. Sitting down, he motioned for Rex to lie down behind him against the wall. The waitress came over with coffee and a menu. When she returned, Luke ordered his dinner and asked if there might be a spare bone for Rex. The waitress nodded and returned shortly with a bone.

While Luke was waiting for his food, the man he had seen talking to the soldier came in with another man and took the table next to Luke. Luke could see that the man was still upset and figured that there was more to it then what had happened with the soldiers. When he saw Rex lying there eating a bone, he got up and said, "What's that mangy dog do'n in here?"

He started toward Rex, and Rex dropped his bone and started growling.

Luke said, "I don't think I'd go near him. He don't take kindly ta strangers."

The man turned, looking at Luke. He started to say something but changed his mind and sat back down. Turning to his friend, he grumbled about the dog being in the café. While he was talking, he kept looking back at Luke and then at Rex.

When Luke's dinner came, he ate, not paying attention to the two men. Luke overheard them saying something about one of the men who had been captured. The man who had been talking to the soldier was saying that he knew the one man. He believed that he had served with him during the war. He wanted to know what they had been doing when they caught him.

The one man said, "Them blue bellies have taken everything from a lot of da farmers here about. Now when they ain't got noth'n left, they want ta hang them. Next they gonna come after us. It's no wonder that some of da boys have gone ta stealing from them blue bellies."

"They come by my place look'n fer some fellas da other day. Said they had killed a soldier while holding up a pay wagon. I done thought they were gonna tear ma place apart look'n fer them. If they don't start treat'n us better, there's gonna be more of us kill'n them soldier boys," said the second man.

Luke finished his dinner, and the waitress came over with a bag. She said, "I brought you some bones for your dog to eat later if you don't mind."

Luke said, "Thanks, ma'am. I am sure he's gonna like them."

Getting up, Luke kept an eye on the man who kept looking at Rex. As Rex walked by the table, the man continued to watch him without moving as they left.

After eating, Luke decided to go to the gunsmith, but first he had to stop by the stable. Going through his gear, he picked up the two rifles and pistols. Leaving the stable, he went to the general store. As he entered the store, he saw that the clerk was working with a lady at the back of the store. On the other side of the store, he saw rifles in a rack under the gunsmith sign. Walking over to the counter, he laid his guns on the counter, waiting for the clerk. While waiting, he started looking at the guns being displayed. Luke noticed a new Henry 44–40 lever action rifle. He had heard about them but had not seen one.

When the clerk finished with the lady, he came over to help Luke. "What can I do for you?" he asked.

"Do ya buy guns, or will ya do some trading?"

"We don't usually buy guns, but we might work out a trade. What did you have in mind to trade for?"

Luke said, "I see ya have one of them Henry rifles I heard about. Mind if I take a look at it?"

The clerk reached up to the rack and took the Henry down and handed it to Luke. Luke looked it over, working the action. Laying it on the counter, he asked, "How's it work? What does it shoot?"

The clerk picked up a box of cartridges and showed Luke how to load the gun.

Luke asked, "What kind of trade ya willing ta make fer this here rifle?"

"What have you got to trade?" asked the clerk.

Luke showed him the two rifles and pistols he had brought in with him.

"How did you come about having these extra guns?" asked the clerk.

"A couple of days ago, two men tried to jump me for mah gear and horses. They didn't need their guns no more, so I brung them with me. I got mah own, so I thought I might sell these. But if yer willing ta trade them fer this Henry, I'd be much obliged."

The clerk looked the rifles over before the pistols. When he had finished, he said, "These are not in too good of shape. I'll take them off your hands in trade for the Henry and fifteen Yankee dollars."

Luke looked at the Henry and back at the clerk before he said, "I'll give ya these four guns and ten Yankee dollars fer da Henry and three boxes of cartridges."

The clerk thought for a while before he reached down and brought out two more boxes of cartridges and put them on the counter. Looking up at Luke, he said, "You got a deal there, young man."

Luke thanked the clerk and picked up his new rifle and cartridges. Calling Rex, they left the store, going back to the stable. At the stable, Luke loaded his new rifle and put the extra cartridges with his gear.

Luke figured that the new rifle would give him an edge if he got into a situation again where someone tried to ambush him. He would have to practice with it when he got a chance. Leaving the stable, he was walking past the soldiers and heard one of them say, "I sure wish the captain would get on with this here trial so we can hang these fellas and be done with them."

The other soldier said, "I heard the captain say that they would hold the trial as soon as they could get a place set up at the edge of town. He wanted to wait till some of the townspeople seen them first."

Luke went to the hotel and put his rifle in the room and sat down watching. He could see it looked like tents were being set up near the edge of town in the direction that the soldiers were taking the prisoners. Never seeing how a trial was held, he decided that he would go and check it out. That way he would know what to expect if they ever caught him.

It was late in the afternoon before the soldiers who remained in town started moving toward the tents. Getting up, Luke told Rex to stay. He left the hotel and headed for the edge of town. It was easy for him to see where the trial was being held. There was a large group of people headed in that direction. He could see the tent that had been set up with the sides open so anyone who was interested could stand outside and watch.

Luke stayed in the back where he could hear what was being said and still be out of the way. The man from the café walked past Luke, moving closer to the front of the crowd before sitting down.

A table was set up just inside the tent with a chair behind it. The three prisoners were seated to the left side of the table facing the people. Guards stood behind them as well as on the outside of the crowd to make sure no one in the audience tried anything during the trial.

Once everyone seemed to be seated, the captain came in and sat down. Turning to the prisoners, he said, "This trial will now come to order." He turned to the audience and said, "During this trial, there will be no outrage coming from you. If you do not remain quiet, I will have you removed. Any gunplay, and that person will be shot."

Turning back to the prisoners, he said, "You three have been charged with robbing an army payroll and killing the guard. How do you plead?"

The three men all started talking at once, and the captain stopped them. He pointed to the first man and asked, "How do you plead?"

"I ain't been near no payroll wagon. I have been working on da Breacher place since da war ended. Yer men come and got me there and said I done it."

The second and third man both followed the same story as the first.

The captain called for the sergeant to come forward and state his case.

The sergeant came forward to tell his story. He started out by saying, "Sir, we were on patrol when we heard shooting. Leading the troops toward the sound, we come across five men riding away from a wagon. Reaching the wagon, we found the guard dead, the pay master wounded, and the payroll missing. Leaving some men to look after the pay master, the rest of us took up pursuit of the men we had seen leaving. Their tracks were easy to follow as they were still riding hard as we pursued them. When we came to a narrowing in the road, they had stopped to set up an ambush. They wounded two of my men, and we killed two of theirs. The three remaining rode out, and we followed them. We heard shots off in the distance, and we figured they were trying to get fresh horses. When we came over the hill, we saw this one lying on the ground and the other two nearby. We told them to raise their hands and surrender. They gave up. When we told them they were going to hang for killing the guard, they said they didn't kill anyone. They said that three men had taken their horses and almost killed them. We tied them to their horses and brought them in. They were the horses we had followed. We were able to match their prints to the ones on the trail."

The captain asked, "Did you find the payroll money on them when you captured them?"

The sergeant said, "No, sir. We figured they hid it somewhere along the way. We looked on the way back but couldn't find it. They wouldn't tell us where they hid it."

The captain excused the sergeant. The captain called several of the men who had been with the sergeant, and they all said the same as the sergeant. The captain then asked the people in the audience if anyone knew these men. The man from the café stood up.

Walking to the front, he addressed the captain. "Sir" he said, "I know'd this man, and he ain't one ta kill someone. Times are hard fer all of us, but he didn't do what ya said he did. I know'd of them other two as well. All three of them boys are hard workers from Mr. Breacher. If they said they didn't rob the pay master, they didn't do it. You need to let them go and find the ones who did do it."

The captain asked, "Did you see this man this morning, or were you with him?"

The man said, "No, I ain't seen him in a week or so. Been busy with my own place."

The captain then asked, "Does anybody else know any of these men?"

When nobody else could vouch for the three men, the captain pronounced sentence. "This court finds the three of you guilty as charged. You are to be hung at sunrise tomorrow. May God have mercy on your souls. Take them away."

The man from the café said, "Did anyone get in touch with Beacher? He should be able to identify them."

The captain didn't answer but turned, leaving the man standing.

Luke knew that they did not have a chance, and if they were telling the truth about there being three others who took their horses, they were going to be executed wrongly. He kept an eye on the man who had gotten up to talk for them. When the captain announced that they were to be executed at sunrise, Luke saw the look in the man's face.

Luke wanted to see what he was up to, so when he left, he followed him. The man got his friend, and the two of them rode out of town. Thinking that they were going to get Mr. Breacher, Luke went back to the hotel.

Entering the hotel, he could hear a commotion going on upstairs. Starting up the stairs, he could hear Rex growling, so he hurried to see what happening in his room. The door to his room was open, and Rex had a man pinned to the floor, standing over him. The clerk from down stairs was at the door, looking at both Rex and the man on the floor. Rex continued to stand over the man until Luke entered the room and called him off.

Looking down at the man, Luke asked, "What ya do'n in mah room?"

The man said, "I came in by mistake. I … I didn't mean nothin.' Honest, mister. Your dog jumped me as soon as I got the door open. I just got in the wrong room."

Luke said, "Ya sure did get ta da wrong room."

Turning to the clerk, Luke asked, "Do ya know this man? Did ya rent him a room or what?"

The clerk said, "No, I didn't rent him a room. I told him not to come up here. He must have come up when I went in the back room."

Luke said, "Get the sheriff."

The clerk turned and left while Luke took the man's gun, leaving him on the floor with Rex standing by. It wasn't long before the clerk returned with the sheriff.

Luke said, "This man broke inta mah room, Sheriff. What ya gonna do about him?"

The sheriff looked at the man and said, "Lucas, I've been locking ya up fer being drunk. Now yer gonna spend the next thirty days in jail. Now get up."

The man got up and walked out with the sheriff. Luke checked the room over and saw that the man didn't have time to take anything. Looking out the window, Luke watched the sheriff take his prisoner to the jail.

Luke decided that Rex needed to go for a walk. Maybe they would hear some news about what was going on in the area. He wanted to find out why the army was still in the area. As he came down the stairs, he told the clerk that he did not want to see anyone else in his room.

As Luke walked toward the saloon, he passed two men sitting on the walk reading a paper. "I wonder how things are gonna change now that Johnson is president," said one of the men.

Luke stopped and asked, "What happened ta Lincoln?"

The man said, "Ya ain't heard he was shot? Some fella by the name of Booth shot him one night in a theater near da capital. Andrew Johnson is now da president."

"What happened ta this Booth fella?" asked Luke.

"Dang fool jumped out of the booth and broke his leg. The law caught up with him in a barn," said the man. "He's gonna hang fer sure if someone don't shoot him first."

Luke turned and continued walking. When they reached the edge of town, he saw where the army had set up camp. Not wanting to raise any questions, he turned, going back to the hotel. He stopped by the stable and checked on his horses. Looking down at Rex, he said, "We might as well eat fer we turn in."

The same waitress was working, so when she seen them sit down at the same table, she went to the kitchen before coming over. When she got to the table, she gave another bone to Rex and waited for Luke to order. After Luke ordered, she walked back to the kitchen.

While he was waiting, he heard some men talking about the trial. They were saying that they didn't think that the men got a fair trial. When the sergeant said that they didn't find any money on them, how could they still be guilty enough to be hung? If they were guilty, where was the money, or did the Sergeant and his men take the money? They continued talking when the waitress brought Luke his supper.

After eating, Luke went back to the hotel to get an early start in the morning. He wanted to get away from town and people. The longer he stayed in one place, the better chance he had of being caught. After seeing the trial the three men had he knew that he would not have a chance if he got caught.

Going up to his room, he found it was warm, so he opened the window to let in fresh air. With Rex there, no one would be able to enter the room without him knowing it. He still had the package the waitress had given him at supper for Rex, and Rex had eyed it before he lay down. He would save it for tomorrow. Luke decided that they would not eat before leaving. Once he was away from town, they would stop and eat.

Lying there, he started thinking about the trial. It wasn't long before he fell into a restless sleep. As he was drifting off, he could hear the piano from the saloon playing. It was starting to get cool outside as the sun went down.

On the edge of town at the army camp, the three men were in a tent guarded by two guards, one at the front and one at the back of the tent. Inside the tent, the men were lying on bunks but not sleeping. The two guards would walk around the tent to prevent escape.

Suddenly there was an eruption of gunfire coming from the far side of the camp. They both turned to see what was going on, and when they did, two men jumped them from behind and hit them on their heads, knocking them out. They cut the back of the tent open, taking the three men out. Once they were out, they ran toward the edge of the camp. A soldier saw the men running and opened fire, missing them as they reached cover.

Luke was suddenly awake, hearing the gunfire. Going to the window, he could see lamps being lit in several houses as he continued to hear gunfire coming from the edge of town. He saw the sheriff running up the street to see what was going on as well.

The gunfire lasted for about ten minutes, and then everything fell silent. Luke heard several horses running. Soon he heard more horses leaving and figured that must be the army following the first ones.

In the morning, Luke got ready to leave. The town was still quiet after what had happened last night. He walked to the stable and was saddling his horses when the stable owner came in. He said, "I see you're getting an early start. You didn't have anything to do with the noise last night, did you?"

Luke looked at him and said, "Naw, it woke me. What went on anyway?"

"The three men on trial yesterday escaped from the army last night. There ain't too many sad people here about this morning because of it. They said that they killed one of the men trying to free them, but no one's seen a body. Someone said that they got a body set up by their camp. No matter. It's not going to do much good. Most of the people who were at the trial believed these three men were innocent."

"Then did da three men get away?" asked Luke.

"Yup, all three. The army is still out looking for them," said the stable owner.

Luke thanked him and mounted his horse. Leaving, he had to ride by the army camp. As he got near, he could not see anyone that they had shot last night. Luke was not surprised to see that the army had lied about that as well.

Riding for about half an hour, Luke met the army returning. They looked beat. Even their horses were walking with their heads down. As they approached, the Sergeant looked at Luke and brought the troop to a halt. Luke recognized the sergeant as the one who had started to stop him when he first entered town. His heart started racing thinking that the sergeant was going to ask him who he was.

"Didn't I see you in town at the trial?" he asked.

"Ya, I was there," said Luke.

"Where you been?"

"I been in da hotel all night."

"Do you know any of the men who were on trial?"

"Nope. I ain't seen them befer," said Luke. "I just went ta da trial ta see how they go 'cause I ain't seen one befer."

"Did you see any of the men who attacked the camp last night?" asked the Sergeant.

"Can't say I did," said Luke. "I was in mah room during da time."

"I feel like I should know you from somewhere, but I just can't place you," said the Sergeant. "You can go on."

Luke rode on, fighting the urge to spur his horse into a run. If the sergeant thought he should know him, maybe he had read the dispatch about him. As he rode passed the troops, it looked like some of them were so tired that they were sleeping in the saddle. Some of the horses looked like they might not make it back to camp. If the sergeant did remember him and decided to come after him, with his horses being fresh he should be able to out run them.

Once past the troops, he again relaxed. What if the men who had rescued the three last night were raiders? Then they could be the raiders that the captain had talked about. Or it could have been some of the local people who did know the three men that came and helped them escape.

If they were the raiders, he would have to be on the lookout for them as well. Maybe the raiders didn't go after individual travelers on horseback. They might figure that only those in a wagon were worth going after. Then again maybe they were only after the northern army supplies and payroll. No matter. He would have to remain alert.

Luke ate some of his jerky as he rode. Now more than ever he wanted to put some distance between himself and the army. If they sent out another patrol that would mean that the sergeant had recognized him and they might not wait to ask questions if they caught him but shoot first.

It was noon when Luke stopped to rest the horses. Finding a hidden place off the road, he unsaddled the horses and let them roll. He started a fire and made coffee. Taking some of his jerky, he made a stew that was hot and wet. When he and Rex had eaten, he took out his new rifle. Aiming at some target he had set up, he found that the rifle was quite accurate. He should be able to hit anything that he could hit with his old rifle and faster. With that, he put it away.

Saddling the horses, he again was on his way.

the dailys

The next few days Luke and Rex traveled without any problems, and he was seeing fewer of the Union soldiers. The people that he did run into paid him little or no mind. Then a week and a half out of London, Luke came across a family just as evening was coming on.

Luke could see that a wagon had stopped for the night and had their campfire going near where the wagon sat. As he rode into the camp, he saw a woman and three kids duck behind the wagon. The man picked up his rifle. "Can I help ya?" asked the man.

"Mah name is Luke Taylor. Seen yer fire and thought I might stop and see if ya might have some coffee ya could spare."

"We got some coffee on. Where ya headed fer?"

"Ah heading fer Independence, Missouri, hope'n ta join up with a wagon train heading west."

"Step down and grab a cup. Mah name is Frank Daily. Ya can tie yer horses over by mine and help yaself ta the coffee."

Luke went over and tied his horses. Getting his cup off his pack, he returned to the fire. By now Mrs. Daily and the kids had come out from behind the wagon and were standing by the fire.

"Luke, I want ya ta meet mah wife, Jenny, and mah kids. This is mah oldest, Mathew, our daughter, Samantha, and our young'n, Peter. Family, I want ya ta meet Luke Taylor."

"Glad ta meet ya, ma'am, kids," said Luke.

Jenny went and got the pot and poured Luke some coffee. "Have you had supper yet? We're about to sit down, and you're welcome to join us," said Jenny.

"Thanks, ma'am. We ain't et yet and sure would be obliged," said Luke.

"We?" asked Jenny.

"Yes, ma'am. We, me and mah partner, Rex," Luke said.

Taking a look around, he did not see Rex. Looking over at the horses, Rex was lying on the far side watching what was going on. Luke called for him, and he timidly came to him. The kids got excited when they saw Rex, but their excitement caused Rex to hide behind Luke and let out a growl. Luke knelt down and patted Rex's head. Once he was calmed down, Luke had the kids come over and pet him. Rex still didn't take to the kids and stayed close to Luke.

Frank asked, "Seem strange fer a dog not ta like kids. Did something happen between him and some kids?"

Luke said, "Don't know. He came ta mah camp one night. He was hurt, and I helped him, and we been friends since then. Sometimes he takes ta kids, and others he don't. Stopped one night at da Green farm, and he took right off ta them kids. Might be on da trail something happened ta him ta not want ta be with people. It took time fer him ta trust me."

Frank asked, "That weren't Isaac Green's place ya stopped at, was it?"

"I believe it was," said Luke.

"We done stopped by their place," said Frank. "We had a nice visit with them. They seemed ta be all right folks."

"Come ta think of it, he mentioned a family by da name of Daily had stopped by. That was y'all, wasn't it?" asked Luke.

Frank said, "Well, I'll be if that don't beat all."

Jenny called that supper was ready. She served the kids and then dished up a plate for Luke and Frank before dishing up her own.

Everybody found a spot around the fire and sat down. Rex stayed close to Luke.

Mathew asked, "Mr. Taylor, can we give yer dog some food?"

Luke said, "Ya can try, but be careful. I don't know how he's gonna act. I ain't seen him act like this befer, but we ain't been around many people either."

Mathew got some food together, and he started toward Rex. As Mathew approached, Rex moved closer to Luke and started growling again. Luke reached down and put his hand on Rex's head, and he quieted down. Continuing to hold Rex, he told Mathew to come closer. When Mathew got next to Luke, Luke could hear a low growl coming from Rex. Making sure that Rex wouldn't bite Mathew, he told Mathew to put the food down but not too close. Once Mathew had put the food down, he stepped back. Rex kept an eye on Mathew and then looked at the food. Luke still held him until he was sure that Rex was not going to go after Mathew.

When Luke let go of Rex, Rex stayed by him, looking at the food. Luke told Rex it was okay, and Rex got up and went to the food. Mathew continued to stand where he was, watching Rex. Rex did not forget about Mathew either; as he ate he kept an eye on Mathew. Whenever Mathew moved, Rex would growl and stop eating until he was sure that Mathew was not a threat. When Rex finished, he lay down next to Luke.

While they were eating, Frank asked, "If that don't beat all. I ain't seen a dog that loyal ta one man as that one. Ya say ya come across him on da trail. Well, I'll be. Say, ya don't happen ta be that Luke Taylor we heard them army fellas saying they have been looking fer? Are ya?"

"I am," said Luke.

"Mind me ask'n what they look'n fer ya fer?" asked Frank.

"They done said I murdered a man in Virginia who come ta our place with one of them carpetbaggers. Truth is, they were gonna kill mah pa and I shot him. I didn't think I'd get a fair trial with da army, so I headed west.

Frank asked, "If ya kil'd him defending yer family, why didn't ya go ta da army?"

"Mah family didn't think I had a chance, and they didn't want ta see me hung. Come ta think of it, I didn't want ta see mah-self hung either. Then I saw what da army trial is like when I was come'n through London. They done tried three men fer kill'n da payroll master with no proof. They even had a man stand up fer them, and da Army still found them guilty. After seeing that, I know'd that mah pa was right. I didn't have a chance with them. It was good that I left," said Luke. "I take it ya are headed west as well."

Frank said, "Ya, we're head'n west. I wouldn't blamed ya fer kill'n them if they had'n been taking yer place. They done took mine. That's why we're headed west. We got word from Jenny's brother that they were go'n west after their place was burned out by da Union soldiers. Cole told us that if'n we couldn't make a go of our place, we should meet up with them in St. Louis. We could then head west together."

"By da time ya get ta St. Louis, winter will be setting in. What ya gonna do fer da winter?" asked Luke.

"Jenny's bother said that we could build a small place fer da win-ter and work fer some of da farmers around St. Louis," said Frank. "Cole said that they would be there befer us and would be able ta grow some food fer the winter, possibly even enough fer us. What ya gonna do?"

"I ain't thought much about it. I was hope'n ta find some work where I could talk ta some wagon train ta get hired on in da spring."

When they had finished their supper, Frank invited Luke to camp with them. Luke thanked them and went to unload his horses. Rex stayed with Luke, keeping an eye on the kids. Luke fig-ured that there had to be a bad time that one of the kids reminded him of. Taking the horses to the stream, he watered them before giving them some grain.

When Luke returned, he said, "Well, kids, it seems Rex just don't know what ta make of ya. Did ya have a dog befer?"

Frank said, "When we were on da farm, we had a dog. When the carpetbagger came and started my troubles, they done killed him along with burning mah barn. I didn't see da need ta get a new one seeing how we were leaving."

"Mind telling me what happened ta yer place?" asked Luke.

Frank started at the beginning of the war and how his place was making a good living for him and his family. They would have been happy to stay there had the war not come along. He had gone to fight, and while he was gone, there was a raid that came down from the North. It seemed that the Northerners' supplies had been running low, so they killed the few cows and raided their cellar, leaving the family without enough food to last until they could grow more.

Then before they rode off, they burned his fields and barn and drove off any of the remaining livestock. If it hadn't been for the neighbors, his family would have starved. By the time he got word on what happened to his place, the war was coming to an end. Getting permission to return home, he left and found his family just barely alive. He was able to get some meat by stealing a cow, and his wife had started the garden over. Then he had gotten word that it looked like the war was coming to an end, and he began to think that things were going to get better. That was before the carpetbaggers showed up demanding taxes for the war. With no crop, livestock, or money, they could not pay the taxes. That didn't seem to bother those who were collecting it. So getting together what little they had left, they set out to follow his brother-in-law.

Frank went on, saying, "Cole's family had gone through da same problems as our place had. Only Cole had been wounded and had been sent home earlier ta recover. When he saw that there wasn't anything left of his farm, they decided ta gather what was left and start west. They had stopped by our place and laid out a plan ta meet if we decided ta leave as well. If we don't arrive by spring, they're going ta go on without us."

By now it was getting dark, and everyone was ready to turn in. Luke put his bedroll on the far side of the fire away from the family. Rex lay down with him. Prior to lying down for the night, Luke made one more check on the horses.

Looking at Rex, he said, "Ya don't trust them kids much, do ya fella? I wonder if ya didn't have some problems from kids befer."

Rex laid there wagging his tail while Luke talked to him. Reaching over, he scratched Rex's head. When Luke stopped, Rex crawled closer to Luke, resting his head on him. Luke's hand was still on Rex when they both went to sleep.

In the morning, Luke woke when Rex growled. Before he moved, Luke caught the smell of fresh coffee brewing. Looking over toward the Dailys' wagon, Luke could see Mrs. Daily busy at the fire and the kids running round doing their chores. He couldn't see Mr. Daily anywhere. Getting up, he noticed that the horses were missing. He couldn't believe that everyone was up and he had not heard them until Rex growled.

Looking back at Mrs. Daily, he asked, "Did Frank take da horses this morning?"

Jenny said, "You were sleeping so well he didn't want to disturb you. Come and get some coffee; it will help you to wake up."

"Thanks, but I think I'll go give Frank a hand first."

Going to the stream, he saw Frank with the horses all lined up. Seeing that Frank had everything under control, as he walked up, he said, "Let me give ya a hand with them ponies."

Frank jumped when Luke spoke. Turing around, he said, "Ya as quiet as an injun. Ya done scared da life outa me."

"Didn't mean ta scare ya. I guess it's become a habit ta just walk quietly. Done it since I was just a kid hunting."

Taking the ropes for his horses, they finished watering the stock and returned to the camp, tying them where they could eat.

Luke went to his pack and took out some of the deer meat that he had and gave it to Mrs. Daily.

"Here, ma'am," said Luke. "I got this deer da other day and figured that ya could use da meat."

"Thank ya, Mr. Taylor," said Jenny. "We haven't had fresh meat for a while."

While they were eating, Frank said, "I seen ya got yerself one of them new Henry rifles. How do ya like her?"

Luke said, "Ain't had her long. She seems ta be a good one though. I done some practicing with it and got ta where I can hit a rabbit. If needed, I guess I could hit a deer with her as well."

"Recon ya could if ya can hit a rabbit," said Frank. "We're gonna be going on this morn. Ya welcome ta ride along."

"Thanks. I just might take ya up on yer offer."

While Luke was getting his gear together, he decided to ride along with them. The army was looking for a man traveling alone, and if he stayed with the Dailys, they may not pay any attention to him.

Frank said, "Ya can tie yer packhorses ta the back of da wagon."

"Thanks," said Luke. "I'll ride ahead looking fer any problems that ya need to know about."

Luke tied his packhorses to the back of the wagon and started out, leading the wagon. Everything was going along fine until one of the wheels started to squeak and smoke. Frank stopped to see what was wrong and saw that it had run out of grease.

When they started, Rex ran along with Luke. Luke had gotten far enough ahead that he did not see them stop. Finding a place where they could rest, he turned to head back to tell them. Not seeing them as soon as he expected, he got worried. A mile back, he saw the wagon stopped. At first he thought that something had happened to them before he saw Frank working on one of the wheels.

Riding up, he asked, "What happened?"

Frank said, "Had a wheel go dry. Guess I should'a checked them last night when we stopped."

He had already unloaded part of the wagon and cut a tree to use as a lever. Luke and Jenny got on the end of the lever while Frank removed the wheel. Putting grease on the axel, he replaced the wheel. He decided to check the other wheels while they were stopped as well. A wheel on the other side was also going dry, so he greased it as well.

Looking at Luke, Frank said, "We need ta grease da others when we stop fer da night."

They reloaded the wagon, tying the pole he had cut on the side of the wagon. Because they had stopped to grease the wheels Luke knew that they didn't need to stop at the place he had found. They drove on, only eating jerky for the noon meal and making up some of the time they had lost.

In the middle of the afternoon, they finally stopped to rest the horses. The kids enjoyed getting out of the wagon and ran around, getting rid of some of their extra energy as well. Rex even seemed to enjoy stopping and resting. He watched the kids as they played but did not join them. Luke was watching Rex when Rex spotted a rabbit. Maybe he wasn't as tired as Luke thought, as it didn't take Rex long before he took off after it. The rabbit must have had a hole that he got into because Rex returned without it.

When the horses were rested and the kids worn out, they started. This time Luke rode just in front of the wagon, and only toward evening did he ride ahead to find a place where they could camp. By the time the wagon caught up to where he stopped, he had gathered wood for the fire and had watered his horse.

Rex alerted Luke to the arrival of the wagon as the wagon came into view. Frank drove the wagon close to the where Luke had stacked the wood, and Luke helped him unhitch the team before putting up his horses for the night. Unloading his packhorses, he led them to water before hobbling them on some fresh grass.

When he returned to camp, Mrs. Daily was cooking the meat he had given her. Luke could smell the coffee cooking. He figured that they had enough fresh meat to last them a couple more days.

By now the kids had finished their chores and were playing in the near field. Rex, still not trusting the children, remained with Luke. At times, Luke thought that Rex wanted to join them but didn't leave his side.

Frank had removed the lever while Jenny was making supper so he and Luke could grease all the wheels. They were just finishing up putting the last wheel back on when Jenny called for supper. Frank and Luke let the wagon down and tied the lever back on the wagon.

Jenny called out, "Frank, come and eat."

"As soon as we wash up," said Frank.

By the time Frank and Luke returned from washing up, Jenny had dished up the kids' plates. When the men sat down, she made their plates. As she approached Luke with his plate, Rex watched but made no sound. Mathew again asked his mother for food for Rex. Mathew brought it over to where Luke and Rex were sitting. Rex watched as Mathew put it down. This time Rex did not growl as Mathew approached. He looked at Luke and at the food, and when Luke said it was okay, Rex went to it and started eating. Mathew remained near Rex while he was eating but did not try to touch him. When Rex finished eating, Mathew reached down, picking up the plate.

The evening was cool, and the fire felt good. They all sat around until Jenny told the children it was time for bed. Mathew had worked on Rex by trying to feed him leftovers from supper. Rex would catch the food if Mathew tossed it to him but would not take it out of his hand. When Mathew went to bed, Rex got up and walked around the wagon before returning to Luke. Luke was puzzled by the way Rex was acting after being so friendly with the Greens' children.

In the morning, Mathew asked, "Mr. Taylor, could I ride with you on one of yer horses taday?"

Luke said, "I don't mind, but ya need ta ask yer pa."

Mathew ran off to find his father. When he found his father, he asked if he could ride with Mr. Taylor.

"What ya gonna ride?" asked Frank.

"Mr. Taylor said I could ride on one of his horses," said Mathew.

Frank walked over to Luke and asked, "Mathew was wondering if you would let him ride one of yer horses."

Luke said, "I would be happy ta let Mathew ride with me. If'n it's all right with ya."

"Da boy done rode some befer, and ah don't mind if'n ya don't mind him tagging along with ya," said Frank. "Ya can put yer pack in da wagon, and we got a saddle in da wagon he can use."

Luke decided he would let Mathew ride the horse that he had picked up on the trail. Once saddled, he helped Frank hitch up the team while Jenny and the kids loaded the wagon. When everything was ready, Mathew and Luke mounted and rode out.

Luke could see that Mathew had ridden before and was a good rider. As they rode, Mathew asked a lot of questions about Rex that Luke could not answer. Luke asked him what his dog had been like. Mathew said that their dog had looked a lot like Rex.

When noontime came, Luke let Mathew find a spot that he thought would be a good place to stop while they ate. Stopping and dismounting, Luke let Mathew take the horses to get water while he gathered some wood. Luke was surprised when Rex went with Mathew. *Maybe Rex is loosening up to Mathew,* Luke thought.

While Luke was gathering the wood, he heard Mathew call out. Luke dropped the wood and went running to see what had happened. When he got close, he could see Mathew looking into the water and not moving. Rex was standing next to Mathew, looking at whatever Mathew had found. When he got closer, he could see a body in the stream. Kneeling by the side of the stream, he reached down and pulled the body from the water. From the looks of the body, it had been in the stream for some time. He could see that whoever it was had been shot in the back. Turning to Mathew, he said, "Ya need ta move da horses up stream."

Luke checked the man's pockets; they were empty. Mathew meanwhile had taken the horses a little farther up the stream. While Luke was still checking the body, Frank drove in with the wagon.

Luke called out, "Frank, don't let the wife and kids come down here."

Frank asked, "What's up?"

"Mathew found a body in da stream, and they don't need ta see it."

Frank had Jenny start unloading the wagon and build a fire while he went to see who Luke had found. When Frank arrived at the body, he agreed with Luke that the man had been shot in the back. Whoever murdered him had taken everything but his clothes.

Frank said, "We need ta let the sheriff know that we found this man."

Luke said, "I wonder how far ta da next town where they have a sheriff. I seen a farm back about a mile. They might know. I can ride back and talk ta them."

Frank said, "While ya do that, we can get camp set up."

Luke mounted and headed back down the road. It didn't take him long before he rode into the yard. A man came out of the house carrying a rifle as he approached. Luke stopped and asked, "Can ya tell me where I might be able to find da nearest sheriff?"

"What ya need a sheriff fer?" asked the man.

"We stopped fer da night up da road about a mile, and when we went ta water da horses, we found a man shot and lying in da stream. We believe he was murdered."

The farmer said, "Ya gotta go inta Shepherdsville ta find a sheriff. That's ten miles. Ya wouldn't have much a chance ta gett'n there tonight. Let me get mah horse, and I'll come with ya and see if I know'd da man."

Luke waited for the man to tell his wife and get his horse. As they rode back to where the wagon was, Luke said, "Mah name is Luke Taylor, and I am traveling with da Daily family."

The famer said, "Mah name is Allen Webb. Me and mah family have lived here since mah folks moved here in da early eighteen hundreds. Why do ya think da man was murdered?"

Luke said, "It looks like he was shot in da back."

As they rode into camp, Frank greeted them. Luke introduced Frank to Allen before taking him to where he had laid the body. Allen took one look and said it was his neighbor, Hezekiah Muller.

Allen said, "I'd heard Hezekiah was have'n trouble with some men who wanted his land. Ah think he mentioned a fella that calls his self Ike. I never thought they'd come ta murdering him. Where did ya find him?"

Luke showed him the spot where Mathew first saw him. Allen said, "Hezekiah's place is up da stream. We had some rain a few days ago that would have raised da stream, allowing him ta float down here. We need ta leave da body here until da sheriff can come out."

Luke said, "We can head on inta town in da morning and have da sheriff meet ya here if that's okay with ya."

Allen said, "I can do that. Maybe befer he gets here I can find out where they shot him."

Allen said good-bye, returning home, while Luke and Frank decided to move farther down the road away from the body for the kids' sake. Hitching up the teams, Luke rode ahead about a mile where he found another spot where they could make camp. By the time Frank arrived, Luke had a fire going.

That night was a restless night for the Daily family. Mathew had nightmares about the body he had seen, which woke the other kids. Jenny tried to comfort him, so she didn't get much sleep herself.

In the morning, they didn't wait to eat but hitched up the horses and started for Shepherdsville. It was midmorning when they arrived. As they rode in, Luke asked the first person he saw where they could find the sheriff. The man pointed to the café and said that was where the sheriff would be.

Luke rode over to the café and tied his horse. Entering the café, he looked around until he found the sheriff sitting near the wall talking with another man. Walking over, he said, "Sir, may we talk?"

The sheriff said, "What ya need, son?"

Luke said, "We made camp about ten miles out of town last night and found a man floating in da steam. Sheriff, it looks like he had been shot in da back. We talked ta a fella by da name of Allen Webb. He said it was his neighbor Hezekiah Muller. Mr. Webb said he would meet ya at the spot where we found him."

The sheriff asked, "I heard he was having trouble with someone who wanted to buy his place. Ya might have been hired to kill him for all I know."

Luke said, "I've been riding with da Dailys. Ya can ask da Dailys; they're out front on their wagon. It looks like this Mr. Muller has been dead fer a couple of days."

The sheriff got up, walking out with Luke.

Frank was sitting on the wagon next to Jenny when Luke introduced the sheriff to them. The sheriff asked who had found the body, and Mathew stuck his head out from behind his ma and said that he had been the one to first see the body.

The sheriff said, "All right, folks, I need ya ta stay here till I get back in case I need ta ask ya some more questions."

Frank said, "We will be here, Sheriff."

"Ya can put yer wagon over by da livery. Tell Josh that I told ya ta," said the sheriff. "Where did ya say da fella is?"

Luke said, "About a mile befer ya get ta Allen Webb's place. He said he would be there waiting fer ya."

The sheriff said, "Thanks," then turned and walked away.

Luke watched the sheriff walk to his office and go in. It wasn't long until he returned carrying a rifle, which he put on the horse, and rode out of town.

Frank drove the wagon to the livery where Josh came out and started to tell him that he couldn't leave his wagon there. Frank said, "The sheriff told us ta wait until he returned and that we could leave da wagon by the livery."

Josh said, "If the sheriff wants you to wait, it's okay. Where did he go that you have to wait for him?"

Frank said, "He went to look at a body we found near Allen Webb's place."

"If ya want, ya can turn yer horses loose in that empty corral over there, as da Sheriff is gonna be awhile," said Josh.

Frank said, "Thanks. I don't mind if I do."

After turning the horses loose in the corral, Luke said, "Let's head fer da café and get some dinner while we wait."

Frank said, "We don't got da money ta spare fer eating in da café. Jenny will just fix us something by da wagon."

Luke said, "Na, it will be mah treat fer all ya have done fer me. Now let's go."

The kids were excited as they entered the café. Rex followed Luke in. They found a table off to the side where the family could sit and Rex could lay down by the wall.

Being it was early for dinner, the café was not busy. While they sat and waited for their meal, other customers started to come. Three men, who looked to be ranch hands, came in and sat down at the table behind Luke. They looked and acted like they had already been drinking that morning and were half drunk. Luke did not pay much attention to them but was watching Peter, who was looking at everything in the café.

Luke asked Frank, "Has Peter ever been in a café befer?"

Frank said, "Na, none of da kids have ever been in a café. This is quite a treat fer them."

While they were eating, Luke overheard one of the fellas at the table behind him mention the name Ike. With the mention of the name Ike, Luke started to listen closer to what they were saying, as that name had been mentioned by Allen, until Mathew asked, "Mr. Taylor, do ya eat in cafés a lot, sir?"

Luke said, "Na, but I done ate in a few."

All three of the kids thought that this was as good as Christmas. Jenny was enjoying herself as much as the children. By the time they had finished eating, all of the plates were as clean as if they had been washed.

Luke looked at the children and asked, "Does anyone want a piece of pie?"

All three of the children looked first at their pa and then their ma to see if it was okay. When they both nodded their heads, they broke into the biggest smiles that Luke had seen and together said yes just as the waitress walked up to the table.

The waitress asked, "What is all this excitement about?"

Samantha said, "We get to have a piece of pie." Then lowering her head, she said, "If ya got some."

"Well," said the waitress, "I think we got us some fresh pie baked just this morning. What would you like, apple or blueberry?"

Mathew looked at his ma and said, "Ma, I ain't never had a blueberry. Can I try it?"

Jenney looked at Mathew and said, "What if you don't like it? Who is gonna eat it for you? And you will go without pie."

Mathew said, "Well then, I am gonna have a piece of apple."

Jenny said, "That's a good idea, Mathew."

Everyone ordered apple except for Luke, who ordered blueberry. When the pie was delivered, Luke asked Mathew if he would like a taste of the blueberry. Again he looked at his ma, who gave him approval, before saying, "May I, sir?"

Luke said, "Sure, and if anyone else would like ta taste it, ya sure can."

Each one of the children took a taste of it. Only Peter thought that the blueberry was better than the apple. Luke asked him if he wanted to trade his apple for the blueberry.

Luke gave Peter his blueberry pie and ate Peter's apple. By the time the waitress came back, she said, "I can see that no one liked the pie by all the pie left on the plates."

Peter said, "Ma'am, there ain't any pie left on da plates."

She laughed and said to Peter, "Well, I'll be. You're right. All the plates are clean."

As they were getting ready to leave, Luke heard the men behind him say that they were going to head back to the saloon and wait for Woodson to show up. Hearing the name Woodson, Luke began to wonder if these men might be the ones who killed Mr. Muller.

Luke paid for their dinner. As they left the café, Jenny said, "Frank, while we're in town, let's let the children walk around and see what Shepherdsville looks like. Would you like to join us, Mr. Taylor?"

Luke said, "Thanks, ma'am, but I want ta check out some information befer da sheriff comes back."

While the Daily family walked up the street, Luke headed for the saloon.

The sheriff arrived where Luke told him that Allen would meet him. He stopped to look around before Allen came walking out of the woods, greeting the sheriff.

Allen said, "Over here, Sheriff."

The sheriff turned with a start, not hearing Allen at first. Seeing it was Allen, he said, "You came up on me kinda quiet. Where's Hezekiah's body?"

Allen said, "Follow me, Sheriff. We put him near da stream where he was found."

The sheriff went with Allen and looked at the body. He agreed that it looked like he had been shot in the back. Now he needed to find out where he had been dumped into the stream. He could tell from looking at the body that it had been in the water for at least three days, so any sign may have been wiped out by now.

The sheriff asked, "Allen, while ya were looking around, did ya find where they put him in the stream?"

"No, I ain't been up that way at all."

"Maybe I can find some trace of where he was killed. Allen, I need ya ta get a wagon so we can at least take his body home."

"All right, Sheriff," said Allen. "It'll take a little while, an I'll tell da wife what's go'n on."

While Allen went to get a wagon, the sheriff rode up the stream looking for where Hezekiah was killed. After a mile, he saw tracks on the ground that indicated a struggle. Getting down from his horse, he looked the area over, being careful not to step on any of the signs. First off, he saw where three men had been standing, facing a fourth man. He made out where a fourth man had fallen and a fifth man walked up from behind him. Looking at the ground where the man had fallen, the sheriff could see that there was blood on the ground. He figured that this must be where Hezekiah was shot. He could also see where the three who had been facing Hezekiah walked over to where he had fallen. Two of the men dragged Hezekiah to the stream and then returned to where the others waited. Searching the area further, he only counted a total of five people.

By the time the sheriff had finished looking the ground over, he had determined that Hezekiah must have come upon the three men who were on his property, surprising them, when the fourth man came up behind him. It must have been the fourth man who had shot Hezekiah. He checked for signs left by the horses to see if there might be something that would help identify the killers. Any marks that were left by the horses had been wiped out by the wind.

Returning to Hezekiah's body, he noticed that Allen had already returned. They loaded Hezekiah into the wagon. The sheriff said, "I found where he was killed. It looks like there were four of them. Do ya know of anyone who wanted Hezekiah dead?"

Allen said, "Well, he told me once that there was a man that had tried ta buy his land but he wasn't gonna sell."

"Did he say who the fella was asking fer his place?"

"Seems I recall a name of Ike or something like that was mentioned. He also mentioned the name of Woodson."

"I recall hearing a name like that in town over da past couple of weeks. Word around town was he has been look'n fer land ta buy," said the sheriff.

They mounted and rode to Hezekiah's place. Hezekiah's wife came out as they rode in. Their boy came out of the barn, and seeing the sheriff and Allen, he hurried toward his mother. The sheriff got down, walking over to them.

"Martha, Isaac," said the sheriff, "I got some bad new fer ya. Hezekiah has been shot. We got his body in da wagon."

Isaac caught his mother as she started to collapse. The sheriff hurried to help Isaac.

Isaac asked, "What happened ta Pa?"

The sheriff said, "It's a long story. Let's get yer ma inside."

When they got Martha in the house, the sheriff said, "Ya stay with her until Mr. Webb and I can dig a grave fer yer pa."

The sheriff and Allen dug a grave in the family cemetery. When they had completed it, Martha was by Hezekiah's body saying her good-byes. Taking a blanket from the house, they wrapped the body before placing it in the grave. The sheriff apologized for not waiting for a proper funeral, but due to the length of time the body had been in the water, he felt it necessary to bury him as soon as possible. Both Martha and Isaac agreed with the sheriff.

Once Hezekiah had been buried, Allen said good-bye before heading home. He told them that he and his wife would come by to see if there was anything that they could do. After Allen left, Martha, Isaac, and the sheriff went into the house.

Inside the house, Martha said, "Sheriff, please sit and tell us what happened."

"Thank you, Martha," said the sheriff. "I don't have a lot of information, but I will tell you what I know. This morning a family rode into town and said they found a body Allen had identified. The young man who reported it said it looked like he had been murdered. When I found yer husband, I could see that he had been shot in the back. Following the stream, I found the spot where Hezekiah had been killed. It looks like there were four men at the site when it happened. Can ya tell me of anyone who might have wanted Hezekiah killed?"

Martha said, "No, Sherriff. I can't think of anyone who might want my Hezekiah dead."

Isaac said, "Ma, what about them four men who came to see Pa three weeks ago? Remember, Pa said that they wanted to buy our place but he wasn't going ta sell. They didn't take too kindly to what Pa said. He said they told him that they would see to it that he would sell or else."

"Do ya know what the men's names were?" asked the sheriff.

Martha said, "I believe Hezekiah said it was a Mr. Woodson. He did not say any of the other men's names."

"Did they ever come back again?" asked the sheriff.

"Not that I know of," said Martha.

"How about you, Isaac? Did ya ever see them around here again?" asked the sheriff.

"No" said Isaac.

"Martha, didn't ya think it strange that Hezekiah had been gone for several days?" asked the sheriff.

"When Hezekiah left, he said that he wanted to keep watch on the herd. When he does that, he could be gone for a week. So when he didn't come back these past few days, we didn't think much about it," said Martha.

Isaac said, "Pa did tell me to keep a look out fer any strangers coming by before he rode out. Did you find Pa's horse?"

"No," said the sheriff, thanking them for the information. He told them that he would find out who had killed Hezekiah.

Isaac said, "I want ta go with ya."

The sheriff said, "Isaac, ya got ta stay with yer ma and let me do mah job. I'll let ya know when I find da men."

"Sheriff, I didn't see Pa's watch in his pocket. Did ya happen ta find Pa's watch while ya were out there?"

"No," said the sheriff. "If they took it, how would I know it was his watch?"

"It plays a little tune of bells ringing when ya open it."

"Thanks. I'll sure keep an eye out for it."

"It also had Pa's initials on da back. HRM."

With this, the sheriff went to his horse and rode to town.

ike woodson

After Luke left the Daily family, he and Rex headed for the saloon. He followed the three men from the café. After hearing the name Woodson mentioned by them, he wanted to find out more about them. If they were some of the men who had killed Hezekiah, he might be able to overhear something before the sheriff returned. Entering the bar, he spotted the three men sitting at a table near the bar. Luke walked to the bar and ordered a beer. He was close enough to hear what they were saying without looking like he was paying attention to them.

The men seemed to have been doing a lot of drinking that day. The more they drank, the more they talked. Luke heard one of the men say something about how they had eliminated him but they still had his family to worry about. They didn't mention any names that would tie them to the murder.

One of the other men asked, "Has anyone heard about his death in town? I ain't heard a thing, and it's been go'n on four days."

The first man said, "I ain't. Have ya heard anything, Cody?"

"Na, I ain't heard a thing neither."

The first man said, "Well, according to Ike, when we hear about his death, we can go after his wife and son. They should make easy targets, and Ike feels we should be able ta get their land without any problem. Where is Ike anyway? He said he was gonna meet us here by noon."

Ike Woodson had gotten up early that morning and headed to the Muller ranch to look around. During the past three days he had not heard anyone talking about Hezekiah being dead, and he was wondering if anyone had found his body. When he got close to the spot where Hezekiah had been shot he got off his horse and hid him before going on. He wanted to make sure that no one was in the area before he went into the open to check for any signs they might have left. Stopping and listening while remaining out of sight, he thought he heard someone coming. He saw the sheriff following the stream. Ike continued to watch as the sheriff got close to the spot where they killed Hezekiah. The sheriff was not paying any attention to what was around him but was watching the ground. Ike figured that he was looking for any sign they might have left. Ike waited and watched as the Sheriff followed the stream. When he saw the sheriff stop at the spot where they had killed Hezekiah, his heart went to his throat. Remaining hidden in the trees, he watched the sheriff look the ground over. When the sheriff knelt down to take a closer look at the ground, Ike figured that he must have found something of interest to him. It wasn't long before the sheriff remounted, riding back the way he had come. Ike followed behind the sheriff to the spot where Allen and Hezekiah's body were. He watched as they loaded Hezekiah into the wagon. When they rode out, he saw that they were headed for the Muller ranch. Once the sheriff and Allen were out of sight, Ike headed for town. While riding to town he wondered what the sheriff had seen on the ground that had been so interesting to him.

It was the middle of the afternoon before he rode up to the saloon. Dismounting and tying his horse, he went into the saloon. Seeing his men, he went to their table and sat down.

Luke was still standing at the bar when Ike walked in. He looked up and not knowing who the man was didn't pay much attention to him until he heard the first man say, "It's about time, Ike. Where ya been?"

Looking over at the bar where Luke was standing, in a low voice that Luke could not hear, Ike said, "I rode out to the Muller place to see why we ain't heard about him. I saw the sheriff while I was there. He found our tracks and the body. Something caught his interest on the ground where we shot him. He took his time looking the spot over before leaving. Webb was with him. Now we have to be careful if we are going to get the Webb place as well. When the sheriff gets back to town, the word about Hezekiah should get out."

Luke was only able to hear part of what Ike was saying, but he had heard enough. Finishing his beer, he left and went looking for the Dailys. He found them walking toward their wagon. He joined them and told Frank what he had heard.

Luke said, "If da sheriff doesn't get back befer they leave, I'm gonna follow them. Ya will have ta let da sheriff know where I went."

Frank said, "I will let da sheriff know."

Luke went and got his horse. Tying him to the wagon, he waited. It was getting late in the afternoon, and the men had not left the saloon.

Frank said, "We need ta move ta set up camp fer da night. We will take yer other horses with us."

Frank went to find Josh. When he entered the stable, Frank found Josh cleaning out stalls. Looking up, he greeted Frank.

Frank said, "Da sheriff has not returned, and we can't stay here in town, so if ya don't mind, when da sheriff gets back, would ya tell him we will be camped at da edge of town?"

Josh said, "I will."

After thanking Josh, Frank returned to his wagon to hitch up his team. Luke joined him, getting his own horses ready for travel.

Once they had the team hitched to the wagon and Frank and his family in the wagon, they drove off.

A while after Luke had left the bar. Ike turned to Cody and said, "Go look out the window to see where that fella that was just at the bar goes."

Cody got up and walked to the window. Looking out, he watched Luke meet the Dailys and head for the stable. Not seeing anything strange, he went back to the table and told Ike that he must be with the family in the wagon.

Ike asked, "How much have you fellas been talking? I think you said enough to get the interest of that stranger. Does anyone know who he is or where he comes from?"

All three of the men said they had not seen him before. They first saw him in the café eating with the family and thought it a little strange that he would come into the saloon by himself if he was traveling with that family, but they thought no more about it, as he only had one beer.

Ike decided to wait for a while before they headed out. He wanted to make sure it was late enough that this stranger was gone. If he was still around, he would have to make sure that he didn't follow them. If he did follow them, he would have to be killed. If he found that his men were talking too much in the wrong places, he might have to take care of them as well.

Ike ordered another drink and sat back to relax and wait. When it was getting close to dark, he decided that it was time to leave. Going to the window, he noticed that Luke was still standing by the corral with his horse; the wagon was now gone. The question in his mind was, if he had ridden in with the family, why hadn't he ridden out with them? Reaching their horses, they mounted and rode west out of town.

Ike made sure that they left tracks that anyone could follow. He didn't want the stranger to suspect that he knew they were being followed.

One of the men asked, "Why we gon this way with da camp east of town?"

Ike said, "We're being followed, and I don't want him to find where we are staying."

When the Dailys left, Luke took his horse and went back to the corral to wait. Rex lay down in the shade of a tree nearby and waited with Luke. It was near dark when the men left the saloon. Mounting, he followed the men out of town. It wasn't hard for Luke to follow them. They stayed on the road and left tracks that anyone could follow. About three miles out of town, they left the road. With it getting dark, Luke got down and followed on foot, taking his time and making sure that he didn't catch up to them. If they did know that they were being followed, he didn't want to run into an ambush. Rex stayed near Luke and kept sniffing the air. Luke figured that if there was anyone around, Rex would let him know. About a quarter mile off the road, Luke lost the tracks at what looked to be an old campsite. He searched around the camp site looking for any tracks leading away from the site. It was like they had vanished into thin air. With it getting dark, he decided to go back to town. Going back to the road, Luke put up a marker at the spot where the men had left the road before heading back to town. At the edge of town, he saw the Dailys' campfire.

When, the four men came to the place where there had been a campfire some time back, they stopped before going on. Ike was sure that they were being followed, so he hung back to wipe out any sign of them leaving the area. Not far from the old camp there was solid rock. Wiping out their tracks between the camp and rock, Ike knew that anyone following them would not be able to track them on the rock. Once they had crossed the rocky surface, they entered a stream and headed south back toward town. Following the stream for a mile, there Ike found another rocky area where they exited the stream. They continued to stay off the road until they were past town. After Ike and his men were back on the road, they did not waste any time heading for camp. Once in camp, they ate supper and waited for morning. Ike said, "I'll go inta town and find out what the sheriff knows in da morning."

Cody said, "Do ya think they have an idea who done it?"

Ike said, "Don't know, but I should be able ta find out."

Ike continued to wonder about the stranger who had followed them. What was his interest in this? Was he working with the law, or was he a relative to Hezekiah? He would go back into town in the morning and see if either the wagon or the stranger were still in town. He was sure that the sheriff didn't have any evidence that would tie him to Hezekiah's murder unless his men had said too much in the saloon or the sheriff had found something on the ground at the scene.

As the sheriff rode into town, it was getting dark. The first thing he noticed was that the wagon was missing from the stable. As he arrived at the livery, Josh came out greeting him.

"What happened ta the folks in da wagon?" asked the sheriff.

Josh said, "They asked me ta tell ya that they would be camped at the edge of town."

The sheriff thanked Josh and decided that as long as they were camped he would get some supper before going out to see them. When the sheriff finished eating supper, he rode out to the Dailys' camp. Riding up, he called out to the camp and identified himself.

Frank said, "Howdy, Sheriff. Would ya like some supper and coffee?"

The sheriff said, "Don't mind if I do take some coffee. I ate in town before coming out."

By the time the sheriff had tied his horse, Jenny had poured him a cup and was waiting for him. When she handed it to him, he thanked her. Frank motioned for the sheriff to sit down before he asked, "What did ya find out?"

"Allen met me and showed me the body, and like you said, he was shot in the back. I followed the river back to where it looked like there was a struggle. Besides Hezekiah's tracks, I figured there were four others. There were three that confronted him and one who came up behind him."

Frank asked, "Have ya got any idea who done it?"

"Allen and I took the body to his house and talked to his wife and boy. They said something about a Mr. Woodson wanting to buy their ranch, but Hezekiah wouldn't sell it. I had heard there was a man in town who was trying to buy land."

Frank said, "Ya got ta talk ta Luke about what he heard."

"Where is he?" asked the sheriff.

"He followed some men out of town late taday. He did say ta tell ya he would be back."

As the sheriff and Frank sat and talked, they heard a horse coming just before they heard someone calling out. Frank looked up as Luke rode in. Seeing it was Luke, he said, "Howdy, Luke. Did ya find out where their camp's located?"

"Lost them in da dark about three miles out of town. Good ta see ya, Sheriff."

Frank said, "He has been here fer a while. We been talk'n about what he found. Have ya had anything ta eat?"

"Na," said Luke, "been too busy looking fer their trail."

"Glad to see you returned. Frank said you might have some information for me," said the sheriff.

Before Luke could answer, Frank called out to Jenny. "Jenny, ya still got some of that good supper left fer Luke?"

Jenny came out of the back of the wagon and went to the fire. She said, "I put some aside knowing that Luke would probably want to eat when he got back."

Picking up a plate, she started dishing up some food. Luke went to put up his horse when Mathew came over and offered to put Buck up for him. "Rub him down fer me, will ya, Mathew?" Luke asked.

"Sure thing, Mr. Taylor," said Mathew.

When Jenny finished fixing Luke's plate, she handed it to him. When Luke finished eating, he told the sheriff what he had heard when they were in the café and in the saloon.

"What you heard is interesting, but it's not proof that they killed Hezekiah. What I need for you to do is take me out ta where you lost them so I can see if we can again pick it up again in the morning. Would you be able to do that?"

"I can head out with ya in da morning. Do ya need the Dailys ta hang around, or can they be on their way? They are going ta meet relatives in St. Louis, and winters a com'n on."

"Na, they can be on their way," said the sheriff.

Frank said, "We can wait fer ya if it ain't too long, Luke."

Luke said, "Ya need to be gon. This may take longer then ya can wait. I may catch up ta ya farther down the trail."

The sheriff said, "I'll ride out in the morning and meet you here."

"I'll be waiting, Sheriff," said Luke.

The sheriff thanked Frank for the coffee. He recovered his horse and rode back to town.

Frank said that they would miss Luke's company and hoped that he would be able to meet up with them farther down the trail.

Luke rolled out his bedroll and lay down. Rex came in from the dark and lay down next to him.

In the morning, Frank told Jenny and the children that Luke would not be going on with them and that he would be helping the sheriff.

Mathew asked, "Can we take Rex with us?"

Frank said, "Son, we can't do that. Luke needs company, and da only company he has now is Rex."

Mathew understood that it wouldn't be fair to Rex or Luke to take Rex with them. He turned and walked back to the wagon. He was sad that after making friends with Rex he was now losing him. Frank knew that Mathew was going to miss riding with Luke as well, but if all went well, they would meet again farther down the trail.

Jenny made breakfast while Luke got his horses ready to travel. Maybe he could take his two packhorses into town and leave them at the stable. They would be able to track faster without them, and his gear would be safe at the stable. He would mention it to the sheriff when he arrived.

Jenny called out, "Come and get it while it's hot!"

Everyone showed up at the campfire, and Jenny started passing out plates filled with food. Luke sat next to Frank, and they talked about the route that they would be taking. It sounded like if all went well Luke could get caught up in a week or two. Traveling with horses was faster than a wagon.

Just as they were finishing breakfast, the sheriff rode in. Luke stood up and greeted him before turning to Jenny and said, "Ma'am, I want ta thank ya fer all yer mighty fine meals over da past weeks. I'll be look'n fer them again."

"Thank you, Luke. We will be counting the days till you rejoin us."

Each one of the children came over and gave Rex a hug and said good-bye to Luke. Frank said, "We sure are gonna miss ya fer a spell. Be looking forward ta ya rejoining us."

Luke shook hands with everyone, including the children, before getting his horses. As he mounted, he turned to the sheriff and said, "I been think'n that it might be better if I leave mah extra horses at da stable."

The sheriff said, "It's just a short ride to the stable, so let's do it."

The sheriff and Luke rode back into town, and when they got to the stable, Josh came out and asked, "What's up, Sheriff?"

"Josh, we need to leave Mr. Taylor's horses with you for a while. The sheriff's office will pay for their keep. Take good care of them, as Mr. Taylor is helping me with tracking some murderers."

"Who's been murdered?" asked Josh, surprised.

"Hezekiah," said the sheriff. "Hezekiah Muller. It happened a few days ago out at his place."

"Well, I'll be. Who would want to do a thing like that to Hezekiah?" asked Josh.

"Don't know for sure, but we got us a lead," said the sheriff.

Josh took Luke's packhorses and told Luke that he would store his gear in the stable. Luke thanked him as he and the sheriff rode back out of town. As they rode, the sheriff told Luke what Hezekiah's wife and son had said about the four men coming out wanting to purchase their ranch. They had mentioned that the man's name was Ike Woodson, the same man that Luke had talked about. He also mentioned that Hezekiah's watch was missing.

Luke asked, "What's special about da watch?"

The sheriff said, "When you open it, it has bells ringing, and it has Hezekiah's initials on the back. HRM."

"Well," said Luke, "if we can find da watch, we will know fer sure we got da killers."

When they reached the spot that Luke had marked, they dismounted and tied their horses. Luke showed the sheriff where he lost their trail at the sight of the old campfire. Going on, Luke showed the sheriff where the ground turned to solid rock. When they got to the rocky area, Luke pointed out that there were marks left by the horses' iron shoes. These were marks that he could not see last night. Now that it was daylight, they were able to look the rock over. It wasn't long before the sheriff found another spot where one of the horses had left a mark on the rock.

"It looks like they rode across the rock until they got to the stream. Now we have to find out which way they went in the stream."

"Seeing that they have gone to all this trouble to avoid being followed, they must have something to hide," said Luke.

"Let's get our horses. You go west, and I'll head east. If you see where they left the stream, fire two shots, and I'll do the same. When we hear the shots, the one who fired them will wait there for the other to show up."

Luke agreed. Now that they knew the four men had entered the stream, they did not have to be as careful. Luke turned west and followed the bank, looking for where the men might have left the water. The sheriff did the same only heading east.

It was slow going as there were a lot of rocks at the edge of the stream, and they would have to get down and examine the rocks looking for a mark. It was noon before Luke heard the two shots from the sheriff. He had been examining an area when the first shot was fired. Not knowing for sure if it was a gunshot, he waited a little then heard the second shot. Mounting, he knew it was a ways off, but all he had to do was follow the stream. He had gone two miles before he caught sight of the sheriff, who had lit a fire and had coffee by the time Luke arrived.

The sheriff showed Luke that he found the spot where they left the stream. He said, "We'll have to take it slow, so I figured we should eat before going on. I done followed it back to where they stayed off to the side."

Finishing their dinner, they mounted, following the trail. Sure enough, they stayed off the road until they were east of town. Once they were back on the road, Luke and the sheriff lost them again due to heavy traffic on the road during the morning.

"It looks like they knew I was following them," said Luke.

"Yup, and I'd say that their camp is east of town instead of west of town. Let's head back to town."

In the morning after they ate breakfast, Ike saddled up and headed for town. As he rode, Ike watched the road to see if anyone had followed them. Not seeing any tracks that stayed with theirs, he felt that they had lost him. As Ike got closer to town, he saw that their tracks from last night had been wiped out by others that morning. As he entered town, he did not see the sheriff's horse that was usually tied in front of his office. He continued on to the saloon where he tied his horse.

Walking up to the bar, Ike asked, "Barkeep, have ya seen da sheriff taday?"

"Seen him ride out of town this morning. I ain't seen him since."

Ike ordered a bottle and sat down. He took a seat near the window so he could keep an eye on the street. While he sat looking out the window, he saw Josh come from the stable and into the saloon. Josh walked up to the bar after looking around the room and seeing the barkeep behind the bar.

"What will ya have this early?" asked the barkeep.

"Too early fer me," said Josh. "The sheriff stopped by mah place this morning, said that Hezekiah had been killed, that he had been murdered. He and that fella named Taylor were going look'n fer the fellas that done it."

"Did he say how it happened?" asked the barkeep.

"Na, just that he had been murdered and he had a lead," said Josh. "If I know'd the sheriff, he's onto something. He'll find out who done it."

"Thanks. If I hear anything, I will be sure to let the sheriff know," said the barkeep.

Josh turned and walked out, heading back to the stable. *This war sure has messed us all up if good people like Hezekiah are killed for no reason,* thought Josh as he returned to the stable.

Ike had heard some of what Josh had said to the barkeep but did not hear it all. When the barkeep came over to see if he wanted anything, Ike asked who had been killed. The barkeep repeated everything that Josh had told him. When the barkeep turned and walked away, Ike sat thinking what his next move would be. He had to find out what clue the sheriff had gotten from the scene. He went back over everything that had taken place when they killed Hezekiah. They did not leave anything that would lead the sheriff to him. That was unless one of the men had talked too much or the sheriff had found something on the ground.

After Ike left for town, the three men sat around the cabin wondering what to do. By midmorning, they were restless and didn't want to just sit. Cody finally said, "Let's go ta town. We ain't got noth'n ta do here, and besides, da sheriff don't know it was us who killed Hezekiah."

The other two agreed; they wanted to get a drink, and they didn't have any liquor in the cabin. They got up and rode into town, arriving only an hour or so after Ike had. Seeing Ike's horse at the saloon, they rode over and tied their horses next to his. When they entered the saloon, they found Ike sitting by himself.

Ike was still sitting at a table thinking things over when the three men came into the saloon. At first he didn't realize that it was his men. It wasn't until they were walking toward him that he looked up and realized who they were. When they reached his table, he asked, "What are ya do'n here? I done told ya ta stay at the cabin."

Cody said, "We ain't got noth'n ta do and ain't got a bottle, so we come ta town to get one."

"Sit down," said Ike, upset that they couldn't follow orders. Getting over his anger, he said, "Da man from the stable was here this morning and said da Sheriff has a clue on who killed Hezekiah."

"I don't know how he could," said Cody.

"What did ya men say yesterday when ya were in here drinking? Did ya talk about it?" asked Ike.

"We didn't say nothing, boss," said Cody. "We were just wondering why we ain't heard nothing."

"Who was in the saloon when ya were here?"

"There weren't no one except this young stranger," said Cody. "He had a beer then left after ya came in."

"Ya fools, he's da one that followed us out of town last night." Turning, Ike called to the barkeep, "Barkeep, three more glasses."

The barkeep brought the three glasses and left them. Ike poured each man a drink, and they sat there in silence.

They continued to sit in the saloon. It was late in the afternoon when Ike saw the sheriff and Luke ride into town. He continued to watch them ride up to the sheriff's office and go in.

As Luke and the sheriff rode in, Luke saw the four horses tied by the saloon. He recognized them as the ones he followed. Inside the office, Luke said, "Sheriff, I think da men were look'n fer are in da saloon."

"I noticed the horses by the saloon when we came in as well and was wondering about them," said the sheriff. "We'll wait fer a while then go over and have a beer. Maybe we'll be able to find out if they are interested in Hezekiah's murder."

Entering the sheriff's office, they went over what they knew about Hezekiah's murder. The one thing that they had to go on was the watch. If one of the men in the saloon had the watch, that would at least put him at the scene where Hezekiah was found.

After a while, they got up and went to the saloon. Luke told Rex to stay. Rex went over and lay down by the wall.

Ike was watching as Luke and the sheriff approached the saloon. He said, "You boys keep yer mouths shut and listen to what the sheriff and that stranger talk about."

Luke and the sheriff entered the saloon and sat at a table where they could keep an eye on the four men and close enough so they could hear what they were talking about.

The barkeep came over and asked, "What'll ya have, Sheriff?"

"A couple of beers, Vern, and this time make sure they're cold."

"Right away."

When Vern the barkeep returned, he set down the beers and said, "Josh stopped by this morn and said ya found Hezekiah murdered. Do ya know who killed him?"

The sheriff said, "Got us a clue on who did it."

"Do you need the townspeople to help ya?" asked Vern.

"Na. Mr. Taylor here is all the help I'll be needing."

Luke had been keeping an eye on the four men while the sheriff was talking to Vern. He saw that they had quit talking and were trying to hear what was being said.

The sheriff and Luke sat there for a while before Ike asked, "Sheriff, what's this I heard about Hezekiah being killed? You know that I talked ta him about buying his place, but he wasn't ready ta sell."

"I heard something about that from his wife and son," said the sheriff. "Did ya happen ta go out ta his place a few days ago?"

"We have been in town most of the time. Hezekiah was to come to town and let me know if he decided to sell," said Ike. "We been waiting to hear from him but ain't seen him. When and how did it happen?" He got up and walked over to the table where they sat.

"A few days ago," said the sheriff. "He was shot in da back."

"That's too bad," said Ike. "I kinda thought he was interested in selling. With him dead, maybe I should be talk'n ta his wife ta see if she wants ta sell."

The sheriff said, "I wouldn't count on Martha selling out. His boy Isaac will run the place now that his pa is gone. If I was you, I wouldn't go near there. You might be shot by the boy, and then I'd have to go after him."

"We ain't done nothin' against the law, Sheriff. I'm just looking for some land to buy," said Ike. "Say, heard you had a clue as to who did it. What kind of a clue you got? Maybe we can help you."

The sheriff said, "Yes, we have a clue, and we'll find them. You can bet on that."

Not getting any satisfaction from the sheriff, Ike went back to the table and sat back down. The sheriff and Luke finished their beers and ordered a second one before leaving and going to the sheriff's office. Back in the sheriff's office, they sat down. The sheriff didn't want to tip his hand anymore than he had already done. Luke got up and was looking out the window when he saw the four leave the saloon. They stood by their horses for a while talking. While they were talking, they kept looking toward the sheriff's office before mounting. Like Luke suspected, they headed east out of town, not west like they had the night before.

Luke said, "Sheriff, da men are leaving. I'll wait till they're out of town; then I'll follow them ta see if I can find where they're camped. Maybe I can get near enough ta hear them talking."

"Before you leave, I better make you a deputy. Raise your right hand. Do you swear to uphold the laws of Kentucky?"

"I do."

"Here's your badge. You are now my deputy," said the sheriff. "While you do that, I'll check around town to see if anyone has seen Hezekiah's watch."

Luke pinned on his badge before going to his horse. While Luke and Rex followed the four men, the sheriff went around town to ask questions about Hezekiah's watch. At the edge of town, Luke picked up their trail. This time Ike and his men felt safe about not being followed, so they didn't hide their trail. About four miles out of town, Luke found where they turned off the road. Following their trail, they came across the cabin hidden in a grove where Luke saw their horses tied.

Tying his horse, he and Rex made their way to the side of the cabin. At the side of the cabin, he found a window. Looking in the window, he saw the four of them sitting at the table. Now knowing for sure where they were hiding out, he needed to report what he found to the sheriff. As he turned to leave, he bumped a stump behind him, knocking over a bucket that was sitting on it. Without stopping to see if they had heard, he made his way back to his horse. Once back with his horse, he turned and looked back.

Cody said, "I think we need to think about getting out of here. I think the sheriff might be on to us. We can't go back out to Hezekiah's place unless we kill the boy as well as his ma." While he was talking he heard a noise outside. "What was that?"

Ike had heard a noise outside as well. Going to look, he noticed that the bucket that had been sitting on a stump near the cabin was now lying on the ground. Maybe the wind had knocked it over, or maybe someone had been out there.

"Cody, go take a look," said Ike.

When Cody left, Ike said, "The sheriff doesn't know who did it, or he would have arrested us today when we was in town."

When Cody got outside, he walked over to where the bucket lay and picked it up. Looking at the ground, he saw tracks made by a dog or coyote and decided that there must have been an animal near the cabin that knocked the bucket over. He went back into the cabin, saying, "There was an animal out there. Must have knocked da bucket over."

Ike said, "We need to take a couple of days and figure out what to do. At least the sheriff doesn't know where we're at. We should be safe here for a while."

Cody said, "Ike, yer da one who shot him in da back. We were do'n what ya told us ta do. We thought ya were just gonna ruf him up some. If da sheriff finds out we were all involved, he's gonna hang us."

Ike said, "After thinking about it, I think that the sheriff and that stranger suspect that we might have had something to do with it but cannot prove it. We need to make sure that he does not find out that we did do it. The only way he would is if you did too much talking while you were in the saloon."

"Do ya plan on kill'n da sheriff as well?" asked Pete.

"Not unless we have to," said Ike.

Before leaving Ike's hideout, Luke waited by his horse and watched the house. It wasn't long before he saw Cody come around the back of the house and pick up the bucket. He watched as Cody looked at the ground and then looked in the direction that he had gone. Luke could tell that he did not see him, but there was something on the ground that made him look in their direction. He thought he had been careful to not leave tracks, but maybe Rex had. Luke continued to watch as Cody went back into the cabin. He waited and watched the cabin for another ten minutes before heading for town.

Arriving at the sheriff's office, he tied his horse before going into the office. The sheriff was sitting at his desk working on some papers before looking up.

"Did you find out where they are staying?" asked the sheriff.

"They're about four miles out of town," said Luke. "They're staying in a cabin about a quarter mile off da road."

"I know the place," said the sheriff.

"Did ya find out anything about da watch?" asked Luke.

"No one's seen it," said the sheriff. "Henry at the general store remembers Hezekiah ordering it and when it came in. He said Hezekiah had him put his initials on it, and if he saw it, he would know it."

"That don't give us anything ta go on."

"No, it don't," said the sheriff. "I'll need you to spend some more time here until we can make sure they are the ones who did it. Now that you are my deputy, you can stay in the room out back and get paid five dollars a week."

"I'll get mah gear and bring it over," said Luke. "If we are not going out after them tonight, I'll put mah horse up."

"Go ahead," said the sheriff. "We'll get some supper when ya get back."

Luke got up, and Rex followed as he led his horse over to Josh's stable. Josh met him as he got to the door.

"Ya come'n fer yer horses?" asked Josh.

"Na," said Luke. "Da sheriff made me a deputy ta help out fer a few days. I'll be leaving mah horses here till he says I can be on mah way. Do ya mind if I leave some of mah gear here as well?"

"Na, I got plenty of room," said Josh.

"Would ya give Buck here some grain? He's been long on the trail and short on grain," said Luke.

"Do ya want me ta grain yer other horses as well?"

"I'd be pleased if ya would."

Luke took his horse in and put him in a stall near his other two horses. He unsaddled him and gave him a good rub down before going to his gear. Taking what he would need for the next few days, he packed everything else away. Returning to the sheriff's office, he put his gear in the back room. They headed for the café.

During supper, the sheriff and Luke worked out a plan on how to capture the ones who killed Hezekiah.

revenge

Luke woke in the morning and lay there for a while looking around before getting up. It seemed strange to be sleeping in a bed again. Rex was lying on the floor next to the bed and looked up as Luke moved.

"Well, Rex," said Luke, "what do ya say we get some breakfast?"

Luke washed his face before heading to the café. Rex followed Luke into the café and lay down next to the wall. The waitress came over and said, "Good morning, Luke. What can I get for you?"

"I'll have a steak and eggs. Do ya happen ta have any scraps fer Rex taday?"

"We figured that you would be back this morning and saved some food for your dog," said the waitress. "By the way, the sheriff was just in but said he would be back and asked us to have you wait for him if you showed up."

"Thanks," said Luke as the waitress headed for the kitchen.

It wasn't long before the waitress returned with a dish full of food for Rex. As she approached Rex, he stood up and started wagging his tail. He watched her as she put the dish down in front of him, and once she moved away, he started eating.

"Rex, ya getting lazy not having to hunt fer yer food. I ain't seen him take ta anyone that quick since we got together," said Luke. "He don't have nothing ta do with most folks."

"I get along with dogs," said the waitress.

Rex never looked up while they were talking; he just kept eating.

While Luke was waiting for his food, the sheriff came in and sat down.

"I have been checking all over town. No one has seen Hezekiah's watch. Either the ones who took it are not the ones we're watching, or they are being very careful," said the sheriff.

"What are ya planning on doing now?" asked Luke.

"If they don't come into town today, we will go visit them."

After finishing their breakfast, they went back to the office to wait out the morning. Luke had a problem just sitting, so he went for a walk, checking on his horses. Rex got up and followed Luke. Entering the stable, he saw Josh feeding the stock. Luke went over to his horses and checked each one. He took a look at their shoes to make sure that none were loose. The packhorse had worn shoes, and a couple were loose. Leading him out to the front of the building, he asked Josh to replace the shoes on him when he got a chance to.

"I can get ta it this afternoon if that's soon enough?" Josh asked.

"I don't think I'll be needing him taday," said Luke.

Luke turned, heading to the sheriff's office. On the way back, he saw the four men ride into town. He stood watching them until they entered the saloon. Entering the office, the sheriff looked up and nodded at Luke.

"They're back in town," said Luke. "They just rode in and are at the saloon."

"Why don't ya keep an eye on the saloon to make sure they stay there? I'll be along as soon as I get done with this paperwork," said the sheriff.

Luke left the office and found a chair where he could sit across from the saloon. It wasn't long before the sheriff came and joined him. While they were sitting there, a wagon came into town with a man and a woman in it.

The sheriff said, "There's going ta be trouble. That's Isaac and Martha Muller, Hezekiah's son and wife. If Isaac finds Woodson in the saloon, he may try to start something, and Isaac could end up dead."

Isaac had gotten up that morning and started his normal day when his mother said that they needed some supplies from town. After they had finished breakfast, he went out and hitched up the wagon. Martha had made up a list of what was needed for the house while Isaac checked on what was needed for the farm. He would check with the blacksmith while he was in town to see if he had gotten the plow fixed that his pa had taken in. Bringing the wagon to the house, he sat and waited for his mother. Once Martha was seated, they headed for town.

"Ma," said Isaac, "since Pa was killed, we ain't seen anything of Woodson around our place. I wonder if da sheriff arrested him or what. Seems to me that if they hadn't had anything to do with the killing of Pa that they would of been comin by again."

"Now, Isaac," said Martha, "the sheriff said that he would take care of it. We got enough problems taken care of the ranch with your pa gone. If something was to happen to you, we would lose the ranch for sure, so you just leave it up to the sheriff. If you see them men in town, you just ignore them."

As they drove into town, Martha said, "Remember, Isaac, don't you do anything if you see those men today."

They stopped in front of the general store, and Isaac saw the sheriff talking to a stranger on the walk. Getting down, they both entered the store, nodding to the sheriff as they entered. Inside the store, Martha greeted Mr. Magee, the storeowner, and gave the list to him.

"This will take us a little while to fill your order, Mrs. Muller. If you have other business to tend to and want to come back later, we'll have it ready for you then," said Mr. Magee.

"Thank you," said Martha. "We do have some other things to take care of. We'll be back later to pick up our supplies."

As they left the general store, Martha saw that the sheriff and the man he was talking to had crossed the street. She did not recognize the man. Martha decided to ask him what he found out. Stepping off the walk, she started crossing the street with Isaac following.

The sheriff turned to look when Luke said, "Sheriff, I think that da Mullers are lookin fer ya."

"Mrs. Muller probably wants to know what's happening about her husband's killer," said the sheriff.

"Howdy, Mrs. Muller," said the sheriff as she approached. "How are you and Isaac doing these days?"

"Fine, Sheriff," said Mrs. Muller. "I was wondering if you caught the men who killed my husband."

"Not yet," said the sheriff. "We got an idea who did it, but we haven't found the evidence we have been looking for. We feel it's just a matter of time. By the way, this is my new deputy, Luke Taylor. He was with the family who found Hezekiah."

"Nice to meet you, Mr. Taylor," said Mrs. Muller. "This is my son, Isaac."

"Sorry about yer husband, Mrs. Muller. Nice ta meet ya, Isaac," said Luke as he reached out his hand to shake Isaac's hand.

Isaac extended his hand. Taking Luke's and shaking it, he said, "It's good ta meet ya as well."

"Isaac," said the sheriff, "Woodson and his men are in town, and I don't want any trouble between you and them. I told you at the ranch that I would take care of it, and I mean it."

Isaac asked, "Where are they?"

"They're in the saloon," said the sheriff. "Now unless you took up drinking, there is no need for you to go in there. We're keeping an eye on them, so you just leave them to us."

Isaac didn't say anything. He just turned to his mother and said before he started walking toward the stable, "I need ta talk to Josh at the stable. Pa had left some equipment there to get fixed. Where will ya be? I'll come get ya when I am done."

Martha said, "I am going to visit Mrs. Brown. You can pick me up there."

The sheriff continued to stand with Luke watching Isaac until he went into the stable. Seeing him entering the stable, he knew that Isaac would not go looking for Woodson. He wasn't as sure that Woodson wouldn't go after the Mullers if he saw them.

"Luke, you stay here and keep an eye on Woodson and his men in the saloon. I need to get something from the office," said the sheriff.

Entering the stable, Isaac called out, "Josh!"

"Back here!" called Josh.

Isaac went back to where the voice came from. Seeing Josh, he asked, "Pa left some equipment fer ya ta fix. I was wondering if it was ready."

"Ya, finished it. It's out back waiting for ya to pick it up. Sorry to hear about yer pa. Did ya hear anything?" asked Josh.

"Thanks," said Isaac. "Da Sheriff said that they had an idea who done it and they were watching them. He said da fella who wanted to buy our place was in the saloon as well and I was ta stay away from them. He's afraid I might start something. Ma don't want me do'n nothing as well. I don't think the sheriff knows fer sure who done it, nor can he prove it."

"The sheriff got himself a deputy to help find the ones who killed yer pa. Fella is a stranger to us. Said he found yer pa. Maybe he's da one who killed yer pa," said Josh. "He ain't been here before, and if he had, what would he be hang'n around here fer? Anyway, I don't think da sheriff would of hired him if he thought he might have killed yer pa."

"Well, having him as his deputy would sure be a way of keep'n an eye on him," said Isaac. "Besides, da sheriff told us that it was four men who killed Pa, so I don't think it was him either."

"Suit yerself," said Josh.

"I'll come back befer long and pick up the equipment befer we leave town," said Isaac.

"It'll be here," said Josh.

Isaac walked across the street going back toward the general store. Walking by the saloon, he looked in and could see Ike Woodson and his men sitting at a table. Ike looked up and saw Isaac as he walked by.

Isaac saw that Ike looked at him. Turning to avoid any contact with them, he headed for their wagon. Before he got to the wagon, Ike and his men had come out of the saloon and were following him.

When Luke saw Isaac come out of the stable and walk across the street he thought that he should stop Isaac. Instead he decided to wait and see what he did. He watched as Isaac paused while looking in the saloon. Getting up, he started to cross the street, but then Isaac started walking toward their wagon. Luke sat back down. He had no more than sat down when he saw Ike and his men come out of the saloon. They stood by the door talking for a minute before they started walking toward Isaac.

When they started walking toward Isaac, Luke again got up, this time crossing the street to try and intercept them before they got to Isaac.

When Isaac reached the wagon, he looked back in time to see Ike and his men coming toward him. Standing by the wagon, he waited. He also noticed that Luke was following Ike and his men.

"Sorry to hear about yer pa," said Ike as he caught up to Isaac. "If you're a mind to sell yer place, I still would like to buy your ranch."

"Yer da one who killed mah pa, and as soon as I can prove it, I am gonna kill ya," said Isaac. "While yer at it, da ranch ain't fer sell, so stay away. If ya come ta our place, I'll shoot ya on sight."

Luke came up to them just as Isaac was finishing.

"Something I can do fer ya fellas?" asked Luke.

Ike turned along with his men to see who was talking.

"Na, deputy," said Ike. "We were just telling Mr. Muller we were sorry to hear about his pa."

"Well, I don't think Mr. Muller wants ta talk ta ya. Why don't ya go back ta what ya were doing and leave him alone," said Luke.

"Now, deputy," said Ike, "we ain't doing nothing wrong. We were just paying out respect ta him."

"Isaac and his ma have enough trouble without you. I suggest ya stay away from them and their place," said Luke.

"Come on," said Ike to his men, turning back toward the saloon. While Luke was watching them, he saw Cody pull a watch out of his pocket and open it. Luke thought that he heard bells playing as the watch opened. He looked at Isaac to see if he had heard it, but Isaac had turned away, ignoring them, and did not see Cody take out the watch.

"Are ya all right?" Luke asked Isaac.

"Ya, I'm fine," said Isaac. "They thought now that pa is gone we would sell da ranch. Someday I'm gonna kill that man."

"Ya need ta do what the sheriff said about leaving Woodson ta him. If ya got enough supplies, I suggest that ya stay at da ranch until we get this cleaned up, and stay away from Woodson and his men. They would not give you a chance, and with you being dead, what would yer ma do?"

"Thanks," said Isaac. "I'll keep ta da ranch as long as Woodson and his men stay away from us. I done told him that if he comes ta our place, I would shoot him fer trespassing, and I mean ta do it."

Isaac went into the general store to see if their supplies were ready.

Luke headed for the sheriff's office. Entering, he found the sheriff. He waited for him to finish before he said, "Sheriff, I think I found Hezekiah's watch. I believe that the fella Ike calls Cody has it. When he walked away from Isaac just now, he took a watch out of his pocket, and when he opened it, I thought I heard bells. If we can get the watch, we can see if it has Hezekiah's initials on it."

"Where are they now?" asked the sheriff.

"When I left Isaac ta come here, they were going back toward da saloon."

Getting up from his desk, the sheriff and Luke headed out just in time to see Ike and his men riding out of town. Luke also noticed that Isaac's wagon was missing from in front of the general store. Much to his relief, he saw Isaac and his mother coming up the street from Mrs. Brown's house.

"Sheriff, I think I need ta follow Isaac and his mother back ta da ranch. At least until they get past the turn off ta where Ike and his men are staying," said Luke. "Ike may try something along the road."

"I think I'll ride along," said the sheriff.

Mounting, they followed the Muller wagon out of town. They caught up with them just outside of town. As they rode up, Isaac pulled their horses to a stop to see what the sheriff wanted.

"What's up, Sheriff?" asked Martha.

"We want to make sure that you don't run into any trouble on your way home taday."

"What make you think we might run into trouble?" asked Martha.

"We saw Ike Woodson and his men ride out just before you did. We wanted to make sure they don't try anything. Luke here thinks that one of the men has Hezekiah's watch. If he does, then we have reason to believe that they had something to do with Hezekiah's murder. The proof we are looking for would be Hezekiah's watch," said the sheriff.

"All right, Sheriff, you're welcome to ride along with us as far as you think you need to," said Martha.

Leaving Luke and Isaac at the general store, Ike and his men went back to the saloon. Instead of going in, they stood out front until they saw Isaac and Mr. Magee load the supplies into the Muller wagon. After Isaac drove up the street, they mounted their horses and rode out of town.

"We need to keep an eye on the Mullers," said Ike. "I think that the sheriff and that deputy of his suspect that we were the ones who killed Hezekiah. About three miles out of town, there's a spot where we can watch fer them. If the Mullers come alone, we can jump them."

They rode in silence until they got to the spot that Ike had mentioned. Turning off the road, they hid their horses and got into a position where they could watch the road. Settling down, they waited. About half an hour later, they saw the Muller wagon coming down the road. Only they were not alone. The sheriff and his deputy were riding with them. Ike continued to watch as the party approached where they had left the road. The sheriff and deputy were not paying any attention to the road, but the dog that always tagged along was sniffing the road and started to follow their trail. Drawing his gun, he waited. If they started to follow the dog and found them, the sheriff would have all kinds of questions that he couldn't answer about why they had been waiting for the Mullers, and they would have to kill them all. He relaxed when he saw the deputy call his dog back.

Luke had kept an eye on what Rex was doing. About three miles out of town, Rex started to follow a scent off the road. Looking at the ground, Luke saw the tracks of four horses. Not wanting to give away that he had seen their tracks, he called Rex back. The sheriff noticed a change in Luke and rode up alongside to find out what was going on.

"There were tracks of four horses leaving da road back there," said Luke. "I believe that Ike and his men are somewhere about watching us. If we hadn't ridden with them, Ike may have tried to stop them."

"This would be a good spot to try and stop them if they wanted to. I don't think they will try anything as long as we're with them," said the sheriff. "Keep an eye out for them, and if you see anything, don't hesitate to shoot."

Luke kept watching Rex as they rode. Rex kept looking off to the side of the road, sniffing the air. Luke figured that they must be close.

Luke and the sheriff rode another five miles with the Mullers before heading back to town. Luke decided that he wanted to spend a little time looking the area over where they believed that Ike and his men had waited. When they returned to the spot, they got down and followed the tracks Luke had spotted. They found where Ike and his men had tied their horses and where Ike and his men had waited. Not seeing which way they had gone, Luke and the sheriff decided that Ike and his men must have gone back into town or they had stayed off the main road, heading for their cabin.

Arriving back in town, they did not see Ike's men or their horses. Going to the office, Luke said, "Sheriff, I know that da one they call Cody must have Hezekiah's watch. I am sure that I heard da bells that Isaac talked about when Cody looked at the watch when he was in town befer. I think we ought ta go get them and bring them in."

"If I know them, they will be back in town in the next day or two. We can wait to question them then," said the sheriff.

Seeing that Luke had called the dog back, Ike put his gun away and just watched until they were out of sight.

Cody said, "We can take them. There are four of us, and it's just da Sheriff, his deputy, a boy, and a woman."

"Don't be stupid," said Ike. "I think they know that something might be up. Did you take a good look at how that deputy was acting? If we tried anything now, they would be prepared for it. It's better that they think something might happen and not have anything happen. The next time they won't be so alert."

Ike and his men remained hidden until they were completely out of sight. Once the Mullers, the sheriff, and Luke were out of sight, Ike and his men rode back to their cabin. Ike didn't want to go back to town. The sheriff had seen them ride out just before the Mullers. If the sheriff returned and saw them, he would suspect that it had been them waiting by the road.

After Ike and his men returned to their cabin, they put up their horses and went in to cook supper. While they were eating, Ike said, "Tomorrow we will go out to visit the Webbs and see if they heard anything from the sheriff."

That night while Ike sat around the cabin, he thought about leaving the area before the sheriff got any wiser. But before he did that, he sure wanted to get his hands on the Muller place. He had heard that their place was a prime spot that could allow him to make a good profit. If the Mullers wouldn't sell out, maybe the Webbs might. His place was a second choice spot that Ike had found.

In the morning after breakfast, Ike and his men saddled their horses and rode to the Webbs' place. It was the midmorning by the time they arrived. Allen was working in the barn as the four rode up. Hearing the horses, he looked out to see who had come. Seeing it was Ike and his men, he grabbed his rifle before going into the yard to see what they wanted.

Holding his rifle on them, he asked, "What do ya want, Ike?"

"Now that ain't neighborly of ya holding that rifle on us. We just want some information. We done heard yer neighbor was killed, and we wanted ta know what you knew about it."

"I don't know nothing about it," said Allen.

"Do ya think that Mrs. Muller would be willing ta sell her place now that her husband is gone?" asked Ike.

"I don't think she's gonna sell ta ya or anyone else."

"Ya got a nice place here. Maybe ya would consider selling it. What would you take ta sell it?"

"Mah place ain't fer sell neither," said Allen. "Now if ya don't mind, I got work ta do, and ya ain't welcome here. Next time I see ya on mah place, yer trespassing, and I'll shoot first and ask questions later. Do ya understand?"

"We hear ya," said Ike. "Ya might reconsider later."

"Is that a threat?" asked Allen. "Is that what ya told Hezekiah befer ya killed him? Now get, and don't bother come'n back." Allen cocked his rifle and pointed it toward Ike.

Ike did not say another word but turned and rode away. Allen stood with his rifle ready, watching them as they left. His wife came out when they were gone. "Who was that, Allen?" Kathy asked.

"That was the men who the sheriff thinks might have killed Hezekiah," said Allen.

"What did they want with us?" asked Kathy.

"They wanted ta find out what I knew. When I told them nothing, they asked if I wanted ta sell our place. I told them no and told them ta get off and stay off," said Allen. "We need ta keep an eye out fer them. If they are da ones who did kill Hezekiah, then they may be back and try to kill us as well."

"When you finish in the barn, hitch up the team, and we will go over to the Mullers. I have some baked goods for them," said Kathy.

"I'll be done shortly," said Allen.

With Ike and his men gone, Allen went back to the barn to finish his chores. Kathy went back into the house to finish her baking. When Allen finished, he hitched up the team and drove up to the house. By then Kathy had finished her baking and had put together a basket of food for Martha and Isaac. Getting into the wagon, they drove to the Muller's.

When they drove into the yard, Martha came out and greeted them.

"Kathy, Allen, it's good to see you. Get down and come on in," said Martha.

"Thank you," said Allen. "Kathy has been doing some baking and thought ya could use some of it."

"We can always use some fresh baking," said Martha. "I haven't had time to do any baking since Hezekiah was killed. Seems like Isaac needed more help than he thought finishing up some repairs they had started. Come on in. There's a fresh pot of coffee on the stove. We'll cut some of your fresh bread. Allen, would you go down to the barn and fetch Isaac?"

"Sure," said Allen.

"Come on, Kathy. We can set the table," said Martha.

Allen walked down to the barn and looked in. He did not see Isaac inside the barn, so he figured that he must be behind the barn, as he did not come out when they drove up. As Allen rounded the corner, he saw Isaac with his rifle near the edge of the grove making his way into the trees like he was hunting. Not knowing for sure, Allen went back to the wagon and got his rifle before following Isaac.

Isaac had been working on the corral behind the barn when he heard a horse nickering in the grove. Knowing that they did not have any of their stock in the area, he wanted to know who was out there. Getting his rifle, he made his way toward the woods. At the edge of woods, he stopped and listened. It wasn't long before he heard the horse again. This time he could tell that the sound came from the center of the grove just ahead of him. He waited to see if he could find out where the owner of the horse was before going on.

Ike decided that they should pay a visit to the Mullers while they were out there. He remembered what Isaac had said about shooting them if he found them on their place. Because of that, he didn't want to just ride in, so when they got close to the Mullers, they circled around to the grove so they could see any activities going on at the Mullers. Tying their horses in the middle of the grove, they made their way to the edge, keeping the barn between them and the house. Ike was sure that they had remained out of sight of anyone in the yard. Not seeing anyone, they continued along the edge of the trees until the house came into view. The move had taken them some distance from their horses. While they were moving along the edge of the grove, Ike spotted Isaac working on the corral. If they had to get back to the horses in a hurry, they may be in trouble. Not liking the idea of being separated from their horses, he decided to send a man back to get them.

"Lance, go back ta the horses and wait fer us. If ya hear some shooting, bring the horses up in a hurry," said Ike. "Be careful. The boy is behind the barn and might see ya if ya get in a opening in the trees, so stay back in the woods."

Lance headed back to the horses when he heard one of them snort. Stopping, he looked toward the barn, seeing Isaac stop working and look up. Lance continued to watch Isaac as he turned and went back into the barn. Not waiting, Lance hurried to the horses.

He knew that he needed to keep them quiet or Ike would take it out on him if the Muller boy found them. Before losing sight of the barn, Lance looked back toward the barn where he saw Isaac coming out of the barn. Lance figured that Isaac must have heard the horses as well. Making it the rest of the way back to the horses, he got there before Isaac but not before the horses snorted again.

Ike, seeing Isaac heading for the woods, knew that Lance would be in trouble if they did not get there as well. Motioning to the men to move back into the woods, he said, "Be quiet as we head back to the horses. The boy is making his way toward Lance. If Lance gets inta trouble, we will come in behind him befer he can get Lance."

Because Ike and his men had started for the horses before Allen came around the corner of the barn, they did not see him leave, nor did they see him return with his rifle to follow Isaac.

Isaac made his way toward the sound of the horses. As he approached the area where the horses were tied, he saw one of the Ike's men standing with them.

"What's going on here?" asked Isaac, holding his rifle on Lance.

Lance turned at the sound of Isaac's voice. Bringing his rifle around, he saw Isaac standing there with his rifle pointed at him. Lowering his rifle, he stood there, not moving.

Isaac asked again, "What are ya doing here, and who is with ya?"

About that time, Ike and the rest of his men came up behind Isaac.

"Drop yer rifle," said Ike.

Isaac turned, dropping his rifle to face Ike.

Cody asked, "What are we gonna do with him?"

"We're gonna hold him until his ma sells the ranch," said Ike. "If she don't sell, we will kill him like we did his pa."

Allen, following where Isaac had gone, soon spotted Ike and his men holding guns on Isaac. "Drop your guns," said Allen.

Hearing Allen's voice, they froze. Ike thought that he could turn and shoot whoever was behind them before they would be able to shoot. But seeing Lance, who was facing him, drop his gun and shake his head, he had second thoughts and dropped his gun.

"Isaac, pick up their guns and bring them over here," said Allen.

Isaac turned and picked up Lance's gun before getting the others. As he walked around them going toward Allen, Cody grabbed Isaac, shoving him into Allen. When Ike saw Cody shove Isaac, he turned, ran, and jumped on his horse. Lance was right behind and was able to mount and ride off before Allen could recover.

When Isaac was shoved into Allen, he fell back but kept hold of his rifle, and as Cody ran for his horse, Allen shot at him, wounding him in the leg and knocking him to the ground. Brent stopped before he got to his horse and raised his hands.

"Pick up yer friend and put him in da saddle," said Allen.

Brent helped Cody up, and with the help of Isaac, they got Cody in the saddle. Isaac tied Cody's hands to the saddle so he couldn't try to escape before they could get their horses. Getting some more rope, he tied Brent's hands while Allen continued to keep his gun on Brent. Gathering the horses' reins, Isaac led them back to the house. Allen walked behind the horses and kept a gun on them in case they tried anything.

Kathy and Martha were standing on the porch as Isaac, Allen, Cody, and Brent came around the corner of the barn. They looked at each other with surprise on their faces before looking back. The women waited until the men got up to the house, and Kathy asked, "We heard shooting. What happened? Are you two all right? We heard a shot, and now you come up with two of Ike's men?"

Isaac said, "When I was working on the corral, I heard a horse in the grove. When I found da horses, Ike's men were there and got da drop on me. Allen came along in time ta save me and got da drop on them. Ike and Lance got away, but we got these two. While they held me, I heard Ike say they were gonna kill me like they killed Pa if Ma didn't sell da ranch."

"Kathy, I want ya ta stay here with Martha while Isaac and I take these two inta da Sheriff. Isaac, go saddle a couple of horses, and we will be gon ta town. Brent, ya and Cody set yerself down over by da porch, and don't move. I'd just as soon shoot ya as well as look at ya."

While Isaac went to saddle a couple of horses, Brent and Cody sat by the porch not moving. Allen kept his gun on them to make sure they stayed put. Cody's leg was continuing to bleed, so Martha got some bandages to stop the bleeding.

"I don't know why yer fix'n his leg. They're going to hang him anyway," said Allen.

"I want him to live long enough to know he is going to hang and suffer waiting for it," said Martha.

When Isaac returned with the horses, Allen made Brent help Cody mount before he could mount. Tying their hands to the saddle horn, they were ready to go. Mounting the horse Isaac brought for him, Allen took the reins of Brent's horse while Isaac led Cody's horse. They rode off heading for town.

Ike and Lance rode as fast as they could in getting away from Allen and Isaac. After riding for a couple of miles, they pulled up to see if anyone was following. Not seeing anyone, they continued on.

"What about Brent and Cody?" asked Lance.

"They're on their own fer now," said Ike. "We got bigger problems. If they're still alive, we will break them out of jail befer they can be hung. If they're dead, we need ta get out of the area 'cause da sheriff is gonna be after us now."

They headed back to the cabin and started packing their gear. Ike figured that the sheriff still didn't know where they were staying, so they should be safe for the time being. They wouldn't be able to go to town during the day without running into the sheriff, so they would have to go in by night to find out if his men were in jail or dead.

Allen and Isaac took their time riding into town, keeping a sharp eye out for an ambush. Whenever they came on a place where an ambush could take place, they would stop while Allen or Isaac circled around to check it out. It was getting late in the afternoon when they finally rode into town. One of the townspeople saw them coming and ran to the sheriff's office.

The sheriff, Luke, and Rex came out of the office just as they rode up.

"Allen, Isaac, what have you got here?" asked the sheriff.

"A couple of men who killed mah pa," said Isaac.

"How do ya know that they killed yer pa?" asked the sheriff.

"Ike said that he was gonna kill me like he had killed mah pa," said Isaac.

"Did Ike say that, Allen?" asked the sheriff.

"Well, I didn't hear him say that, but they were holding a gun on Isaac when I came up on them," said Allen. "When I told Isaac ta pick up their guns, they made a break fer it."

"Who shot him?" asked the sheriff.

"I done it," said Allen.

"Luke, take these two and lock them in a cell. I need da two of ya ta come on in and make a statement on what happened," said the sheriff.

Luke untied Brent while Allen untied Cody and helped him off the horse. "This man needs a doc," said Allen as he helped Cody into the sheriff's office while Luke put them in a cell. Luke returned to the main office just as the sheriff, Allen, and Isaac were entering. "Luke," said the sheriff, "would you go fetch da doc so he can look at Cody's leg?"

"Right away," said Luke as he walked past them and out the door. Returning, he took the doctor to where Cody was lying on a cot. Cody was just taking a watch out of his pocket and was opening it when they walked in.

Luke, hearing the bells, went to Cody, saying, "Let me see that watch." When Cody handed it to Luke, Luke turned it over and saw the initials HRM engraved on the back.

"I'll just hang on to this," said Luke.

When the doc finished patching up the leg, Luke locked the cell before going back into the main office.

In the office, he walked over to the desk where the three men were sitting. He waited until they had finished talking before he laid the watch on the desk.

"I think this belongs ta ya, Isaac," said Luke.

Isaac picked it up and looked at it. "Ya, this is da watch they done took off Pa when they killed him," said Isaac. "Where did ya get it?"

"Ya brung it in with ya when ya came in," said Luke. "Cody had it on him."

"Between what you just told me about what Ike said and finding your pa's watch on Cody, we have the proof we need to hang Ike and his men," said the sheriff. "Luke, you and I will go out in the morning and pick them up. By now it should be all over town that we have some of Ike's men in jail."

"Sheriff," said Allen, "we will be heading back ta da ranch. Kathy and Martha are out there alone, and we don't want Ike and his other man ta harm them."

"You two keep an eye out for them. If he's going to go after anyone now, it might be you for what happened out at the farm and putting Brent and Cody into jail."

"We sure will, Sheriff," said Isaac. "If ya need any help, just call us."

"Thanks, Isaac. I will keep it in mind," said the sheriff. "But I think that Luke and I can take care of those two."

The sheriff and Luke walked out with Allen and Isaac and watched as they rode off.

Taking Cody's and Brent's horses, the sheriff and Luke walked down to the stable to put them up.

Entering the stable, the sheriff said, "Da county's got a couple of customers for ya, Josh."

"Put them in those empty stalls," said Josh.

When Luke and the sheriff left the stable, they headed for the café. One of the customers at a table they passed asked, "We saw some goings on at the jail. What's up?"

"We might have a couple of the men who killed Hezekiah," said the sheriff.

As the sheriff turned, they congratulated him on catching the men that killed Hezekiah. The sheriff nodded and kept on walking to the table.

"Word will surely get around fast now about da men we have locked up," said the sheriff.

"That's fer sure. Da ya think that Ike will try and get his man out of jail?" asked Luke.

"Right now I don't think that Ike will be doing much. I am not sure if they will even be at their cabin when we get there in the morning," said the sheriff. "Once we get Ike and the one he called Lance locked up, you can be on your way again."

"I'll be look'n fer it," said Luke. "I may be able ta catch up ta the Dailys again if they ain't got too far."

"What are you planning on doing when you get out west?" asked the sheriff.

"I don't rightly know. I thought maybe I might do some guiding for a wagon train heading west," said Luke. "I done thought about da west since I was a kid. I use ta go ta town and listen ta da men who came back from da west while they would tell their stories. I started dreaming about da west and wanting ta go out there ever since. Da war stopped me earlier, but now I am on mah way."

"Did you fight in the war?"

"Na, mah pa did. Got hisself wounded while riding with Jackson," said Luke. "I been look'n fer a man name of Fry who raided our farm and killed mah brother while mah pa was gone. He leads a bunch of men who raided farms in Virginia during da war dressed as a Union soldier. He also killed a couple friends of mine. We thought we had him, but he got away. Last I heard, he was heading west. Someday I will run inta him, and when I do, I will kill him."

"I can understand how you feel. Why don't you let the law take care of him?" asked the sheriff.

"The law won't do nothing 'cause he did it during da war," said Luke.

"There were a lot of folks who were hurt during the war," said the sheriff. "Seems like there were a few who broke the law for personal gain. I don't think you are going to be able to find your man, but good luck to you."

They ordered their meal and some scraps for Rex. While they were eating, several customers came up and congratulated the sheriff about catching the man who killed Hezekiah. Seems the man who had asked what was going on when they entered had left and was spreading the word around town.

Ike and Lance ate supper after they had packed their gear. While they ate, Ike told Lance that they would go into town and find out what happened to Cody and Brent. Loading their gear on their horses in case they couldn't return, they headed toward town. On the edge of town, they avoided the main street and entered through a side street, staying out of the main traffic. Keeping to the shadows, they made sure that no one would see them.

Tying their horses in the alley, they made their way between two buildings, one being the saloon. In the dark, they waited until they saw a man walking along the boardwalk. When the man reached the opening between the two buildings, Ike moaned and bent over. When the man came to see what was wrong, Lance pulled a gun and told the man to raise his hands.

"Hey, what do you want from me?" he asked.

"Where's the sheriff?" asked Ike.

"In the café eating supper with his deputy."

"How do ya know?"

"I just come from there."

"Lance, go check the café and see if they are still there," said Ike. Turning back to the man, Ike asked, "Does the sheriff have anyone in jail?"

"I heard that he had a couple of men in jail," said the man.

Ike had the man turn his back to him before taking his gun and hitting him over his head, knocking him out. It wasn't long before Lance returned and said that they were still eating their supper. Going to their horses, they rode around to the jail, picking up two more horses on the way. At the jail, Ike went in, leaving Lance watching the horses. Finding the key to the cell, he unlocked the cell, letting Brent out, and was unlocking the cell for Cody when they heard a shot coming from in front of the jail.

The sheriff and Luke heard the shot as well. Getting up, they ran to the front door to see where the shot had come from. Looking toward the jail, they heard a second shot coming from in front of the saloon. Rushing to the man who fired the shot, he pointed toward the jail. Looking at where the man was pointing, Luke saw Lance sitting on his horse in front of the jail holding three other horses. He and Rex started running for the jail.

Lance saw Luke and Rex running toward him. He fired and missed Luke and fired a second time, missing again. Luke returned fire, hitting Lance and knocking him from his horse just as Ike, Cody, and Brent were coming out of the jail.

Ike saw Lance falling from his horse and all the horses running off. Turning toward Luke, he saw both him and the sheriff running toward the jail. Ike fired at the sheriff, hitting him in the arm. Luke fired, hitting Ike and knocking him down. Rex, in the meantime, had reached Brent and had him on the ground. Brent was helping Cody, so when he saw Rex jump for him, he let Cody fall to the ground to protect himself from Rex. When Luke got to the jail, he took Ike and Cody's guns away before calling Rex off Brent.

Before Luke had finished collecting their guns, the sheriff had arrived and was holding his gun on them. After Luke had the guns, he checked on Lance. The shot that Luke had fired killed Lance. Seeing that Ike was only wounded, he grabbed him. Taking the three of them into the jail, they put Ike, Cody, and Brent into separate cells.

"Sheriff, yer wounded," said Luke.

"Just a scratch," said the sheriff. "Go get the doctor 'cause I think Ike is going to need him worse than I will."

Luke left Rex with the sheriff and went to get the doctor. Returning with the doctor, he took a look at the sheriff first before taking a look at Ike. Luke went with him to make sure that Ike didn't try anything. When he finished working on Ike, they returned to the office.

"Well, doc, will he live to hang?" asked the sheriff.

"He'll be okay in a couple of days and able to stand trial by the time the judge gets here," said the doctor.

"That's good," said the sheriff. "I would hate to not be able to hang this one."

"Sheriff, now that ya got all da men who killed Mr. Muller, do ya need me ta stay around?" asked Luke.

"Na. With Isaac's testimony and catching them trying to break Brent and Cody out of jail, they will hang," said the sheriff. "You can get started in the morning if you want."

"Thanks," said Luke. "I would still like ta get ta Independence befer winter sets in too hard."

In the morning, the sheriff and Luke, along with Rex, went to the café for one last breakfast before Luke and Rex were on their way. During breakfast, the sheriff thanked Luke for his help and paid him for the days he worked as his deputy.

Before they were done eating, the waitress came up to Luke and handed him a package, saying, "This is for Rex. I heard you say you would be leaving this morning."

"Thanks," said Luke. "I am sure he will enjoy it." The waitress walked over to Rex and scratched his head before leaving them alone again. Rex stood there wagging his tail. After breakfast, Luke said good-bye to the sheriff and headed for the stable.

"Josh," Luke called out as he entered the stable.

Josh came out from the office he had in the rear of the stable. "What can I do for ya?" he asked.

"I came ta get mah gear and horses. Da sheriff got the men who killed Hezekiah in jail and said I could be on mah way," said Luke.

"I am glad that the sheriff got the men who killed Hezekiah," said Josh. "Let me get your horses for you. Your gear is where you left it."

Once Luke had his gear loaded, he mounted. Saying good-bye to Josh, he rode out of town. As he and Rex headed down the road, he was wondering how far the Dailys had gotten and if he would be able to catch up to them before they reached St. Louis.

indiana

The Dailys had been traveling since Luke and the sheriff left. They missed Mr. Taylor and Rex and tried to take it easy so that they could catch up soon. What they had heard in town about people being killed by robbers made Jenny worry, but Frank assured her that they would be all right. They followed tracks that looked like they belonged to another wagon, hoping to find another family to ride with. They knew they would be much safer with another family. Luckily, when they caught up to the other wagon, it did belong to another family—the Hermans.

The Dailys told the Hermans that they were headed for St. Louis and told them about Luke. The families agreed to travel together and look out for each other until they reached St. Louis or until Luke came back to help the Dailys. After a few days of traveling together, one of Frank's horses developed a stone bruise. The families rode together into Mitchell to see if Frank could trade for a new horse. The morning before they went into town, they saw some strange men ride past their camp. After seeing these men, the Dailys wanted Luke back by their side more than ever.

As Luke and Rex left town, the word that the men who had killed Hezekiah had been caught and there was going to be a hanging had spread. As he rode, he saw more and more people heading into town. One man stopped and asked Luke why he wasn't staying for the hanging. Luke just told him that he did not need to see anyone hung. He had seen enough dead men to last him a lifetime during the war. By the end of the day, there must have been an additional hundred people who had come to town to see the hanging.

Luke noticed that Rex seemed to be happy that they were away from all these people and traveling again. Even the horses that had been in the stable for the past few days were glad to be stretching their legs. Luke checked his supplies before loading his gear at Josh's stable and saw that he had everything that he needed to last him for the next month. He could kill fresh game as he went, but he still had plenty of jerky for during the day so he could make up some time trying to catch up to the Dailys.

The first night back on the trail Luke found a spot off the road with shelter. Building his fire, he knew he would stay warm with the nights getting colder. Rex ran out and caught himself a rabbit and lay by the fire eating it while Luke cooked his own supper.

"I see ya ain't lost yer appetite fer rabbit since we been in town," said Luke.

Rex just wagged his tail and kept eating.

Lying down for the night, Luke went over in his head about what had happened in town. He had helped the sheriff catch the men who had killed Hezekiah. Maybe if he had worked closer with the marshal in Panther Gap, his friends Helen and Hicks would still be alive.

Rex must have sensed that Luke needed someone near him. He came over and lay down next to Luke and put his head in Luke's lap. Luke reached down and started petting Rex while he was thinking. Finally he looked down at Rex and said, "Ya are still with me, mah friend. "

Rex looked up at Luke and barked like he knew what Luke was saying. That night Rex lay next to Luke for most of the night. During the night, Rex woke up and growled, waking Luke. Luke sat up and listened. He could hear what sounded like men on horse-back moving on the road. By now his fire had died down and was not giving off much light. Getting up, he and Rex made their way toward the road. Luke watched as several men rode by. From the way they were traveling, it looked like both the men and horses had been traveling for a long time.

Going back to his camp after they had passed, Luke thought to himself that it was strange that men would be traveling this late at night. He would have to keep an eye out for them. Traveling late at night was either an emergency or someone up to no good. By the way they were traveling, he figured they were up to no good.

Luke finally went back to sleep. He and Rex slept the rest of the night without being disturbed. In the morning, Luke made break-fast, giving some to Rex. They ate and prepared to get started. The Dailys had been on the road for over a week since Luke had last seen them, and if they were making between fifteen and twenty miles per day, it would take Luke at least a couple of weeks to over-take them. Hopefully nothing had happened to them.

When he and Rex started out, Luke again began thinking about those men who had ridden past their camp during the night. He could see the tracks that they had left. There must have been ten or twelve men riding together. He figured that they would have stopped not too long after they had passed his camp for the night or they would kill their horses. He would keep an eye out for any tracks showing where they left the road.

About an hour on the trail, Luke saw where they had left the road. Not taking time to follow, he continued on. He had not gone half a mile when he saw their tracks where they again entered the road. Stopping to take a closer look at them, he determined that the tracks were about an hour old. So they were still ahead of him, and it looked like they were still traveling fast.

"I hope they turn off before they catch up to the Dailys," said Luke to Rex. "We need ta keep an eye out fer them as well."

Luke continued to see their tracks all day. He would have to be careful not to run into them. At noon, Luke stopped, and he saw that the tracks appeared to be less than an hour old. That could only mean one thing. Their horses were tiring, and they were not traveling as fast. Now he would have to be extra careful.

"Rex," said Luke, "ya need ta keep yer nose ta da air and look out fer them."

Rex took off like he understood what Luke had said. They traveled on for an hour when Rex came to a halt with his ears up, looking off to the side of the road. Luke stopped, getting down. He worked his way toward where Rex was looking. Making his way into the brush, he stopped to listen. Not hearing anything, he continued on. Suddenly he stopped, smelling smoke.

Tying his horses where they were out of sight, he made his way toward the smoke. When he got to the opening, smoke was still coming out of an abandoned campfire. Looking around, he noticed that it had to have been the camp of a dozen or so men. From the looks of the campsite, they had not been gone long. Putting out the fire, he went back to his horses.

Entering Louisville, he didn't see anything that was unusual for the town. Seeing that it was dinnertime, he stopped in front of the café. Tying his horses, he and Rex entered the café. Taking a table near the windows, he sat down. Rex lay down next to the window with Luke between him and anyone who might come over to the table.

When Luke ordered his dinner, he asked if they would happen to have any scraps or a bone for Rex. The waitress returned with a bone from the kitchen and gave it to Rex. He started to chew on it.

While Luke was eating, there was a sudden burst of gunfire coming from the street. Looking out the window, he saw men coming out of the bank with guns drawn. He guessed that there were about twelve men in front of the bank. Some of the men on horseback were holding spare horses for the four men who just came out carrying what looked to be saddlebags. The last fella to leave the bank turned and fired back into the bank as he left while the other three ran to their horses and mounted. While he made his way to his horse, the other men who were already on their horses started firing at anyone who was on the street. The sheriff, hearing the gunfire, came out of his office and started firing at the robbers. One of the robbers returned fire, hitting the sheriff and causing him to fall back through the open door and drop his gun. Some of the townspeople were returning fire as the robbers started to ride out.

Luke got up from the table and ran to the front door, drawing his pistol as he went. Opening the door, he ducked outside and started firing as the robbers rode past him.

Luke noticed that it looked like a couple of them had been hit as they rode past the café. Luke continued to fire at them as they rode by. He was almost hit by a bullet as he stood there shocked when he recognized some of the men as the same men who had been with Captain Fry. With the last bullet in his revolver, he fired at the last man. He saw the man jerk as the bullet hit him, causing him to fall forward on his horse. He continued to watch as they rode out of town. The man he had hit slid from the saddle before he made it out of town. Luke assumed that he was dead. Some of the townspeople who were near the edge of town approached the man with their guns drawn. When Luke saw that they put their guns down, he knew that the man had to be dead.

Looking back up the street, he saw that people were running to the sheriff's office to see how bad he was hit. Returning to his table, he sat down and finished his meal. Rex had gone out with Luke but was now lying down by the table with his bone again. While Luke was finishing his meal, he thought about Fry. So this was where he and his men had headed when they were driven out of Virginia. Now the question was, should he go after them or try and catch up to the Dailys? The direction that Fry had taken was the same direction that he and the Dailys were headed. Finishing his meal, he paid for it and left. On the street, Luke could see that the sheriff was now standing, meaning that his wound wasn't too bad. From where Luke stood, it looked like the sheriff had been hit in the shoulder. It looked to be bad enough that he would not be the one leading the posse on the chase, but Luke could see that he had a deputy.

When the sheriff finished talking to the deputy, the deputy turned and started to round up men for a posse to follow the bank robbers. Luke stood by the café watching them as they gathered and rode out. Once they had ridden by, he went to his horses. Luke checked his horses to make sure that they had not been hit during the gunfight. While Luke was checking his horses, the sheriff, with the help of another man on his way to the doctor's office, stopped where Luke was standing.

The sheriff asked, "How come you didn't go with my deputy? I saw you firing at the robbers when I got hit."

"Ain't none of mah business. I just lent a hand when I saw yer troubles," said Luke. "Anyhow, yer deputy looks ta be able ta take care of hisself."

"Which way are you headed?" asked the sheriff.

"West," said Luke.

"Well, I can't force you to help, but if you come across the posse, maybe you can give them a hand if they need it," said the sheriff.

"If I come across them, I'll see if I might give them a hand," said Luke. "Right now I need ta catch up with some friends of mine befer this gang gets ta them."

"Well, thanks for your help, and good luck on finding your friends," said the sheriff.

As Luke reached the edge of town, he could see that Fry's men and the posse were traveling fast. What Luke couldn't figure out was why Fry and his men hadn't headed back the way they had come. When Luke ran into them the last time, they had a camp that they were based out of that they did their raiding from. Now he began to wonder if they were still on the move and had robbed the bank because they needed some quick cash.

During the robbery, the townspeople had wounded two of Fry's men. Luke had shot and killed a third. The two wounded would slow them down.

As they rode out of town, Fry did not see that three of his men had been hit. When he found out about it, he did not have time to see how badly they were hit. The report he had received from Jack was that the Blain had been hit badly and fallen from his horse before they got out of town, but the other two were still riding okay, as they were keeping up. During the robbery, he saw the sheriff go down. With the sheriff out of the way, he figured that they had gained the time they needed. It would take them some time to get a posse together to follow them. Fry was not aware that the sheriff had a deputy who would take up the chase. The extra time that he figured he had was needed to give their horses a rest. The robbery was a last minute decision after seeing what looked to be a sleepy town without much law and their need for cash. Not wanting to take any chances, he called Jack and told him to drop behind and keep an eye out for anyone following.

Jack dropped back and waited. He didn't have long to wait when he saw the posse coming. Turning, he rode hard back to Fry and reported that the posse was right behind him and moving quickly.

Fry had his men increase the pace, knowing that their horses could not keep it up for long. They were able to ride for a couple of miles before the horses started playing out. Finding a place where they could wait in ambush, they stopped and spread out.

The posse, wanting to overtake the outlaws, continued to follow at a fast pace and rode right into the ambush. Several of the posse members were wounded in the first volley of gunfire, and a couple men were killed, being caught in the open. Those that could still move found protection behind some rocks and returned fire. They were still in a gun fight when Luke rode up.

As Luke rode farther west, he heard the gunfire. Taking his time, he got close to where the posse was pinned down before dismounting. Being careful to not be shot by the posse, Luke made his way to where the deputy was calling out who he was before coming into the open. He saw that the deputy was hit, and it looked like the rest of the posse was starting to lose their nerve.

"What happened?" asked Luke.

"They were waiting for us," said the deputy. "They just about wiped us out. Can you give us a hand? I need to get these men out of here."

Taking the Henry, he started shooting in the direction where Fry and his men were holed up.

Fry noticed that the firing coming from the posse had died down. Then all of a sudden there was an increase in the firing, but it seemed to be coming from only one spot. The two men who had been wounded in town were not doing well. Fry decided that he would sacrifice these two men by having them stay while the rest got away. Going to them, he said that if they were captured by the posse, they could get the help that they needed in town, and it would allow the rest of the men to get away. Knowing that was the only chance they had to live, they both agreed to stay. Calling the rest of his men together, they mounted and slowly rode out, leaving two wounded men covering their escape.

Luke noticed that the firing had almost stopped except from a couple of men. If most of Fry's men were not returning fire, he began to wonder if they had pulled out, leaving only a couple to cover for them.

"Deputy," said Luke, "ya have yer men give me cover, and I'll make mah way around behind them. I think that there are only a couple of men left up there pinning you down. Rex, ya stay here."

Luke moved back down the trail until he could make his way around and get behind the men. Getting in close to where the gunfire was coming from, he saw the two men who had been left. Luke recognized that they were the same two who had been wounded in town during the gunfight.

Getting in behind them, Luke said, "Drop yer guns." Both men dropped their guns and raised their hands.

Calling out to the posse, Luke said, "Hold your fire. I have them. Stand up, and walk out in da open where da posse can see ya."

Helping each other, they were able to get up and walk into the open.

Luke followed them. "Here's two of da men who robbed yer bank," said Luke.

"Thanks," said the deputy.

A couple of the posse men tied the two up and looked after their wounds. Luke stayed and helped with the wounded before he rode on. Because it was getting late, he didn't make it far before he stopped for the night. Finding a nice, quiet spot, he and Rex settled down for the night. In the morning, he made breakfast. When he and Rex finished, he cleaned up camp and started out. By now, Fry and his men must have traveled to wherever they were going and should be off the trail, Luke thought.

Luke rode at a faster pace, trying to make up some of the time he had lost helping the deputy. Two days later he was getting close to Mitchell. He stopped outside of town, making camp.

In the morning when he rode into town past the smithy, he thought he recognized one of the horses in the corral. Stopping, he dismounted and went inside the stable. As he entered the stable, the smithy greeted him.

"What can I do for you?" asked the smithy.

"I seen one of yer horses in da corral that looks familiar ta me. Where did ya get her?" asked Luke.

"A family came through here yesterday and traded me for a new horse. This one had a stone bruise," said the smithy.

"Did ya happen ta see a bunch of riders come through town da other day?"

"There were some the same day that the family you are asking about came through. It seemed that they were interested in those men as well. Looking at those men, they didn't look real friendly to me. What do you know about them?"

"They robbed a bank in Louisville a couple of days ago," said Luke. "They killed some of da posse who followed them but got away. Da family who traded the horse, did they leave town befer those men did?"

"They were camped just east of town, and when they picked up the new horse, they asked me to keep an eye on the men. When they came back through town, the men had left, and that's what I told them," said the smithy. "They then headed west out of town, but not in a hurry. Those horses the men were riding were about played out. Now I know why. They were not going to get far on them. I sure hope your friends didn't run into them."

Luke thanked the man and headed out of town. So the Dailys were closer than Luke thought. When he reached the outside of town, he noticed another camp that had been recently occupied; only this camp had two wagons. Following the tracks, he could see that the wagon tracks were on top of Fry's tracks. The wagon tracks were fresh. That morning, Luke figured that he could catch up to them by noon. If he had gone through town the night before, he might have caught up to them last night.

"Come, Rex," said Luke. "Da Dailys ain't that far ahead of us."

the reunion

Leaving camp, Luke felt that they could be meeting the Dailys before the day was over. Luke was concerned with Fry heading in the same direction that they were. On their worn-out horses, they would be looking for fresh horses.

Traveling until late in the morning, Luke thought he smelled smoke. At the same time, Rex's ears perked up, and he started barking and wagging his tail. Luke watched as Rex ran off ahead of him into some trees.

The Dailys and the Hermans were taking their time not pushing their teams for fear of coming across the men who had gone by their camp just that morning. Stopping early for a noon rest, Jenny and Isabel made dinner while Frank and John took care of the stock.

"Come and get it!" called out Jenny.

The children came running and were sitting by the fire before John and Frank could get there. They were eating when they heard a dog barking. Mathew jumped up.

"That sounds like Rex!" cried Mathew.

He took off running in the direction of the barking.

"Come back here!" called out Jenny. "You don't know whose dog that is."

Mathew didn't pay any attention to his mother but kept running. He didn't have to run far before he saw Rex running toward him. Stopping, he waited. Rex did not stop but jumped up on Mathew, knocking him to the ground. He was standing over Mathew, licking his face, when Samantha and Peter arrived. They both dropped to their knees, hugging Rex. Luke rode up and started laughing at what he saw. Getting down, the kids came over to him and said that they were sure glad to see him again.

"Pa is sure going to be glad yer back," said Mathew.

Luke walked with the children back to their camp. As they arrived all four adults were watching for the children. It was Jenny who was the first one to recognize Luke.

Turning to Frank, Jenny said, "Look, Frank! It's Luke." Turning toward Luke, Jenny said, "Luke, it is sure good to see you."

Frank got up, walked over to him, and shook Luke's hand.

"It's good ta see ya," said Luke. "Who's that ya got there with yer?"

"Come. I want ya ta meet da Hermans," said Frank. "This is John, his wife, Isabel, and their two children, Patty and Richard. We caught up ta them a couple of days out of Shepherdsville. We been traveling tagether ever since."

John got up and shook Luke's hand. Turning, Luke said hello to Isabel and the children. Rex was sitting with Mathew and Peter, who kept petting him. He looked happy to be back with the children.

"Luke, have you had anything to eat?" asked Jenny.

Luke said, "Not since this morning, ma'am."

Jenny said, "You just set yourself down while I put together a plate of this here bear meat and get you some coffee."

Luke sat down with John and Frank and waited while Jenny fixed a plate for him.

"What happened ta the men who killed Hezekiah? Did they get caught?" asked Frank.

"Well, da sheriff caught them. One of da men was killed. Da other three were tried and sentenced ta be hung," said Luke. "Have ya seen a group of men riding this way?"

"We saw them the other day in town when Frank picked up a new horse. Their horses were near wore out. With them ahead of us, we held up for an extra day so we wouldn't run into them. What do you know about them?" asked John.

"They are da men that robbed a bank. Do ya remember me tell'n ya about the men who raided our farm, Frank?" asked Luke.

"I recall ya tell'n us about them."

"I believe they are da same men. I recognized a couple of them when I was in Louisville when they robbed da bank."

"We are sure glad that ya caught up ta us," said Frank. "With them in front of us, we didn't want ta run inta them. We figured that if ya were with us, ya could scout ahead like ya did befer."

"I can tell ya that ya don't want ta come across them. They would kill ya and the children, and it's hard ta say what they would do ta yer womenfolk befer they had finished with them," said Luke. "Jenny, that was some mighty fine bear fix'n ya made fer me."

Getting up, they loaded the wagons, getting ready to leave. Frank told Luke that he could tie his extra horses to the back of his wagon. When everyone was ready, he started. Rex ran with Luke, keeping his nose to the ground.

Luke made good time without his packhorses. He could get far enough ahead and move quickly if he had to. Rex would help him to sniff out any trouble. He did not find a lot of horse signs on the road. Maybe Fry, if it was him, had left the main road and was holed up.

Luke continued to ride ahead of the wagons for the remainder of the day. Near evening, he found a spot where the wagons could stop with feed and water. By the time he heard the wagons, he had cut wood for a fire.

Once the wagons were in place, Luke helped John and Frank with the horses, watering them and putting them out where there was grass. By the time they got back to camp, the women had supper going. Rex was back playing with the children. Supper smelled mighty good to Luke. He was glad to be back with these folks, not only for the company, but also for the good cooking.

Luke found a spot and rolled out his bedroll. He had just finished setting up his bed when Isabel called that supper was ready. The women had fried some of the bear steaks and made some fresh bread and beans that were making Luke's mouth water.

Taking his plate to the fire, Jenny and Isabel dished it up. John and Frank had already gotten their plates filled, so Luke joined them.

"I didn't see any sign of those men taday," said Luke. "I am hoping that they have moved off the trail and have gone into hiding somewhere. If we don't see any sign of them tomorrow, we may be safe."

"That would be good," said John. "I heard that maybe there are others who go after lone wagons."

"I don't think that some of the smaller gangs would attempt ta stop us now," said Luke. "No matter what, we need ta keep an eye out fer any strangers we come across."

"Pa," said Mathew, "do ya think I could ride with Mr. Taylor tamarrow?"

"Well, son, I don't rightly know," said Frank. "Have ya asked Mr. Taylor?"

Hanging his head, Mathew said, "Naw. Can I ride one of yer horses like I did befer, Mr. Taylor?"

"Well, Mathew," said Luke, "if yer pa will allow me ta put mah gear inta yer wagon, ya can ride da sorrel."

"Gee, thanks, Mr. Taylor," said Mathew. "Pa, can Mr. Taylor put his gear in our wagon?"

When Frank said yes, Mathew ran off to the other children to brag to them how he was going to be able to ride one of Luke's horses. Richard was jealous and wanted to hear more. Mathew had told Richard a little about riding with Luke and how he had found a man floating in the river, but Richard did not believe him. Now that Luke was back and he was going to ride with Luke again, Richard was curious about what Mathew had said.

After they had finished supper, Luke moved the horses to new grass. By the time he got back from moving the horses, the women had cleaned up the camp and were putting the children to bed. Luke headed for his bedroll, looking for Rex.

"Did ya happen ta see where Rex went?" asked Luke.

"I think he got in the wagon with Peter," said Jenny. "Do you want me have Peter send him out?"

"Naw, he can stay with da children if ya don't mind," said Luke.

Turning, he opened his bedroll and lay down. He pulled the blanket up to his chin and went to sleep.

In the morning, he woke up before the others and took care of his horses and had a fire going. It wasn't long before Jenney joined him and asked him to get water. Luke took the bucket and went to the river. When he turned, Rex was sitting there looking at him.

"Well, what do ya want?" Luke asked. "Ya didn't want ta stay with me last night."

Rex just sat there looking at Luke. Luke reached down and scratched his head as he started for the camp. Rex got up and followed. Back at camp, he put water in the coffee pot while Jenny added the coffee grounds. Putting the pot on the fire, he went to roll up his bedroll. By now, Frank and John were busy with their horses and the children were doing their chores. Mathew came over to Luke and watched him as he was putting his gear away.

"Mr. Taylor?" Mathew asked. "Do I get ta ride with ya this morning?"

"Mathew, I said last night that ya can ride the sorrel taday," said Luke. "Have ya got yer chores done?"

"I got them done," said Mathew.

"Good," said Luke. "Ya need ta get yer saddle after ya finish yer breakfast. We are gonna be out fer a while this morning and may not get back fer dinner, so make sure yer ma gives ya some jerky ta bring along."

"Thanks, Mr. Taylor," said Mathew. "I'll be ready ta go."

Mathew went running, meeting the other kids for breakfast. By the time breakfast was ready, Frank and John had the horses waiting. They walked over to Luke and sat down.

"Luke, I'm sure glad yer back with us. I don't know how ta tell ya this, but we been mighty scared traveling without ya," said Frank.

"Well, I am glad ta be back as well. I kinda got use ta having company traveling with me," said Luke. "If we're lucky, we won't run inta that bunch again."

"I know'd ya said something about these being the ones who raided yer farm and killed yer brother," said Frank. "Did ya consider going after them when ya recognized them?"

"I thought I might but knew that da law was after them fer robbing da bank," said Luke. "I figured that they would take care of it fer me."

Everyone pitched in to help load the wagons after finishing breakfast. Luke tied his spare horse behind the Daily's wagon. Turning to Mathew, Luke took the reins to the buckskin while Mathew mounted the sorrel. Checking the wagons, Luke saw that everyone was ready, so he and Mathew rode out.

They made good progress during the day. Luke did not find anything on the trail to cause him concern. That night they camped by a stream. Everyone seemed to be relaxed when they sat down to supper. It was good to have someone that he could trust.

While they were eating supper Rex stayed with the children. He would sit and look at one of the kids begging until they gave him something to eat. Then he would sit in front of one of the other kids and beg for more food.

Traveling for the next two weeks everything went smoothly. Mathew rode with Luke and was getting good at tracking. While they rode, Luke would point out tracks and have Mathew identify what made them. When they arrived at Sandoval, Illinois, they saw that there was a celebration going on. As they rode through town, there were banners strung across the street welcoming home the Illinois soldiers. It looked like the celebration had been going on for some time. One of the signs indicated that there was a dance that evening.

"Jenny," said Frank, "ya know'd we haven't been ta a dance fer some time. What ya say we come ta it tonight?"

"Well," said Jenny, "what we gonna do with the children? You know that maybe Isabel and John might like to go to the dance as well. Then who is going to take care of the children?"

"Maybe we could get Luke ta keep an eye on them fer us," said Frank.

They drove through town, and when they reached the outskirts, Luke spotted a good camp spot. Setting up camp, Luke helped get fires going before stating that he wanted to go into town and check things out.

"Luke," Frank called out, "while ya are in town, can ya check on da location fer that dance? Maybe if we get a chance we might get ta hear some of da music."

"Luke," John asked, "do you mind if I ride along with you?"

"No, ya can come along," said Luke.

"Jenny and I are thinking about going ta it tonight if'n yer will'n ta stay with da children," said Frank.

Riding into town, they took a closer look at what was going on. Luke didn't see anyone he recognized. They tied their horses to a hitching rail near the general store, as John wanted to pick up a couple of items. Entering, there were a few customers looking at the merchandise with a woman standing behind the counter helping a lady. There was a man with an apron on behind another counter. Luke overhead him talking about the dance tonight.

"Gus, it is going to be a good dance tonight. Martin and his boys are going to be playing. I think the whole town is going to show up," said the shop owner.

"Well, Richard," said Gus, "I just don't know if Ma is up to it. You know that she has not been feeling that well lately."

Gus picked up the bags on the counter, putting them under his arm. He walked out and put the bags in the buckboard.

Richard went to help another customer while Luke waited for John to find what he needed. While waiting, two of the ladies who were standing behind him started talking about an attack on a wagon.

"Sally, did you hear about that attack on those poor people heading for St. Louis just over a week ago?" Joan asked.

"Yes, I did. From what Jeremy was saying, no one was left alive. Some were saying that they thought it might have been Indians, but others were saying that it looked more like outlaws. You know how there have been so many robberies since the war ended," said Sally.

"I know what you are saying, Sally. We are all suffering from the war," said Joan.

John finished getting his supplies and was ready to leave. Going to their horses, John tied his supplies to his horse.

Luke said, "John, how about a beer before we go back ta camp."

"That sounds good."

They walked over to the saloon. Entering the saloon, they walked up to the bar and ordered two cold beers. When the barkeep brought their beer, Luke said, "I heard talk about some robberies hereabouts."

"Ya, there has been some robberies going on around here," said the barkeep. "What kind of robberies have you heard about?"

"I done heard of a wagon being burned and da folks killed. I heard someone mentioned a fella name Fry was involved with da robbery. Have ya heard about him?" asked Luke.

"Heard some talk from some of the fellows who come in here now and again," said the barkeep. "They seem to be new to the area. No one heard of him before a couple of weeks ago. The sheriff has been looking for him but has not had much luck. The sheriff also received a telegram a few days ago from Louisville about a gang robbing their bank and heading this way."

"Ya say he has only been around here fer a couple of weeks?" asked Luke.

"Before that, we had not heard of anyone being shot up and robbed," said the barkeep.

Another customer came in, and the barkeep went to wait on them. Luke stood there for some time sipping his beer and thinking. If they headed out, maybe they would be in danger of running into Fry. But it had been over a week since they had hit that wagon, and they didn't stay around Louisville long after robbing the bank. Luke was wondering if they had some destination in mind.

"Luke," John said, "it looks like yer a long ways away. What are you thinking about?"

"I was just thinking about what da barkeep was saying," said Luke. "Them fellas are da ones who killed mah brother."

"What makes you think that you can find them if the sheriff can't?" asked John.

"I followed them fer a long time befer heading west mah self," said Luke. "If they be around here, there would be sign of them. After Louisville, they did not stay put, but they kept moving west. In fact, they were moving a lot faster than we were with da wagons. Something tells me that they are still heading west."

They finished their beer and headed back for their horses. Mounting, they rode back to camp. By the time they arrived, the women had the camp set up.

After putting up their horses, Frank asked, "What did ya find out in town?"

Luke told him about what they had heard in the general store and in the saloon. "From what we heard, we should not have any trouble between here and St. Louis," said Luke.

"I say that gives us all cause to celebrate tonight," said Jenny. "Let's all go to the dance."

Everyone hurried to get cleaned up before heading to town. The dance was in full swing by the time they arrived. While everyone else was dancing, Luke stood by the wall listening to the music and asking questions about Fry. The people from town were not able to offer any additional information as they had only seen them passing through. By the time they arrived back at camp they were all exhausted from traveling and dancing. Everyone slept well that night.

In the morning, everyone woke refreshed. After eating breakfast, life was back to normal. Luke and Mathew saddled their horses and scouted ahead of the wagons. Luke told Frank and John that he did not think that they would run into any problems before they reached St. Louis.

"Luke, did ya find out if they had a telegraph office in town?" asked Frank. "I think I should send one ta Jenny's brother and let him know'd that we should be arriving in St. Louis within da next couple of weeks. I'll tell him that we got another family with us."

"Mathew, let yer pa use yer horse. We need ta go inta town befer we leave," said Luke.

They rode into town and found the telegraph office. Frank sent off a telegram to Cole. After sending the telegram, they rode back to camp where everyone was waiting.

During the next week, they made good time and arrived in St. Louis during the middle of the second week. From what Luke could see, it was none too soon, as the bad weather was starting to set in. It had snowed the night before they arrived, making the last day of travel hard on the horses. St. Louis was a welcome sight. Stopping just outside of the livery stable, Frank inquired about Cole. At the general store, he learned that Cole lived about two miles west of town. Back where they left the wagons, Luke was gone, so they waited until he returned.

It took them less than an hour, and they were at a road leading to a house. There was a wagon standing by the barn and horses in the corral. Frank drove his wagon into the yard just as someone was coming out. Jenny was the first to recognize her brother and called out to him. Cole came running up, greeting them. As he came, he called for Ester, his wife. It wasn't long before the door opened and a woman with a boy came out to see what was going on. When Ester saw Jenny and Frank, she almost dropped the dish she was holding. Setting the dish down, she and her son, Hank, came out.

Cole said, "I got yer telegram, and we were not expecting you fer another few days. Ya made good time and got here befer all da bad weather set in."

"Cole, Ester, Hank, I want ya ta meet Luke Taylor," said Frank. "Those in da other wagon are the Hermans, John, Isabel, and their children, Patty and Richard."

Cole said, "Glad ta meet ya. This is ma wife, Ester, and our boy, Hank. Pull yer wagons inta da yard, and I'll help ya unhitch."

Jenny and the children had gotten out of the wagon and were greeting everyone. Ester said, "Jenny, it's good to see you. It's nice meeting you, Isabel. Hank, take the children to the house. Ladies, come in. I was just going to start making supper. We will just have to make room for everyone."

Luke said, "If ya don't mind, I will put mah horses up in the barn and I will stay in da loft. In da morning, I'll be leaving."

"Yer not spending da winter with us?" asked Cole.

"Na, I want ta get ta Independence," said Luke.

After the stock was cared for, everyone went to the house. The women had finished setting the table and had supper ready. There was not enough room for everyone at the table, so the children made up plates and found a place to sit on the floor. During supper, Frank caught Cole and Ester up on what had happened since the last time they had seen them. Cole told Frank that they put up enough supplies for the winter and there was enough hay for the livestock, even with the extra horses. What they would have to do is add on to the house to make room for everyone to sleep. John and Frank said that with the three of them they should be able to make the additional room without a problem with the wood in the area.

The women cleaned up the dishes and started working on places to sleep. Ester said that Hank and the boys would sleep on the floor in the main room. Frank and Jenny could have Hank's room, and Isabel and John could have the spare room. The girls would have to sleep on the floor in their parents' room. "I don't know where you are going to sleep," said Ester, looking at Luke.

"Don't worry about me," said Luke. "I'll be fine in da barn. Come morn, I'll be on mah way."

Luke got up and went to the barn. He picked up Rex and carried him to the loft. He put his bedroll in the loft where the hay was. His bed was soft lying on the hay. Having Rex with him helped to keep him warm. It wasn't long before he was sound asleep. In the morning, he woke before the sun came up. Getting down from the loft, he gave the horses hay. He was putting hay in the corral when Cole came out. Seeing Luke already feeding the stock, he helped him finish.

"Come on in. Ma has breakfast on," said Cole.

"Thanks," said Luke.

They went into the house and washed up. It wasn't long before Frank came out of the bedroom and joined them. John came out a little later. Isabel and Jenny came out shortly after that. It seemed that everyone slept in, as it was the first time they had slept in a house in a while. The women went to the kitchen to help Ester finish breakfast.

"What are ya gonna do when you get to Independence, Luke?" asked Frank.

"Don't know fer sure. Maybe check around ta find out if I might be able ta hook up with a wagon train in da spring," said Luke.

"Where are you going to stay?" asked Cole. "You know you are welcome to stay the winter with us."

"Thanks," said Luke. "I need ta keep going. At da dance da other night, I heard talk about Fry and talk about a fella who killed some government men in Virginia that they were looking fer. I don't want ta cause y'all any trouble."

The women put breakfast on the table, and everyone started eating. When they finished eating, Luke got up. Ester came over and handed him a bundle of food. Thanking her, he said good-bye to the children. He thanked Cole and Ester for their hospitality; he said good-bye to the Hermans before the Dailys.

"I want ta thank ya fer yer kindness over these past weeks. I sure enjoyed travel'n with ya," said Luke.

Putting his coat on and gathering his package, he went to the barn. Rex, John, and Frank followed Luke into the barn. Rex sat and watched while Frank and John helped Luke get ready. Mathew came running out to say good-bye to Rex.

Luke knelt down, patting Rex and looking at Mathew. "Rex, ya are gonna stay here with Mathew," said Luke.

"Ya mean yer given Rex ta us?" asked Mathew.

"If Rex wants ta stay, he's all yers," said Luke.

"He's your dog," said John. "Aren't you going to miss having him along?"

"Rex came ta me hurt and alone, and he picked me ta tag along with. I seen how he likes ta hang out with da children and how the children like ta play with him, so I figure that they would be good fer each other," said Luke. "Now, if'n ya don't want ta keep him, Frank, I'll take him with me."

"We would be happy ta keep Rex fer ya," said Frank. "Da children will take good care of him, and it will be a way of having a little of ya with us as we travel."

Luke tied his packhorses together. Mounting Buck, he took the lead rope of the front packhorses and rode out of the barn. Rex got up and followed him out of the barn. Once outside, he stopped and looked back at Mathew and then again at Luke riding away. Mathew called Rex and waited until he came back to him. He bent down and petted him. Rex relaxed and started wagging his tail.

Luke rode away from the farm. Looking back, he saw Rex by Mathew. Luke smiled knowing that Rex would be better off with the Dailys. Luke rode until noon when he stopped to eat. This was the first chance he had to look at what Ester had packed for him. Opening the package, he found a couple of loafs of bread and several donuts. Cutting some of the bread, he ate it with some of his jerky. He would save the donuts for the morning. He didn't have to worry about finding any meat between here and Independence. The Dailys had given him plenty.

It was close to a week before he made it to Fulton. The second day after leaving, it started to snow. He was lucky finding shelter. The snow lasted all night, leaving about a foot of snow added to what was there from before. Luke decided to take an extra day to make sure that it was not going to snow again as long as he had the shelter.

The next day he finally decided to leave. The snow made it harder for the horses to walk, so he couldn't travel as long as before. Luke decided the best way to save his horses was to swap the lead horse each time they stopped. By using a different horse to break the trail, it allowed the other horses to follow and not work as hard. Riding into Fulton two days later, Luke went straight to the livery to put up his horses. Getting down in front of the livery, the owner came out and asked, "How are you doing?"

Luke said, "I'm doin' fine now that we made it ta town. Can ya put mah horses up?"

"Sure enough can. How long are you planning being in town?" asked the livery owner.

"I am only gonna be here long enough ta rest mah horses fer we head out again. Have ya got some grain ya can give them? They been work'n hard traveling through that snow. Can I leave mah gear here?" asked Luke.

"You are welcome to leave it in the corner," said the livery owner.

"Thanks," said Luke. "Is that hotel across da street open fer business?"

"If I was you, I would use the hotel down the street if you want a clean bed," said the livery owner.

In the morning, it was still snowing. Looking out the window, he could see that the snow had come down all night. He wasn't going to be going anywhere soon. The horses had a hard enough time yesterday traveling, and with this added snow, it would be impossible for them to travel without becoming totally exhausted. Luke decided that the best thing to do was wait it out.

Leaving the hotel, he saw that some of the walks had been shoveled, but the snow in the street was deep. He walked down the walk until he saw a spot where someone had crossed before him. Following where they had walked, he made his way across the street. Luke continued on to the café. Taking a table, he sat down and ordered his breakfast.

While waiting, the front door opened, and the sheriff came in. Luke watched as the sheriff headed toward his table. "Mind if I join you?" asked the sheriff.

"Na. Help yerself. It might be nice ta have some company," said Luke, wondering why the sheriff wanted to sit with him.

The sheriff sat down and called out to the waitress, "Dolly, I'll have my usual. I see you are new in town. Do you plan on staying long?" he asked.

"Just passing through, but this snow may cause me ta stay fer a few days," said Luke.

"It ain't snowed like this since sixty. Kept people locked up in their homes for over a week. Most people could not travel for two weeks," said the sheriff. "What got you traveling so near winter?"

"The war got me traveling," said Luke, wondering if the sheriff regonized him from a flier or what.

"Where are you headed?" asked the sheriff.

"I planned ta get ta Independence fer da winter set in," said Luke. "I didn't make it befer da snow but hope ta go on when it clears."

"Where are you from?" asked the sheriff.

"I hail from Virginia," said Luke, watching the sheriff closer to see if it brought a reaction. Not seeing one, he relaxed some.

The waitress brought their breakfast. After she left, they both became silent and started eating. They were close to being done when Luke asked, "Have ya heard anything about a man called Fry?"

"Seems like a poster crossed my desk about a man named Fry some time back. I believe it said something about them heading this direction," said the sheriff. "What's your interest in him?"

"They killed mah brother and a couple of mah friends," said Luke. "When we get done with our breakfast, come back to the office, and we can take a look at that poster," said the sheriff.

They finished their breakfast and went to the sheriff's office. Inside the office, the sheriff poured Luke a cup of coffee and handed him a stack of posters to look through. Luke sat in the chair going through the stack of posters. About halfway through he stopped when he saw a flier with his name that had been sent out by the army. *The sheriff must not look at these that often if he didn't remembered this one,* Luke thought. Taking the flier, he put it on the bottom and continued to look for the one on Fry. Finding the one on Fry Luke read it over, but it didn't give him any more information than what he already had. It did say that there was a reward for the capture of Fry and his men. The last sighting had been at De Soto, which was South of St. Louis. Maybe Fry was going further south. If that was the case, he would have to go south to find Fry if he wanted him. While the sheriff was busy Luke took the flier about himself and put it in his pocket before giving the stack of posters back to the sheriff.

Back at the hotel Luke put the flier he had taken into the stove and watched it burn. He was going to have to be careful from now on around the law knowing that there was a flier sent out by the army to them.

an old enemy

On the morning of the fourth day after it stopped snowing, Luke checked out of the hotel. After loading his packhorses, Luke saddled Buck. He could tell that they were ready to travel. The horses were well rested and had been eating grain for three days. They had plenty of energy.

Most of the snow on the road was gone, making it easy for the horses. Luke rode till noon when he stopped to eat. He found a place where the wind had blown the snow, leaving grass for the horses to eat. From what he had learned in town, he figured it would take him about two weeks to reach Independence if the weather held out.

Two days later outside of Boonville, Luke spotted a nice doe in an open field. He could use the fresh meat. Taking his rifle, he made his way through some trees and dropped her. After cleaning her, he loaded her on his packhorses until he could find a place to camp. Keeping his eyes open, he found what he was looking for. He came across a spot where there was protection for him and the horses in case the weather changed. There were trees around where he could hang the deer while he cut her up. The snow had melted, leaving plenty of grass available for the horses, as well as water.

After taking care of the stock and hanging the deer, Luke built a fire and started to make coffee. Now he wished he had Rex back with him. It was going to be lonely without having that flea-bit dog around. Going over to the deer, he cut himself a steak for his supper. With it being as cold as it was, he figured that when he cut the deer up he would keep some of the meat to cook. The cold weather would keep it longer without it spoiling.

After eating supper, Luke cut up the deer, wrapping some of meat in the hide. Cutting the rest in strips, he hung it where it would dry for jerky. He would spend the next day preparing his meat before going on. The next morning he checked the meat drying, making sure no animals had gotten to it during the night. Finding that the meat was okay, Luke cared for the horses, making sure they were okay. Back at camp, he built up his fire and started making breakfast. Today was going to be a quiet day waiting for the meat to dry. Leaving it hanging in strips overnight with a fire under it would mean that it should be ready to pack up by late afternoon.

Late that afternoon Luke had finished drying the deer meat and put it into his packs. He now had enough meat to last him for some time. Sitting back, he was thinking about what he could do when he got to Independence. He did not know anyone, and it was late in the year. He would have to find something to do to earn some money to make it through the winter. He could live off the land if there was enough game in the area. He had heard that Independence had grown and there were more people there than there had been back in Virginia.

The next morning, Luke packed up his gear and saddled his horses. When he brought the packhorses to camp he noticed that the sorrel had a bad shoe that needed replaced. Checking his pack, he did not have one to replace it. Looking at the shoe and doing what he could for it, he decided that at the next town he would have to have it replaced. Luke finished loading the horses and rode out.

Coming into Boonville, Luke looked around the town for the livery. Not seeing one, he stopped and asked one of the men walking down the street. The man said that the livery was at the other edge of town. Luke thanked him and rode through town. Reaching the edge of town, he found the livery. Riding up to it, he dismounted and tied his horses. Walking inside, he found the smithy working on a shoe.

Looking up, the smithy asked, "Howdy. What can I do for you?"

Luke said, "I got a horse with a bad shoe. Can ya replace it fer me?"

"When I finish here," said the smithy.

Luke found a bale of hay and sat down to wait.

"You're new around here," said the smithy. "I haven't seen you in town before."

"Just passing through," said Luke.

"Where are you headed for?" asked the smithy.

"Independence," said Luke.

"Traveling kind of late in the year, ain't you?" asked the smithy.

"Got held up some time back," said Luke. "I planned ta make Independence befer da snow set in. Ain't that far now."

"Well, you can make it if the weather holds up," said the smithy. "You're going to have to be on the lookout as you travel. I heard that we have some raiders back in the country. We had some a year or so ago, and when the sheriff tried to get help from the army, they couldn't help. The folks here about had to take matters into their own hands. Several were killed, but the rest got away."

"Have ya heard who da ones do'n da raiding are?" asked Luke.

"No, it seems that they only came about in the past few weeks. No one knows for sure when they actually came," said the smithy.

"What have they been targeting?" asked Luke.

"Seems they been raiding some of the farmers around here," said the smithy. "They been going into a farm killing the family and their stock. They take anything of value after spending a couple days on the place and then burn it when they leave."

"What are y'all do'n about it?" asked Luke.

"The sheriff's been out hunting them, but they seem to disappear," said the smithy. "Folks don't know that they are in the area until they see the smoke coming from a neighbors' place, and by the time they get there to see what is going on, it's too late."

"Where's your sheriff's office?" asked Luke.

"Back up the street," said the smithy, "but you ain't gonna find him there. He rode out this morning after Gus Lancer came in and told him that the Meyer farm had been raided."

"Where does Gus Lancer live?" asked Luke.

"Just west of town about three miles or so," said the smithy. "What's your interest in these raids?"

"It seems I been following these fellas fer some time now," said Luke. "If they be da same ones who robbed da bank in Louisville, they are an old enemy of mine."

"Can't say if they be the same ones," said the smithy. "If what you say is true, the timing could be right for them to be in this area."

"All I know is that they were driven out of a town called Panther Gap after trying ta burn da town down," said Luke. "They were headed west at that time, and da marshal sent out notices fer others ta be on da look out fer them. I thought I was done with them till I got ta Louisville when I saw them rob da bank."

"You may want to hang around until the sheriff comes back so you can tell him what you just told me," said the smithy.

The smithy finished putting the new shoes on the horse, and Luke went and brought in his sorrel. The smithy took a look at the sorrel's shoes and determined that there were two shoes needing replaced. Luke sat back down and waited while the smithy went to work. When the smithy finished with Luke's horse, Luke asked about purchasing extra shoes. The smithy made up a couple of sets of shoes for Luke to take with him and some nails.

"When do ya think da Sheriff might be back?" asked Luke.

"He should be back before dark," said the smithy. "If you want, you can leave your horses here while you wait for him to return."

"Thanks," said Luke. "Could I get some hay fer them while they're here?"

"Why don't you bring them in and put them in those stalls over there. I'll get some hay," said the smithy.

Luke went out and brought the other two horses in, putting them in the stalls where the smithy had put hay. He left them saddled but loosened the cinches, not knowing when the sheriff would get back. Leaving the livery, Luke walked back toward town looking the place over. He hadn't gone far when he found a saloon and went in. Inside the saloon, there were several customers. Going to the bar, he ordered a beer, taking it to a table where he could watch the street. Luke was on his second beer when he saw a fella riding into town. The barkeep came over to see if Luke wanted anything.

"Is that the sheriff riding in?" asked Luke.

"Ya, that's him," said the barkeep.

"Thanks," said Luke. "I need ta talk ta him."

Luke watched to see where the sheriff went. Seeing him stop in front of his office, Luke got up and went to the sheriff's office. Luke opened the door and saw the sheriff sitting behind his desk.

Looking up, the sheriff asked, "What can I do for you?"

Luke said, "I've been talk'n ta da smithy at da livery about da raids ya been having. I think it might be da same fella who robbed da bank at Lousiville."

"What makes you think that?" asked the sheriff.

"From what da smithy said it sounds like da same men who were raiding in Virginia during da war," said Luke. "If it is, they robbed da bank in Louisville. Da Sheriff there sent out a poster. Did ya get one?"

"I believe I did. Let me take a look," said the sheriff.

He got up, walked over to a cabinet, and started going through a stack of papers. He was about halfway through the stack when he stopped and came back to his desk. "Is this the one you were talking about?" he asked.

"Ya, that's da one."

"It doesn't say much about the men," said the sheriff.

"They raided mah folks place and killed mah brother during da war," said Luke. "I thought I was done with them till I saw them rob da bank." Luke paused for a while before he went on.

"During the war, they did a lot of raiding in Virginia, taking anything of value from da farms they hit and killing da families," said Luke. "Befer they rode out, they would burn the place. The smithy was saying that da raids go'n on here followed da same. I think it's da same men raiding here."

"From what you are saying, it does sound like it could be the same ones. At least they are following what you're saying," said the sheriff.

Luke said, "If'n ya a mind ta, ya can contact da marshal in Panther Gap. He can fill ya in on more of what happened there."

"Are you willing to give us a hand?" asked the sheriff. "I'll make you one of my deputies while you're here."

"I can't promise that yer gonna find them," said Luke. "If'n things get ta hot, they may take off again like befer."

"Right now, you're the only one hereabouts that know how they work," said the sheriff. "That would be a big help to us."

"Thanks," said Luke. "I'll think on it some."

Luke left the sheriff's office thinking about what the sheriff had asked. If he stayed in Boonville, how would he hook up with a wagon train? Arriving at the livery stable, he tightened the cinches on his horses. He was just finishing when the livery owner came in.

"What do I owe ya?" asked Luke.

"Two dollars for the new shoes and hay," said the livery owner.

Luke paid for the horses and led them out of the stable. Mounting, he rode out of town. He figured he would ride to the burned-out farm and looked it over. No one would be there, so he could camp nearby.

After Luke left, the sheriff waited a bit before going to the telegraph office. If what Luke had told him about Fry was true, the marshal at Panther Gap would be able to back it up and maybe give him some additional information. Entering the telegraph office, he handed his note to the operator.

"I want this sent right away, Jerry," said the sheriff. "When you get an answer, let me know as soon as it comes in. I don't care if you have to wake me up. Do you understand?"

"Yes, sir, Sheriff. I'll get on it right away," said Jerry.

The sheriff left, going back to his office, but first he stopped by the livery and asked if Luke had picked up his horses. When the livery owner said yes, the sheriff asked, "Did he say where he was headed?"

"No," said the livery owner. "When I was working on his horse, we got to talking about the Meyer family that was killed and their place burned out. He seemed to be really interested in them. He even asked directions to Gus's place. Maybe he headed out that way."

"He came by and told me quite a story," said the sheriff. "If he comes back, I need to talk to him some more. If you see him, let him know."

"Will do, Sheriff," said the livery owner.

Leaving the livery, he changed his mind about going to the office and stopped by the café. While he ate, he continued to think about how Luke seemed to know how they would act and hide out if they were still in the area. If it was Fry who had raided the Meyer farm, he could be a big help. Hopefully the marshal at Panther Gap could shed some light on what was going on. From what the livery owner had said, maybe this fella was that interested in the Meyer place. If so, that might be where he went. Maybe he would find something that would give them a clue where they were holed up. If he came back into town, he definitely would try and make Luke a deputy if the marshal from Panther Gap could vouch for him.

Finishing his meal, he went to his office, waiting for a response from Panther Gap.

Luke rode into the yard of the burned-out farm. Tying his horses at the gate, he walked in looking at the ground. It wasn't long before he found what he was looking for. There was a partial hoof print with the same marking as the one he had followed out of Louisville when Fry robbed the bank. This meant that at least one of Fry's men was here, and if one was, he would bet that the whole gang had been there.

Luke continued to look around and found the tracks left by the livestock as they were driven from the corral. Most of the tracks had been wiped out, but it looked like they had been driven west. Following them on foot for a ways, he did find where they did head west. If he had the sheriff with him, they could follow them and find the hideout that Fry was using.

Going back for his horses, he looked for a place to camp for the night. He would head back to town in the morning. Mounting his horse, he remembered a spot on the way out of town that would make a good camp. Turning, he rode toward town. It wasn't long before he found the spot.

The spot he had found was on a small hillside that had trees, and there was a small overhang that would allow him some shelter if it snowed. Once he had his fire going, he put on a pot of coffee before taking out the meat to cook. When he had finished eating his supper, he poured himself a cup of coffee and sat back. It was now time to think of what he was going to do.

The sheriff had mentioned something about helping to find the men who had raided the Meyer farm. This might be the chance he had waited for to get revenge on Fry. After seeing that partial hoofprint, he knew that Fry had to have been behind it. If the directions that the livery owner had given him were correct, Gus, the fella who reported the raid to the sheriff, lived just up the road. He would stop and talk to him in the morning.

Luke slept late the next morning. Getting up, he built up his fire and started making fresh coffee before checking on his horses. After making sure that the horses were okay, he made breakfast. After breakfast, Luke headed for town. While he was getting ready to leave, he thought he heard a rider go by. Stopping to listen, it sounded like whoever it was had kept going. Not thinking anymore about it, he mounted. Working with the sheriff might not be bad. When he and Hicks tried to do it alone, it didn't work out. He had been lucky to get away alive, but Hicks wasn't so lucky. Maybe with the help of the sheriff he could bring this to a closure.

The first place he came to he thought must be Gus's place. Riding into the yard, a man came out of the barn carrying a rifle with two boys behind him. They, too, were carrying rifles. As Luke brought his horses to a stop, a third boy came out of the house carrying a rifle as well.

The man from the barn asked, "What do you need, stranger?"

Luke said, "I'll be look'n fer a fella calls hisself Gus. Do ya happen ta be him?"

"That's my name. What do you want with me? I don't know you," said Gus.

"Mah name's Luke Taylor, and da fella who owns da livery in town said ya reported da raid on da Meyer place," said Luke.

"I told the sheriff about it," said Gus. "What's your interest in it?"

"I just want ta ask ya some questions. I think da men who did this raided our place during da war," said Luke.

Luke started to step down when Gus said, "If it's all the same, you stay on your horse. What kind of questions do you want to ask? I told the sheriff all I know already."

Luke asked, "Did you see anyone ride by yer place befer the raid?"

"No, we didn't see anyone go by," said Gus. "I even asked the boys here if they had seen anyone."

"How about after ya saw da smoke. Did ya see anyone?" asked Luke.

"I don't think they came this way at all. When we went over to see what was burning, we found the Meyers lying in the yard, dead. Larry, my oldest, said that he saw some tracks that looked like the livestock had been driven west," said Gus.

"Has anyone come by yer place look'n fer infermation that didn't seem too important ta ya in da past week or so?" asked Luke.

"Now that you mention it, a fella did stop by about a week and a half ago asking for directions to town. Seemed odd to me at the time that the fella on the road would be asking directions. I didn't think any more about it after the fella rode off. Mike, my other boy there, thought he saw the fella head west instead of east toward town," said Gus.

"Thanks fer da infermation," said Luke.

Turning, he rode out of the yard and headed for town. Looking back, he saw that Gus and his boys stayed in the yard watching him until he was out of sight. Gus had confirmed that the men were staying west of the Meyers' place. If they had been closer to town, they would have had to drive the livestock past Gus's place, and Gus or one of his boys might have seen them.

The next morning at the sheriff's office, he built up the fire. The office had cooled down overnight. He would have to show the deputy how to bank a fire so it would stay burning. Going into the back where the cells were, he found the deputy asleep in one of the cells. Looking around, he saw that the other cells were all empty. Nudging the deputy, he called out, "Earl, get up! It's time to make rounds."

Earl stirred. Looking at the sheriff, he said, "Huh? What the— Oh, it's you, Lloyd. I guess I really went out last night."

"Get up, Earl. It's time to make your rounds," repeated the sheriff as he turned, going back into the office.

It wasn't long before Earl joined the sheriff after washing up. The fire was getting hot, and the pot of coffee on the stove was starting to warm up. Earl walked over to the pot and felt it. It was still cold so he sat down to wait for it. The sheriff gave him a dirty look but said nothing. He figured that things had been quiet, so Earl could have a cup of coffee before venturing out.

"Did you get your answer from Panther Gap?" asked Earl.

"Came in this morning," said the sheriff.

"Did it confirm what that Luke fella said?" asked Earl.

"It said that if anyone could help me find these men, it was him," said the sheriff. "He also said to say hello to him."

"What are you going to do if he doesn't come back?" asked Earl.

"I don't know, but if he does come back, I'll ask him to hire on as a deputy to help catch these fellas," said the sheriff. "Now drink your coffee and make your rounds."

Earl got up, put on his coat, and headed for the door. The town was still partially dark. Most businesses had not opened, nor had the owners arrived. He walked down the street, taking a look in the window of each business. The café was open, and as he walked by, he saw that there were several people eating breakfast. He saw at one table several of the businessmen were having their usual weekly gathering. There were lamps lit in the saloon as he walked by, and he could see Herb, the barkeep, sweeping the floor. Walking past the bank and looking between two buildings, he thought he saw someone duck behind the bank. Walking to the back of the building, he didn't see anyone. Either he was seeing things, or whoever it was must have gone into the bank. Checking the door, it was locked, so no one went into the bank. Just as he was about to go on, a dog came running out of the shadows and headed down the street. *That must be what I saw,* Earl thought to himself. Turning and walking back to the front of the building, he swore that he had seen a person and not a dog going around that corner. When he completed his rounds and returned to the office, he would mention it to the sheriff.

Oliver was making his way around the bank, doing what Fry had ordered him to do, looking for a way into the bank. He knew that they could hit the bank during the day, but if he could find a way in at night, they could be in and out before anyone knew. When he saw the deputy coming up the street, he headed for the back of the bank. The deputy was stepping down off the walk between the buildings just as he was going around the corner. Finding a dark corner behind a water barrel, he was hoping that the deputy hadn't seen him. He didn't have long to wait before he heard the deputy coming. Drawing his gun, he waited. Next he heard the deputy try the back door and find it locked. He was afraid that the deputy would come farther when a dog came up behind him, scaring him. The dog took off running out across the street. Oliver waited with his gun. It wasn't long before he heard the deputy turn and walk away. Because he had slept late, he almost got caught. Feeling relieved, Oliver waited until the deputy could not be heard before moving. He went to get his horse. Mounting, he stayed in the back streets and rode out of town. Once out of town, he relaxed. He had found a way into the bank. That would make Fry happy. Camp was several miles from town, and after they had raided that farm, things were still a little stirred up in town. Fry would also like the other information he had heard in the saloon. Dave from the bank had been drinking and was talking too much.

Everything looked normal as Luke rode into town. He went straight to the sheriff's office. Tying his horses in front of the office, he went in. Entering, the sheriff was sitting behind his desk with a second man sitting behind the other desk. When the door opened, the sheriff looked up.

"Glad to see you again, Luke," said the sheriff. "I wasn't sure you would be coming back after talking to George at the livery. This is my deputy, Earl."

Luke walked over and shook Earl's hand. "Have a seat. I have a message from the marshal in Panther Gap. He said to say hello to you and was glad to hear you're still alive," said the sheriff. "When I talked to George at the livery and saw your horses were gone, I figured you were long gone. What brought you back?"

"After talk'n ta ya yesterday, I went out ta da Meyer farm ta look around," said Luke. "Well, I done found a hoof print of one of da horses I followed out of Louisville. I knowed he rode with Fry. I decided to come back. They drove off da stock ta da west when they left. I follow'd some tracks fer a while ta make sure. Then I stopped by and talked ta Gus on da way inta town, and he confirmed that they didn't come by his place."

"Well, the marshal in Panther Gap said you know more about Fry than most. How about hiring on as a deputy and helping us find them?" asked the sheriff.

"Sheriff, da last time I did anything against Fry, I got mah friend killed and he almost burned down Panther Gap. Are ya sure ya want me as a deputy?" Luke asked.

"You have more knowledge about him and his men than anyone around here, and if they try to burn our town, the townspeople won't let it happen. Now, what do you think? Will you join us?" asked the sheriff.

"After what I found out taday, I figured ta hang around and see if Fry could be stopped," said Luke. "I might as well be paid fer it."

The sheriff took out a deputy's badge and swore Luke in. After pinning the badge on Luke, he welcomed him to the office. Earl, likewise, shook his hand and welcomed Luke.

"Where can I put up mah horses?" asked Luke.

"See George at the livery," said the sheriff. "The county will pay for their keep while you're my deputy. Why don't you take him down there, Earl, in case George has any questions."

Luke and Earl left the office. Earl led the two packhorses while Luke led Buck. At the livery, George was coming out just as they arrived.

"I see the sheriff found you," said George.

"I done stopped in ta see him," said Luke. "He told me ta bring mah horses here for boarding. He said da county was gonna pay fer them."

"I thought I saw a badge on you," said George. "I got to run over to the general store for some supplies. You can put them in the same stalls that they were in yesterday. If you want, you can store your extra gear in the tack room. Earl can show you where it's at."

"Thanks," said Luke as George walked away. While they were unsaddling the horses, Earl told Luke about what he saw this morning on his rounds.

"Did ya see anyone ride out of town after that?" asked Luke.

"No, can't say I did," said Earl. "Why do you ask?"

"When I was getting ready to come ta town, I heard someone riding west go past mah camp," said Luke. "Where do ya all bunk?"

"Most of the time I stay at the jail," said Earl. "If the jail is full, I sleep on the cot in the office. The sheriff has his own place, and he stays there. He has a housekeeper who cleans and cooks for him."

Picking up Luke's gear, they headed for the office. Earl was eyeing Luke's Henry. "I ain't seen many of them around here. Where did you get it?"

"It's a Henry 44–40," said Luke. "Sure beats mah old rifle. Ya can shoot a long time fer ya have to reload. I bought it back on the trail. Seen it in a general store and traded in some older guns I had fer her."

"I see you have several revolvers as well," said Earl. "How come you wear two and carry two spares?"

"Got inta da habit during da war," said Luke. "Traveling alone look'n fer mah pa, I never knew when I would run inta bad company. An extra gun comes in mighty handy at times."

They walked back to the sheriff's office. When they entered, Luke put his gear in the corner. When he was putting the Henry down, he saw the sheriff looking at it, but he didn't say anything.

"Do you have any thoughts about going after Fry and his men or how to find out where they might be holed up?" asked the sheriff.

"First, we need ta go back ta da Meyer place and follower da tracks where they drove da stock away," said Luke. "If'n their tracks are still there, we might follow them ta where their holed up. It looked ta me like there had been a lot of people going over da ground after they drove da stock away. Da tracks I followed headed west, and maybe no one followed them. Da print I found was only a partial print, but I'd know'd it anywhere. I was lucky ta spot it. Someone had walked on part of it."

"The first thing in the morning you and I will ride out there," said the sheriff. "Now I want to introduce you to some of the town folks so they know who you are. One of the first places we will stop is the bank. You said that Fry had robbed a bank in Louisville so they might try it here if we don't find them first."

At the bank the sheriff introduced Luke to Mr. Olson, the owner of the bank. Mr. Olson, in turn, introduced Luke to all other employees at the bank. Leaving the bank, the sheriff stopped at each business along the street to introduce Luke. When they got to the café, they decided to eat dinner, as it was already past noon. Most of the noon crowd had eaten, so they didn't have a problem finding a table where they could talk and not be overheard.

"What do ya make of what Earl saw this morning?" asked Luke.

"Could be nothing," said the sheriff.

"I think we need ta go back ta da general store and da saloon," said Luke. "Them are da places Fry or his men would head fer. They will either want supplies or liquor. Da Barkeep and Mr. and Mrs. Graves would be da first ta know'd any strangers coming ta town. In Panther Gap, they left da townspeople alone until one of his men was put in jail. If they are still around, they will be showin' up."

"With them raiding in the area, why do you think they might still be here?" asked the sheriff.

"They had been moving further west, robbing as they went," said Luke. "They robbed a bank, raided wagons, and only took what they could carry. Now they done raided a farm and drove off their stock. With winter upon us, I suspect that they are holed up near here."

Oliver rode into the farm that Fry had taken over. When they were going through the country, they had come across the place and found it deserted. They had seen other abandoned farms coming out of Virginia where the family had just picked up, leaving their farms behind. Finding this one was good for Fry. Now that they had gotten some stock, if someone came by, they would say that they were homesteading. The place was laid out almost like the place they had had during the war. The barn had hay in it, which would support the stock through the winter. Setting up camp there was perfect for Fry.

"What did you find out about the bank?" asked Fry.

"The bank can be gotten into fairly easy," said Oliver. "I need to go into the bank and see the layout so we will know what we will need to open the safe, but that ain't the good news."

"What's the good news?" asked Fry.

"When I was in the saloon last night, I heard a fella from the bank talking about a large shipment of money coming in," said Oliver.

"When did he say the shipment was coming in?" asked Fry.

"He got up and left before he said when," said Oliver. "But I understand that he goes to the saloon all the time, so maybe we can get someone in there. When he gets good and drunk, we can find out when."

"If we can find out when that shipment is coming in, we will wait," said Fry. "Did you have any problems while you were in town?"

"When I was checking out the bank, the deputy was making his rounds and almost saw me," said Oliver. "I seen him coming up the street and ducked behind the bank. I was able to get out of town without being seen."

"Good," said Fry. "We don't want to attract attention to any of us while we're in town."

Fry sat down to think about his next move. Since Panther Gap, they had been on the run. It seemed like the marshal had known where they were heading and had sent fliers out to all the towns in their path. They had been lucky to find this place, but then the raid they pulled on the farmer had brought attention to them again. If they could remain out of sight, the interest may die down. By not pulling any more raids, the local law may think that they had moved on. If so, they would be able to stay throughout the winter and move on in the spring. The money Oliver talked about could be enough to give them a start out west. If he bought the land and cattle, it may keep people from suspecting them of any raids they might pull, and they could operate like they did during the war. They might become leading citizens. He would wait for a week before allowing anyone back in town. If they needed any supplies, they would go to Arrow Rock.

Luke and the sheriff walked back to the saloon to warn the barkeep to look out for any strangers in town. When the sheriff told the barkeep to keep an eye for any new people in town, the barkeep said, "Sheriff, there was a stranger in here last night. He sat over in the corner drinking by himself. Dave from the bank come in and sat down at the table next to him. He did seem to take an interest in what Dave and Larry were talking about. He managed to drink quite a bit, and when Dave and Larry left, he followed them out. I ain't seen him since."

"Let me know if he comes back," said the sheriff.

"Will do, Sheriff," said the barkeep.

Leaving the saloon, they went back to the general store and told the Montgomerys to be on the lookout as well. When they finished, they walked back to the office. On the way back, Luke asked, "Where could I bunk?"

"You can bunk at my house," said the sheriff. "Maria and I would like the added company."

"I thought ya weren't married," said Luke.

"I ain't," said the sheriff. "Maria's my housekeeper. She comes to clean and sometimes cook for me. She got her own place where she stays."

"I got me some deer meat down at da livery," said Luke. "I was wondering what I was gonna do with it. I'll bring it over ta yer place. Won't Earl be upset with me bunk'n at yer place?"

"Naw, he has his own place but spends most of his nights at the jail," said the sheriff. "Seems he don't like stay'n in the house since his ma died."

They spent the rest of the day at the jail going over their plan for in the morning. Late in the afternoon, the sheriff and Luke picked up Luke's gear and went back to the livery to get the meat. When they opened the door to the sheriff's house, they could smell fresh bread being baked. It reminded Luke of being back home and his mother making bread. Going into the kitchen, the sheriff said,

"Maria, this is Luke Taylor. He will be staying here for a while. He also brought us some fresh deer meat."

"Nice to meet you, Mr. Taylor," said Maria, "Thanks for the meat."

"Nice to make yer acquaintance," said Luke.

"How about cooking some of that fresh deer meat for supper, Maria?" asked the sheriff. "Come with me, Luke, and I will show you where you can put your things."

Maria got busy cooking supper while the sheriff and Luke put up Luke's gear. She took the remaining meat and put it in the root cellar where it would keep. When supper was ready, she called to the sheriff and Luke to wash up.

After supper, Luke got up, thanking Maria for one of the best meals he had eaten in some time. The sheriff wanted to make his rounds before it was too dark. Putting on their guns and coats, they headed for the main street while Maria cleaned up.

The town was quiet. Most of the businesses were already closed for the night. As they walked by the bank, Mr. Olson was just locking up. "Working late tonight, Mr. Olson?" asked the sheriff.

"Huh? Oh, yes, Sheriff," said Mr. Olson. "You know how it is when you get behind."

"Yes," said the sheriff. "You have a good evening."

"Thanks. You too," said Mr. Olson.

They continued on their rounds, stopping in the saloon. Nothing looked out of place. The usual people were sitting around drinking. The sheriff walked over to a table where two men were drinking and said, "Don't you think you should go home, Dave? Margaret ain't gonna like you not coming home again tonight."

"I'll be going soon," replied Dave.

Finishing their rounds, they went back to the house. "Feels like it's going to snow tonight," said the sheriff.

"If'n it snows tonight, we won't be see'n noth'n at da Meyer place," said Luke. "It could wipe out da tracks that I found as well."

"Hopefully it will hold off till we get back," said the sheriff.

Luck was not with them. When Luke woke up, he looked out the window and saw that it had snowed about a foot during the night. He thought they had lost their chance of locating Fry. When the snow went away, they would still have to check it out just in case it didn't wipe out all the tracks. He smelled fresh bread baking coming from the kitchen. Getting dressed, he went and washed up. When he entered the kitchen, the sheriff was sitting at the table drinking coffee and Maria was cooking bacon. When Maria saw Luke coming through the door, she got the coffee pot to pour him a cup and brought it to him as he sat down. "Good morning, Luke. Did you sleep all right last night?" she asked.

"Thank you, Maria. I did," said Luke. "It felt good ta have a soft bed ta lay on. At first, mah body didn't know how to take it without a rock poking me in mah back all night."

The sheriff waited until Luke sat down and had his coffee before saying, "Snowed some last night."

"I saw that," replied Luke. "That much snow could wipe out any sign."

"That's what I was thinking," said the sheriff. "Now we will have to think on what to do next."

"Well, we know that they ain't gonna be traveling in this weather. If they're still in da area," said Luke, "I don't think they will be goin' anywhere. They may lay low till spring befer they head out again. My guess is they done found a farm or ranch where they are holed up. If'n they found a place abandoned, they could hole up where no one would be interested in them. Are there any abandoned places hereabouts?"

"I ain't heard of any places near here," said the sheriff. "That doesn't mean that there ain't any. The war's been hard on everyone. Some of the farmers lost everything, including family. We saw several families coming through here last summer trying to make it out west so they could start over. Seems like all the people I talked to heading west had the same story to tell. They had little or no money. Their farms had failed or been burned out. Some had gathered a little money from selling their farms; others had just rode away, taking whatever they could carry and leaving the rest."

"Da family I was traveling with had just upped and left their place," said Luke. "Mah folks have a chance ta keep our place, if'n da Yankees don't take it from them. Still, I heard out west is not fer da weak. If'n it's harder than what we have been through with da war, then no one can make a life out there either."

Maria had finished cooking and brought them their breakfast. She had made enough that she sat down with them. Luke noticed that she kept looking at the sheriff with a look that said she was more than just a housekeeper. Luke began to think that she had a liking for the sheriff. Luke also noticed that the sheriff seemed to not pay any attention to Maria. When they finished eating, they left. Maria asked, "Will you be stopping in for dinner at noon?"

"We will today, Maria, as we won't be able to ride out this morning," said the sheriff.

Leaving the house, they made their way through the snow to the office. "Why don't ya marry that gal?" asked Luke.

"What gal? You mean Maria?" replied the sheriff, surprised at Luke's comment.

"Ya, that's da gal," said Luke. "I saw how she looks at ya. If'n ya were ta ask her, she'd agree." Luke went on saying, "I done saw that look in mah own eyes some time back."

"Then how come you ain't married?" asked the sheriff.

"She was killed back at Panther Gap," said Luke.

"Now I understand why you're so interested in getting him," said the sheriff. "Not only did they hurt your family; they killed your gal as well."

Entering the office, they saw Earl sitting behind his desk drinking coffee. He got up, saying, "I think I'll go to the café and get some breakfast. We got a couple of guests in the back who wanted to break up the saloon last night. They should be sobered up by now."

The sheriff nodded to him as he headed for the door. "Luke, go up to the saloon and see how much damage was done," said the sheriff.

Herb was sweeping the floor when Luke walked in. Looking up, he asked, "We won't be open for business for a while."

"The sheriff sent me over ta see how much damage those two drunks did last night," said Luke.

"Sorry, deputy, I didn't recognize you when you first walked in," said Herb. "They only broke a couple of bottles on each other. Earl was coming in on his rounds just as the fight got started. He broke it up and took the two to jail to sleep it off. Funny those two getting into a fight. They have been drinking together every Saturday night for as long as I can remember."

"Thanks," said Luke. "I'll tell da Sheriff."

Walking back to the office, Luke noticed that the shop owners were trying to clear the snow from in front of their shops. When he got back to the office, he told the sheriff what Herb had said. The sheriff got up; taking the keys, he went to the back. Before long, he returned with two men that did not look like they were in too good of shape. Luke recognized one of the men as Dave from the bank. The other he figured had to be Larry.

"You're free to go," said the sheriff.

"Ah, Sheriff, let me stay. You know how Margaret is. She ain't going to leave me be with it being Sunday and in the condition I'm in," said Dave.

"Dave, you know better. You should have behaved yourself and gone home last night when I told you. If you go back to the saloon, I personally will take you home," said the sheriff.

Dave hung his head, and the two of them walked out. Luke watched from the window as they left. He saw them look toward the saloon, but they thought better of it and headed for their homes.

Turning from the window, Luke said, "I think I'll walk down and check on mah horses."

"Fine," said the sheriff.

Luke took his time walking to the livery; not much was going to happen today being Sunday and with the fresh snow that fell last night. When Luke entered the livery, Buck saw him and nickered. Luke went to his stall and started petting him.

Luke was startled and jumped when George said, "I ain't seen that kind of affection between a man and his horse for some time."

"You sure walk quietly," said Luke. "Most people can't come up behind me without me know'n it."

"I didn't mean to startle you," said George. "I like to see a man take care of his animals."

"Buck and I have been through a lot," said Luke. "We went all over Virginia look'n fer mah pa during da war. He saved mah hide more than once."

"I can tell by the way he acted when you came in that he likes to be near you," said George.

"Ya might say he's like mah family," said Luke. "I raised him from a colt."

George turned to go do some work while Luke got a brush and brushed all three of his horses. When Luke finished brushing the horses, he noticed George was watching him. Luke went over to him and asked, "Have you seen a shoe with this marking?" Luke drew the marking in the dirt.

"That almost looks like a star," said George. "I can't say that I have seen it."

"If'n ya do, let me know," said Luke. "The horse it belongs ta is one of da men we are look'n fer."

"If I see it, I will let you or the sheriff know," said George.

Luke left the livery and decided to have a look around town before going back to the office. Not seeing much activity in town, he went back to the office. Luke took the wanted posters off the wall and started going through them. When he finished, he hung them back without recognizing any of them. He was also looking to see if there was a poster on him. Not seeing it, he thought maybe the army had given up on him. The sheriff, seeing Luke looking at the posters, said, "There is a stack of old ones in the corner, if you're looking for someone."

Luke picked up the old stack and found the poster on Fry as well as the flier the army had sent out. He took the flier of himself and put it in his pocket. He would get rid of it later.

The sheriff thought he saw Luke folding one of the posters out of the corner of his eye but put the thought aside when Luke showed him the poster on Fry. Maybe it was the one on Fry that he had seen him set aside.

The sheriff finished his paperwork and looked up at the clock. "Time for dinner," he said. "Let's go see what Maria has cooked up for us."

As they got up to go, Earl came walking in. "Just finished breakfast?" asked the sheriff.

"No. Been over at the saloon. Some of the men from town were in there playing checkers," said Earl. "I didn't see anything going on in town, so I stopped and watched for a while. They were doing some talking, and word has gotten around about the raid on the Meyer farm. One of the fellas said that he had talked to Gus and that Gus was concerned about his own family. At least he has them three older boys to help out if there's trouble. Some of the other men wanted to know what you were doing about it. I told them that we were doing all we could and had a new deputy who's been following them."

"We're going to dinner," said the sheriff. "You can go when we get back."

As the sheriff and Luke walked toward the house, the sheriff asked, "So you think Maria has an eye for me, do you?"

"I sure do," said Luke. "Ya need ta notice her look'n at ya when you're around. I'll bet she'll be look'n at ya while we're eat'n dinner."

When they entered the house, Maria had the table set for three and dinner was almost ready. "Wash up before you sit down," she called from the kitchen.

By the time they had washed up, Maria had finished and was setting dinner on the table. Everybody sat down. The sheriff did his normal thing of eating and not paying any attention to Maria. When he remembered what Luke said, he glanced at Maria, who quickly turned her head away and blushed. The sheriff smiled to himself, thinking about what Luke had said about her having eyes for him. He went back to eating, and every once in awhile he would glance over at Maria out of the corner of his eye without moving his head. Whenever he looked, he saw that she was watching him as well. After they finished eating, he noticed that Maria had hardly eaten any of her food. *Well, maybe she will eat after we leave,* he thought. Getting up, he said, "That was a mighty fine meal, Maria."

"That sure was," added Luke.

"Well, thank you," said Maria. "A woman doesn't mind cooking for men who can eat like you two can."

They left, and while walking back to the office, Lloyd said half to himself and half out loud, "Now what does she see in me?"

Luke asked, "What did ya say?"

"Oh, I was just thinking out loud on what she could possibly see in me," Lloyd said.

"Well, I'd say she sees a lot from da way she keeps looking at ya," said Luke. "Why don't ya do something about it, or ain't ya got feelins fer her?"

"I've done some thinking about her," said the sheriff. "I don't want to cause anyone sorrow if something was to happen to me."

"Ya don't think yer not gonna cause her sorrow if'n something happened ta ya now?" asked Luke.

They walked the rest of the way without talking. When they got back to the office, Earl got up to leave. As he was going out, the sheriff told him not to be gone till suppertime.

The afternoon was just as quiet as the morning. When suppertime rolled around, Luke and the sheriff made their rounds before going home. The sheriff had not said any more about Maria that afternoon or on the way home. When they entered the house, supper was waiting, only Maria had only put two plates on the table.

"Aren't you going to join us?" asked the sheriff.

"I didn't know if you would want me to," said Maria.

"Please get another plate, and come join us," said the sheriff.

Maria said thank you as she went to get another plate. Supper was quiet. Luke noticed that Maria was not as obvious when she looked at the sheriff, but she still looked. Luke finished his supper and excused himself, leaving Maria and the sheriff alone. As he walked away, he heard the sheriff start talking.

"Maria."

"Yes, Lloyd," said Maria.

"How long have you been working here, cleaning my house and cooking for me?" asked the sheriff.

"Ever since you became Sheriff," said Maria. "Why are you asking?"

"Well," said the sheriff, hanging his head, somewhat embarrassed, "I've been thinking about you a lot but was afraid to say anything. I would like to get to know you better. Now, I don't want to force you into anything because I don't want you to think wrong of me. If things work out, I would like you to stay here permanently."

"I don't know what to say," said Maria. "I've done a lot of thinking about you as well. I was afraid that you did not like me. You never said anything before."

"That wasn't the case," said the sheriff. "I am afraid that I could get killed in this job and leave you alone. I would hate to cause you hurt."

They continued to talk for some time. Luke had gone into his room and closed the door, shutting out any more of their conversation. Looking out the window, he saw that it was starting to snow again.

In the morning, Maria had gotten there extra early and seemed to be very happy. When Luke walked into the kitchen, Maria was humming as she was making breakfast. Looking at Luke, she smiled, telling him to sit. She was still humming when she brought him coffee. Luke had finished drinking his coffee when Lloyd came in. Lloyd had a smile on his face as well. Sitting down, Maria brought him coffee; only this time they kept looking at each other. Maria said, "Good morning, Lloyd."

"Good morning, Maria," said Lloyd. "Did you sleep well last night?"

"No," said Maria. "I was awake most of the night thinking about what you said last night."

"Me too," said Lloyd.

Maria turned, walking back to the stove. Luke said, "Do ya mind if I have another cup of coffee?"

Maria's face turned red as she came back with the coffee pot.

Luke didn't say anything during breakfast but continued to watch Maria and the sheriff. He would smile every once in a while. After breakfast, Luke and the sheriff got up and went to the office. On the way to the office, Luke said, "I see ya and Maria come ta an understanding last night."

"Yes, we did," said the sheriff. "I am sure glad you convinced me to talk to her. It could be that if all works out I might consider getting married."

When they arrived at the office, Earl noticed right off that the sheriff was in a good mood. "Well, I see the weather hasn't gotten you down," said Earl.

"He come ta an understanding with himself last night," said Luke as he walked away, laughing.

Earl looked at Luke and shook his head, not knowing what Luke was talking about. He looked at the sheriff and asked, "Did you make the rounds this morning on your way in?"

"No, we didn't," said the sheriff. "Why don't you make them this morning and take Luke with you? He could use the exercise."

Earl and Luke left the office with Luke still laughing. "What's so funny?" asked Earl.

"I think da Sheriff is in love," said Luke. "If not, he sure looks like a love-sick puppy ta me."

Earl decided not to ask any more questions about the sheriff while they were making their rounds. With all the snow that had fallen, no one from the country would be in town for a while. That also meant that they would not be able to get out to the Meyer place.

"What are you thinking about, Luke?" asked Earl.

"I was just thinking about how ta find Fry again," said Luke. "I know'd of one horse that they have with them. It left a different mark. If I saw it again, I'd recognize it. I done followed their trail ta their camp once befer, and I think I can do it again."

"When do you plan on looking for him?" asked Earl.

"We gotta wait till da snow is gone," said Luke. "I don't think we're gonna find any sign left at da Meyer's."

For the next few weeks, the temperature remained cold. The trains were delayed for a week while they sent out a special engine to clear the snow off the track. Luke continued to make the rounds with either the sheriff or Earl. He made regular trips to the stable to see his horses, and they were getting restless, as was Luke.

the hunt for fry

The second night after Oliver returned, it snowed. When Fry woke up and saw all the snow on the ground, he felt relieved knowing that the snow would cover any tracks that they might have left when they moved the livestock. Between the livestock and the supplies they had taken from the raid, they could remain for weeks without having to go to town for supplies. The only thing that he was thinking about now was how they were going to get the information about the money. If the money came in and it was late enough in the year, they would be able to rob the bank and head out. If it came in earlier, they would have to rob the bank at night, make their escape, and hide out until they could travel again.

He was the first one into the kitchen except for the cook. He took a seat at the table, and the cook came over with a cup of coffee. When he set the cup down, he asked, "Did you see the snow that came down last night?"

"I looked out and saw that there must be at least a foot of snow on the ground this morning," said Fry. "I don't think anyone will be going anywhere for a while. Looking at the sky, I would say that there is more snow on the way. What have you got cooking this morning?"

"How about some steak and eggs?" said the cook.

"Sounds good," said Fry. "Where did you get the eggs?"

"Found them in the root cellar at the place we raided," said the cook. "They also had some chickens that we brought with us."

While Fry was waiting for his breakfast, some of the other men started to come in and sit down. They were talking about what had happened during the raid. "Seemed like old times like it was during the war," said one of the men.

After breakfast, the men got up with most of them going to the bunkhouse. Some of the men lay back down; others decided to play cards. Someone pulled out a bottle and started drinking, passing it around to the others. It didn't take long before the bottle was empty. One of the men asked if there was any more. Not finding any, they got quiet while the rest continued with playing cards. Oliver found an old newspaper and started reading it. He found an article about their robbery in Louisville.

"It's too bad about Blain getting killed back there," said Oliver.

"Well, we all know that is the risk," said Cody. "He ain't the first one that we lost."

"No, he ain't the first one we lost, but thanks to Peter and James who held off the posse, we got away. How many others of us would have done that?" asked Oliver.

Fry called Oliver back to the house after breakfast. When Oliver arrived, he said, "I want you to go over again what you found out in town. I want you to tell me about the bank's layout as well as what you heard in the saloon," said Fry.

Oliver went to the stove and got himself a cup of coffee before he sat down and started talking. "Well, I decided that I needed to spend the night in town. After checking into the hotel, I found a place where I could put my horse out of sight in an abandoned barn and didn't have to use the livery. Being it was close to suppertime, I went to the café to get something to eat. They were getting busy, so no one paid much attention to me. During supper, I heard the man from the livery talking about a fella who rode into town asking a lot of questions about the place we raided."

"What about this stranger who was asking the questions?" asked Fry. "Did anyone say who he was or what he looked like?"

"Na, no one mentioned his name; only the man from the livery said that he looked to be a young fella but old for his age," said Oliver. "He went on to mention something about him talking to the sheriff some as well. Before he finished, the man from the livery said that the sheriff had come by and wanted to talk to the stranger again, but he told the sheriff that he had ridden out of town heading west and didn't know if he would be coming back."

"You had to ride past the place we raided on your way back. Did you see anyone along the way?" asked Fry.

"No, I didn't see a soul," said Oliver.

Finishing what he had to tell Fry, Oliver got up, leaving Fry to do his thinking. Fry thought about how they could get a look at the inside of the bank. They also needed to find out when the money would arrive, how much money was coming in, and how it was being shipped. Even without knowing for sure when the money was to arrive, he could go ahead with their planning to rob the bank. At least then they would be prepared for it if it happened. As soon as the weather cleared up, he would send men out to different towns to see if they could find information about the money.

Setting aside his thinking about the money, he began to think about the stranger who had asked so many questions about the raid. *A young fella with a Virginia accent,* he thought. He sat there for some time before he said to himself, "It couldn't be." Not that fella they ran into at Panther Gap. He had been badly wounded. With his wounds as bad as they were, he surely would have died. *If it is him, what is his name? I know that we heard them talking about him while we were there. Maybe one of the men might remember what his name was.*

The men spent the rest of the day in the bunkhouse until supper was ready; then they came back to the house. While they were eating, Fry laid out his plan.

"Oliver said that there was a man in town asking about our raid. He heard something about him being from Virginia. Does anyone remember the name of the fella that caused us all our problems when we were in Panther Gap?" asked Fry.

"Well, Cap," said Cody, "I seem ta recall something about da fellas being called Luke or Hicks."

"Ya, that was da names I recall," said Herbert. "One was called Luke, and the other I believe was called Hicks."

"Well, we got us a couple of names that we can listen for," said Fry. "Oliver done said that the stranger in town asking about us had ridden out and it wasn't known for sure if he was coming back. I was sure that we had gotten rid of him, but he is the only one I could think of who would take an interest in us out here."

"When we were in Louisville," said Reynolds, "I done thought I seen a fella by da café that looked familiar, like I had seen him someplace befer. It was only as we were leaving, so I weren't sure about it."

"If it is him, that means that he has been trailing us ever since we were in Louisville or even from Panther Gap," said Fry.

"Could be, Cap," said Reynolds.

"We need to find out for sure," said Fry. "Reynolds, I want you to go into town as soon as the weather clears and see if you can find out anything about who this fella is. I want to know if it is the fella from Panther Gap."

"Sure enough, Cap," said Reynolds.

The weather did not cooperate with Fry's plans. The added snow that came in locked them down tighter than before. They would not be traveling anywhere for some time. After two weeks of being snowed in, the men were really getting restless. Fry was feeling the effects as well. He began jumping on the men for no reason. Not knowing for sure when the money was coming made it worse for Fry. What if the money had already been arrived? Even with all the snow, the trains might still be able to get through. They needed to get back to town and find out what was going on.

It was three weeks after the snow had started before anyone could travel. Fry had made up his mind he was going to send Oliver to Boonville so he could find out what the inside of the bank looked like. In order for Oliver to get into the bank, he gave Oliver a large bill, which he would have him change at the bank. With the money, Oliver was to get some supplies as well.

Fry decided to send Jack to Boonville to board the boat to Jefferson City. While he was on the boat, he needed to look around and find out if they had any means for keeping a large sum of money locked up.

The next day Jack left for Boonville, taking a route that would allow him to enter the main road a couple of miles east of town. His first stop as he entered town was to go to the dock to find out when the next boat was headed for Jefferson City. Looking at the schedule, he saw that he had to wait until tomorrow morning before the boat was scheduled to leave. Talking to the ticket agent, Jack asked, "Is the boat still running with winter here?"

"Been running on time," said the ticket agent. "The river stays open for most of the winter, and it hasn't been cold enough to freeze over even with the snow. Where do you want to go?"

"I need to go to Jefferson City for a few days," said Jack. "Where can I put up my horse?"

"There's a livery near the edge of town," said the ticket agent.

Jack paid for his ticket and headed to the livery. Riding up to the livery, he dismounted and tied his horse. In the livery, George was working on a horse. Looking up, George asked, "What can I do for you?"

"I need to leave a horse for a few days while I go to Jefferson City. The fella at the dock said I could put him up here," said Jack.

"How long you going to be gone?" asked George.

"No longer than a week," said Jack. "The missus doesn't cater to me being gone too long; she gets a little lonely."

"My missus don't like to be left for long neither," said George. "Why don't you bring your horse in, and I'll put him in the stall back here."

Jack went out, and bringing him into the livery, he took him to the stall that George had indicated. Taking his saddlebags and bedroll, he headed for the hotel. He would have to spend the night in town waiting for the boat. At the hotel, the clerk gave him a room with a window facing the street. In the room, he left his saddlebags and bedroll. Now that he had the day to kill, he decided to take a walk around town and get a drink.

George didn't think much about the man who had come into the livery. He had said that he was from the Fayette area. There were a lot of people, especially from that area, that he did not know. Anyway, the people that Luke and the sheriff were looking for would come in from the west. He went back to shoeing his horse.

Jack walked into the saloon and went up to the bar. "What can I get for you?" asked Herb.

"Give me a whiskey and a beer," said Jack.

Herb poured Jack a shot of whiskey and then got him a beer. Returning with his beer, he asked, "Your new around here, aren't you?"

"I live up by Fayette. Me and my wife got a farm up there," said Jack.

"What brings you to Boonville?" asked Herb.

"I need to go to Jefferson City to look at some new equipment," said Jack. "I figured to take the boat it would be easier than riding there this time of the year."

At that time, a new customer came into the saloon, and Herb went to help him. Jack took his beer and went to the table near the window and sat down to watch the street. He didn't know when Oliver was going to come into town, but he wanted to keep an eye out for him so that they didn't meet. Jack stayed in the saloon throughout the afternoon drinking beer. Near suppertime, he headed for the café. Entering the café, he took a table near the window. After ordering his supper and looking out the window, he saw a deputy going into the saloon.

Earl walked into the saloon and looked around. Herb called him over to the bar and said, "There came a new fella into the saloon today. Said he was from Fayette."

"How long was he in here today?" asked Earl.

"He spent most of the afternoon here," said Herb.

"Seems strange that he would not have traveled, don't it?" asked Earl.

"Na. He said he was waiting for the boat to take him down and it didn't leave till tomorrow," said Herb.

"Okay," said Earl. "I'll mention it to the sheriff when I get back to the office. Did you happen to see where he went?"

"I think he's over at the café," said Herb.

"Thanks," said Earl. Maybe he would take a walk by the café and see if he could get a look at this new fella. As he approached the café, he saw the fella that Herb had talked about sitting near the window. Earl opened the door to the café and looked in, taking a good look at the man. He would remember who this man was if he saw him again. Before he could turn to leave, the waitress asked, "Are you going to eat, Earl?"

"Na, I'll be back later," said Earl. "I'm just doing my rounds." Back at the office, he told the sheriff about the new man. The sheriff didn't think any more about it either. It wasn't long until Luke came into the office. He had been walking on the other end of the town doing his rounds. He didn't see anything out of place either.

Earl said, "I think I'll go get some supper."

"Go ahead," said the sheriff.

Earl went to the café. When he arrived, he noticed that the stranger had already left. Taking the seat that the stranger had, he ordered his supper. When the waitress returned with his meal, he asked, "Did the stranger say anything when he was in here?"

"No, he just ordered his supper and left after he ate," said the waitress.

Earl thanked her and ate his supper, watching the street. Everything was quiet.

It wasn't long after Earl had left that the sheriff and Luke headed for the sheriff's house. Maria was waiting for them when they arrived. Things had changed at the sheriff's house. Maria seemed to be a lot happier, as well as the sheriff. *Who knows? Maybe they will get married,* thought Luke.

"Wash up," said Maria. "Supper's on the table."

They washed up and joined Maria at the table. "Maria," said Luke, "when this is over, I don't know if I'm going ta be able ta leave. If da Sheriff here doesn't want ya, ya sure can come with me."

Maria laughed and winked at Luke. "Well, if Lloyd don't want me, I would be happy to go with you."

"Now what brung this on?" asked Lloyd. "Aren't you happy here?"

"Now, Lloyd, we're just fun'n you," said Maria.

Luke and Maria continued to give Lloyd a hard time while they ate supper. When they were done, Luke told the sheriff that he was going to take a walk. He wanted to check on his horses. He got his coat and headed for the livery. At the livery, he took his time and brushed all three of his horses. Buck was glad to see him and kept rubbing his head against Luke whenever he got the chance. "One of these day we're go'n get a chance ta get some exercise," said Luke. When done, he headed for the saloon.

Entering the saloon, he went up to the bar and ordered a beer. After Herb gave him his beer, he took a look around and saw the stranger sitting by the wall by himself. The ticket agent from the dock was sitting at the table next to him, and it looked like the two of them were talking. "Is that da fella who came in from Fayette, Herb?" asked Luke.

"Ya, that's him," said Herb.

"Has he been in here long?" asked Luke.

"Been here since supper talking to Bill," said Herb. "I understand that he has a ticket on the boat tomorrow."

"Has he been talk'n ta any one else since he came in?" asked Luke.

"Na, he's been staying to himself," said Herb.

"Thanks," said Luke. He finished his beer and went back to the house. Lloyd and Maria were still sitting at the table talking when Luke came in. "I see da dishes are still on da table," said Luke. "Ya must have had some mighty important things ta talk about."

Maria just looked at Luke with a big smile as her face got red and she shook her head.

"Da cat got yer tongue?" asked Luke. "Ya look like ya swallered something."

"I asked her to marry me," said Lloyd, "and she has been like that ever since. I don't know if she is going to say yes or no."

"Well, if'n ya were ta ask me," said Luke, "I'd say she is gonna agree ta marry ya as soon as she gets herself tagether."

Luke started picking up the dishes and taking them to the sink. Maria up got up to help him. Maria finally turned to Lloyd and said, "Yes, I'll marry you." She then turned back to the sink and started washing the dishes. Lloyd stood there in disbelief. Luke just started laughing.

"Well, I'll be," said Lloyd. "She done said she would marry me."

"When do ya plan on getting married?" asked Luke. "I need ta know how long I got ta find a place ta live, if'n ya are getting hitched."

"It's up to Maria," said Lloyd. "You can stay here in that extra room you're in till we get Fry, if Maria doesn't mind."

Maria had finished washing the dishes and putting them away when she said, "I would like to get married as soon as possible. Luke, you can still stay in your room. I know that you want to go on as soon as you can."

"I guess that settles it," said Lloyd. "I guess I need to tell Earl in the morning as well. Maria and I will go talk to the preacher tomorrow and see when he can do the honors. Luke, I want you to stand up for us since it was you that got me talking to Maria."

"Now wait, Lloyd. Ya ain't gonna go and blame me fer what ya did," said Luke. "All I done was told ya that ya needed to open yer eyes."

"And I'm glad you did," said Maria.

Luke got up and excused himself, going to his room for the night.

After Luke had left the saloon, Jack asked who the man at the bar was. "I don't know what his name is, but he's a new deputy for the sheriff. He came into town a couple of weeks ago," said Bill. "Why do you ask?"

"Oh, nothing important," said Jack. "He looked like someone I've seen before. If he just got to town, I guess I don't know him. He just looks like someone I know'd." There was something familiar about him, but he couldn't remember where he might have seen him before. He did not get a good look at him, and with that coat and hat on, it could have been anyone. Anyway, he would mention it to Fry when he got back to the farm.

In the morning, he got up and went to the café before going to the boat. While he was eating, Earl came in. Jack kept an eye on Earl, making sure that he was not paying too much attention to him. Earl wasn't paying attention to anyone except the waitress whenever she would come by his table. When Jack finished his breakfast, he paid and headed for the dock. Walking down the street, he saw a rider coming in from the east end of town leading a packhorse. At first, he did not recognize the rider. As the rider got closer, he saw that it was Oliver. Looking around, he saw that the deputy had come out of the café as well and was watching him. Jack looked away from the rider as Oliver neared him, trying to show that he had no interest in him.

Oliver had left the farm early that morning hoping that he would be able to get into town before there were many people moving around. As he rode down the main street, he saw Jack come out of the café. It wasn't long after Jack came out that he saw a second man come out watching him. Oliver continued to ride down the street watching both men. As he got closer to Jack, he saw Jack turn sharply away from him. Still paying attention to Jack, he kept a close watch on the second man. As he got close enough to the second man, he could see that the man was a deputy, and it looked like he was taking an interest in both him and Jack.

Earl hadn't thought much about seeing the stranger while sitting in the café. It was the same man he had seen yesterday and who he had heard was catching the boat this morning. What did catch his interest was the way he went out of his way to avoid looking at the new stranger. He continued to watch the man riding as he rode up to the café and got down. After Oliver tied his horse and packhorse, he stepped up on the walk. The deputy said, "You're new in town."

"Just passing through," said Oliver. "Need to pick up some supplies and have the shoes on my horse replaced. Do you have a good blacksmith in town?"

"He's down at the livery," said Earl. "You ain't going to find him there now. He's in the café eating. He'll be back at the livery a little later."

"Good," said Oliver. "I can get me something ta et first."

Earl watched the man as he went into the café before heading back to the office. Once back at the office, he put a fresh pot of coffee on the stove and sat down, waiting for the sheriff.

After breakfast, Lloyd told Luke to go ahead to the office. He and Maria were going to go talk to the preacher and see if they could get a wedding set up. Luke was thinking that Lloyd was acting like a little schoolboy who just found out what candy was for the first time. Nodding to the sheriff, he got his coat and headed to the office. Entering the office, Earl looked up and asked, "Where's the sheriff? Didn't he come in with you?"

"The sheriff will be in later," said Luke. "He done got some personal business ta take care of. What's up?"

"I ain't sure," said Earl. "I seen that new fella who came to town yesterday at the café. Something he did just didn't seem right to me."

"What was that?" asked Luke.

"When he left the café, he headed for the dock, but this other fella came riding into town. The fella from yesterday went out of his way to not look at the fella riding in," said Earl. "I talked to the new fella when he got down by the café, and he said that he was just passing through."

"What's so strange about that?" asked Luke.

"Nothing except the way they seemed to try and avoid each other," said Earl. "Do you know how long the sheriff will be before he arrives?"

"It shouldn't take him that long," said Luke. "When he gets here, we'll see what he wants ta do. Maybe I'll take a walk down ta da livery ta check on mah horses once he gets his horse down there."

Deciding not to go until the sheriff arrived, Luke got himself a cup of coffee. While he was waiting, he got to wondering why these two had avoided looking at each other. Maybe they did know each other. If they did, why did they want to avoid each other unless they were up to something?

Earl and Luke had only to wait about an hour until the sheriff came into the office. When the sheriff entered, he looked at Luke and said, "It's all arranged for Sunday afternoon."

Earl looked at the sheriff and then at Luke before he asked, "What's going on?"

The sheriff looked at Luke before turning to Earl. He said, "Luke didn't tell you what I was doing this morning?"

Earl said, "The only thing that Luke said was you had some business to take care of."

"It weren't none of mah business ta be tell'n what yer up ta," said Luke.

The sheriff shook his head and said, "Well, Earl, Maria and I are going to get married this Sunday."

"Congratulations, Lloyd. I've been wondering why you haven't done something like this before. I know that you have had an eye for her since she started keeping your house for you," said Earl. "Well, while you were out making your plans, another fella rode into town this morning. I think the fella that came in yesterday and the new fella know each other."

"What makes you think that?" asked the sheriff.

"When they met on the street, they tried too hard not to notice each other," said Earl. "The new fella told me that he was passing through and needed to take his horse to the livery. He also needed supplies, but he was going to eat some breakfast first. We might be able to meet up with him at the livery."

"I'd like ta take a look at his horse's shoes," said Luke. "I could go ta da livery and check on mah horses and see if'n I'd know'd him."

"If you know him, don't you think he will know you as well?" asked the sheriff.

"He might," said Luke. "I think that's a chance I need ta take."

"Okay, why don't you go down and take a look," said the sheriff.

Luke headed for the livery. Earl walked out of the office with Luke. Earl pointed out that the new fella's horses were gone from in front of the café. Earl stood watching Luke before going back into the office.

When Luke entered the stable, George was working on the stranger's horse. Looking around, Luke did not see the stranger. George said, "Good to see you, Luke. Did you come to spend some time with your horses again?"

"Thought I'd stop by and take a look at them and check out da shoes yer take'n off this horse," said Luke. "Ya haven't seen that horse shoe print I told ya about, have ya?"

"No, I haven't," said George. "This horse has been in town before though. I remember seeing him a few weeks back. About the time you came to town."

"Do ya know'd where the fella went?" asked Luke.

"He said something about needing some supplies," said George. "He may be at the general store."

"Thanks," said Luke, turning and going back to see Buck. "One of these days, Buck, we'll get out fer a spell."

Leaving the livery, Luke went by the general store but did not see any strangers in there. He also stopped by the saloon, but it was empty as well. Looking up the street, he saw the stranger coming out of the bank. *Now that's a strange place for him to be,* thought Luke. He stood watching him coming in his direction. Luke did not recognize the fella, but that didn't mean anything. Walking up the street, he went around the corner of a building. When he came out from behind the building, he saw that the man was going into the saloon. Continuing on, he went to the bank. Seeing Mr. Olson's office door open, he walked over and knocked. Mr. Olson looked up and, seeing Luke, said, "Oh hi, deputy. What can I do for you?"

"The fella that was just in your bank, do you know what he wanted?" asked Luke.

"I think Dave took care of him. Let's ask him," said Mr. Olson. "Dave," Mr. Olson called out, "would you come in here for a minute?"

Dave came into the office, looking at both Luke and Mr. Olson, and said, "Is there something wrong, Mr. Olson?"

"No, Dave," said Mr. Olson. "The deputy was wondering what business that stranger had in the bank."

"He came in to get some change for a large bill," said Dave. "Once he got his change, he left. By the way, I saw him in town once before."

"When was that?" asked Luke.

"It was back before we got all this snow," said Dave. "Larry and I stopped for a beer one night after work, and he was sitting in the saloon drinking a beer by himself. This is the first I have seen him since then."

"Thanks," said Luke.

Dave went back to the teller window, and Luke headed back to the sheriff's office. As he entered the office, the sheriff asked, "Well, did you find out anything?"

Luke told him what George had said at the livery and that he saw him coming out of the bank. He told the sheriff what Dave had told him and about the time that Dave had seen him in the saloon.

"I wonder if that ain't about da time Earl thought he saw someone around the bank," said Luke. "Is there something go'n on at da bank?"

"They have a large shipment of cash coming in next month," said the sheriff.

"Who knows about da shipment?" asked Luke.

"Our office and the bank," said the sheriff. "Did you recognize him as one of Fry's men?"

"Na, I don't recall see'n him before," said Luke. "Several of Fry's men were killed back in Virginia, so he probably has gotten more men since then."

Luke stayed in the office the rest of the day. Earl took a couple of walks around the town to check things out but did not find anything. While sitting there, Luke mentioned to the sheriff that he would take a ride out to the Meyer place and look around in the morning.

Herb thought he recognized Oliver as one who had been in before and kept an eye on him as he entered the saloon and went to a table. When Oliver sat down, Herb remembered him sitting at the same table when he first stopped in. After serving Oliver his drinks, he kept watching, and when he saw that Oliver had finished his beer, he walked over to see if he wanted anything else. As Herb approached, Oliver turned a piece of paper over so Herb could not see what he was drawing.

"Would you like another?" asked Herb

"I'll have another beer," said Oliver.

When Oliver finished his second beer, he got up, going to the livery. He paid for his shoeing before saying, "I decided that I would be staying in town. Can you put them up for the next couple of days?"

After George said that it would not be a problem, Oliver got his saddlebags and bedroll before going to the hotel. At the hotel, he checked in and went to his room and lay down for the afternoon. He would wait until later before going back to the saloon. Maybe he would run into Dave from the bank.

Before the stores started to close for the day, Oliver got up and went back to the café to eat supper. While he was sitting there, Earl walked in. Earl walked over to him and asked, "Didn't George have time to get to your horses?"

"You mean the fella at the livery?" responded Oliver. "He got the shoes on my horses, but I decided to spend a couple of days in town before leaving. I don't think the weather's going to stay nice, and if I can have a warm bed for a couple of nights, it would be good."

"Well, enjoy yourself," said Earl. Walking away, he found himself a table and sat down where he could keep an eye on him.

When Oliver finished eating, he went to the saloon. As he was about to enter the saloon, he noticed Dave and the other teller coming out of the bank. He paused just long enough to see which direction they headed. Seeing that they appeared to be heading toward the saloon, he went in and found the table where they had sat the last time. Herb was just giving Oliver his drink when Dave and Larry came in. They looked at Oliver, and Oliver waved to them, motioning for them to come over. When they got to the table, Oliver offered to buy them a drink. Sitting down, they both ordered a beer.

"That's kind of you to buy us a drink," said Dave, "but I don't understand why you would want to buy us a drink."

"I don't like to drink alone, and you two are the only ones that I have met in town," said Oliver. "If you don't want my company, you're free to sit somewhere else." Both men remained, still questioning in their minds why this fella was being so friendly.

"I didn't mean to offend you. It's just that strangers don't usually buy us drinks," said Dave. "By the way, this is Larry."

"Glad to meet you," said Oliver. "My name's Oliver. Me and a couple of mah army buddies are on our way west. We found a place abandoned and decided to winter there. It sure was a good thing, too, with this snow coming in on us. I had to come in to town to get some supplies. With it getting late, I decided ta wait till tomorrow before riding back."

Dave and Larry seemed to accept what Oliver was saying. After a few more drinks, they both were well relaxed and started talking about some of the bank's goings on. Oliver asked how the area was doing after the war, saying that where he came from there was no money. Dave made a slip and mentioned that they did not have the same problem, as they had a shipment coming into town next month. Larry carelessly asked if he was talking about the one during the middle of the month without thinking, and when Dave said yes, Oliver knew he had what he had been sent to town to find out. He sat with the two until they decided that they needed to head for home.

The next morning after eating breakfast, he stopped by the general store and told them that his plans had changed and he would be leaving that morning and wanted to know if they could have his supplies ready. They told him that by the time he got his horses they could have everything ready to go. By the time he returned with his horses, they did have everything ready. Paying for the supplies, he loaded them on his packhorse. Leaving the general store, he stopped by the saloon and bought several bottles of whiskey before riding out of town. When he arrived at the farm, he stopped by the house and unloaded the supplies before putting up his horses. He kept a couple of bottles of whiskey to take to the bunkhouse. The men there would be happy to get that. The remaining whiskey he left hidden in the barn.

Fry told Oliver to come in and talk to him once he had gotten his horses put up. Entering the house, Oliver sat down with Fry before saying, "I think I found out what ya needed ta know. Last night I sat in da saloon with the tellers from da bank, and they said that da money is due in da middle of next month." Reaching into his pocket, he took out the drawing of the bank he had made so Fry could see it.

"Is this the layout of the bank?" asked Fry.

"Ya," said Oliver. "Your plan worked well. He had ta go ta da vault, so I had enough time ta look da place over good befer he got back. I'd say that da best way ta get da money would be ta go through da window in da spare office through this door. If we go in at night, we can hold da horses in the back, and when we come out, we can head out of town da way I went da night da deputy almost saw me."

Fry went over the drawing, asking detailed questions of Oliver before he felt that he had an understanding of bank layout as well as Oliver. He also had Oliver draw a map of the escape route from the bank to out of town. After Oliver left, Fry continued to sit and refined the plan.

Arriving back at Boonville, after not finding out anything, Jack went directly to the livery and got his horse. He headed out of town, going east before circling around and heading to the farm. Arriving at the farm, he saw that Oliver had returned. Going into the house, he found Fry sitting at the table. He told him that he found out that the money would not be coming in by boat, nor would it be coming from Jefferson City. Fry told him that he had already found out that the army would be escorting it, and Oliver found out that it would not be arriving before the middle of next month.

In the morning, Luke got up with the sheriff and the three of them ate breakfast. Luke said that he was going to ride out to the Meyer place and take another look around. "What do you think you'll find seeing how it snowed?" asked the sheriff.

"I'm not sure if I'll find anything," said Luke. "Maybe we missed something."

"I'll ride with you," said the sheriff.

The sheriff and Luke spent the morning riding out to the Meyer farm. Most of the snow had melted, but in the process of melting, it had wiped out most of the tracks that had been left. Luke walked through the ashes of the house and barn looking for anything that might tell him that the raiders were indeed part of Fry's men. Not finding anything in the ashes, he and the sheriff walked the way Luke had, following the cattle trail, and again the tracks had been wiped out. It was late afternoon when they mounted and rode back to town.

Fry called Reynolds into the house and told him that it had been long enough since they had sent others into town that he needed him to go into town and see if the fella that was working with the sheriff was one of the men from Panther Gap. Reynolds got up and left for town, riding into town from the west. On the way into town, he heard riders coming his way, so he moved off the road to avoid them. While he waited for the riders to pass, he thought that maybe he should go around and come into town from the east as well. When he left, he stayed off the main road and did come in from the east.

By the time he had entered town, it was past noon, so he went straight to the saloon. Tying his horse in front of the saloon, he went and ordered a drink at the bar. Once he had his drink, he sat down at one of the tables where he could watch the door. While he was sitting there, Earl walked in and looked around. Reynolds did not look directly at the deputy but kept an eye on him. He did not recognize the deputy. If he was the person that Fry was concerned about, he was not known to him. He saw that the deputy had spent extra time looking in his direction and checking the room out before going to the bar and talking to the barkeep. He also noticed that the barkeep looked over his way when the deputy talked to him. He figured that they must be checking out anyone new to town. That would mean that they might have been warned by the fella Fry was concerned about.

Earl turned from the bar and walked over to where Reynolds was sitting. When he arrived, he asked, "Did you just get into town?"

"Arrived about noon today," said Reynolds.

"Are you planning on being in town long?" asked Earl.

"Na," said Reynolds. "Just passing through and thought I might spend the night before going on. Where can I put up my horse?"

"You can put him up at the livery just up the street," said Earl.

"Thanks," said Reynolds as Earl turned and left the saloon. Reynolds continued to sit in the saloon for some time before taking his horse to the livery. George met him as he approached the livery and put up the horse while Reynolds went to the hotel and got a room. The room was in front of the hotel, giving him a view of the street. He decided that the best place for him to wait now would be in his room. From there he could see anyone on the street. It was getting late in the afternoon when two riders rode into town from the west and went to the stable. From where Reynolds was sitting, he could not get a good look at them, so he did not realize that it was the sheriff and the man he was to check out.

When Luke and the sheriff entered the stable, Luke took time to rub his horse down before putting him in his stall. The sheriff had finished and was waiting for Luke before they headed to the office. Walking to the office, Luke was on the opposite side of the sheriff from the hotel, and Reynolds could not see Luke's face. He did notice that the second man was wearing a badge as well. That meant that there were at least two deputies in town.

When the sheriff and Luke entered the office, Earl asked, "Did you find anything new out there?"

"No, we didn't," said the sheriff. "The snow had wiped out any of the tracks that would have helped us. How have things been in town?"

"There's new fella that came to town today," said Earl. "He said that he was just passing through. He did plan on spending the night and took his horse to the livery. Did you see it there?"

"No, we didn't," said the sheriff. "I'm surprised that George didn't say anything about it when we came in. Do you know where he is at now?"

"I ain't seen him since he was in the saloon," said Earl. "I saw that his horse was not at the saloon, so I assumed that he took it to the livery."

"I'll keep an eye out fer him," said Luke. "Did ya get his name?"

"Na, I didn't think to ask him," said Earl.

"It seems that we are getting a lot of new people in town all of a sudden," said the sheriff.

"It sure does," said Earl.

They all sat in the office for a long time while the sheriff went through his paperwork in silence. Luke was doing some thinking that maybe he would walk back down to the livery and check out the horse that this new fella rode in before heading to the sheriff's house for the evening. "I think I'll check out that horse befer go'n ta da house," said Luke.

"Okay," said the sheriff. "I'll tell Maria that you're going to be a little late for supper."

Luke got up and left the office. Stopping in front of the office, he decided to walk past the saloon to see if he happened to be in there. Walking across the street, he was underneath the porch when he walked by the hotel. Reynolds was still sitting in his room and didn't see Luke walk by. Luke went on to the livery, and when he entered, George was just finishing feeding the stock. "Hi, George," said Luke as he entered. "I come ta look at da horse da new fella rode in. Is he here?"

"Ya, he's back here," said George. "I checked his print but did not see the marking you are looking for, but it does look like he has new shoes on."

Luke went to the stall where the horse was tied and looked it over. George stood and watched Luke as he checked the horse. Looking up at George, Luke asked, "Have ya got a file?"

"Sure do," said George. "What are you planning on doing with it?"

"Thought I'd mark one of his shoes," said Luke.

After marking the shoe, Luke left the livery and went to the sheriff's house. Maria and the sheriff were already eating when Luke entered the house. Maria, hearing Luke coming in, got up and fixed a plate for him. Sitting down, he thanked Maria for fixing his plate and said hello before he started eating. Maria and Lloyd went back to talking about the upcoming wedding. Maria wanted to invite most of the town, but the sheriff wanted to just keep it small, and it didn't sound like they were coming to an agreement. Luke chuckled to himself, thinking about his ma and pa and how in the end it seemed that his ma would always win. He figured that in the end Maria would have her way as well.

Finally the sheriff asked, "Luke, did you find out anything about the horse?"

"Just that it was not one I recognized," said Luke. "The fella who owned it had put new shoes on him. I did take a file and marked one of da shoes so he would be easy ta follow."

"You have an idea that it could be one of the fellas who raided the Meyers then?" asked the sheriff.

"I couldn't say fer sure," said Luke. "I'd like ta lay eyes on him befer he leaves town. Maybe I'll take a walk down by da saloon later and see if'n he decided ta get a drink." Looking at Maria, he asked, "Are y'all ready fer yer wedding?"

"No," she said. "Lloyd doesn't want to have a big wedding, and I do." Maria looked back at Lloyd with big, sad eyes. Lloyd saw the look in Maria's eyes and quickly looked down at his plate.

Luke laughed and said, "Well, Maria, I am sure ya gonna have yer wedding da way ya want it."

Lloyd gave Luke a look that Luke had not seen before. Part of the look was anger and then softened as if to say, "I give up." He then looked at Maria and said, "Between the two of you, I don't have a chance. You do what you need to get it set up."

Maria got a big smile on her face and said, "Oh, thank you, Lloyd. Mama and Papa will be so happy too."

They finished eating, and Luke got up, going to his room for a while. He decided that he should put his things together and get ready to move to the hotel. Coming back to the kitchen, Maria was just finishing up the dishes and Lloyd was still sitting at the table reading the paper. When he looked up, Luke said that he was going to take a walk around town. Lloyd nodded as Luke turned, leaving the house. Leaving the house, the first place he headed for was the hotel. At the hotel, he made arrangements to move into one of the rooms before the sheriff's wedding.

Leaving the hotel, Luke made his rounds, checking doors of the businesses as he went. At the café, he went in and looked around. The café was almost empty. It looked like there were two couples just finishing their supper when he entered. Luke asked the waitress if there had been any strangers in for supper this evening. She told him that there had been one, but he had finished and left already. Luke thanked her and continued on his rounds. He walked into the saloon and saw who he was looking for. He was sitting in the back of the room with his back to him playing poker with some men from town. Luke stood by the bar for a while and watched without getting too close to the table. The man didn't turn around, so Luke couldn't get a good look at him. Stepping back in the shadows where the fella could not get a good look at him, he ordered a beer and waited. Finally the man turned to the bar to order another drink, and Luke got a look at his face. When he saw the face, it brought back memories of Panther Gap. He recognized him as one of Fry's men. If he recognized him, that meant he might also recognize Luke. Finishing his beer, he waited till they were all concentrating on their poker game before he left.

Reynolds had returned to the saloon after eating supper and got involved in the poker game. After a few drinks and winning a few hands, he was in a good mood. Turning to order another bottle, he did not pay much attention to the person standing in the shadows at the bar, or he might have recognized Luke. After ordering another bottle, he went back to their game.

Luke, instead of heading directly to the house, went to the office first to see if Earl was still there. Entering the office, Earl was sitting at his desk playing cards. He looked up, surprised to see Luke. He asked, "What are you doing here?"

"I got ta think'n about that stranger who come ta town," said Luke. "I done seen him in da saloon just now. I recognized him as one of Fry's men. I don't think he got a look at me 'cause he was play'n poker. Maybe ya should make your rounds and stop by da saloon and keep an eye on da fella fer a while."

"Do you want to come with me?" asked Earl.

"Na, I think it's better he doesn't see me," said Luke. "Let me and da Sheriff know what ya find out in da morning. I marked a shoe on his horse, so we might be able ta track him ta their camp when he leaves."

"Okay, I'll go keep an eye on him," said Earl.

When he got back to the house, Maria was gone, and the sheriff must have gone with her or gone to bed because the house was dark. Going into his room, he decided that he could wait until the morning to tell the sheriff about the man in the saloon. He had just lain down when he heard the sheriff come in. He would still wait until the morning to tell him.

It wasn't long before the house was completely quiet, and Luke fell asleep.

reynolds

Earl got up after Luke left and made his way to the saloon. Walking over to the bar, Herb came over and said, "Seems like you deputies have a big interest in my place tonight. Your new fella was just in here before you."

"We got more of an interest in the stranger playing poker," said Earl. "Luke seemed to think he might have seen him before."

"Well, Luke was here earlier but stayed back where the stranger couldn't get a good look at him," said Herb. "What's up?"

"Luke seems to think that he could be part of the men who raided the Meyer farm," said Earl. "Has he been in here long?"

"He's been here since suppertime," said Herb. "Came in and was sitting by himself until some of the boys came in and started playing poker. He got up and joined them."

"How's his luck been running?" asked Earl.

"He's been winning some and losing some," said Herb. "I'd say he was holding his own. He ain't go'n away a big winner unless his luck changes."

"How are the others doing?" asked Earl.

"About the same," said Herb.

"Has he been asking any questions?" asked Earl.

"I heard him ask'n the boys if they knew who the new deputy was," said Herb. "I thought it was funny that he should take an interest in the deputy until what you just said, that Luke might know him. None of the boys playing poker have met Luke."

"If Luke is right, they might be planning something, and we don't want them to know he's in town. If it is who he thinks he is, he had a run-in with them before," said Earl. "If he asks you about him, just say you ain't been introduced to him."

"Will do," said Herb.

Earl walked over to the table and watched the game for a while. He stood opposite of the stranger so he could get a good look at him and remember what he looked like. He noticed that the stranger was looking him over as well. Seeing that nothing unusual was going on with the game, he went back to the office. He would go out later and see if they were still playing.

Close to midnight, Earl went to the saloon. Instead of going in, he watched through one of the windows and saw that the game was breaking up. As the men came toward the door, Earl went around the corner. He wanted to see where the stranger went as he left the saloon. The stranger was the last one to leave. Earl stood in the shadows and watched as Reynolds went directly to the hotel. Earl continued to stand in front of the saloon watching the hotel. It wasn't long after Reynolds had entered that a lamp went on in the room facing the street. He would tell Luke in the morning what room the stranger was in. If Luke didn't want the stranger to see him, he would have to be careful on the street. Earl went back to the office and went to sleep.

In the morning, Luke woke early. When he went into the kitchen, he saw that Maria had not arrived. Luke built a fire in the stove and put on a pot of coffee. While he was setting the pot on the stove, Lloyd walked in. "You're up kinda early this morning," said Lloyd. "Did you have a problem sleeping last night?"

"I slept well last night," said Luke. "Coffee will be done befer long. Did ya and Maria get yer plans worked out?"

"I think my life is going to change more than I thought," said Lloyd. "I declare that woman is as hard-headed as any two men I know. The way things are going, she is gonna get her way with this wedding or else."

Luke laughed and said, "Mah pa told me how mah ma had changed his way of thinking. Seemed he had thoughts of going out west befer he met Ma. Once he met Ma, she changed his thoughts into settling down on da farm and raising a family. He couldn't talk Ma into going out west, so ya might say that I am carrying his dream."

Luke checked the coffee and moved it off the fire so the grounds would settle. While he was moving the pot, the front door opened and Maria made her way back to the kitchen. She was surprised to see both of the men already in there waiting for their coffee. "You two are sure up early. Are you going somewhere that you forgot to tell me?" she asked.

Lloyd said. "Na, Luke here couldn't sleep and was so noisy out here he woke me as well."

Maria laughed, shaking her head at Luke. "You go set yourself down, and let me fix breakfast before you burn yourself."

Luke went to sit down when there was a knock at the front door. Instead of sitting down, he went to see who was there. "Come on in," said Luke when he opened the door, seeing Earl. "What brings you here? Do you want some coffee?"

"I could go for some coffee," said Earl. "Is the sheriff up yet? I need to talk to both of you."

"Ya, he's in da kitchen," said Luke. "Come on in."

Walking into the kitchen, Lloyd looked up surprised to see that it was Earl this early. "What's up?" asked Lloyd.

Earl, seeing Maria, said, "Hello, ma'am. I hear congratulations are in order."

"Thank you, Earl," said Maria. "It's nice to see a man with manners. Would you like some breakfast? I was just starting some for Lloyd and Luke."

"Thank you, ma'am," said Earl. "I sure would like that."

"Have a seat," said Maria. "I'll get you some coffee."

Sitting down, Earl looked at Luke and asked, "Did you tell Lloyd what you told me last night?"

"Na, I ain't had a chance as yet," said Luke.

After Earl and Luke had sat down, Lloyd said, "Well, are you going to fill me in on what is going on around here, or do I have to guess?"

Luke said, "Ya remember mah go'n out ta check out that fella last night?" Lloyd nodded before Luke went on. "I found him in da saloon playing poker. He had his back ta me, so I stood back in da shadows where he couldn't get a good look at me. When he turned to order a bottle, I saw his face. Well, I done seen him befer. He was one of da men I saw with Fry. So I done told Earl that he ought ta keep an eye on him ta see what he did."

"I did like you said," said Earl. "About midnight, the game broke up. I was just going back to the saloon and saw it breaking up, so I waited outside to see where he was headed. He went right to the hotel, and it looks like he's got the room up front. If you don't want him to see you, you're going to have to be careful going to and from the office.

"Maybe you should stay away from the office until he leaves town," said Lloyd.

Maria brought breakfast over, placing the ham and eggs on the table with fresh bread. She sat down with them and filled her plate after the men had filled theirs. Everyone started eating quietly, thinking about what to do next.

Luke was trying to figure out the next move Fry would make if he knew that he was in town. Would they try and come after him, or would they act like they didn't know him and make other plans?

If they didn't find out about the shipment of money, then they were just waiting out the winter. If that was the case and they found out about Luke, they may try and ambush him, thinking that he might be following them again. If they knew about the money, they might be waiting until it arrived. They needed to find out what Fry was up to.

"How long do you think he will stay in town if he doesn't see you?" asked Lloyd.

"I don't know," said Luke, "but when he leaves, I should be able to follow him ta where the rest are. The mark I put on his shoe should be easy ta follow."

"I think we need to keep you under wraps for a while and see what he does," said Lloyd.

"What about our wedding on Sunday?" asked Maria.

"His being here won't affect the wedding," said Lloyd.

"Won't he see Luke if he is still in town?" asked Maria.

"You may have something," said Lloyd. "Maybe I can help him along so he will leave town before Sunday. Luke, I think we can find a place where you can stay out of sight until he leaves and still see what's going on in town."

Earl said, "The Longs have a barn nearby that would allow Luke to see most of the street. No one has been using it for some time. We could check it out on our way back to the office."

Finishing breakfast, they went to the Long's barn. Its location was just what Luke needed. From there, he could watch the main street. With the door in the back of the barn, he could come and go to the sheriff's, remaining hidden from the main street. Luke went into the barn while Lloyd and Earl went to the office.

Reynolds got up early and was watching the main street when he saw two men walking toward the sheriff's office. He recognized the sheriff and thought that the second man looked familiar but couldn't make him out. That must have been the new fella they heard about. He must have been the one he saw leaving the office last night. Reynolds decided to wait to see if he would come out again. After an hour of seeing no one coming or going, he decided to go eat breakfast. Leaving the hotel, he went straight to the café, where most of the morning crowd had finished their breakfast. Sitting down, he ordered breakfast and started thinking about how long he was going to be staying in town.

Luke entered the barn and took a look around. Looking around, he saw where a horse had been tied and left standing for some time. There were droppings not over a month old. Making his way to the loft, he found a spot where he could watch the street. While he was sitting there, he saw Reynolds leave the hotel and go to the café. It was some time before he saw Reynolds leaving the café. Luke figured that Reynolds was not in a hurry to leave town.

When the waitress came with his food, Reynolds asked, "Have you seen any strangers in town lately?"

"Only a couple besides yourself," said the waitress.

"I heard talk that the sheriff has got himself a new deputy. Have you met him?" asked Reynolds.

"I saw him a few times but haven't met him," said the waitress.

"You don't happen to know where he might be from, do you?" asked Reynolds.

"I heard someone mention once that they heard he might be from Virginia, but they couldn't say for sure," said the waitress. "What's your interest in him?"

"Thanks. I was wondering if he might be someone I knew during the war," said Reynolds. He sat and ate his breakfast, thinking about what the waitress had just told him. He needed now more than ever to get a good look at him. Maybe he would just stop in at the sheriff's office and see if he was there.

Earl was looking out the window when he saw Reynolds go to the café. Maybe Herb at the saloon had overheard the stranger talk about why he was in town or mention his name. Leaving the office, he decided that he would go to the saloon and talk to him. Herb was just finishing sweeping the floor when Earl entered. "Mornin,' Earl. What can I do for you?" asked Herb.

"Mornin,' Herb," said Earl. "That stranger that was in here last night, did you happen to get his name?"

"I recall one of the fellas playing poker called him Reynolds or something like that," said Herb.

"You didn't happen to hear why he was in town, did you?" asked Earl.

"Na. With the poker game going on, most of the talk was just about the game," said Herb.

"Thanks," said Earl, turning to leave. As he reached the door, he looked back at Herb and said, "If he comes back in and you hear why he's here, let us know."

"If I hear, I'll come and tell you," said Herb.

Earl went back to the office, where he found the sheriff still sitting at his desk. When he looked up, the sheriff asked, "Where did you run off to?"

"I went over to see Herb at the saloon to see if he found out who the stranger was," said Earl. "Herb said he thought the man's name was Reynolds or something like that."

"Did you go by and tell Luke?" asked the sheriff.

"Na. Figured we could tell him later when we saw him," said Earl.

"I'll be seeing him at dinner," said the sheriff. "I'll mention the name and see if it means anything to him."

They spent the rest of the morning working in the office. At one time while they were in the office, Earl thought he saw Reynolds stop and look through the window long enough to see who was inside before going on.

Later in the morning, Mr. Olson came in from the bank to tell them that the money shipment would be arriving on the fifteenth of the month. He figured the sheriff needed the extra time to prepare for it.

The sheriff asked, "Are you putting on guards at the bank once you receive it?"

"It will be safe once it is put into the vault," said Mr. Olson. "We haven't had anyone get into it yet."

"You know once the money is in your bank you are responsible for it," said the sheriff. "We won't be putting on extra deputies to watch it for you. If you want any extra protection for that money, the bank will have to get it."

"We haven't had any problems in the past, and I don't expect any now," said Mr. Olson. "The only ones who know about it in town are here in this office and the bank."

"I hope you're right, Mr. Olson," said the sheriff. "I know what that money means to the people hereabout."

After Mr. Olson left, no one else showed up at the office before noon. At noontime, the sheriff told Earl that he was going to go home for dinner and he would pick up Luke on the way.

When Luke saw Reynolds go into the café, it was a short time later when he saw Earl walk to the saloon. Earl wasn't in the saloon long before he left to go back to the office. Sometime after that, Luke noticed Reynolds leaving the café. He continued to watch him as he walked around town, stopping and looking in all the business windows. Reynolds seemed to be spending a lot of extra time when he got to the sheriff's office before moving on. The only thing that

Luke could think of was that he was looking for him. Seeing that Luke had recognized him in the saloon, there was a good chance that he would recognize Luke if he saw him.

At noontime, Luke saw the sheriff leave the office and walk toward the barn. As the sheriff approached the barn Luke got down from the loft and met the sheriff at the door. "Lloyd," said Luke, "I want to show ya that someone had used this barn a month or so ago."

Going back into the barn, Luke showed the sheriff the horse droppings.

"That's interesting," said the sheriff. "That was about the same time you came into town and Earl thought he saw someone by the bank. By the way, Earl told me that Herb said his name was Reynolds. He heard it last night when he was playing poker. One of the fellas at the table called him that when he brought a bottle over to the table."

"Reynolds," said Luke. "That was a name of one of Fry's men. If it's da Reynolds I'm think'n of, I killed one of his friends when Hicks and I raided their hideout. If I recall, he was none too happy about it and swore ta kill us."

"If it is him, he may try and get even if he sees you," said the sheriff. "Let's go get some dinner. I am sure Maria has it ready by now."

They continued to talk as they walked to the house. Luke was glad to be back in a warm building after spending the morning in the barn. Maria was glad to see Lloyd as she had come up with more ideas that she wanted for the wedding. Lloyd just shook his head and said okay. Maria had beaten him down to where all he said was yes, and they weren't even married yet.

Luke wondered if his pa went through the same thing before he married his ma. "If mah pa went though this, then I can tell ya it gets better after da wedding," Luke said, laughing.

When Lloyd and Luke entered the house, Maria had dinner ready for them. They sat down and waited for Maria to join them. Maria and Lloyd talked about the upcoming wedding while they ate. Luke just sat quietly eating.

Reynolds spent the morning in his room watching the street. When the sheriff left the office at noon heading for his home, Reynolds decided to follow him. Hurrying down to the street, he waited until the sheriff was out of sight before leaving the hotel, looking up and down the street to see who might see him. Not seeing anyone, he crossed the street. After crossing the street, he took one last look before going around the corner. Rounding the corner, he caught sight of the sheriff heading toward a barn. Stopping back in the shadows where he could watch, he waited. He didn't have long to wait until he saw another man come out of the barn and motion for the sheriff to follow him. Reynolds continued to wait until the sheriff and the other man reappeared.

Reynolds followed them, staying some distance behind until the sheriff and Luke entered the house. Reynolds figured that the house must belong to the man that had joined the sheriff. Waiting to see if anyone came out, he just stood there for some time. When no one came back out, he decided to go get himself something to eat. At the café, he took a table near the window where he could watch for the sheriff's return. While he was sitting waiting, Earl came in and took a table near the wall where he could keep an eye on everyone in the café.

Earl was looking out of the window after the sheriff left when he saw Reynolds come out of the hotel and cross the street. At first Earl thought that Reynolds was going to the saloon, but as he kept watching, he saw Reynolds following the sheriff. Earl started to leave the office and was going after Reynolds when Dave from the bank came walking up. Dave stopped and talked to Earl while Earl was trying to get away. By the time he got away, he had lost track of Reynolds, so he returned to the office to finish his work. As he was leaving for the café, he saw Reynolds returning from the direction the sheriff had gone, going toward the café. He continued to wait and watch as Reynolds went in the café. While he was watching Reynolds, he wondered what Reynolds had been up to. There were no businesses, only that empty barn, unless he was following the sheriff. If he had followed the sheriff, he might have seen Luke. Walking to the café, he entered, taking a seat where he could keep an eye on Reynolds. After ordering his meal, he didn't pay attention to Reynolds. He did notice that Reynolds was taking an interest in him. Earl could see that Reynolds kept watching him as he ate.

When Luke and the sheriff finished eating, they left the house and Luke went back to the barn. The sheriff decided to walk around town before going back to the office. The sheriff wanted to find out where Reynolds was keeping himself. It seemed that no one had seen him since breakfast. Maybe he was holed up in the hotel. If he ran into him, he wanted to know how long and what he was doing in town. People did not just come to town and stay without some purpose. As the sheriff walked around, he missed seeing Reynolds in the café. Back at the office, he sat down to wait for Earl to return.

Reynolds saw the sheriff coming back onto the main street by himself. He continued to watch as the sheriff made his rounds checking each business. When the sheriff went into his office, Reynolds left the café and went to the saloon.

Earl watched Reynolds get up and leave the café. Getting up, he went to the window and watched where Reynolds went. Seeing him go into the saloon, Earl went back to the office. At the office, Lloyd asked, "Have you seen Reynolds lately?"

"I was just in the café where he was eating. He just went into the saloon," said Earl.

"I thought I'd ask him what he was doing in town. Seeing he is new to these parts, it would be proper for me to check him out," said Lloyd.

"After you left to get Luke, I saw Reynolds come out of the hotel going down the street after you. I started to follow but got stopped by Dave, so I didn't see where he went. He was gone for some time before he returned, like he might have followed you to your house. Do you want me to come with you?" asked Earl.

"Naw," said Lloyd. "I'll just stop by the saloon and talk to him friendly like."

The sheriff got up, putting on his coat before leaving. Entering the saloon, there were a couple of men standing at the bar talking to Herb. Taking a look around, he saw Reynolds sitting near the window where he could watch the street. The sheriff knew that Reynolds saw him when he left the office, and he was still watching as he entered. Looking around after entering, he saw that Reynolds kept watching to see what he would do next. Walking over to where Reynolds was sitting, Reynolds looked up at him and said, "Howdy, Sheriff. What can I do for you?"

"I've seen you in town these past couple of days and was wondering what we can do for you," said the sheriff. "Wondering if you're passing through or what?"

"Just passing through," said Reynolds. "I was to meet up with my partner here, but he hasn't showed up yet. He might have got himself held up with the snow that we been having."

"What's your partner's name?" asked the sheriff. "I'll ask around and see if anyone heard of him coming through town."

"Thanks," said Reynolds. "I'd appreciate it. His name is Herbert. He's a big fella with dark hair and a scar on his face. You can't miss him if you see him."

"I'll keep an eye out for him," said the sheriff. "Are you at the hotel, or where should I tell him where he can find you if I come across him?"

"I'll be at the hotel," said Reynolds.

The sheriff turned, leaving the saloon, and went back to his office. Earl was in the back sweeping out the cells when Lloyd opened the door. When he heard Lloyd enter, he went back to the office to make sure that it was Lloyd. Seeing that it was the sheriff, he asked, "Did you find him?"

"Yes, I did. He was in the saloon like you said."

"What did he have to say for himself?" asked Earl.

"He said he was in town waiting for his partner," said Lloyd. "He may be waiting for a partner, but I think he is still trying to find out if he knows Luke. Since you told me that he looked like he might have followed me at noon. We will need to keep a closer watch of him."

Leaving the house, Luke decided to go to the livery to check on his horses instead of the barn. As he entered the stable, Buck recognized him and nickered. Luke went to him first and started rubbing him down. He could see that George must have put all three of the horses in the corral, as they had mud on them from rolling. At least they had a chance to do more than stand in a stall. Getting a brush, Luke took his time brushing each of the horses.

After the sheriff left, Reynolds finished his drink and left. He decided that he would make his way to the barn to see if the second man had returned. He was thinking that if the other man was there, he would get a chance to see what he looked liked. If it was the fella from Virginia, he could leave town before raising any more suspicion from the sheriff. Not wanting anyone to see him going into the barn, he started up the street in a direction taking him away from the barn. Once he was far enough up the street, he circled around. He made his way back to the barn, staying out of sight. Once he got to where he could see the barn, he stopped, looking for any movement before going on. Making his way to the back of the barn, he found a door open. Quietly entering the barn, he stopped and listened. Not hearing any movement, he looked around the barn. Not seeing or hearing anyone, he decided to go back to the hotel. Walking out the front of the barn in the open, he went straight to the hotel.

Luke was leaving the livery when he saw what he thought might be Reynolds coming out of the barn. Stepping back, he watched through the open door of the stable as the man leaving the barn went straight to the hotel. When he saw the man enter the hotel, he figured it had to be Reynolds. If it was Reynolds, why would he be checking out that barn unless he had been following the sheriff and saw the two of them leaving it? He would mention it to the sheriff. It was a good thing that he decided to check on his horses or Reynolds might have seen him at the barn. He might be better off staying at the livery. While he was standing there deciding, George walked in. Seeing Luke, he asked, "What's up?"

"I just stopped by ta see mah horses," said Luke. "I was about ta leave when I saw Reynolds and decided ta watch fer a while. Do ya mind if'n I sit a spell?"

"Help yourself," said George. "I'll be glad to have the company. What's up with this Reynolds fella anyway?"

"We're trying ta figure that one out ourselves," said Luke. "I think I know'd him from Virginia, and if I do, he's no good."

"Well, make yourself at home. I got some work to do," said George as he picked up a pitchfork and went to the back of the barn. Luke continued to stand by the door for some time watching the street. Not seeing anything out of the ordinary, he decided to go to the office. This sitting and hiding was not his way. Maybe he just needed to face Reynolds and see what happened.

When Luke entered the office, Lloyd and Earl both looked up, surprised to see him. "What are you doing here?" asked Lloyd.

"Figured no sense hiding," said Luke. "I might as well face him and see what happens. If he sees me, he may lead us ta Fry."

"You might want to go over to the saloon where I talked to him earlier," said Lloyd.

"He ain't there," said Luke. "I saw him go inta da barn befer he headed back ta da hotel. He might have seen me come in here. If he did, maybe he will come out."

"Earl, you head on over to the saloon and see if he comes back," said Lloyd. "Luke, you can stay here and watch the front of the hotel to see if he leaves."

Reynolds went directly to his room after entering the hotel. He looked out the window in time to see Luke going into the sheriff's office. This time he got a glimpse of Luke's face and was almost sure it was the fella from Panther Gap. Sitting down, he had to think of what he would do next. As he sat there, he thought about the time that the dynamite blew up the bunkhouse, killing Frank. When the dynamite went off, it drove splinters of wood into Franks face, knocking him back into the lamp and catching him on fire. Reynolds still remembered the screams that Frank made as he burned to death. The longer he sat there thinking about it, the madder he got. If he got the chance, he would kill Luke. Getting up, he decided to go back to the saloon and get a bottle. When he got to the saloon, he went straight to the bar and got a bottle before finding a table where he could sit with his back to a wall near the back of the saloon. He was still thinking about Frank when he got to the saloon and didn't pay any attention to the deputy he passed.

Pouring a drink, he downed it without tasting it. He continued to pour drink after drink until half the bottle was gone.

Earl watched Reynolds as he went through half the bottle. Seeing that it looked like Reynolds was bothered by something, Earl decided to go back to the office and let Luke know what was going on. Luke was waiting when Earl entered. "Saw Reynolds go inta da saloon," said Earl.

"What's he do'n?" asked Luke.

"He got himself a bottle, and he's sitting at the back of the room drinking," said Earl. "It looked like he's got something on his mind 'cause he had gone through half of the bottle without stopping."

"Maybe I need ta go have a talk with him," said Luke.

"I'll go with you," said Lloyd.

When they got to the saloon, Luke told Lloyd that he wanted to go in alone. He didn't want Reynolds to think they were ganging up on him. He wanted to find out for sure if he was one of Fry's men. Lloyd agreed to let Luke go in by himself. He would wait and try to come in unnoticed.

Luke entered the saloon, stopping long enough to look around. Seeing Reynolds still sitting where Earl had said, Luke walked over to the table.

Through the window, Lloyd watched as Luke approached Reynolds. Lloyd could see that Reynolds was shocked when he recognized Luke. Taking advantage of Reynolds's concern about Luke, he entered the saloon and stepped off to the side, keeping to the shadows but keeping Reynolds in sight.

Reynolds looked up at the person who had approached him and was about to order another bottle, thinking it was the barkeep, when he recognized Luke. At first he was too shocked to say anything. Once he collected himself, he asked, "What do you want, deputy? I've already been questioned by your sheriff."

"I want ta know where Fry's hiding," said Luke.

"I don't know any Fry. What makes you think I would know that?" asked Reynolds.

"'Cause ya ride with him," said Luke. "Ya were with him at Panther Gap, and ya were with him during da raid at da Meyer place."

"You don't know what you're talking about," said Reynolds. "I ain't never heard of that fella, nor have I ever been in Panther Gap. Like I told the sheriff, I am waiting for my partner to meet me here."

"As soon as da wire comes back from da Marshal at Panther Gap, we'll see who ya are," said Luke. Turning his back to Reynolds, he started for the door when a shot rang out. Looking at where the shot came from, Luke saw the sheriff holding his still-smoking gun. Turning and looking behind him, he saw Reynolds holding his shoulder where the sheriff had shot him. Both Luke and the sheriff went over to Reynolds. The sheriff was still holding his gun on Reynolds while Luke picked up the revolver that Reynolds had dropped.

"Get up," said the sheriff. "You have just tried to shoot your last man in the back. You're going to jail for attempted murder of my deputy."

Earl came busting through the front doors with his gun drawn. Seeing that everything was under control, he put his gun away. "Get the doc and meet us at the jail," said the sheriff.

Earl turned to get the doctor while the sheriff and Luke took Reynolds to the jail. The sheriff put Reynolds into a cell while Luke locked up his gun. It wasn't long before Earl returned with the doctor. It took the doctor about an hour to patch up Reynolds's shoulder. When he finished, he went back to his office while Reynolds lay in his cell resting.

After the doctor left, Earl asked, "Now what are we going to do? We just can't let him go so that Luke can follow him."

"I am sure that if he does not return to Fry's camp, they will send someone else to find out what happened to him," said Lloyd. "Luke, you know these men better than we do. What do you think they will do?"

"If they do what they did in Panther Gap, they will try ta get Reynolds out of jail when they find out where he is," said Luke. "We need ta look fer any strangers asking questions about Reynolds."

Now that they had a prisoner, the sheriff decided that Earl and Luke needed to take turns keeping an eye on him. That was okay with Luke, as he wanted to move out of the sheriff's house since he was getting married in a couple of days. The sheriff told Luke to go over to the hotel and gather Reynolds's gear so they could see if they might find any information on where the rest of the men might be located.

At the hotel, Luke told the clerk that he had lost a guest that he was now a guest of the sheriff. The clerk gave Luke the key to the room so he could gather Reynolds's gear. Returning to the sheriff's office, they went through his things, but didn't find anything that would tell them where Fry was hiding. Now they would have to wait and see what Fry did next.

Reynolds had been gone for almost a week, and Fry was beginning to wonder what had happened to him. By now he should have been able to find out if the new man was one of the boys from Virginia. Calling Herbert to the house, he instructed him to go to town and find out what happened to Reynolds.

"Herbert," said Fry, "if you don't see Reynolds around town and have to ask about him, tell people that you were to meet him and you were wondering if he had made it to town before you."

Herbert got his gear together and rode to town. It was late in the afternoon before he arrived. Going to the livery, he put up his horse. While he was taking his gear off of his horse, he saw Reynolds's horse tied in one of the stalls. That meant that Reynolds was still in town, and he should be able to find him. Going to the hotel, he asked the clerk, "Do you have a room?"

"Yes, we do," said the clerk. "You need to put your name in the register."

While Herbert was recording his name in the register, he saw Reynolds's name in room two. When the clerk returned with the key to room three, Herbert said, "I see you have a man staying here by the name of Reynolds. Do you know where he might be?"

"He was staying here until today," said the clerk. "I heard that he is now staying in the jail. Do you know him?"

"The name sounds familiar. What happened?" asked Herbert.

"Word is something about a shooting at the saloon," said the clerk. "If you want to find out more, you need to talk to the sheriff. Here's the key to room three, up the stairs on the right."

"Thanks," said Herbert. "The fella I am thinking of doesn't carry a gun unless he's on the trail, so it's probably not him." Taking his key, he went up the stairs to his room. After he got to his room, he put his gear away before deciding to go to the saloon. If the shooting took place in the saloon, maybe he could find out some information without giving away who he was. Maybe Reynolds did recognize the fella and shot him. When he got to the saloon, he went straight to the bar. Herb was at the other end of the bar to talk to a couple of customers. Herbert caught a few words about the shooting. When Herb came over to see what Herbert wanted, Herbert ordered a whiskey and asked, "Did I hear you say something about a shooting in here?"

"Just today," said Herb. "The sheriff shot this fella who's been hanging around for about a week. Seems he tried to shoot one of the deputies in the back, but the sheriff was here and shot him first.

It's a shame that it all had to happen just a couple of days before the sheriff's wedding."

"Do you know why the fella tried to shoot the deputy?" asked Herbert.

"Can't say why," said Herb. "The deputy came in and talked to him, and when he turned to leave, the fella pulled a gun and tried to shoot him in the back. The sheriff was standing by the bar, and when he saw him pull the gun, he shot and wounded the fella. The sheriff has him locked up in the jail."

"The fella must have had some kind of grudge against the deputy to pull something like that," said Herbert.

Herbert ordered another whiskey and a beer. After serving the drinks, Herb went back to the men at the other end of the bar. Herbert overheard one of the men say, "Herb, I heard that the sheriff was getting married this Sunday."

Herb replied, "Ya, Earl said it should be a big wedding if Maria has her way." All the men laughed, knowing that she would get her way if she was like the other women in town.

Herbert finished his drink and went to the café. He would spend the night in town before going back to the farm. If the sheriff was getting married on Sunday, they might have a chance to break Reynolds out of jail while the town was busy with the wedding. Finishing his supper, he went back to the hotel, staying out of sight.

Earl went to the café early to eat his supper so he could bring back supper for the prisoner. Leaving the café with the meal for the prisoner, he noticed a fella coming out of the saloon that he did not recognize. When he got back to the office, the sheriff and Luke left for supper. Luke told Earl that he would be back later so they could make their rounds.

Finishing their supper, Luke could see that Lloyd and Maria had things that needed worked out for the wedding. Getting up, he went back to the office. Earl was sitting at his desk when Luke walked in. "I'll sit here if you want ta make da rounds," said Luke.

"It might feel good to stretch my legs some, and I can take the tray back to the café," said Earl. Going by the café, Earl stopped and talked to the waitress before going on with his rounds. He stopped by the saloon, and not seeing anyone or anything out of place, he went on. Taking his time, he was gone about an hour before returning to the office. Entering the office, he said, "The town sure looks quiet tonight. I would think it would take some time before anyone came looking for Reynolds."

"Good," said Luke. "I'll just stay here in da office tonight anyway. I'll be moving mah gear ta da hotel tomorrow."

The night went without any incidences. Luke made rounds near midnight and only found the normal customers in the saloon. Come morning when the sheriff arrived, both Luke and Earl went to the café for breakfast. While they were eating, Luke noticed a stranger leaving the hotel and going to the livery. Shortly after he entered the livery, he reappeared with his horse. Without even looking around, he mounted and rode out of town. Luke didn't give him a second thought.

When Luke and Earl finished their breakfast, Earl went back to the office while Luke went to the sheriff's house to get his gear. Maria was surprised to see him at this time of the day. "Is something wrong?" she asked.

"Nah," said Luke. "I just came ta get mah gear to move in ta da jail. Now that we got a prisoner, we need ta make sure he stays there." Luke went to his room and returned with his gear. Leaving the house, he went to the office and put his gear in the corner.

"What's this?" asked the sheriff.

"I thought I'd move in here now that we got one of Fry's men," said Luke. "Ya might want ta go home early taday ta get ready fer yer big wedding day tomorrow."

"I think I might do that. All seems quiet here," said Lloyd. With that, he got up and left.

the wedding

Herbert went to the house after putting up his horse. Fry had seen Herbert ride up alone, so he was in the frontroom waiting. As Herbert entered, Fry asked, "Did you find Reynolds?"

"I didn't see him, but the clerk at the hotel said he was in jail," said Herbert.

"Now what did he do?" asked Fry, thinking about what had happened in Panther Gap.

"According to the barkeep at the saloon, he tried to shoot a deputy in the back but got shot by the sheriff instead," said Herbert.

"Did the barkeep say why Reynolds tried to shoot the deputy?" asked Fry.

"He just said that the deputy had been talking to Reynolds while he was drinking, and he had gotten drunk. When the deputy turned to walk away, he pulled his gun," said Herbert.

"Did anyone connect you with Reynolds?" asked Fry.

"The clerk at the hotel knows I was looking for him," said Herbert. "But the barkeep was talking to some customers about the shooting when I walked in, so he figured I was just curious when I asked."

"Now we need to get Reynolds out of jail," said Fry. "I hope he hasn't messed up our chances for that money coming in. The only reason Reynolds would try and shoot the deputy is if he recognized him."

"I heard some other news about the sheriff," said Herbert. "It seems he is getting married tomorrow, and it sounds like the whole town may be at the wedding. If that's so, we might be able to get Reynolds out of jail while the wedding is going on."

Fry sat thinking for a while before he said, "If we can get Reynolds out of jail without the town seeing us, we can still hit the bank when the money arrives. Call the boys together."

The sheriff finished some paperwork he had started before getting up to go home. There were a lot of unfinished tasks that Maria had wanted him to do for their wedding tomorrow. Leaving the office, he stopped by the general store to pick up some items that she needed for the reception. He was thinking as he headed to the general store that this was going to be a bigger celebration than the Fourth of July. Maria had done a lot of organizing in the short time she had.

The Graves had his items waiting for him when he arrived. Mr. Graves said to the sheriff as he paid, "Well, Sheriff, are you a bit nervous about tomorrow?"

"Not sure if I should be nervous or if I should just run," said the sheriff.

"We want to congratulate you anyway," said Mr. Graves. "You don't worry about a thing. Maria is a fine woman. We will see you at the church tomorrow."

"From what I heard, it sounds like most of the town plans on being there," said the sheriff. "Even Herb at the saloon said he was closing down to attend." Picking up his supplies, he left the store.

Entering the house, he found it full of the town's women. Some were decorating while others were cooking. Maria was nowhere to be seen. Mrs. Johnson saw the sheriff come in, and she stopped him, asking, "What are you doing here?"

"Last I looked I lived here and come to help," said the sheriff. "Here are the supplies that Maria ordered from the general store. Where is Maria anyway?"

"You can't see her," said Mrs. Johnson. "She is in the bedroom with some of the women finishing her dress for tomorrow. You give me those things, and you go back to your office. We have everything under control here."

"Should I come back tonight?" asked the sheriff.

"No. Maria is going to be staying here, and you can't see her until the wedding," said Mrs. Johnson. "You need to stay with a friend or at the hotel tonight. I'll have one of the ladies bring your suit by for tomorrow. Now get." She was pushing him out of the house.

When he got back to the office, Earl looked at him, surprised to see him, and asked, "I thought you were going home to help. What happened?"

"They kicked me out of my own house and told me to stay at the hotel," said the sheriff.

The sheriff put his hat and coat on the coat rack before going to his desk. When the sheriff sat down, he said, "Why don't you two go check the town?"

Getting their coats, Earl and Luke left the office to make their rounds. As they headed toward the livery, Earl said, "It sure looks like Maria has Lloyd on the tame."

"Seems ta me that a woman can do that ta a man," said Luke. "Mah pa said that mah ma tamed him fer he know'd it."

They walked to the livery without talking. Entering the livery, George was working on a plow for one of the farmers. Looking up when they entered, he stopped and asked, "What are the two of you up to?"

Earl said, "The sheriff kicked us out."

George looked at them with a puzzled look, asking, "What's the sheriff gone and done now?"

"Since he asked Maria to marry him, it seems that he has gone and gotten himself roped and hog tied," Earl said, laughing. "He went home to help and got kicked out of his own house."

George laughed and went back to working on the plow.

Luke asked, "Have ya seen any strangers lately?"

"A fella rode in late yesterday and left early this morning," said George. "I figured he must have been passing through."

"Did he ask any questions while he was here?" asked Earl.

"No. Just paid for his horse and rode out," said George.

"Thanks," said Earl. Both Luke and Earl turned, leaving. They stopped by the café. Earl talked to the waitress while Luke stood listening. The waitress said much the same that George had. Next they went to the saloon. When they entered the saloon, Luke said, "Let me buy ya a beer."

Earl nodded as they walked to the bar. Herb asked, "What'll it be, gents?"

"Give us a couple of beers," said Luke.

When Herb returned with their beers, Luke asked, "Did ya see the stranger who come ta town in here yesterday?"

"Ya, the fella came in late yesterday. He had a couple of drinks and left," said Herb.

"Did he ask any questions while he was in here?" asked Luke.

"He asked about the shooting," said Herb. "I was talking about it with some of the boys when he came in. I figured he probably heard us talking about it and got curious. He did ask if I knew what caused it, but that's all. I ain't seen him since."

"Nobody saw much of him while he was in town. I take it he must have been passing through," said Earl. "Even George said he didn't see anything about the man to cause a concern."

"It sure seems ta be that way," said Luke.

They finished their beer before finishing their walk around town. They were careful checking each of the businesses as they finished their rounds. When they got to the hotel, they didn't go in, figuring that they would hear the same story about the stranger that they had already heard. Going back to the office, they told the sheriff what they had found. He agreed that it must have been someone just passing through.

The rest of the afternoon was quiet. Both Earl and Luke noticed that as the day went on Lloyd was acting more and more nervous. Lloyd would get up and go check on the prisoner.

Reynolds was up moving around in his cell when Luke looked in on him. He had continued to refuse to talk even when the sheriff questioned him on why he tried to shoot Luke in the back. The judge was due in the first part of next week, and the sheriff knew that if they couldn't get him for the Meyer raid, they still had him for attempted murder.

After the sheriff finished questioning him, Reynolds sat in his cell thinking about Fry. If he did get out of jail, Fry would be very upset with him for trying to kill Luke and failing. He remembered what had happened at Panther Gap when some of the men tried to kill him in the café and failed. Now how was he to get word to Fry about the deputy and him being in jail?

Near suppertime Lloyd, Earl, and Luke decided to go to the café to eat. Locking the door, they walked to the café. Entering the café, they found that there were several customers eating. Making their way to the table, several customers stopped the sheriff and congratulated him.

Luke and Earl got to the table ahead of the sheriff and sat down. By the time he arrived, the waitress was standing there talking to Earl. When the sheriff sat down, she congratulated him. After taking their order, she left. Earl asked, "So Lloyd, is everything ready for the wedding?"

"When I went by the house, it looked like the womenfolk were busy," said Lloyd. "They told me to get out until after the wedding. So I have to assume that they have everything in hand."

"What are you going to do with your last night of freedom?" asked Luke.

"Hadn't thought about it," said Lloyd. "I guess I'll just spend the time at the office."

"Earl, we need ta take Lloyd ta da saloon fer a drink," said Luke. "Maybe we can get rid of some of his fears about get'n hitched."

"What do you know about being married?" asked Lloyd. "You ain't never been married."

"Nope. I ain't never been married and don't plan on it for some time," said Luke. "But ya look like a stallion in a pasture full of mares da way ya been prancing around da office taday."

When their food came, the sheriff was glad as the two deputies started eating and left him alone. When the sheriff wasn't being congratulated, they talked about what they were going to do about the prisoner during the ceremony. Finally the sheriff said, "We'll lock the jail like we did tonight. We haven't seen any strangers around town that would cause us concern. The only one you heard about left again. If he had hung around and asked a lot of questions, then we would have to make sure someone stayed with him. Seeing how he didn't, we can relax."

The sheriff ordered supper for Reynolds. The waitress brought a tray of food, giving it to Earl as they were leaving. As they walked back to the office, the sheriff said, "Earl, you had better look out. I think that Kaitlin has her eyes on you. If you ain't careful, you'll be marching down that aisle as well."

"Naw, her and I are just friends," said Earl.

"I'd say she's got that look like Maria had fer Lloyd," said Luke. "Ya better watch yer step."

Now it was Lloyd's turn to laugh while Earl's face turned red. "Heck, Earl," said Lloyd. "It ain't so bad."

Entering the office, Earl took the food to Reynolds. When Reynolds was done, Earl collected the tray, taking it back to the café. When Earl finally returned from the café, Lloyd said, "Luke, I think it might be sooner than later for Earl."

Luke just laughed. Earl tried to ignore them, acting like he was working. About ten o'clock, Earl said, "I think we need to get the sheriff out of the office so he can get the rest he is going to need. We don't want him to fall over during the ceremony.

"Sure enough," said Luke. "I think he needs a drink or two to relax so he can get some sleep tanight. Come on, Lloyd."

With Luke on one side and Earl on the other, they headed for the saloon. Entering the saloon, they could see it was full of customers. Going to the bar, Earl ordered drinks for all three. Once their drinks were served, Earl said, "You know that tonight is the sheriff's last night of freedom. So let's make sure he has a good one."

Several of the men came up to congratulate the sheriff. It didn't take long before the sheriff had several drinks lined up. Seeing that the sheriff was going to be well taken care of, Luke went back to the office. At the office, Luke saw that Reynolds was lying on his cot. Putting the bar on the front door, Luke lay down.

Sometime later, he woke with a start. He lay still trying to figure out what had woken him. Hearing a gunshot followed by several more, he jumped up to see what was going on. Looking out, he saw several drunk cowboys in front of the saloon firing their guns in the air. He went out to try and quiet them down. He saw that Earl was one of them. Looking around, he didn't see the sheriff. Maybe he was still in the saloon. Before going into the saloon, he was able to get the men to start for home. He told Earl to go to the jail.

Inside the saloon, the sheriff was still standing by the bar more asleep than awake. It looked like everyone in the saloon had been celebrating since he had left. Herb said, "He ain't going to be feeling too good come morning. I ain't seen the sheriff drink like he did tonight. It's a good thing that he's got you."

Luke took the sheriff by the arm and led him to the hotel. Once he got him to his room, he went back to make sure Earl had made it to the jail. There were only a couple of them still standing by the front door. Before going to the office, he went over to make sure that the men headed for home as well.

When Luke went into the saloon, some of the men got up and headed for the door. After the saloon had emptied out, he went to the office where Earl was standing by the desk, not knowing where to go next. Luke led him to one of the empty cells. Going back to the office, he lay down.

Lloyd woke in the morning with his head hurting. He was wondering what he had gotten himself into. With the wedding not starting till noon, he had time. Washing up, he got dressed and went to the office. When he arrived, he found the front door barred. Rapping on the door, Luke opened it. Entering the office, Lloyd saw that Earl was still sleeping. It appeared that Reynolds was in better shape this morning than Earl or himself.

Back in the office, Luke said. "Ya sure look like ya had a rough night last night. How are ya feeling?"

"I'll live," said Lloyd. "I see the prisoner is doing better this morning."

"He'll be all right," said Luke. "He slept through da night and woke up asking fer food this morn."

"I could use some food myself," said Lloyd. "Wake Earl, and we can go get some breakfast."

When they came from the back, Lloyd locked the door before going to the café. While they were walking, Luke looked up at the sky and said, "It looks like yer gonna have a good day fer da wedding."

Lloyd grunted, keeping his head down and shading his eyes from the sun. Maybe after he got some food in his stomach he would feel better. He had not done any drinking like he did last night since he was young. Entering the café, Kaitlin noticed that Lloyd and Earl did not look too good. By the time they got to a table, she had their coffee ready for them. Looking at Lloyd and Earl, she asked, "What was all the shooting about last night? Did someone do too much celebrating?" She waited without getting an answer before she asked, "What can I get for you?"

Luke ordered first, and Kaitlin said, "At least it looks like one person didn't celebrate too much. Now what will you two have?" After taking their order, she went back to the kitchen. Lloyd was glad that there weren't any other customers in the café. He didn't want the townspeople to see him in the condition he was in. When they finished eating, Kaitlin brought out the breakfast for the prisoner. Leaving the café, they returned to the office. Luke decided to wait till Reynolds finished eating before making his rounds. He figured that both Lloyd and Earl didn't want to go out in the sunlight anytime soon.

When Reynolds finished his breakfast, Luke took his tray back to the café and ordered a dinner to be picked up before the wedding. His first stop after the café was the livery. He saw that George had already fed all the stock. Checking his horses, he gave each of them some grain. He also noticed that the horse belonging to Reynolds was still tied in a stall. Walking around town, he heard singing as he walked by the church. He figured that most of the townspeople would be in the church this time of the morning. He also figured that most of them would be back for the wedding. When he got back to the office, it looked like Lloyd and Earl were going to live after their night out. The three of them spent the rest of the morning in the office. When it got closer to noon, Lloyd went to the hotel to get ready, putting on his suit while Luke went to get Reynolds' dinner.

Sunday morning after breakfast, Fry called the three men he wanted to go to town with him. Saddling their horses, he laid out his plan. They would not go into town until they saw that the people had gone into the church. Once the wedding had started, they would be able to get Reynolds out without being seen. As they approached town, they saw that there were several people still on the street. Stopping before coming into full sight of town, they found a place where they could watch the town. When it was getting closer to noon, Fry saw a man coming out of the café carrying a tray and going to the jail. He figured that it had to be Reynolds's dinner.

From where they were sitting, they could see the church. Shortly after the man carrying the tray had left the café, the owner of the café came out and locked the door. Not long after that, they saw some women going into the church. One of the women looked like she was the bride. Fry figured that it wouldn't be long before the wedding would start. Fry and his men continued to watch as people started entering the church. After most of the people had entered the church, only three men remained outside. One of the men had to be the sheriff, and the others were his deputies. When the three men entered the church, Fry put his plan into motion.

Herbert went to the livery while Fry and the other two men made their way to the jail. Placing one of the men outside to watch the street, Fry and the other man entered the jail.

Herbert entered the livery from the back. Finding Reynolds's horse, he saddled him and took him to the jail.

Fry was surprised to find the front door of the sheriff's office unlocked. Opening the door with guns drawn, they had a second surprise when they found the office empty. Finding the door leading to the cells locked, they tried the keys hanging on the wall. It didn't take them long to find the key that unlocked the door. Taking the keys with them, they went to the cell that Reynolds occupied and let him out. Fry took time to roll up Reynolds's blanket to make it look like someone was sleeping and relocked the cell door. Going back into the office, he closed and locked the door leading to the cells, hanging the keys back on the wall. Looking out the front door, they made sure nobody was on the street. Leaving the office, they made their way to the back of the jail to Herbert and the waiting horses. Mounting, they rode out of town. As they passed the church, they heard singing, which told them that the wedding was still going on. Once out of town, they rode hard back to the farm.

Back at the farm, Reynolds told Fry that the new deputy was one of the boys from Virginia. Fry asked, "How much did you tell the sheriff?"

"I didn't say a thing to the sheriff," said Reynolds.

"Does he know where we're holed up?" asked Fry.

"He knows I am connected to you by that deputy, but he don't know where we're at," said Reynolds.

Fry began thinking on how he could get rid of Luke and still get the money. If they didn't get rid of this fella, he was sure that he would continue to follow them.

Lloyd, Earl, and Luke waited outside the front door of the church. When the preacher opened the door and said they were ready for them, Luke thought that Lloyd looked like he was ready to run. Once he got to the front of the church, he seemed to calm down some. When the music started and Maria started down the aisle, Lloyd began to smile. Seeing Maria in her wedding dress was the first time he realized that she was a lot more beautiful that he thought.

To Lloyd it felt like the ceremony went on for a lifetime. With all the music, the ceremony lasted just over an hour. The ceremony went without any problems. After the preacher pronounced them man and wife, Maria and Lloyd walked down the aisle and waited outside the doors to greet everyone. As they greeted everyone, they invited them to their house where Mrs. Graves and the town's ladies were preparing for the guests. Luke said he would take a walk by the office to make sure that Reynolds was okay.

Walking to the jail, he didn't see anything out of place. The street was empty with all the townspeople at the church.

Opening the front door to the office, he saw that the door between the office and the cells was still closed, and it appeared that nothing had changed since they had left. Checking the door, he found it locked, so instead of going in, he looked through the window in the door. Seeing Reynolds's cell, it looked like Reynolds was lying there asleep. Not wanting to disturb him, Luke left, going to the sheriff's house. By the time he arrived, it looked like the whole town was there celebrating. Not knowing most of the people, Luke got some food and sat down.

Luke saw that Earl was talking with Kaitlin from the café. Watching them, it reminded him of how he and Helen use to talk. Earl, seeing Luke by himself, walked over. "Was everything okay at the jail?" asked Earl.

"It looked like Reynolds was sleeping," said Luke.

"You need to get up and meet some of the people," said Earl.

"Nah, I think I'll go back ta da office," said Luke. "Ya can stay, and I'll keep watch on da prisoner."

Luke had a problem finding Maria and Lloyd with all the people in the house. Once he found them, he congratulated them and told Lloyd that Earl and him would take care of the prisoner and he should enjoy himself.

Arriving back at the jail, he again looked in the back. It looked like Reynolds was still sleeping. Seeing that everything seemed to be okay, Luke decided to go check on his horses. When he entered the stable, Buck nickered for him. Going over to Buck, Luke began to brush him. Once he finished brushing Buck, he brushed his other two horses. Turning to leave, he noticed that Reynolds's horse was missing from where he had been standing earlier that day. Maybe George had put him in the corral seeing that Reynolds was not going anywhere for a while. When he left the livery, he made his rounds before going back to the jail. While making his rounds, he saw that the café was again open. Entering the café, he ordered supper for the prisoner.

Back at the office, Luke put the tray of food down on the desk while he unlocked the door to the cells. Opening the door, he saw that Reynolds still had not moved. With the sun going down, Luke lit a lamp before going to Reynolds's cell. He began to wonder if Reynolds had died. Opening the cell, he entered with the lamp only to find that Reynolds was gone. Taking the lamp with him, Luke went outside to look at the ground for any tracks. Going around the corner of the jail, he saw where someone had been standing for a while, and he was joined by three other men. Following their tracks, he found where a fifth man waited with five horses. Checking the prints, Luke saw the print from Reynolds's horse where he had stood with the other horses. *Fry must have broken Reynolds out of jail while we were at the wedding,* thought Luke. Luke was now upset with himself for not taking a closer look at Reynolds when he first stopped after the wedding.

Following the tracks they left, he saw that they had headed west out of town. They hadn't hidden their tracks, which made it easy for him to follow. He continued to follow their trail for half a mile. It was now getting too dark to continue following them. He needed to go back and tell the sheriff what had happened.

When he arrived at the house, Earl saw Luke as he came through the front door. He could see by the look on Luke's face that something was wrong. Earl asked, "What's wrong? Did Reynolds die or something?"

"He's gone," said Luke. "Where is the sheriff?"

Earl pointed, indicating where he had last seen the sheriff. They found the sheriff talking to a couple of the men. When the sheriff saw Earl and Luke, he excused himself and went to see what was going on. When he got to them, he asked, "Is something wrong?"

Luke said, "Reynolds escaped. It looks like four men came in and got him out of jail while we were out of da office. They got Reynolds's horse from da livery, and I followed his tracks west out of town."

"Do you think you can follow them to their camp?" asked the sheriff.

"We should be able ta follow them come first light," said Luke.

"Keep this to yourselves for now," said the sheriff. "If someone from town is helping them, we don't want them knowing we might be able to track them. They might try and warn them before we have a chance to find them."

Luke said, "I am go'n back ta da office ta get ready ta leave at first light." Luke left the house and went back to the office. Back at the office, he put the gear together before going to sleep.

The celebrating at the sheriff's house went on till late before all the guests left. Earl was one of the last to leave. When Lloyd and Maria were alone, they were exhausted. Maria could see that something was bothering Lloyd. She was wondering if he was having second thoughts about getting married. Looking at him, she asked, "Are you sorry we got married today?"

"Huh?" said Lloyd. "No, I am not sorry we got married."

"What's wrong?" she asked. "You have been quiet ever since Luke came back. Is there something wrong at the jail?"

"Our prisoner escaped sometime today," said Lloyd. "We thought he was our lead to who raided the Meyer farm. Luke thinks he can track him come morning if there isn't too much traffic on the road. He wants to get started at first light."

"Come. Let's go to bed," said Maria. "I'll get this mess cleaned up in the morning."

Lloyd was awake before first light. Getting up, trying not to wake Maria, he got dressed. Stopping before leaving the bedroom, he took a last look at Maria sleeping and smiled to himself. When he got to the office, Luke was up and had made a fresh pot of coffee. Lloyd helped himself to a cup before Luke said, "Let me show ya what I found last night."

Taking Lloyd out back, he showed him where a man stood with the five horses. Luke also pointed out the print from Reynolds's horse. They followed the prints out of town for a short way. Luke pointed out that they should be able to follow them without too much trouble.

Returning to the office, Luke got his gear before going for their horses. Once they had saddled their horses and mounted, Luke led the way to the spot where he had stopped following the trail the night before. Stopping, Luke got down and double-checked the direction the five men had gone. Mounting again, they took their time following the trail. There had not been any traffic on the road that morning. Since Reynolds and the other four didn't know about the marked shoe, they weren't concerned about anyone following, so the trail left by Reynolds's horse was easy to follow. Luke could tell that the men were in a hurry. They rode hard for some time before they slowed down. Reynolds's horse continued to leave clear prints.

Having to take their time making sure that they didn't lose Fry's trail, it was late in the morning when they were near the Meyer farm. The trail continued past the farm and looked like it was following the same direction Luke had seen the cattle going. Stopping to give the horses a short rest, they chewed on some jerky. "When we find Fry's camp," said Luke, "if we find cattle there with Meyer's brand, then we will know they were da ones who killed da Meyers."

After they tightened their cinches, Lloyd and Luke mounted and continued to follow the trail. As they rode, Lloyd was feeling more confident that they were going to find out where Reynolds was hiding. He didn't have any proof on who had killed the Meyers, but if Luke was right about the cattle, it could be the proof he needed. It was only a couple of miles west of the Meyer farm where the trail turned south, following a small road.

Turning south, they rode for about a half a mile when Lloyd stopped. "Seems to me I heard of an abandoned farm about a mile or so from here," said Lloyd. "If it's the place I recall, it stands out in the open. If they are there, they would be able to see us coming from a ways off."

"Are ya familiar with da area?" asked Luke.

"I ain't had much call to be out here," said Lloyd. "If I remember right, when we top that hill up ahead, we should be able to see the place."

Luke started forward again, being more alert to their surroundings. If what Lloyd had said was true, they may need to find a place to get undercover. When they were near the top of the hill, they stopped and dismounted. Leaving the horses, they crawled to the top of the hill where they could see. Looking over the top of the hill, they did see the farm off in the distance. Luke could see men walking around the place, but they were too far away to make out who they were. Searching the countryside around the farm, they couldn't see any way that they could get close enough to spot Reynolds without being seen first.

While they were watching the farm, they saw one of the men mount a horse and start riding toward them. Falling back to their horses, they rode to a spot that Luke had spotted and waited. If the man continued past them, he would pass close enough to them that Luke would be able to see his face. When the man went by, Luke did not recognize him. They needed to get closer to the farm, but how?

After the man passed by, they decided to make a wide circle around the farm to see if they could get closer from the south. By the time they were mounted and before circling the farm, Lloyd decided that they wouldn't have enough time to circle the farm and get back to town before late. "We need to go back to town and return when we're better prepared," said Lloyd. "Now we have a good idea that it is them and where they are. We don't have to take the time following their tracks. I have some field glasses that will help us to see who's at the farm even if we are not able to get as close as we would like."

They cut across country wanting to avoid running into the man they saw leaving the farm. Once they were back on the road, they increased their pace to town. It was past suppertime before they rode up to the livery. They put up their horses before Lloyd headed for home and Luke went to the café. When Luke entered the café, he saw Earl sitting at his usual table talking to the waitress. When Luke sat down, the waitress asked, "Would you like some coffee?"

"I could sure use some, ma'am," said Luke.

When she left to get Luke's coffee, Earl asked, "Did you and the sheriff have any luck?"

"We found da farm where they're holed up," said Luke. "We couldn't get close enough to make out if Reynolds was there, but we think he must be."

"What are you going to do now?" asked Earl.

The waitress returned with Luke's coffee and took his order. When she left, Luke said, "We need ta get some supplies befer we go back. In da morn, da Sheriff and I will head back out, and we may be gone fer a couple of days."

"How's the sheriff going to like that, him just being married and all?" asked Earl. "Maybe I should go with you so the sheriff can stay with his new missus."

"Could be," said Luke.

Earl sat with Luke while he ate. Luke told Earl how the farm was situated sitting out in the open. That was their problem with trying to see who was at the farm without being seen. When Luke finished eating, they walked back to the office.

Maria was glad to see Lloyd when he entered the house. Lloyd was surprised to see the house all cleaned up after yesterday. Maria, seeing the look on Lloyd's face, said, "Some of the women stopped by and helped me pick up this morning. Did you find the man you were looking for?"

"Luke tracked Reynolds's horse to the farm where we think they are holed up," said Lloyd. "We didn't see the man we had in jail, but we have a strong feeling he's there. We are going back in the morning, and we may be gone for a couple of days.'

"Can't Earl and Luke do that?" asked Maria.

"I am the sheriff, and he got away from my jail," said Lloyd. "How do you think the townsfolk would like it if I just sent my deputies out there? They may begin to think they don't need the sheriff and only the deputies if I can't do my job."

"Come sit before your supper gets cold," said Maria. She knew what Lloyd had said was true, and she resigned herself to the fact that even though they had gotten married he still had his duty to the town. She was glad at least he had made it home this night and they would have the whole evening, just the two of them. They still had so much to learn about each other.

In the morning, Maria put together a supply of food for both Lloyd and Luke that would last them for a week. Lloyd went to the office only to find that Luke had already gone to the livery. When he arrived at the livery, Luke was just finishing putting a pack saddle on one of his packhorses. He looked up as Lloyd came in. "Maria put together food for us," said Lloyd. "We can ride by the house and pick it up on the way out. I also have my gear there with the field glasses."

Luke nodded as he finished putting the saddle on. When he finished, he said, "Earl thought ya might stay home, letting him and I go out there. Ya can keep an eye on town, and if they go ta leaving, we could follow them."

"Maria wanted me to stay as well," said Lloyd. "It's my job as sheriff to go after escaped prisoners, and that's where I need to be."

Lloyd saddled his horse. With the packhorse, they would have all the supplies they needed for the trip. Leaving the livery, they went by the office where Lloyd left instructions for Earl before going by the house to get his gear. While Luke put Lloyd's gear along with the food Maria had put together on the packhorse, Lloyd said his good-byes to Maria.

Lloyd turned and waved to Maria as they rode away. Maria stood on the front porch and watched until they were out of sight before going back into the house. Knowing where they were going, they made good time. When they stopped before coming into sight of the farm, it was still an hour before noon. First off, they had to find a place where they could set up camp and not be seen by anyone coming or going from the farm. Next they had to find a spot where they could watch the farm without being seen. Lloyd figured the best place to find what they needed was on the south side of the farm. Anyone coming from town would be riding in from the north or east. Staying out of sight of the farm, they circled far to the west. When they were about a quarter of a mile south of the farm, they came across a deep ravine. Going down into the ravine, Luke found a deer trail that they followed. The ravine seemed to circle around the farm going in the direction they needed to go. Luke knew that when the trail left the ravine, there was a good chance that they would find shelter where they could set up camp.

As they followed the deer trail, Luke stopped and crawled to the edge of the ravine. Looking in the direction of the farm, he found himself to be within a quarter of a mile. From this spot, they could watch the farm and they could see anyone approaching them from a long way off. That would give them enough time if they needed to move. With the field glasses, they should be able to make out the faces of the men. Going back to the horses, he told Lloyd what he had found. They rode on until the trail came up out of the ravine.

Luke had guessed right; there was a grove of trees that the trail went into as it left the ravine. Riding through the trees, he found an opening that would give them shelter and would hide any smoke from a campfire. Unloading the packhorse, Luke gave him water while Lloyd set up camp. After picketing the packhorse, Lloyd had finished setting up camp, and they rode back to the spot Luke had found for watching the farm.

Lloyd took the first watch. Taking the field glasses, he could see the faces of the men as they moved about the farm. He spotted cattle in the corral, but they were too far away to make out the brand on any of them.

After a couple of hours, Luke relieved Lloyd. While he was watching the farm, he spotted the big man, Herbert, with the scar on his face. Seeing him brought back memories of the raid on their farm; he knew for sure that they had found Fry. He was determined not to let Fry get away this time. They spent the rest of the day without seeing Reynolds. Luke was positive that Reynolds had to be at the farm.

When the sun started to go down, they went back to their camp. Maybe they would spot Reynolds tomorrow. Luke built a fire and started supper while Lloyd took care of the horses.

After they ate, sitting by the fire, Lloyd asked, "You're sure that the big fella you saw is one of Fry's men?"

"I ain't about ta ferget that face," said Luke. "He was one of da fellas who killed mah brother."

"If we find that Reynolds is at the farm, we will have cause to go in there," said Lloyd. "If we don't see Reynolds, we may have to wait for something else to happen before going after them."

"From what ah saw taday, it looks like they might be getting ready ta move again," said Luke.

"What makes you think that?" asked Lloyd.

"I was watching some of da men mending their gear and gathering supplies together, like one does befer getting ready ta head out," said Luke.

"You may be right," said Lloyd. "If we don't see Reynolds soon, we may have to just watch them leave."

The next morning before light, Luke had breakfast ready. By the time Lloyd was up, he had also watered the horses. By the time they finished breakfast, it was getting light enough to see. They were back watching the farm by the time the men first started moving around. Lloyd called Luke to take a look at a man he believed to be Reynolds. When Luke confirmed that it was Reynolds, Lloyd was ready to go after him. First, they would have to take a look at the north side of the farm to see if there was a way they could get to the farm without being seen. Fry had an army with him, so it would take an army of men to capture him.

"We need to move fast if we are going to get Reynolds," said Lloyd. "We'll have to put a plan together and get more men to help us."

Back at camp, they packed up their gear. Instead of going back to the ravine, they circled through the grove till they were farther west of the farm. Circling to the north, Lloyd was looking for a way that they could approach the farm without giving them a warning, not seeing any, they continued until they reached the road. Turning toward town, they rode in silence, each deep in his own thoughts.

When they arrived in town, they rode straight to the office. Earl was surprised to see them back so soon. "Did you find Reynolds?" he asked.

"We saw him at the farm this morning," said Lloyd. "Now we need to get men who will fight before going back."

"How soon do you want to go after him?" asked Earl.

"We need to put together a plan before we go back out there," said Lloyd. "The farm they are staying at sits in the open, and they will be warned long before we can get close to them. While I was there, I counted at least a dozen men, and there could be more."

They spent the rest of the day putting together a plan. Lloyd wanted to go after Reynolds within the next day or two.

That night Lloyd, Earl, and Luke had their plan that they hoped would get Reynolds, as well as Fry, for the raid on the Meyer farm. Now all they had to do was get the men and put it into action.

the fight

Things at the farm had remained quiet since they broke Reynolds out of jail. Fry had sent out scouts to see if there had been any activity in the area. On their return, they hadn't seen anyone near the farm. Sending the new guy, Trevor, to town, he had not heard of any posse looking for Reynolds. The sheriff must have not been able to follow them, or they figured that Reynolds had left the area. With it being quiet, Fry decided to continue his plans for robbing the bank. If they could pull off getting Reynolds out of jail in daylight without alerting the town, they might be able to rob the bank at night without alerting the town as well.

After they robbed the bank, they wouldn't stay in the area. Fry would take his men farther west. If they could get out of town without alerting the townspeople, they would have a large enough head start by the time the money was discovered gone, and the sheriff wouldn't be able to catch them. The best thing about it was that the townspeople wouldn't have a clue of who had taken their money.

With the information that his men had gathered, Fry knew it would be at least another two weeks before the money would be delivered. That would give him enough time to figure out a way to get the fella from Virginia. If the fella was following them like it seemed he was, he would continue to follow him and his men west. He needed to be stopped here and now before he could cause any more trouble.

Trevor came into the house, interrupting Fry's thoughts. "What do you want?" asked Fry.

"I found some fresh tracks on the road," said Trevor. "They came from the main road but turned west before they topped the hill. It looked like they were looking for something."

"Did you follow them?" asked Fry.

"No," said Trevor. "If they had been looking for us, they wouldn't have headed west before turning back north."

"Okay," said Fry. "Tell the men to keep an eye out for anyone in the area, just in case they were looking for us."

Trevor went out and spread the word to keep an eye out for any strangers in the area and to report to Fry if they saw any.

By now, evening was coming on. The cook called all the men in for supper. During supper, Fry went over the plans for robbing the bank. "We still have a couple of weeks before the money arrives," said Fry. "If the weather holds up, we should be able to get the money and clear out without being followed."

"What will we do if snow sets in like it did a few weeks ago?" asked one of the men.

"We sit," said Fry. "No one will be doing anything if we get snow, and the money will remain safe in the bank.

By the time they had finished supper, all the men knew that they would be on the move again before long. None of the men had many personal items to worry about, so traveling was not a problem. When it came time to move on, they could carry all their belongings in their saddlebags and bedrolls. Any livestock would be turned loose. Someone would find them, or maybe Indians in the area might come across them. Anyway, it wasn't their cattle to start with.

The next morning Fry sent his men out to look for signs of anyone else that might have been in the area. The men were out most of the morning and reported back that they had not seen any signs of anyone else in the area.

Fry began to think that maybe someone might have lost some stock and that's why they were in the area. If whoever it was was looking for stock, he believed that they would still be in the area or it could be one of the local farmers out roaming around. No matter; he decided that they would keep a closer watch on the road over the next few days. If people continued to show up, there would be reason for concern. With the farm being located out in the open like it was, they would be able to see anyone approaching. They would have enough time to prepare for anyone's arrival. If they needed to, they could defend the farm from the buildings; anyone attacking would be caught out in the open. With water and food, they would be able to hold anyone off for a long time. The farmer who built this place knew what he was doing in case they were attacked.

After a couple of days when the men reported that they had not seen any other activity, Fry started to relax again. When Fry called off the scouting, the men went back to doing their normal activities tending to the farm. Some of the men got busy fixing saddles and other gear, again preparing to travel. With the idea that they could be on the move again, they were losing some of their restlessness. Most of the men had wanted to go west when Fry first mentioned it. They had heard stories of men starting a new life, leaving their past behind. The West had not developed much law. People didn't ask a lot of questions about one's past. Fry had promised that they would all be partners in a ranch. Most of the men were getting tired of always being on the run and were looking forward to settling down. The war had allowed them to make some easy money without getting the law involved. Now with the war over and the army available, there was more of a chance of being caught and hung.

However, some of the men were beginning to doubt Fry's plan, and now there was talk of the man from Virginia that caused all of Fry's problems before. If he had followed them this far, what would prevent him from following them out west? Some of the new men were asking questions of the men who had been with Fry during the war and at Panther Gap about what had happened. When they heard the story about how two boys had destroyed their camp and killed several of the men, they began to wonder just what kind of a man it was that was following them. There were more than a dozen men on the farm, and Fry was concerned about one man. If that fella was that good, one would think that his reputation would have preceded him. Some of the new men began to think that once they got the money from the bank, they would take their share and leave. Fry could fight his own battles with his past.

The next morning Fry was sitting in the house when Reynolds came in, saying, "When I was on my way to the barn, I saw a couple of flashes coming from the south near the ravine. It could be that someone might be out there watching the place. Did you send someone out, or what do you want to do?"

"Find Trevor, and send him out to check it out," said Fry. "If it's someone looking for you, we don't want them finding you here. If it's a local farmer looking for some stock, Trevor can give them a neighborly hand."

Reynolds found Trevor in the barn. He said, "Fry wants you to check out a flash of light I saw coming from the ravine. You need to go out around so you don't chase them out before you get a chance to see who it might be. If it's someone looking for stock, you're ta help them."

Trevor nodded and got his horse. Riding east away from the farm, he kept an eye on the ground for any fresh tracks. After he was out of sight of the farm, he came across a set of tracks made by three horses heading west. Turning west, he followed them as they led to the ravine. Getting down from his horse, Trevor led him into the ravine. Coming across a deer trail, he saw that the tracks turned onto the trail heading south. Seeing that they were sticking to the deer trail, he mounted and followed the trail. About a quarter of a mile up the ravine, he saw where the brush had been broken. Getting down to get a closer look at the ground, he found where two horses had been tied for some time. Tying his horse to the brush, he crawled up to the edge of the ravine. At the top of the ravine, he found where two men had spent some time just this morning. If they had been watching the farm, what were they looking for? If they had been looking for Reynolds, they would have gone the way he had come, so they must have continued following the ravine. Going back to his horse, he found where the men he was following had indeed headed west.

Following their tracks, he found where they had camped. Looking the ground over, he confirmed that there were only two men, but they had three horses. The only thing that he could figure was the third horse must have been a packhorse. Trevor followed their tracks for a short way to make sure they had ridden away. They had continued west until they were past the farm where they turned north, going back the direction they had originally rode in from.

Riding back to the farm, Trevor reported to Fry what he found. Fry asked, "You are sure that they were watching us?"

"Yes," said Trevor. "Their trail came in from the north and circled around the farm just out of sight and headed back north on the west side of the farm. What I can't figure out is why anyone leading a packhorse would want to scout us out."

"Could be it was someone on the dodge," said Fry. "They might have been looking for someone easy to rob. When they saw how many men we have, they might have pulled out to look for someone easier to take."

"Might be," said Trevor. "Just seems strange the way they rode around us avoiding any contact with us."

"Do you think it could be the same people we come across the other day?" asked Fry.

"I didn't look that close at their tracks the other day," said Trevor. "If it was, they didn't have a packhorse with them at that time. It could be someone else."

"Maybe it was their packhorse that run off and that is what they were looking for the other day," said Fry. "Looking for their horse, they might have come across us by accident and came back after they found their horse to check us out."

"Couldn't say," said Trevor. "Just seems strange that we ain't seen anybody until we got Reynolds out of jail and then people start showing up."

"How would they find us if they came from town?" said Fry. "No one saw us when we broke Reynolds out of jail."

When Trevor left Fry, he saw Reynolds by the corral brushing his horse. Going over to him, Trevor asked, "Are you sure no one saw you leaving town the other day?"

"Ya, they were all at the church," said Reynolds as he had just finished brushing his horse. He turned to take the brush back into the barn.

Reynolds's horse all of a sudden sidestepped as a pitchfork that had been leaning against the fence fell, hitting him in his side. Trevor bent down to pick it up and saw a strange mark made by one of his shoes.

Going to the leg with the marked shoe, he took a look at the hoof and saw it had been filed. *Someone marked the shoe,* thought Trevor. Now he wanted to find out just how easy it would have been to follow Reynolds. Going to his horse, Trevor mounted and rode down the road leading to the farm. Following the road, he could see where Reynolds's horse had walked when they returned from town. Now the question was whether Reynolds knew about the shoe being marked and made an agreement to help the sheriff. *Getting Reynolds out of jail went too smooth,* thought Trevor. *Maybe the sheriff had set it up so they could follow Reynolds.* He would do some talking to some of the others when Reynolds wasn't around to see what they might know about him and if they trusted him. If they asked him why he was asking about Reynolds, he would just say that there seemed to be a lot of activity around the farm since he returned, and he would not mention the shoe.

Riding back to the farm, he didn't say anything to Reynolds when he put his horse up about why he had ridden out. When Reynolds did ask what he was doing, he just said that Fry had wanted him to go back to check the tracks from the other day.

Reynolds walked away, leaving Trevor to finish putting up his horse. When he finished, he looked around as he was leaving the barn, and not seeing anyone, he went to the bunkhouse. He had heard some talk that some of the men had made concerning the man from Virginia; maybe Fry did not have as much control over the men as he thought.

Fry had spent the day thinking about the events that had happened since they broke Reynolds out of jail. It seemed too much like a coincidence that right after getting Reynolds back people were watching the place. They had made sure no one had seen them while they were in town, and no one had followed them that day, so how was it that someone had been hanging around now? Had Reynolds done some talking to the sheriff that he hadn't told Fry about? Reynolds had been with him throughout the war, Fry had never had any reason to doubt Reynolds's loyalty. He was beginning to have a feeling like he had when things were going badly in the war, and now it was all because of one man.

The morning after Lloyd and Luke had returned, Lloyd put out the word that he needed to put together a posse. He was looking for fifteen men to join him and his two deputies. When word got around, the mayor came to see him. When the mayor came to the office, Lloyd was not there, but when he saw Earl, he rudely asked, "Where's the sheriff?"

"He's out rounding up a posse," said Earl.

"You tell him that I want to see him as soon as he gets back," said the mayor. "I'll be in my office, and I'll be expecting him to be there within the hour with a good reason why he needs all these men. You tell him. Do you hear me?"

"Yes, sir, Mayor," said Earl. "I'll tell him as soon as he gets back."

Earl heard the mayor utter to himself as he walked out, "I don't understand why he needs all these men to go get one fella. That's what we pay him and his deputies for."

It was two hours before Lloyd and Luke returned to the office. When Lloyd entered the office, Earl said, "Boy, am I glad to see you two. I thought that you might be the mayor coming back."

"What did the mayor want?" asked Lloyd.

"He wanted to see you in his office over an hour ago," said Earl. "He wasn't happy when he was here, and with you not getting back before now, he ain't gonna be any happier when he sees you."

"What did he want to see me about?" asked Lloyd.

"He wants you to explain why you need so many men to go after one fella," said Earl. "By the way, did you have any luck?"

"We got the men we need," said Lloyd. "They will be here in an hour to go over the plan. If they show up while I am with the mayor, tell them to wait."

Lloyd left the office to go see the mayor. When he entered the mayor's office, the mayor said, "It's about time. I told your deputy over two hours ago I wanted to see you. Where have you been?"

Lloyd ignored the mayor's comment and asked, "What do you need?"

"Didn't your incompetent deputy tell you anything I said?" asked the mayor. "I want to know why you need all these men to go after one man. It's been three days since he escaped. How do you expect to find him now?"

"We know where he's at," said Lloyd.

"Well, if you know where he is, why didn't you bring him in?" asked the mayor. "Where is he?"

"He's at an abandoned farm west of here," said Lloyd. "He's protected by over a dozen men."

"Why can't you just ride in there and arrest him?" asked the mayor.

"I don't think they would be willing to just hand him over to me," said Lloyd, "seeing how they were the ones to break him out of jail. We also believe they are the ones who killed the Meyers. Maybe you would like to ride along and help us arrest him or show us how to do it."

"Well ah, me?" asked the mayor. "That's what we hired you for."

"If you don't mind, Mayor," said Lloyd, "let me do my job, and we should be able to get these men. If you don't have any other questions, Mayor, I will go do the job you hired me for."

Turning, Lloyd did not wait for an answer from the mayor but went back to the office. By the time he got to the office, all the men had arrived. After swearing them in, he went over his plan. After making sure they all knew and understood the plan, they went their own way until tomorrow. They would meet back in front of the sheriff's office at first light.

That night when Lloyd arrived at home, Maria seemed to be in a quiet mood. She turned and greeted Lloyd as he came in but turned right back to the stove, continuing to make supper. Even as they ate, Maria remained quiet. Finally Lloyd asked, "You are quieter than normal tonight. Is there something wrong?"

"I have been thinking about what you are going to be doing tomorrow," said Maria. "I am worried that you might be hurt or killed. I know you have to do your job, but I can still worry, can't I?"

Lloyd got up and went to Maria. Taking her in his arms, he tried to reassure her that they would be all right. He said, "I have all the men I need to make sure that they won't be trying anything when we go after Reynolds. Luke knows how they work, and that gives us the advantage over them. By tomorrow night, this will all be behind us."

Maria nodded her head and tried to smile, but it had done nothing to stop her from worrying. That night Lloyd lay awake going over the plan in his mind. While he was thinking about the plan, he noticed that Maria was having a restless sleep as well. This was the reason he had not married before. They had only been married a short time, and she could be a widow before tomorrow night.

Lloyd was awake early. Seeing that Maria had finally fallen into a peaceful sleep, he quietly got up out of bed. Trying not to wake her, he dressed. When he finished dressing, he leaned over and kissed her forehead before he left for the office. She stirred when he kissed her forehead but did not wake.

As he approached the office, he could see that a lamp had been lit and there was movement inside. Opening the door, Earl was just pouring himself a cup of coffee. Looking around, he asked, "Where's Luke?"

"He went to get the horses," said Earl. "Do you want some coffee?"

"Thanks. Don't mind if I do," said Lloyd.

As Lloyd was getting his coffee, Luke returned with the horses. Hearing Luke coming with the horses, he poured a second cup of coffee and had it ready for Luke when he entered. Handing the cup to Luke, Luke said, "Thanks. Yer here early."

"Couldn't sleep," said Lloyd. "I spent most of the night going over the plan time and time again."

By the time they had finished their coffee, the men were gathering in front of the office. Luke picked up his Henry and saddlebags on his way to his horse. Earl was following behind him while Lloyd finished gathering his gear. After putting their gear on their horses, they waited for Lloyd to join them. When Lloyd joined them, he said, "I am glad to see you all could make it this morning. If we are lucky, we will be able to do this without a fight. Let's go."

Mounting, the posse rode out of town. It was midmorning when they came to the road leading to the farm. Turning up the road, the sheriff halted the men. "Luke," he said, "I want you to ride ahead and find out if they are still there. The rest of you remain with me."

Luke rode off while the sheriff and the rest of the men followed at a walk. When he got to the bottom of the hill, he stopped. Taking out the field glasses, he left Buck while he made his way to the top of the hill. Looking through the field glasses, he could see that nothing had changed. The activities at the farm looked normal. Returning, he rode back, meeting up with the sheriff and the posse.

Luke told the sheriff that activity at the farm was normal. Now it was time for the sheriff to put his plan into action. He needed Luke to point out Fry, so he sent Earl with five men to circle to the east of the farm in case anyone tried to escape in that direction. It was the closest cover to the farm, and the buildings would hide anyone trying to escape with the men riding up to the farmhouse. They waited for an hour to allow Earl and his men to get into place. Luke remained on watch in case one of Fry's men headed their way.

When the hour was up, they headed for the farm. Lloyd knew that as soon as they reached the top of the hill they would be seen. He hoped that he and his men could get close enough to surprise them before they could react. Taking their time, they topped the hill and headed for the farm. Lloyd saw a man walk toward the barn and turn when he saw them and run to the house. He had hoped they would have been closer before that happened and cursed their bad luck.

The night before at the farm when Trevor was going to the barn, he ran into Herbert. "How long have you known Reynolds?" he asked.

"Why?" asked Herbert.

"Do you trust him?" asked Trevor.

"He's been with the captain throughout the war," said Herbert. "The captain trusts him. What's up?"

"Seems strange to me that after he has been in jail that people started showing up here watching the place," said Trevor. "Fry don't seem to be concerned, but it bothers me."

"Ain't thought much about it," said Herbert. "Fry's done taken care of us for some time."

Trevor had talked to a couple of the other men earlier. None of them had thought the way he was thinking. That night he lay in his bunk thinking on what he wanted to do since he had stumbled onto the farm and joined up with Fry when he got caught in a snow storm. When invited to join them, it seemed like a good idea. Now it looked like they were getting ready to run even before they could rob the bank. Maybe it was the law that was watching the place, and if they returned, he could end up in jail or hung for something he didn't do. After a while, he decided that in the morning he was going to leave before it was too late.

When morning came, he got up and ate breakfast with the rest of the men. On the way to the house, he had taken some of his gear to the barn. He took his bedroll out and hung it over the fence to air it out. From there, he would be able to get it to the barn without being seen. After breakfast, he went back to the bunkhouse and got his rifle. As he came out, he ran into Herbert who asked, "Where are ya going?"

"I got a feeling like someone is watching us," said Trevor. "I thought I might ride out and take a look around the place."

"I think you're wrong, but if that will make ya feel better, then do it," said Herbert.

Trevor got his bedroll on the way to the barn. Saddling his horse, he loaded all his gear and took his horse out the back. Riding toward the ravine, he kept the barn between him and the house so Fry wouldn't see him and he wouldn't raise suspicion with the other men.

Not seeing Trevor come back out of the barn, Herbert decided to see what was holding him up. Just before he got to the barn door, he saw riders coming up the road approaching the farm. Tuning, he hurried to the house to warn Fry. As he climbed the porch, he called out, "Cap, we got company coming."

Fry opened the front door and looked where Herbert was pointing. Seeing a dozen or more men heading toward the farm, he said, "Herbert, go warn the men and tell them to be on the alert. Tell Reynolds to get out of here."

Herbert went to the bunkhouse and told the men to get ready, that they had company coming. Four men ran to the barn, including Herbert. Before leaving the bunkhouse, he saw Reynolds and said, "There's a bunch of men riding up to the place, and the captain said for you to get out of here till they are gone."

Reynolds grabbed his rifle and headed east around the bunkhouse, running for the trees, not knowing that Earl was there with five deputies waiting. Reynolds was watching the men approaching the farm, not watching where he was going, or he might have seen the men waiting.

Earl saw a man running toward them. Moving the men out of sight, he saw that it was Reynolds. As soon as Reynolds entered the trees, he turned, looking back at the farm in time to see that the riders had reached the house and stopped. Hiding behind a tree, he watched the men getting ready for a fight. *Fry must be talking to the riders,* he thought as he could see some of the riders just standing looking toward the front of the house.

Reynolds turned, going further into the trees. As Reynolds turned, Earl stepped out from behind a tree and told Reynolds to drop his gun. Reynolds, not hearing Earl before, jumped, dropping his rifle. Seeing Earl, Reynolds reached for his revolver. Earl did not wait, but shot, killing Reynolds as he drew his gun.

As Lloyd and his men rode up to the house, they saw Fry come out of the house and were waiting for him. By the time they reached Fry, he had been joined by four other men carrying rifles. All the posse members had their rifles laid across their saddles. As they came to a stop, Fry asked, "Oh, it's you, Sheriff. I didn't recognize you at first. What can I do for you, Sheriff?"

"We're looking for a man who escaped from my jail by the name of Reynolds," said the sheriff.

"What did he do?" asked Fry.

"He tried to kill one of my deputies and broke out of jail," said the sheriff. "I have a report that he has been seen here, and I would like for you to turn him over to us."

"Can't say I know anyone named Reynolds," said Fry. Turning to his men, he asked, "Have any of you seen a man call Reynolds?"

They all replied, saying they had never heard of him.

"Whoever said they saw him must be wrong. We haven't seen anyone around here for some time," said Fry. Just at that time, a shot rang out from the grove behind the farm.

Hearing the shot, both Fry's men and the deputies reacted by opening fire. Two of the deputies were knocked from their horses. One of Fry's men was lying on the porch, dead, with two more wounded. Luke took a shot at Fry as he jumped back through the door. The bullet hit him in the shoulder, but he managed to keep on his feet. One of the deputies shot the fifth man as he rounded the corner. Luke dismounted and followed Fry into the house. He followed a blood trail that led to the back of the house.

As Luke followed Fry, the cook came from the kitchen and fired a shot at Luke that went wide. Luke returned fire, killing the cook. Luke continued to follow Fry through the house and out the back door. As he got to the back of the house, he could hear gunfire coming from the trees where Earl and his men were. He saw Fry making his way toward the bunkhouse. Luke called out to Fry. When Fry heard his name, he stopped and turned around. Luke saw that

Fry had a gun in his hand. Both men fired at the same time. Luke felt something hitting him in his side, spinning him around. As he started to spin, he saw Fry jerk when the bullet hit him. When Luke regained his balance, he saw that Fry had fallen to the ground. Fighting to stay standing, he watched as Fry lay on the ground.

Firing was still going on in the barn and the front of the house when Luke saw Earl and his men coming out of the trees. The shooting coming from the bunkhouse had died down. Luke made it the rest of the way to the bunkhouse and only found two men still in there alive. "Drop your guns," said Luke.

The men dropped their guns, raising their hands. Luke held them until Earl arrived with his men. Leaving a man to watch those two, the rest went to help the sheriff.

By the time they made it to the front of the house, most of the fighting had ended. Several of Fry's men were lying dead on the ground. Three wounded men threw out their guns and came out of the barn. Two of the men were helping the third man.

"Where are the rest?" asked Lloyd.

"They're gone," said one of Fry's men. "They went out the back when they saw we couldn't win."

"Earl, take a couple of men and check out the barn," said Lloyd.

Earl took two of the men and went to the barn. Finding it empty, they returned. In the meantime, a couple of men checked out the livestock. Finding the Meyer brand on the cattle, they knew they had caught the right men.

When Trevor left the rear of the barn, he rode to the ravine. He figured once he was in the ravine he could ride west, leaving Fry and his men behind. As he started up the ravine, he heard a single gunshot. Stopping, it wasn't long before he could hear gunshots erupting all over the farm. Not waiting any longer, he rode, following the trail leading up out of the ravine. He followed it until he found himself in trees out of sight of the farm. Finding a concealed spot, he stopped and waited. While he was there, he saw two men following the trail he had taken. Remaining concealed, he saw that they were two of Fry's men who were trying to get away as well, and one of them he recognized as Herbert. *That must mean that things are not going well for Fry,* thought Trevor. At first, he thought about calling out to them but then decided not to. He watched as they continued to run on foot. While he remained concealed, he heard others coming up the trail. It wasn't long after he heard them that he saw two more men following on horseback. Once they got into the trees, they seemed to have lost their trail. After searching without success, they turned, going back to the farm. When they returned, they reported that they had lost their trail in the woods.

Luke went around looking at the dead men to see if Reynolds was one of them. Not seeing him, he said, "Lloyd, Reynolds must have gotten away. I didn't find him here among the dead."

Earl walked up just as Luke had finished talking, and Lloyd asked, "What was that shot coming from the woods that started this?"

Earl said, "When you rode up, Reynolds came running toward us. When he saw us, he pulled his gun, and I had to shoot him. His body is back in the trees."

Lloyd said, "Send someone to bring him back here. Luke, you need to have your side looked at before we go back to town. Some of you men start digging graves. We will bury them before we go." Some of the men, hearing the sheriff, found shovels and started digging graves while the rest started patching up one another's wounds. Those who were not wounded had the graves dug by the time the wounded had been cared for.

All in all, the sheriff and his posse were lucky. Only one deputy had been killed, but they had eight wounded, including Luke and the sheriff. Once the dead men who had been with Fry, including Fry, had been buried, they rounded up the livestock, driving them to town. It was late by the time they reached town. Putting the livestock into a corral at the livery, Lloyd figured he would take care of them in the morning. Earl took Deputy Wilson's body to the undertaker. Lloyd would have to tell his family.

Earl and Luke took the five prisoners to the jail with the help of a couple of the men. Once the prisoners were in jail, the men went home to see their families and take care of their wounds. Lloyd went by the Wilson's place and told them about Jerry being killed during the fight. Once he finished there, he went home to where Maria was waiting. Seeing blood on his sleeve, she made him take off his shirt and cleaned his wound. While she was cleaning his wound, she said, "I was too afraid to come down to the office when you rode in. I was afraid that you might have been killed. I am so glad you are home safe. Did anyone else get hurt?"

"Mine's nothing but a scratch," said Lloyd. "Jerry Wilson was killed, and some of the others were wounded. Luke is one who could use some help. He was shot in the side, but I think the bullet went clean through."

"Where is he?" asked Maria.

"He's at the jail," said Lloyd.

Maria put some things into a basket and said, "Put on a clean shirt, and let's go see how bad it is."

Lloyd got a clean shirt and followed her as she hurried off to the jail. Entering the office, she saw Earl trying to take care of Luke's wound. Going over to them, she shoved Earl aside, saying, "Let me do that."

"Yes, ma'am," said Earl as he backed away.

Lloyd stood back watching, thinking to himself how lucky he had been marrying such a strong woman.

Maria took a look at Luke's wound and said, "You are lucky the bullet went through." Taking a bottle from her basket, she poured some on a rag, cleaning the wound. As she started to wash the wound, Luke jumped as the liquid she was using caused the wound to sting. She smiled and poured some more on the wound. When she finished cleaning his wound, she wrapped his side before saying, "You will be all right if it doesn't get infected."

While Maria was taking care of Luke, Lloyd sent Earl to get the doctor. When he got to the doctor's office, he found two of the posse members waiting to see him as well. Opening the door to where the doctor was, he said, "Doc, when you get done here, the sheriff would like you to come by the jail and take a look at some of the prisoners. We got three prisoners who were wounded and could use your help."

"When I am done here, I'll be over," said the doctor.

Earl went back to the jail. He arrived just as Maria had finished with Luke. Earl told Lloyd that the doctor would be over to check the prisoners as soon as he was done with the patients in his office.

"Why don't you and Luke go get something to eat and bring food back for the prisoners," said Lloyd. "I'll stay here till you get back."

"Lloyd, I'll go finish your supper," said Maria. "As soon as they get back, you come home before it has a chance to get cold."

Maria left at the same time that Luke and Earl did. When they got to the café, they no more than sat down when Kaitlin put a steak in front of each of them. "Larry figured you would be hungry when you got here. He saw you ride into town and started to prepare a supper for you."

Earl said, "Thanks. We'll be wanting five meals to take back to the jail."

Larry had gotten all the meals ready by the time they finished eating. Taking the meals, they went back to the jail. No one was in the office when they came in. Going to the back, they found the sheriff back there with the doctor taking care of the prisoners. While the doctor was finishing with the last prisoner, Earl and Luke fed the others. Lloyd, seeing Earl and Luke, said, "Doc, now that they're back, I'll be heading home myself." As he was leaving, he told them that they would see him in the morning.

When the doctor finished with the prisoners, he turned to Luke and said, "I heard you were wounded as well. Let me take a look at it before I go."

"It's okay, Doc," said Luke. "Maria fixed it up for me."

"Open your shirt anyway," said the doctor.

Luke opened his shirt, and when the doctor saw that it wasn't bleeding and the bandage was clean, he let Luke put his shirt back on.

As the doctor was leaving, he said, "I'll come by in the morning to check on the prisoners."

After the doctor had gone and the prisoners had finished their supper, Earl took the trays back to the café. With the loss of blood and the long day, Luke lay down and was asleep as soon as his head hit the pillow.

When Earl returned, seeing Luke asleep, he barred the door and blew out the lamp. He too was exhausted and went to sleep as soon as he lay down.

Maria had finished making Lloyd's supper and was waiting for him. When she heard the front door open, she dished it up and had it sitting on the table when Lloyd walked into the kitchen. She gave him a hug and a kiss before telling him to sit down and eat. She could see that the day had taken its toll on him as well. When he finished eating, she put the dishes in the sink, and they went off to bed.

In the morning, Lloyd woke refreshed. Maria had already gotten up and was in the kitchen making breakfast. Getting a cup of coffee, he sat down, and she asked, "What happened yesterday?"

While they were eating, Lloyd went through the events from the day before. After hearing what had happened, Maria was more than grateful for their safe return.

When Lloyd finished breakfast, he wanted to see what kind of shape the wounded prisoners were in. Arriving at the office, he found the front door still barred. Lloyd knocked on the door, and it was a while before a sleepy Earl removed the bar and opened the door. Entering, Lloyd saw that Luke was just beginning to move. Luke felt a sharp pain in his side as he sat up. It seemed his side had stiffened during the night. The pain reminded him of what had happened the day before.

Lloyd went back to the prisoners, and he could see that one was badly wounded and was not doing well. "Earl, go get the doc right away," he said.

Earl hurried off to find the doc. Stopping by his office first, he found that the doctor wasn't there. Hurrying to the doc's house, he arrived just as the doctor was coming out. "Doc," Earl said, "Lloyd needs you to come by the jail right away. One of the prisoners ain't doing well."

"All right, all right," said the doctor. "I'll be right there."

Both Doctor and Earl walked together back to the jail. By the time the doctor arrived, the man that Lloyd was concerned about had gotten a high fever and didn't look good at all. The doctor took an alcohol-soaked rag and started to wipe the man down. The man started coughing up blood and died shortly after that. Getting up, the doctor took a blanket and covered the man. Going back into the office, he told Lloyd that the man had died and the undertaker needed to be contacted.

"When Luke and Earl return, I'll have one of them go get him," said Lloyd. "What about the other two men that were wounded?"

"They should be well enough to hang if that's what you intend to do with them," said the doctor.

"That's up to the judge, not me," said Lloyd. "By the way, Doc, if you're going by the café, would you tell Earl that we only need four meals now?"

After the doc left, Lloyd sat down and started going through wanted posters. He found the one on Fry first. There was a five hundred dollar reward for him. Luke had been the one who found him and shot him so he should get the reward, Lloyd figured. He also found rewards on some of the other men. He figured that those rewards would be divided between the rest of the men.

When Earl and Luke returned, they only had the four meals, so the doctor must have run into them.

The rest of the day was quiet. The mayor stopped by and congratulated Lloyd for capturing the men who killed the Meyers. He went off afterward to brag about how good of a sheriff he had selected for Boonville and how he had encouraged the sheriff to go after the outlaws. He also was saying how he suggested that the sheriff had plenty of help with him.

Luke sat down at one of the desks and took out some paper and a pencil.

Dear Ma, Pa, Milton, and girls,

I sit here this day thinking of ya. I have not gotten to mah destination, but I am well. During mah travels, I come across a family who was heading ta St. Louis. They invited me ta join them. I left them with their relatives in St. Louis, and I went on.

Pa, I know'd ya gonna be glad to hear I come across Captain Fry. Da Sheriff at Boonville hired me on as one of his deputies when I come across a farm that was raided. I thought it looked like da work of Fry and his men. We don't got ta be worried about him no more. When we went ta arrest him, he got killed along with most of his men. Those not killed are in jail waitin fer da judge.

Milton, I got me one of them new Henry rifles. It sure shoots nice. With it, ya are like a one-man army. If Pa had one during da war, he would have whipped them Yanks fer sure.

Ma, I got wounded when we went after Fry, but ya not ta worry. Da Sheriff's wife done patched me up fine.

Mary and Sue Ann, I sure miss ya as well.

Y'all take care. Will write again when I can. Fer now, I am getting ready ta move on.

Luke

When he finished writing his letter, he folded it and got up. "I'll be back," he said as he walked out the door.

Lloyd just nodded and watched him go. After Luke had gone, he said to Earl, "Did Luke say anything to you about anything being wrong?"

"No," said Earl. "He ain't said a word to me."

"He has never talked much about himself or his family. Maybe that is who he wrote the letter to," said Lloyd. "The young man's been through a lot for his age."

Luke went to the general store to post his letter. Mr. Graves was somewhat surprised to see that the young deputy was sending a letter. After posting his letter, Luke decided to walk around town and do some thinking. Stopping by the stable, he was glad to see that George wasn't there. Going to his horses, he started rubbing them down. This was where he did his best thinking. While he was rubbing down the horses, he figured out that he needed to move on to Independence. He needed to be there before they started organizing wagon trains if he wanted to get a job with one. By the time he had rubbed all three horses down, he was feeling better knowing he had a plan. As soon as he could get released by the sheriff, he would be on his way.

Both Earl and Lloyd could tell Luke was feeling better when he came back to the office. Neither mentioned anything about the way he looked when he left.

"While you were gone, I've been looking at some posters," said Lloyd. "It seems that there was a reward on some of the men. Seeing how you were the one who found and killed Fry, I figured you for his reward. The rest of the rewards will be divided between the rest of the men."

All Luke could do was shake his head. He had not figured on getting money for killing Fry. He had only wanted revenge for what Fry had done to his family and friends.

"When will da Judge hear their case?" asked Luke after he had recovered.

"He will be here the first of next week," said Lloyd. "By then, those two who are wounded should be ready for the trial. Earl, why don't you go to the telegraph office and send a wire to the marshal in Panther Gap and tell him that Fry is dead. That should make some of the townfolk there happy."

When Earl left to send the wire, Lloyd looked at Luke and said, "I see there's something on your mind. Do you want to talk about it?"

"I've done some think'n, and I think it's time I move on," said Luke. "Ya got Fry and his men, so ah figured ta stay fer da trial and then head out."

"I figured something was bothering you," said Lloyd. "You know you are welcome to stay on here if you like.""

"Thanks," said Luke. "I been itch'n ta go out west fer as long as I can remember. Guess I won't be happy till I see it fer mahself."

When Earl came back, neither the sheriff nor Luke said anything to Earl about Luke's planning on leaving.

The rest of the week was quiet. Luke and Earl took turns watching the prisoners, making sure no one tried to break them out of jail. They didn't have too much of a concern, but they did know that a couple of Fry's men had gotten away. Without Fry to lead them, Luke was sure they would not attempt anything on their own. He had not seen the man with the scar on his face dead or captured. He had to be the one who got away.

On Thursday, the money the bank was waiting for showed up. Lloyd was returning from the general store when he saw the Union troops coming into town. He was surprised to see the army, but then he remembered the money. He turned from going to the office to going to the bank. There he waited for their arrival.

Luke was looking out the window when the troops went by. At first, he tensed up. Earl happened to be looking at Luke when he got tense and got up to see what caused it. Going to the window, he saw the troops and said, "I see the money has arrived."

"I guess you're right," said Luke. "I saw Lloyd head fer the bank just befer I saw da troops.

"Maybe we should see if they need any help," said Earl.

Picking up their rifles, they left for the bank. As they approached the troops, some of them turned and pointed their rifles at Earl and Luke. Lloyd said, "Captain, you can tell your men to relax. Those two are my deputies."

"Stand down, men," said the captain. "They are with the sheriff."

Instead of going to where the troops were, Earl and Luke walked across the street, keeping an eye out for anything that might be out of place. Two of the troopers dismounted and went to the back of the wagon. Opening the back, they took out a chest that contained the money and carried it into the bank. When they returned, the captain said good-bye to the sheriff, and they rode back out of town returning the way they had come.

Earl had been watching Luke ever since he had seen him tense up when the troops first arrived. He seemed to relax when he mentioned the money. Earl started to think that there was more of a mystery to Luke than they knew about him. He would mention it to Lloyd when he had a chance.

After the troops pulled out, the three of them walked back to the office. Restlessness was starting to set in with Luke now that he was thinking that it wouldn't be long before he would be on his way. Getting up, he walked to the stable. After he left the office, Earl said, "Lloyd, when those troops rode in today, Luke got tense when he first saw them. I wonder what he is hiding."

"You know that he is from Virginia," said Lloyd. "Being through the war at such a young age must have left in impression on him. He told us about what Fry and his men had done, and they had done it wearing Union uniforms. I would imagine that it will be some time before he does not react to the Union uniform."

"You may be right," said Earl. "When I first saw his reaction, I thought it looked like it could be more than just a reaction from the war."

"Remember," said Lloyd, "he is the one who told us about Fry and how he worked. If he was running from someone, I don't think he would have stayed around and helped us. Anyway, we have no information saying he is wanted by us."

Earl nodded his head and dropped the subject. He had picked up the wanted posters and was going through them without finding anything that looked or sounded like Luke.

Luke saw George as he entered the stable and said, "Howdy."

"You've done the town a big favor," said George. "I don't think the sheriff would have got those men without your help."

"Thanks," said Luke. "I can't say I did it fer da town as much as fer mah family."

"Are you going to stay around?" asked George.

"I plan on hooking up with a wagon train go'n west dis spring," said Luke. "I heard stories about the country and plan ta see it fer mahself."

"I think Lloyd is going to miss having you around here," said George. "Seems I heard you were the one who got him to marry Maria as well."

"Ah wouldn't say ah was da one," said Luke. "Ah just asked him why he hadn't married her. Anyway, that's probably reason enough ta move on befer he regrets getting hitched."

George was still laughing as Luke walked back to his horses. As he brushed them, he was talking to them. One would think that they could understand what he was saying by the way they reacted. When he was done brushing the horses, he took out the gear he had left at the stable and started going through it. He took time to oil his guns and checked their loads. He made sure all the saddle straps were in good shape. He also began to make a list of supplies he would need before leaving. When he finished, he put his gear away and decided to take a walk around town.

When he arrived at the office, Lloyd and Earl were still sitting at their desks. Not knowing what else to do, he sat down and started cleaning his Henry.

They only had till Monday for the judge to show up, and it was already Saturday. Things had been quiet since they had returned from going after Fry and his men. With it being quiet, the days seemed to be getting longer and longer for Luke. He was not used to sitting in a building just waiting. If he had been hunting that would have been different. He would be able to sit all day and wait.

the trial

On Monday, Luke was ready for the judge to show up. The stage did not arrive until late in the afternoon when he greeted the judge. The judge wanted to get settled into the hotel before going over any cases.

When the judge showed up at the office, Lloyd introduced Luke to him. After they were introduced, he asked, "What have you got?"

"We've got four men who are charged with robbery, murder, and hiding an escaped prisoner," said Lloyd.

"Some of these are hanging offenses," said the judge. "We will set up court and select a jury tomorrow. You will need to let the townsfolk know that we are going to need their help." He left, going to an office the town had set up for him at the courthouse. At his office, he began to prepare for the trial that would start tomorrow.

Lloyd sent Earl and Luke out to notify the people in town that a jury was going to be required and they needed to show up at the courthouse in the morning by nine o'clock.

With the judge in town, Luke knew that it wouldn't be long until he would be back on the trail. This seemed to help his restlessness some. As he was walking around town, he stopped in at the general store. As he entered, Mr. Graves said, "Howdy, Luke. How are you doing today?"

"Howdy, Mr. Graves," said Luke. "I am do'n fine."

"What can I do for you?" asked Mr. Graves.

"I am planning on leaving as soon as the trial is over," said Luke. "I'll be needing some supplies. I got me a list if ya would fill it fer me when ya get a chance."

"I heard the sheriff talking about a reward for the leader of the men you brought in," said Mr. Graves. "He mentioned that you were the one who got him. What are you planning on doing with the money?"

"I am gonna send some of it ta mah folks back home," said Luke. "Da rest will help me ta get a start out west."

"Well, I'll pull your supplies together when I hear that the trial is coming to an end and have them waiting for you when you're ready to leave," said Mr. Graves. "We'll be sorry to see you go. Our town could always use someone like you."

"Thanks, Mr. Graves," said Luke. "I'll be by fer them then."

When Earl and Luke returned to the office, they were sure that there would be enough people available for the judge to select a jury. That evening when Lloyd left to go home, Earl and Luke locked the jail and went to the café for supper. When they entered the café, Kaitlin was busy with other customers. Going to their usual table, they sat down. "Lloyd said you are planning on leaving," said Earl.

"As soon as da trial is over," said Luke. "I hadn't planned on stopping here till I ran inta Fry."

"Where are you going to head to?" asked Earl.

"Someone going somewhere?" asked Kaitlin as she walked up to the table.

"Luke here is going to leave us," said Earl. "I was just asking him where he was going."

"When are you going?" asked Kaitlin.

"Ain't made up mah mind," said Luke. "First off, I am go'n ta Independence. I heard ya could hook up with a wagon train heading west. Figured I'd start there.

"It sounds exciting," said Kaitlin. "Now what would you like to eat?"

After Kaitlin left with their order, Earl asked Luke what he knew about the West. Luke told him not much. What he knew he had heard from men who had been out there or had heard about it from others who had been there.

Earl started thinking about what Luke had told him while he ate. It started to sound like an interesting adventure, but he was not ready to give up what he had. Not that he had that much. If he was to go, Kaitlin would be here. *Maybe we are more than just friends,* he began to think. *Nah,* he thought to himself, shaking his head.

"What ya shaking yer head fer?" asked Luke.

"It was just some silly notion I know ain't true," said Earl.

"It ain't got noth'n ta do with Kaitlin, does it?" asked Luke.

Earl's face tuned a little red as he wondered how Luke would know that. "What makes you ask that?" asked Earl.

"Noth'n sept ya act different when yer around her," said Luke.

Earl's face got redder than it was before. He looked down at his plate, trying to avoid Luke's looks, and started eating again. Luke laughed as he watched Earl turning red.

Kaitlin came over to see if they needed more coffee, and when she saw Earl, she asked, "What are you blushing for, Earl?"

Earl just turned redder and looked away. Luke could not hold it back any longer and let out a loud laugh, causing several of the customers to look to see what was going on. Finally, Luke said, "It seems Earl was think'n about a certain young lady in here. When I asked him about her, he turned red in his face. It seems when that young lady came over, he got redder."

When Kaitlin heard what Luke had said, she did not know whom Luke was talking about at first. When she realized that he was talking about her, she almost dropped the coffee pot and started to turn red herself. The people sitting by their table heard Luke and saw Kaitlin turning red and started to laugh with Luke. By now, both Kaitlin and Earl were ready to kill Luke. Kaitlin turned, leaving the coffee pot, and went to the kitchen. Luke picked up the coffee pot and filled his cup. Earl felt like leaving but figured if he did it would make it worse.

It wasn't long after Kaitlin went to the kitchen that the laughter stopped. Kaitlin composed herself in the kitchen before returning to the dining room. When she came by their table to get the coffee pot, she avoided looking at either Luke or Earl. Earl kept his head down to avoid looking at either Luke or Kaitlin as well. When Luke could get Kaitlin's attention again, he ordered the meals for the prisoners.

On the way back to the jail, Luke said, "I know'd there was something between ya and Kaitlin."

Earl didn't reply but kept on walking. Back at the jail, they fed the prisoners and waited for them to finish. When they were done eating, Luke offered to take the trays back to the café, but Earl said he would do it because he had to straighten out Kaitlin's thinking.

When Earl got to the café, he was relieved to see that it was empty. Kaitlin got up as Earl came in to take the trays from him. Taking the trays and setting them down, she turned to Earl and asked, "What was that all about with Luke?"

"Luke and I were talking about the West, and I got to thinking about how it might be nice to go there," said Earl. "But then I got to thinking about what I would have to give up here, including our friendship. Well, Luke done caught me thinking about you, and I got embarrassed."

"Do I embarrass you?" asked Kaitlin.

"No, it's just that I, well I ... " said Earl.

"Well, you what?" asked Kaitlin.

"Well, I sometimes hope we might be closer than just friends," said Earl.

"What are you saying, Earl? Are you going to ask me to come courting?" asked Kaitlin.

"I've been afraid to 'cause I thought you might say no," said Earl.

"How long have we known each other?" asked Kaitlin. "I've been thinking that you didn't want to be anything but a friend from the way you act around me."

They continued to talk for some time. When they were done, they agreed to get together. Earl went back to the jail happier than when he left. When Earl came into the office, Luke saw the big smile on Earl's face and asked, "Well, what did she say?"

Earl just smiled and went to his desk. Luke got up, getting his hat and coat. "I'll go make da rounds," he said as he went out the door. Luke took his time making his rounds. The town was quiet except for the saloon. All the businesses had locked their doors, and the merchants had gone home. Even as he went by the café, they were closing up for the night. When he got to the saloon, he decided to stop and have a beer. When he entered, he saw that at one table some of the men from town were playing poker. Herb was behind the bar talking to a couple of customers. The other tables had men sitting at them talking and drinking. When Herb saw Luke walking toward the bar, he asked, "Do you want a beer?"

"Sure thing," said Luke. "Da town seems quiet tonight."

Herb got Luke a beer. When he gave Luke his beer, he asked, "Do you think the men you brung in will hang?"

"I don't know what da judge will do," said Luke. "We done found da Meyer livestock at their place, so it seems ta me they done it."

"Well, no matter what happens, folks here abouts don't have to worry about them anymore," said Herb.

"Some got away," said Luke.

"How do you know?" asked Herb.

"When the sheriff and I were watching da place, we counted more men staying there," said Luke. "I'd say maybe three or four made off while everyone else was busy."

"Do you think they will stay around?" asked Herb.

"Nah. Them boys are long gone since their leader was killed," said Luke. "Mah guess is they will stay out of trouble until they can find another gang ta join."

Luke finished his beer and went back to the jail. When he opened the door, he saw Kaitlin inside talking to Earl. Luke said, "Pardon me, ma'am. I'll leave ya alone."

"That's okay. I was just leaving," Kaitlin said.

"In that case, good night, Miss Kaitlin," said Luke.

"Good night," said Kaitlin as the two of them left the office.

After they left, Luke went into the back to check on the prisoners. All four were sitting on their cots talking until Luke came in. One of the prisoners looked at Luke and asked, "You ain't from Virginia, are ya?"

"I hail from there," said Luke as he took a closer look at the fella who asked the question. He saw a bald spot on the side of his head. When he saw that, he remembered seeing it during the raid on their farm.

"How come you are followed us out here?" he asked.

"I didn't," replied Luke. "I was heading west and came across ya."

"You weren't following us?" he asked.

"Nope," said Luke. "But I sure ain't sad about come'n across ya though. Ya killed mah brother and a couple of mah friends back there."

"That was da war," said the man.

"Ya weren't fightin' no war. Ya were raid'n farms, kill'n women and children," said Luke. "Ya would of kil'd all of us hadn't da townfolk stopped ya. Maybe they gonna hang ya here."

The man didn't say anything else as Luke walked back out. Luke sat down at Lloyd's desk, remembering the raid on their farm. He was still thinking about it when Earl returned. Seeing Earl, his mind switched back to what had happened at supper. Looking at Earl, he just smiled and shook his head.

Earl just ignored Luke and sat down. They did not say anything to each other for the rest of the night.

In the morning, Luke was up early wanting the trial to be over so he could be moving on. When Earl got up, they went to the café. Carrying the prisoners' food back, they met Lloyd just arriving from home. "Well, today we will start their trial," said Lloyd. "Do you still plan on going when it's over, or have you changed your mind?"

"Figured I would be on mah way," said Luke.

After the prisoners ate, Earl returned their trays. When he got back, it was time to take the prisoners to the courthouse. Entering the courtroom, they found that it was already full of the townspeople. Escorting the prisoners to their seats in front of the court, they waited for the judge.

They didn't have long to wait until the judge entered the courtroom. Once he sat down, he went over the proceedings before he started selecting men for the jury. As he called each person, he questioned them to make sure they were not related to the accused or part of the posse who captured them. Once the jury was picked, the trial was ready to begin.

"The four of you have been charged by the state of Illinois with the following crimes," said the judge. "You're charges inclued robbery, murder, assault on an officer, and aiding an escaped prisoner. How do you plead?"

All four of the men pleaded not guilty to all the charges. With them pleading not guilty, the trial was to start the following morning at nine o'clock. The judge told the prosecutor to get his witnesses together, and he told the four men that they would need a lawyer to defend them. The judge assigned a public defender to represent the prisoners before recessing for the day.

The lawyer assigned to defend them followed them back to the jail. Once the prisoners were locked up, the lawyer was allowed to be with his clients while the sheriff and his two deputies were in the outer office.

The lawyer spent the rest of the afternoon talking with his clients before going back to his office. At his office, he did some research before going home. When he was done, he felt that he could keep them from being hung, but he would not be able to keep them out of prison.

In the morning, the lawyer showed up at the jail and again talked to his clients before going to the courthouse.

Back in court, the judge asked the prosecutor to call his first witness. The prosecutor called the sheriff to the stand. "Why did you arrest these men, Sheriff?" asked the prosecutor.

"These men were found at the location of an escaped prisoner," said Lloyd.

"What happened when you tried to arrest the escaped prisoner?" asked the prosecutor.

"They opened fire on us," said Lloyd.

"Sheriff, was there any other reason that you were at the farm other than to arrest an escaped prisoner?" asked the prosecutor.

"We believed they were the ones who raided the Meyer farm, killing the whole family and stealing their stock," said Lloyd. "We found Meyers' stock in the corral."

The prosecutor said, "I have no more questions for this witness."

The judge asked, looking at the defense lawyer, "Do you have any questions for this witness?"

"Thank you, Your Honor. I do," he said as he rose and approached the witness. "Sheriff, you said these men were found at the location of an escaped prisoner. Did you see the prisoner before you rode in that morning?"

"No, we didn't," answered Lloyd.

"Sheriff, did these men fire on you first?" asked the lawyer.

"No, there were men at the house who opened fired on us when we arrived," said Lloyd.

"Were these men at the house when the firing started?" asked the defense lawyer.

"No, they were in the barn when we arrived," said Lloyd.

"So for all they knew, you could have been the one who fired first," said the defense lawyer.

"Ya, I suppose so," said Lloyd.

"Do you think these men could have just been defending themselves, not knowing you were the sheriff?" asked the defense Lawyer.

"What about the livestock we found there from the Meyer place?" asked Lloyd.

"Just answer the question," said the judge.

"Again, Sheriff, could these men just have been defending themselves not knowing who you were?" asked the defense Lawyer again.

"Ya, I suppose so," said Lloyd.

"What did they tell you when you asked them about the cattle?" asked the defense lawyer.

"The said they found the stock running loose, and they locked them up in their corral until they could find out where they belonged," said Lloyd. "But we knew that the stock had been driven there from the Meyer farm."

"Are you saying, Sheriff, that you were able to follow a trail from the Meyer farm to where you found the stock in the corral?" asked the defense lawyer.

"Well, no, but we found at the Meyer farm where the stock had been driven in their direction," said Lloyd.

"Did you find any evidence that these four men were at the Meyer farm during the raid, or could someone else have raided the Meyer farm, driving the stock off and letting them roam?" asked the defense lawyer.

"Well, no. We did not find anything that we could tie to these four men," said Lloyd.

"Did you find your escaped prisoner at the farm?" asked the defense lawyer.

"He was shot by my deputy when he tried to get away," said Lloyd.

"What led you to the farm in the first place?" asked the defense lawyer.

"The escaped prisoner was recognized by my deputy as being involved in a robbery," said Lloyd. "He figured he could lead us to the rest of the men, so he marked one of the shoes on his horse. Well, when they broke him out of jail, we followed his tracks, along with four other horses, to the farm where we found him."

"Do you have proof that these four were the four who freed your prisoner?" asked the defense lawyer.

"No, just that they were at the farm that the five rode to," said Lloyd.

"You found wanted posters on some of the men at the farm. Isn't that true?" asked the defense lawyer.

"Yes, I did," said Lloyd.

"Did you find any on these men?" asked the defense lawyer.

"No, I didn't," said Lloyd.

"Did anyone see these men break Reynolds out of your jail?" asked the defense lawyer.

"No," said Lloyd.

"Your Honor, I have no more questions for the sheriff," said the defense lawyer.

"Sheriff, you are excused," said the judge.

The prosecutor called the deputies next. When Luke was called on, he stated that he saw one of the four men on the raid at their farm during the war. The judge told the jury to disregard Luke's statement.

By the time the defense lawyer finished with Luke, it was getting late in the day. The judge called a recess until Thursday morning. The prisoners seemed to be in a better mood after watching their lawyer in court. They were thinking that at least they wouldn't be hung.

After the prisoners were back in their cells, Lloyd went home for the night. Luke and Earl went to the café for supper. Sitting down, Kaitlin came over and asked, "How did it go in court today?"

Earl said, "Not as good as we would have liked."

"What happened?" asked Kaitlin.

"It seems we don't have any evidence to prove they killed the Meyers or that they were the ones who broke Reynolds out of jail," said Earl.

"That's too bad," said Kaitlin. "Now, what do you boys want to eat tonight?"

Earl and Luke ordered their supper and the meals for the prisoners. When Kaitlin left with their order, Earl said, "It's too bad we didn't kill those four when we had the chance."

"We got most of them," said Luke. "At least we don't got to worry that Fry will put another gang together. He was da worst of da bunch. When I shot him, I got mah revenge."

When they finished eating, they took the meals back to the jail. Earl stayed with the prisoners while Luke made the rounds. Going by the bank, he saw that everything was locked up. He stopped looking at the bank and began to wonder if Fry had intended to rob the bank in Boonville.

Luke stopped by the saloon for a beer. Herb said, "I heard things ain't going too good in court."

"I can't say fer sure," said Luke. "Guess we got ta wait fer da judge ta say what will happen."

"It would be a shame if them boys were to get off," said Herb.

"Ya, I'd know'd what ya mean," said Luke.

Luke finished his beer and went back to the jail. By then, the prisoners had finished their supper and Earl was waiting to take the trays back. Earl was gone for some time before he returned. Luke figured that he must have been talking to Kaitlin. *It won't be long,* thought Luke, *before Earl is married.*

In the morning after breakfast, they marched the prisoners back to the courthouse. The prosecutor brought each of the posse members to the witness stand. As he finished, the defense lawyer would try to put doubt into the jury's mind about what they had said. By the end of the day, the prosecutor had run out of witnesses. The judge then asked the defense lawyer if he had any witnesses. Not having any, the judge said he would hear their closing statements on Friday morning.

On Friday morning, the prisoners were again back in court. The judge again asked the defense Lawyer if he had any witnesses before giving their closing statements. Not having any, the judge called on the prosecutor to give his statement first.

Getting up, the prosecutor started, "Gentlemen of the jury, you have heard testimony from our Sheriff and all the posse members stating that these four outlaws were involved in multiple crimes committed within our community. They brutally killed the Meyers. They stole their cattle, and they harbored a known escaped prisoner. They resisted arrest and fired upon our Sheriff and his men, killing one of the deputies and wounding others. These men should not be turned loose but hung by the neck until dead for their crimes. Gentlemen, you have only one choice, and that is to find all four of these defendants guilty on all counts."

The judge turned to the defense lawyer when the prosecutor sat down for his closing statement.

The defense lawyer got up, facing the jury, and proceeded with his closing. "Gentlemen of the jury, what we have here is an attempt to railroad these men to the gallows. There has been no proof presented that would put these men at the Meyer farm during the raid. No one proved that the men were not trying to identify who owned the livestock they found roaming near their farm. There has been no proof that these men had anything to do with the alleged jail break, nor is there any proof these men had been near town before the sheriff and his posse brought them in against their wills. The only thing that the prosecutor has presented as evidence was the resisting arrest and harboring a known fugitive. I ask you, gentlemen, if you were in your barn and heard shooting and went out seeing a bunch of men on horseback shooting at your friends, would you ask who they were or start shooting? Gentlemen, I know that you are logical men and can understand a situation when it is presented to you. That is why you have but the one choice to find these men innocent of all charges."

Finishing his speech, he returned to his seat and sat down. When he was seated, the judge gave the jury members their instructions before sending them to deliberation. The judge told the sheriff to take the prisoners back to jail. He would send someone for them when the jury was ready.

Back at the jail, all three sat in the office not saying anything. Each was in their own thoughts wondering what the jurors were doing. It was four o'clock when the judge sent a runner to the sheriff's office. When he entered the sheriff's office, he said, "The judge wants the prisoners back in court. The jury is ready."

"You can tell the judge we will be right over," said Lloyd.

By the time the prisoners were brought into the courtroom, the room was full of the townspeople. Once the prisoners were seated, the judge came in and quieted the people before asking for the jury.

When the jury was seated, the judge asked, "Foreman of the jury, have you reached a verdict?"

"We have, Your Honor," said the foreman.

"Will the prisoners rise?" said the judge. Once they were standing, the judge asked, "On the count of murder of the Meyer family, how do you find?"

"Not guilty, Your Honor," said the foreman.

"On the count of aiding the escape of a prisoner, how do you find?" asked the judge.

"Not guilty," said the foreman.

The audience let out a groan as the judge banged his gavel on the desk.

"On the count of stealing the Meyers' livestock, how do you find?" asked the judge.

"Not guilty, Your Honor," said the foreman.

Again the people showed their disapproval.

"On the count of harboring a fugitive, how do you find?" asked the judge.

"Guilty, Your Honor," said the foreman.

This crowd let out a cheer, and the judge again banged his gavel on the desk to quiet them.

"On the count of resisting arrest, how do you find?" asked the judge.

"Guilty, Your Honor," said the foreman.

Turning toward the jury, the judge said, "Gentlemen of the jury, the court wants to thank you for your time and consideration in these matters. You are excused."

After the jury left, the judge turned toward the prisoners and said, "You have been found guilty of harboring a fugitive from the law and for resisting arrest. I will see you back in my court on Monday at nine o'clock for sentencing. Sheriff, they are to remain in your custody until then. Are there any questions? If not, court is recessed until Monday morning."

After returning the prisoners to their cells, Lloyd said to Earl and Luke, "Well, we couldn't prove that they were at the Meyers or involved in the jail break. But in my mind, we got most of those who were involved with the Meyers. Luke, you know what kind of men that were killed when we went after Reynolds. How do you feel about it?"

"I ain't thought much about it," said Luke. "Them we killed done a sight of killing themselves. If not at da Meyers' place, then during da war raiding farms in Virginia. It brung closure ta mah family."

"Your reward money will be here on Monday. What are you going to do when it gets here?" asked Lloyd.

"I got no call ta stay here once it arrives. I'll be heading for Independence," said Luke. "Might be I can hook up with a wagon train head'n west come spring."

"Do you know where out west you want to go?" asked Lloyd.

"Ain't thought that out," said Luke. "Figured ta follow wherever mah horse wanders ta. Heard some about gold or land ta be gotten if ya willing ta work fer it. With da reward money, one could get a start with a spread of his own."

Luke spent the weekend checking his gear and then rechecking it. On Monday, the prisoners were taken to the courtroom where the judge announced their sentences. They were sentenced to five years in prison at the state prison in Chicago. Lloyd contacted the state prison, and they would send a prison wagon to pick them up.

The reward money did arrive on Monday afternoon. After Lloyd handed Luke his money, Luke returned the deputy badge to him.

"Luke, I want to thank you for all your help," said Lloyd. "Maria and I would like to wish you the best of luck as you go west. If there is anything I can do for you, let me know. By the way, here is the money you earned as my deputy as well."

Luke thanked him and said good-bye to Earl. He would get his gear together as well as his supplies from the general store and be ready to leave in the morning. First off, he went to the bank and got a bank draft for two hundred dollars to send to his folks before going to the livery. At the livery, he checked his horses over, making sure they were ready for travel again.

Taking his bedroll and Henry, he went to the hotel and got a room. On the way to the hotel, he stopped by the general store where he sent the bank draft off to his folks. After putting his gear in his room, he decided to take one last walk around town before settling down for the night. When he got to the café, he went in and sat down. Kaitlin came over to take his order and said, "Sorry to hear you're leaving. Earl was by earlier and said you were going and would be leaving in the morning."

"I'll be heading out in da morn," said Luke. "I'll miss mah new friends here some I reckon."

They talked a little longer, and Luke ordered his supper. When he finished eating, he paid and said he would be back in the morning for breakfast before he left. Leaving the café, he went to the saloon. He figured he would have one last beer with Herb before he left.

Herb saw Luke entering the saloon. Before Luke could make his way to the bar, Herb had poured a beer and was waiting for him. "On the house," said Herb. "Earl came by and said you were leaving tomorrow. Didn't know if I would get a chance to say good-bye to you or not."

"Figured ta make one last round befer I headed out," said Luke. "I ain't been here long, but da place seems like home."

"Well, the town sometimes ain't the most friendly," said Herb. "But I know the sheriff and Earl are going to miss having you here about."

When he finished his beer, he said, "Thanks fer da beer, Herb. Y'all take care, ya hear."

Leaving, he went back to the hotel and went to bed.

independence

In the morning, Luke woke refreshed and ready to go. Leaving the hotel, he went to the café. Earl and Lloyd were both sitting at a table. When they saw Luke come in, they motioned for him to join them. Walking over to their table, Luke said, "What happened, Lloyd? Maria sleep in on ya taday?"

"No," said Lloyd. "I figured you would stop by for breakfast this morning, so Earl and I decided to have one last meal with you before you left."

Luke sat down and ordered breakfast. Earl started asking questions again about the West, and Luke told him some of the stories he had heard. Lloyd was watching Earl's face as Luke told the stories. He said, "Now just a moment. You got me to ask Maria to marry me, and you got Earl to take a new look at Kaitlin here. Now you don't have to get him to follow you out west as well."

Luke laughed. He was going to miss his new friends. When they finished breakfast, they got up and walked to the livery with Luke. George had brushed and saddled Luke's horses before they got there. Seeing them, George said. "I checked their shoes, and they are ready to go."

"Thanks, George," said Luke. He got together his gear and started loading the packhorses. As he worked with them, they would not stand still. "Ah think they have been standing too long," said Luke. "They're ready ta go."

When he finished tying his gear on the packhorses, he put the Henry in the scabbier. Turning to George, he asked, "What do I owe ya?"

"The county owes me for your horses," said George. "Best of luck to you." George shook his hand.

Luke took the lead rope to one of the packhorses and tied it to the other packhorse before taking the reins of Buck while Lloyd took the lead rope of the front packhorse. They led the horses out and waited while Luke mounted. Once mounted, Lloyd handed Luke the lead rope. As Luke rode west out of town, he turned and waved to the three men standing in front of the livery.

The three men stood watching Luke ride away until he was out of sight. After Luke was gone, George went back into the livery while Lloyd and Earl walked back to the office.

Luke could tell that the horses were well rested and ready to go. They had spent the past few weeks without getting much exercise. Luke knew that they had a ways to go, so he held them back to an easy pace.

By late morning, he was near the Meyer farm. As he rode on, he came to the farm where Gus lived. As he rode into the yard, Gus came out to greet him. When he recognized Luke, he said, "It looks like you are traveling again."

"Yup, sure enough," said Luke. "I wanted ta tell ya that da men who killed da Meyers are dead or in jail. Don't know'd if ya heard or not."

"There was a fella that stopped by here a couple of days ago said something about a trial going on in town last week," said Gus. "Don't suppose that had anything to do with those men?"

"Da captured men were tried last week," said Luke. "Their leader was killed when we tried ta arrest them. So ya ain't got no worry about them coming back this way."

When he finished talking to Gus, Luke rode out. At noon, he stopped to give his horses a rest. After an hour, he was again riding west. That night he found a place that would protect him if the weather changed. Over the past two weeks, the weather had been warmer and had melted most of the snow. It was now becoming more important for Luke to get to Independence. If the weather continued to hold, the wagon trains would want to get an early start. Luke wanted to leave with the first wagon train in the spring—if he could hire on with them.

When Trevor heard the gunfire coming from the farm, he knew he had gotten out of there at the right time. Now he wasn't sure why he had joined up with the gang in the first place. With the snow, he had needed a place to hole up for the winter, and when they invited him to stay, he was glad to accept. When they started talking about robbing the bank, he was broke and needed money if he was going to continue on with his plan to go out west. He decided that the plan that Fry had put together by getting the money at night with no one getting hurt was good, and he needed the money. It also reminded him of the time when he was living on the streets in Pittsburgh. Slowly, he had watched the boys grow restless as the weather remained bad. Some of the boys talked about some of the things they had done during the war. The more they talked, the more Trevor began to wonder if they could be trusted. Then when Reynolds came back with his horse's shoe marked, he knew it was time to leave, even without the money. After leaving the ravine, he stopped when he got to the trees and waited. The gunfire seemed to go on for a long time. He heard someone coming, so he moved farther into the thickets and waited. When he saw that it was two of the men from the farm, he almost called out, but when he saw that one was the big fella with the scar that ran from his forehead to his chin, he changed his mind. Some of the men had called him Sergeant while he was in their camp. Right now, he did not trust them to remain quiet. From the way they were running, Trevor figured that there must be someone after them. He continued to watch until they were out of sight.

It was close to half an hour later that two more men showed up on horseback. They looked around, and, not seeing anyone or any tracks, they turned back riding again to the ravine. Trevor waited until it was dark before he left the trees. Going back to the ravine, he saw that the farm was dark. Not trusting that someone wasn't waiting to make sure that whoever ran might return, he went back to the trees and made camp for the night. In the morning, he would be able to see if anyone was still around the farm.

When the sun came up, he made his way back to the ravine where he could watch the farm. He spent the morning there without seeing anyone; he decided to investigate and find out what had happened. He rode up to the farm from behind the barn. Putting his horse in the barn, he heard a horse come into the yard. Grabbing his rifle, he went to the door and looked out. At first he could only see the back end of the horse standing by the corral. Quietly making his way out of the barn, he stayed close to the barn, ready in case he met someone when he got to the corner. By now the horse had gone into the corral. When he got to the corner, he took a look and saw only a horse with no saddle on. It took him a little bit, but he recognized the horse as the one that belonged to Reynolds. Going back into the barn, he got a halter and lead rope. Putting the halter on the horse, he led him back into the barn and tied him in a stall.

After feeding the horses, he went to the house to look around. In the kitchen, he found food, so he made himself dinner. Once he finished eating, he went through the house looking for anything that he could use on his trip out west. Once he had gone through the house, he walked around the grounds looking at the signs left from the fight. He found the fresh graves of the men the posse had killed. Going through the bunkhouse, he found money that the men had left in their gear that he took. By the time he had finished going through the bunkhouse, it was getting dark. Going back to the barn, he fed the horses before taking his bedroll to the house. In the house, he put his bedroll in the bedroom where he decided that he would stay for the next few days. He saw that there was plenty of food until he decided what he was going to do. The next day he replaced the marked shoe on Reynolds's horse. He figured that he would use Reynolds's horse as a packhorse when he rode out. By the end of the week, he had gone through the root cellar and gathered the food that he would need.

After spending a little over a week at the farm with no one showing up, Trevor figured that he would be able to travel now without any fear of the law following him. On the second Sunday, he was packing up his gear and putting it on Reynolds's horse, not believing his good luck. Maybe running into Fry and his men worked out better than he thought. He didn't have to worry about Fry; the law had taken care of them. Mounting, he rode north, following the road leading from the farm and taking the same road that the posse had taken that day. When he got to the main road, he turned west, heading for Independence.

Not seeing anyone since the posse had shown up, Trevor was relaxed. He wasn't worried about running into anyone on the road, as he was not known in the area and people would think that he was just another soldier going west like so many others had. He took his time along the trail. If he hurried, people might think he could be running from someone.

When Trevor rode into Marshall, he decided that he would get a drink. Tying his horses in front of the saloon, he went in. It was late in the afternoon when he ordered his drink. Looking around, he saw four men playing poker at one of the tables in the back. After the barkeep told him it was an open game, he went and joined them. At first, he started losing and thought that it might have been a mistake to sit in on the game. About the fifth hand, his luck started to change, and he won a few hands. Before long, he was ahead fifty dollars. It was now getting around suppertime, and the men decided to break up the game and go home. With the game breaking up, Trevor figured he would spend the night in Marshall. Taking his horses to the stable, he put them up. Trevor left his gear and took his bedroll to the hotel. At the hotel, he got a room and put his bedroll in the room. When he was registering, he saw that the hotel had a dining room. Leaving his room, he went to the dining room for supper.

After eating, he went back to the saloon where he found another poker game going on. After watching it for a while, he sat in. His luck was still somewhat with him. He won some and lost some, but by the time midnight rolled around, he was ahead another two hundred dollars as the game broke up. When he went to bed, he thought to himself that he had gotten himself a good grubstake from the poker games. He had enough money that he could go out west to make a start. In the morning, he would ride out. During the war, he had become confused on what he wanted and where he wanted to go. Before the war, he had been restless and wild. He had been in and out of trouble with the law. When the war broke out, the law had said, "Join up or go to jail." The war had changed him. After seeing so many men die and the suffering of families, he had lost some of his wildness. Hooking up with Fry and his gang proved to be not what he had wanted after he had said he would stay.

At noon, Trevor stopped when he noticed his horse was favoring one of his hooves. Checking his hoof, he found that he had a shoe coming loose. He would have to fix that before going on. He set up camp and started a fire to make coffee. He figured by the time he repaired the shoe, coffee would be done.

After Luke rode out of Gus's farm, he made good time. The horses were eager to go, and he wanted to get to Independence. It was midmorning of the next day when he rode through Marshall. Not stopping, as he had all the supplies he needed, he continued on. The sun was high in the sky when he started thinking about stopping to give the horses a rest. Looking for a good place to stop, he caught the smell of coffee brewing. It wasn't long before he saw smoke rising from a campfire. Riding in the direction of the smoke, he saw a man nailing a shoe on his horse. He called out as he rode up. The man looked up, and, seeing it was a fella with packhorses, he determined it wasn't the law, so he kept on working on the shoe and said, "Howdy. Sit if you a mind to. I'll be done right soon."

"Thanks," said Luke. "Don't mind if I do." Luke watered his horses and put them where they could get some grass. Losing their cinches, he got his cup and some jerky from a pack before going back to the fire. By the time he returned, the man had finished with his horse and was pouring himself some coffee. As Luke walked up, he said, "Mah name's Luke Taylor."

When Trevor heard Luke's name, he did all he could do to hide his surprise. So this was the fella that Fry was so concerned about. After seeing what had happened at the farm, it looked like he had a right to be concerned. Or was it just a coincidence that this fella had the same name. He figured it must be someone else, not this Luke Taylor. This fella looked too young to have caused that much concern.

"Folks call me Trevor. Trevor Lane," said Trevor. "Pour yourself some coffee, and sit a spell."

"Thanks," said Luke. "Where ya headed fer?"

"Ain't sure," said Trevor. "Thought I might go out west and see what it was like. How about yourself?"

"Independence," said Luke. "Figured on hooking up with a wagon train. Ain't sure where I am headed fer mahself."

"Maybe we could ride together a ways or until we figure out where we want to go," said Trevor.

"I sure would enjoy da company," said Luke.

Now that Luke was riding with someone, he did not feel the eagerness to get to Independence that he had had before. If for some reason he couldn't hook up with a wagon train, maybe Trevor and him would head west by themselves. He had heard about trails leading all the way to Oregon or California from Independence. He was sure that they could get all the information they would need to follow a trail to wherever they decided to go.

That night when they stopped, Luke decided that they could use some fresh meat. While Trevor set up camp, Luke found a young doe. They did have plenty of salt pork, flour, and beans, and with some fresh meat to go with it, it would be nice. Returning to camp with the doe, Trevor helped him cut the doe up. It wasn't long before they were cooking some fresh steaks. It turned out that Trevor was right handy with a frying pan. He even whipped up some fresh biscuits.

After eating, Luke went out to move the horses. While they were riding that afternoon, Luke got to thinking that Trevor's packhorse looked familiar. He was reminded of Reynolds's horse, the one he had marked the shoe on. Checking his hoofs, Luke saw that he had new shoes on, but none of them had the file mark he had put on Reynolds's horse. The new shoes were not a concern, as Reynolds's horse had had new shoes as well. Putting the thought out of his mind that he had seen the horse before, he went back to camp.

That night when they were resting by the fire, they started talking about what had happened to them during the war. Both men had developed a common dream of going west either before the war broke out or during the war. But like so many people, the war had changed their lives.

Three days later as they were getting close to Independence, they had become good friends. When they rode into Independence, they first looked for a hotel. Luke figured to get a room before he started looking for a wagon train. At the hotel, they registered and put their gear away before taking their horses to the stable. At the stable, he asked, "Do ya have some grain ya can give our horses?"

"I sure do," said the blacksmith. "It will be two bits extra per horse."

"They done come a ways without any," said Luke.

Luke and Trevor unsaddled their horses and rubbed them down while the blacksmith got them their hay and grain. When they finished with their horses, they asked the blacksmith, "Where do you recommend a man can get a good meal?"

"The hotel got the best food in town," said the blacksmith.

Going back to the hotel, they went to the dining room and ate their supper. After supper, Trevor said, "How about a drink to top off that good meal?"

At the saloon, Trevor ordered a whiskey and a beer while Luke just ordered a beer. While they were sitting at a table, the sheriff walked in. At first, he went to the bar. After standing there awhile, he looked around and noticed the two new men sitting at a table. When he saw them, he walked over to their table to find out who they were. When he arrived at their table, he said, "Good evening, gentlemen. I see you are new in town. Mind telling me your names?"

"Not at all," said Trevor. "I am Trevor Lane.

Luke said, "I am Luke Taylor."

The sheriff looked at Luke and said, "I got a wire from the sheriff in Boonville. He said you were headed this way."

Trevor looked surprised. He started thinking that he had gotten himself hooked up with the wrong person again before he remembered that Luke had helped the sheriff.

The sheriff when on. "He asked me to put in a good word for you with any of the wagon trains heading west if you needed it. Seems he put some store by you. I don't know what you did, but whatever it was, Sheriff Lloyd felt he owed you and wanted to pay you back some."

"Won't ya have a seat, Sheriff?" asked Luke. "Care to have a drink?"

"Thanks. Don't mind if I do," said the sheriff, sitting down. "I'll have a beer."

When Trevor heard that the sheriff was there to help them, he relaxed and ordered a round of beer for them. The sheriff asked, "Where are you boys headed for?"

"We're headed west," said Luke. "Ain't got no place in mind though. Thought we might hook up with a wagon train and see where they're go'n."

"Several folks been going west ever since the war ended," said the sheriff. "The war sure changed a lot of people's lives. We got a family near here by the name of James. Some folks say they are outlaws who rode with bloody Bill Anderson. Others think they got a raw deal. They ain't wanted hereabouts, so we let them be."

"I know some people who got accused of things they ain't done," said Luke. "It will sure change one's life when that happens."

"You say you would like to hook up with a wagon train?" asked the sheriff again. "You might ride out west of town tomorrow. There have been some wagons showing up since the weather started to get warmer. I don't know if they have a guide yet, but you might be able to get on with them."

"Thanks, Sheriff," said Trevor.

"If anyone has any questions about you, you tell them to come see me," said the sheriff. The sheriff continued to sit with them until he had finished his beer. Once he left, they sat awhile longer, drinking another beer before going back to the hotel.

That night Trevor lay in bed thinking about what the sheriff had said about the wire from Boonville. This was the Luke Taylor that was talked about at the farm. It was a good thing that he had not told Luke that he was staying at the farm and had only left that morning that the posse had arrived. Maybe someday he would tell Luke about his experience with Fry's outfit. He had not been in on any raids with them, he only needed a place to stay for the winter.

In the morning after breakfast, they went to the stable and got their horses and rode west of town to where the wagons were gathering.

Back in Virginia, the weather was getting warmer, and Milton was thinking about getting ready to plant. Since Luke had seen to it that they had the money to pay the carpetbagger, no one had bothered them again. Pa's arm had gotten better, but he would never get full use of it again. That morning at breakfast, he said, "Pa, it's time ta get some supplies from town. We gonna start planting fer long."

"Why don't ya go ta town and see Mr. Hynes at the general store," said Jake. "He will get ya what we need."

After breakfast, Milton hitched up the wagon and drove to town. Stopping in front of the general store, he took his list in and handed it to Mr. Hynes. "Can ya fill it fer us?" he asked.

Mr. Hynes looked at the list and said, "I'll have it ready in a few minutes. Why don't you look around and see if there is anything else you might need?"

When Mr. Hynes had gotten the supplies together, Milton asked, "Can ya put it on our bill?"

"Already have," said Mr. Hynes.

Milton loaded the supplies into the wagon and was about to leave when Mrs. Hynes came running out, waving two envelopes. "Milton!" she called out. "These letters just arrived yesterday for your folks. I was gonna bring them out, but as long as you're here, you can have them. They may be from your brother."

Seeing the letters, Milton got excited. Hurrying the horses, he made them run most of the way home. As he came racing into the yard, Jake came out of the barn to see what was wrong.

"Pa," Milton called out, "where's Ma? We done got a couple of letters from Luke."

Abigail came from the house hearing all the excitement, saying, "What's going on here?"

"Ma, we got a couple of letters from Luke," repeated Milton.

Abigail took the letters and started to open one and stopped. "No," she said. "We will read them tonight when Mary and Sue Ann are here. They need to hear what Luke has to say when we do. Now you go about your chores, and we will read them after supper."

The rest of the day went slow for the family. Everyone was anxious to hear what Luke had to say. When evening came and the girls had returned from school, Abigail hurried with supper.

Mary asked, "What's wrong, Ma? Why is everyone in such a hurry?"

"We got a couple of letters from Luke today, and we will read them after supper," said Abigail.

When Mary and Sue Ann heard that, they, too, were anxious to finish supper to hear what Luke had written.

All through supper no one talked. Everyone was busy eating. When everyone had finished eating, the table was cleaned. Everybody sat down and waited.

Abigail's hands were shaking as she opened the first letter and began to read. "Dear Ma, Pa, Milton, and girls..." When she finished reading and put the first letter down, it was some time before she said, "Thank God that he is all right."

Jake said, "I can't believe he come across Fry again."

Milton and the girls just sat there missing their brother.

Abigail picked up the second letter and opened it. When she unfolded the letter, a smaller slip of paper fell on the table. Picking it up, she said, "It's a bank draft."

"What's a bank draft?" asked Milton.

"I think it's a way to send money," said Abigail. "It says that it's worth two hundred dollars, and it came from Luke."

"Now where would Luke get that kind of money moving on da way he is?" asked Jake. "Come on. Read da letter."

Abigail looked at the letter and began to read.

Dear Ma and Pa,

When I told ya that Fry was dead, I didn't tell ya I was da one who killed him. It seemed there was a reward fer him. Well, da sheriff here in Boonville figured I was da one ta get da reward. I am sending ya some of da money. Figured ya might need it ta get yer crops in. Ma, get yerself some nice material, and get something fer da rest of da family.

By da time ya get this, I will be heading west again.

Luke.

Jake said, "With da money Luke sent, we can pay off Mr. Hynes at da General store and have some money left over. We don't got to worry this year."

Abigail just sat there being thankful that her son was alive. In her heart, she knew he would be okay, but she missed him as much as she missed Tyler, who had been killed.

That night the Taylor family slept a little happier and peacefully.